Advance Praise for

All Up

"*All Up* takes the reader beyond the usual descriptions of the challenges and achievements of the technical teams by describing the human reality behind the extraordinary efforts of intelligence and will that made it all possible. Imagine if we could meet von Braun and Korolev, and hear them speak about their lives, their failures and hopes, and their eventual successes. That is the story told in this exceptional book, a timely contribution and a valuable guide to the stunning voyages to come."

—Dr. Jacques F. Vallée, computer scientist,
winner of the Jules Verne Award for science fiction

"*All Up* takes us behind the scenes of the Space Race—but with a fictional twist. With its fascinating personalities that only Rinzler could describe, *All Up* can't be put down."

—David Mandel, executive producer of *Veep*

"*All Up* ingeniously weaves together the stuff of history and science fiction... of what really happened, and what seems both fantastic and yet almost possible, where fiction lifts off from fact like a rocket achieving escape velocity... So just hang on for the jet-propelled ride of your life. You won't want to stop till you discover how it all comes out!"

—Roy Thomas, author/editor, member of the
Will Eisner Comic Book Hall of Fame

"*All Up* reminds me in some ways of the great novels by James Michener and Leon Uris that teach us history in a fictional manner."

—David Chudwin, author of *I Was a Teenage Space Reporter:*
From Apollo 11 to Our Future in Space

"*All Up*... What a space journey from planet Earth to the Moon! If Stanley Kubrick wove his *Odyssey* into the music of Richard Strauss, Rinzler's has the Faustian spirit of Wagnerian opera in it. I can see dozens of academic research articles growing out of such fertile soil."

—Dr. Hans Volker Wolf, former director of Goethe Institute Malaysia,
Senior Lecturer at University of Malaya

J. W. RINZLER

A PERMUTED PRESS BOOK

All Up

ISBN: 978-1-68261-901-8
ISBN (eBook): 978-1-68261-902-5

Cover art by Cody Corcoran
Author photo by Joel Aron
Interior design and composition by Greg Johnson, Textbook Perfect

Permuted Press, LLC
New York • Nashville
permutedpress.com

Published in the United States of America

To the writers, illustrators, filmmakers, and visionaries who imagined space voyages long before they took place, and to the men and women (and unwitting animals) who took those space voyages, whose work, dedication, engineering, constructions, theories, and rockets made them possible, past, present, and future.

PRINCIPAL PLAYERS

(In alphabetical order; title, rank, or affiliation usually corresponds to the player's first appearance)

The Americans

Quincy Adams, agent, Central Intelligence Agency (CIA)

Buzz Aldrin, astronaut, National Aeronautics and Space Administration (NASA)

James Jesus Angleton, Associate Deputy Director of Operations for Counterintelligence, CIA

Neil Armstrong, test pilot, National Advisory Committee for Aeronautics (NACA)

Henry Harley "Hap" Arnold, General, Chief of the Air Corps

Frank Borman, astronaut, NASA

Vannevar Bush, Chairman of the Joint Research and Development Board of the Army and Navy

Michael Collins, astronaut, NASA

Calvin Cory, Major, Army Ordnance

Walt Disney, cofounder of the Walt Disney Studio

Allen Dulles, Director, CIA

John Foster Dulles, Secretary of State

Frederick Durant III, President of the International Astronautical Federation

Dwight D. Eisenhower, Supreme Commander of the Allied Forces

James Forrestal, Secretary of the Navy

Robert Gilruth, Director, Space Task Group

Robert Goddard, professor, physicist, and inventor/rocketeer

Lyndon B. Johnson, Senator

Theodore von Kármán, aerospace engineer, professor, Director of the California Institute of Technology, cofounder of the Jet Propulsion Laboratory (JPL)

John F. Kennedy, Congressman

Robert F. Kennedy, Attorney General

Chris Kraft, Flight Director, Space Task Group

George Mueller, Director, Apollo Program, NASA

Marvel Whiteside "Jack" Parsons, explosives expert, cofounder of JPL

Al Shepard, astronaut, NASA

Bruce Staftoy, Major, Army Ordnance

Harry S. Truman, President

James Webb, Chief Administrator, NASA

The British

Winston Churchill, Prime Minister

Reginald V. Jones, Assistant Director of Intelligence, Chief of Air Scientific Intelligence, MI6

Frederick "the Prof" Lindemann, Lord Cherwell, physicist, head of S Branch, science advisor to Winston Churchill

Cornelius "Connie" Ryan, journalist

Duncan "Sands" Sandys, Chairman of the War Cabinet Committee for Defense, Churchill's son-in-law

The Germans and Austrians

Karl Heinrich Emil Becker, Lieutenant Colonel, Head of the Ballistics and Munitions Section of the HWA Weapons Testing Division

Magnus von Braun, chemical engineer, Wernher von Braun's younger brother

Maria von Braun, Wernher von Braun's wife

Sigismund von Braun, diplomat, Wernher von Braun's older brother

Wernher von Braun, engineer/rocketeer

Kurt Debus, Flight Test Director/rocketeer

Arthur Dieter, Electrical and Guidance Systems/rocketeer

Walter Dornberger, Captain, Germany Army, rocketeer

Helmut Gröttrup, electrical engineer/rocketeer

Irmgard Gröttrup, Helmut Gröttrup's wife

Heinrich Himmler, *Reichsführer-SS*

Adolf Hitler, *Führer*

Hans Kammler, *Brigadeführer-SS*

Fritz Lang, film director

Willy Ley, rocket and space travel enthusiast/writer

Hermann Oberth, physicist, engineer/rocketeer

Ernst Rees, Electrical and Engines, Fabrication and Assembly/rocketeer

Viktor Schomberger, inventor

Albert Speer, Minister of Armaments

Johannes Winkler, member of the Verein für Raumschiffahrt (early German rocket club)

The Russians

Boris Evseyevich Chertok, communications expert/rocketeer

Yuri Gagarin, cosmonaut

Mikhail Klavdievich Glushko, Engine Designer/rocketeer

Nikita Sergeyevich Khrushchev, Soviet Union Premier

Kseniya Maximilianovna Vincentini Korolev (Lyalya), doctor, Korolev's first wife, Natasha's mother

Natasha Korolev, daughter of Sergei Pavlovich and Kseniya Maximilianovna

Sergei Pavlovich Korolev, Chief Designer/rocketeer

Nina Ivanovna Kotenkova, translator, mistress to Korolev, his second wife

Vasily Pavlovich Mishin, engineer/rocketeer

Joseph Stalin, Soviet Union Premier

Dmitriy Fyodorovich Ustinov, People's Commissar of Armaments

Leonid Alexandrovich Voskresenskiy, engineer

A note to readers of All Up*: Newspaper headlines preceding each chapter did not occur on the exact date of the chapter's events (except for a few instances); the headlines usually occurred days, weeks, or, more rarely, months before the chapter date. However, in all cases the headlines were taken from the newspapers as indicated.*

Prelude

The Free Imperial City of Nuremberg
Friday, April 4, 1561

The little boy backed away from his mother, but she jabbed him in the stomach with a thick wooden cane and he doubled over.

With both hands she swung her heavy stick onto the boy's back and flattened him to the threshing-room floor.

"Do not smile at him, do not relent," growled the boy's uncle from a stool not far from them. "If you are weak in little things, you will suffer in great ones."

The mother screwed up her face in righteous anger and, stained gown fluttering, booted her son in the ribs. The seven-year-old rolled over and blinked at the wooden rafters in the farmhouse ceiling. He gasped for air. In the hazy morning light, he saw dancing dust motes.

"You dare not spare your child this beating." His uncle shoved a poker at red coals in a brazier. He was shaping a metal lamp, and his other hand clenched a small hammer. "The rod will not kill him but will do him good."

The boy tried to rise to his knees, so she smacked him on the side of his head and he tottered over again.

"When you strike the sinful body, you save the soul," his uncle declared, bloodshot eyes rolling upward in a disfigured face. "You must raise your child in fear if you wish to find a blessing in him. You must crush his ribs before he is grown, or he will cease to obey."

The mother grabbed her son by his short brown hair, she yanked and shook him—"Runt!" she shrieked—and flung him into a side stall usually reserved for cattle.

She slammed the wooden door and clapped down its bar.

Inside the dark pen, the boy put three fingers to his head and touched blood. He crawled deep into a corner, accustomed to the odor of piss and manure, and curled up in a pile of hay. His rags couldn't keep him warm, so he held his bent legs close. He lay that way for long minutes, whimpering softly. His body shook with a jolt—his crying might be heard—and a wall shot up in his mind to cut off the pain.

He closed his eyes.

It was quiet when the little boy opened them and he was hungry. He stared at the intricate coiled patterns in the wood slats for a long while, until shafts of light shot through the seams, sheets of orange, yellow, and red. Strange sounds seeped in from the outside—deep rumblings, then a high-pitched whine.

He sat up, wild and desperate.

The Last Judgment?

Curiosity replaced misery.

He recalled that the stall had been left empty because it wasn't sound. He burrowed through the straw and found a small hole. He kicked at the rotting boards to loosen them, then rammed through with his good shoulder. Once through the opening, he ran in the direction of the flashes and booms.

At the top of a neighboring hill, he gazed above him in astonishment.

On the same mound of the Reichsstadt Nürnberg, merchants and farmers had already assembled, and a number of wealthy men and women dismounted from horses held by liveried servants. Behind them the walled city with its many towers straddled the river. From its eastern gate, others hurried to join them. They, too, looked up at the sky. Their place afforded an unblocked view of the extraordinary sight: white lights and large globes as big as a rich man's house. The undersides of the globes glowed a dark crimson red, their tops shimmered blue and black. They dived and swooped like falcons before the afternoon sun.

The boy marveled at the appearance of two great silver tubes. Their noise grew louder, more threatening, and he looked to his betters for guidance.

"Tricks and illusions!" murmured a learned craftsman.

"Blood-colored crosses," said a lean candlemaker.

"Like floating cannons," another remarked. "They come arrayed for battle."

The boy glanced back at his thatched farmhouse, afraid he might be missed and pursued, but no one stirred.

He moved closer to one of the finely dressed gentry, who had a black stiletto beard and a twisted stance. He'd never come so close to a rich man, and admired the man's clothes nearly as much as the strange objects cartwheeling above. Surely the aristocrat descended from the ancient nobility, with his crimson cloak, black vest, and puffed sleeves. A gold band hung around his neck, with a circular gem, a crooked golden spiral set in red clay.

Feeling the boy's eyes, the bearded man cocked his head sideways. "Perhaps I've arranged this whole theater," he said.

The boy's blue eyes widened, but a bright yellow flash made him look to the west.

"One of the globes disappeared!" someone shouted.

Seven more pale-blue orbs sprinkled the sky, darting in and out of long white clouds. The bright lights of the strange objects reflected orange in the alabaster faces of the wealthier men and women. At least a hundred people had gathered.

"It is a dreadful apparition!" a peasant exclaimed.

"It is a sign of rods and whips," moaned the candlemaker. "The Last Judgment is upon us."

The candlemaker scurried off. Yet his words confirmed the boy's secret desire, so he stayed and summoned the courage to request of the bearded man, "If you arranged it, tell me what is happening."

"Is it not a cavalry battle, or are you stupid?" he answered. "A skirmish between demons of warring factions," he sniffed. "I smell yellow crystals…"

"Are we in danger?"

The aristocrat didn't say. He strutted away and took the reins from his groom, who inclined his head in deference. The rich man mounted his black steed and rode off. His retinue followed, and the child noted their foreign manner of dress, with knee-length heavy skirts of salmon and lemon. They, too, wore strange jewels.

When one of the globes split into flames, three women wailed. It dived silent and low over their heads, so closely pursued by a spear-like silver tube that the remaining men cowered. The boy stood fast and even reached up to try to touch its underbelly.

The orb crashed beyond the fields of planted barley. A cloud of steam-like vapor rose from the long gash it had made in the ground.

The sky flashed white and the remaining globes were catapulted toward the Sun. Fiery red, they disappeared in a burst of light that made the spectators shield their eyes. When the boy looked again, he saw the spear jump heavenward and shake the throne of earth with its thunder.

Then, silence, except for gusts of wind and prayers muttered in dread.

The more curious, or brave, trotted down the hill and across the pastures. The young boy ran ahead of them all.

On a berm of upturned dirt, he gawked at the half-buried smoking globe; its surface shone to him like a giant's glistening armor. He'd forgotten his beating and the blows he'd receive for leaving home without permission.

In the years afterward, he made charcoal drawings of the flying ships without fins that could churn away whole hillsides. At thirteen, he left home to learn how to read so he could study in the great libraries.

But no one, not the church fathers nor the wise scholars, ever said or wrote anything that satisfied him. His scars unhealed, he died at the age of twenty-two. The violence he'd experienced went on, wreaked on a vast multitude of children on the hour, if not every minute, throughout that troubled land, throughout that continent, overseas, on both sides of the equator and across the whole surface of planet Earth.

During that little boy's short, painful life, however, his fervent desires had migrated to invisible fields radiating around the planet and fused with those of others who had beheld similar wonders. There, in the cyclic depository of time, their kindred yearnings for love and knowledge waited with patience to be acted upon by souls with similar dreams.

ACT I

Chapter 1

"Russian Social Democratic Party Looks to the Destruction of the Czar and His Political System"

—The New York Times

Nizhniy, the Russian Empire
Saturday, March 25, 1911

Sergei Pavlovich Korolev was punched and scolded by a cousin bigger and stronger than he. Although Sergei Pavlovich's nose was bleeding, his nurse sent him to the attic of his grandparents' tilted house, where he plopped down on a dusty floor to watch the other children in the wide street below. The four-year-old had golden hair to his shoulders and round, abnormally black eyes. He didn't have any friends. His parents had separated. His mother, Mariya Nikolaevna, had told him that his father had since died. The intelligent child suspected that she lied, for his grandparents always kept the front gate locked in case an ogre came to steal him away.

One night in the attic, looking up instead of down, he saw seven stars floating like sky wagons. Strange lights, they darted sideways, this way and that. The bright amber dots went higher and higher, so high he thought they would fly over the tallest mountains, and vanished.

He wished he could follow.

Berlin, Germany
Saturday, March 22, 1924

Twelve-year-old Wernher von Braun lashed long cylindrical fireworks securely to the rear of his red wagon.

His four-year-old brother, Magnus, snuggled into its midsection.

Wernher struck a match, lit the wicks, and straddled the front. Holding on tight, they blasted down a cobblestone street—in their minds, faster than Odin's eight-legged fiery steed—jostled and jerked as they careened into a narrow lane and saw shoppers leap out of their way. They sped by shaken fists and outraged shouts.

Clattering into a town square, they cut off the legs of a fruit stand before swerving out of control, tumbling out and skinning their knees in short pants.

Magnus wasn't held in custody, but, as the elder, Wernher was hauled in front of the local constable. At day's end the constable took the lad's hand and walked him home. Two large ink-black ravens watched them from high atop an oak tree.

The constable and his charge were greeted at the magnificent double doors of an aristocratic chateau by Wernher's father, Baron Magnus Freiherr von Braun. The constable sported a fine mustache and had been in the service long enough to know it wasn't his place to lecture the baron on childrearing. He politely handed over the youth, whose slicked blond hair was still tousled from the breakneck flight.

The constable started back down the path.

"Go to your room," the baron told Wernher.

His son nodded and obeyed. He knew the drill.

When his father arrived with the switch, he was bent over the foot of his bed, pants down, bare buttocks exposed.

"*Am Anfang war Erziehung*," the baron said.

After all, it will only help the rambunctious boy, he thought to himself.

A few hard strokes; the youth held back his tears.

"Please, my dear Wernher, do not pull any more *verrückte* stunts," his father respectfully asked. "Think of our family's honor. Think of your mother."

"*Ja, mein Vater.*"

The baron clicked the door shut and, undeterred, Wernher promptly pulled out of a trunk the telescope his mother had given him. He trained it on the darkening sky. While waiting for the stars to appear, he thought about how he might make his next vehicle so powerful that he would one day visit the planet Mars.

Chapter 2

"Europe Solves Her Greatest Problem—Germany Will Pay Through an International Bank War Debts to America"

—*The New York Times*

Berlin, Germany
Tuesday, October 15, 1929

Five years later, perched on its four fins, a rocket three stories high towered over a crowd. Searchlights strafed it, attracting a steady stream of passersby who gathered round, all bundled up against the chill of a fall evening. They pondered the glistening silver obelisk made of wood, concrete, and steel, and debated its purpose.

Silent-film director Fritz Lang, the brains behind the spectacle, adjusted his monocle on a fourth-floor balcony. Above the Romanisches Café, across from the Ufa-Palast am Zoo cinema, he looked through the skeletal limbs of autumn trees in the plaza and could make out the title of his latest film, *Frau im Mond*, lit in garish yellow bulbs. Next to Lang stood his imperious wife, Thea, with the rocket's architect, Hermann Oberth, who had traveled far since leaving his native land of the seven castles. She sipped her aperitif.

"We are getting a large audience," Lang remarked. "Too bad your space train will not work as you had promised, Herr Oberth."

Oberth frowned. He had a high forehead and a thin mouth so wide it seemed to cut the lower part of his face in half. "I told you from the start that launching a rocket of this size and complication had never been done before. I told you it would be a case of trial and error."

He rubbed his aching head, the result of a test fire gone wrong.

"It's not my fault you almost lost an eye!" cried Lang, who removed his monocle and stiffened. "What about my eyes, eh?"

"For a film director, your eyes see very little."

Oberth delivered his sarcastic barbs in a thick Transylvanian accent, which made them all the more irritating to Lang.

Below the trio on the balcony, two members of the German rocket club—Verein für Raumschiffahrt, of which Oberth was president—examined the tall missile. The club's vice president, Willy Ley, held a letter in his hand. Johannes Winkler drew near, not as tall, wearing a straw hat and a long, thick double-breasted black coat with a fur collar.

"Good news, Willy?" he asked. "A response to your endless grasping letters?"

"*Nein.* Only a polite note of no consequence from the American inventor Goddard," replied Willy, reading through wire-rimmed glasses.

"I hear Wernher even placed a long-distance call to the other American rocketeer, that crazy Jack Parsons."

"*Ja*, but he is not giving away anything either." He put the letter into a deep pocket.

"Never mind that, Willy. The missile you constructed with Professor Oberth is a wonder. We are all impressed. But will it fly?"

"You'll see."

They surveyed the crowd that had filled the plaza, searching for their friend. New arrivals climbed the steps of a church for a better view. Hundreds of hats of many kinds bobbed up and down in the searchlights.

"I see a banker or two," Willy noted.

"What we need is an eccentric millionaire banker who wants to go to Mars."

More Berliners in fashionable attire and sables queued up on a red carpet that led to the ticket booth. Some of them stared at the film's stars who lingered beneath the trees in tuxedos and top hats, sequined gowns and furs.

An usher placed a sign on the box office window announcing that the theater's two thousand–plus seats and its proscenium boxes had sold out.

Wernher von Braun had purchased his ticket earlier. At seventeen, tall and athletic, he was unimpressed by the celebrities and didn't feel the cold. The rocket, however, thrilled him. His rocket society associates had kept their work a secret, a surprise, until today. He was quite amazed to see it at last.

He moved in for a closer look, and one of the powerful searchlights caught him in its beam. Those nearest, struck by his polished demeanor and sure stride, mistook him for one of the film stars. With his slick blond hair and pronounced chin, he seemed to some a young avatar of the god Wotan.

On the top steps of the church, Captain Walter Dornberger, dressed in civilian clothes, eyed the rocket with envy; his two aides scanned the plaza.

"Do you see them?" Dornberger asked, his eyes fixed on the missile.

"*Ja.*" His junior officer pointed in the direction of Willy Ley and Johannes Winkler. "Over there."

They waded into the throng like starved wolves.

On the balcony, Fritz Lang welcomed Joseph Goebbels, an influential fixture in the National Socialist German Workers' Party. "How good of you to come."

"Not at all, Herr Director. I would not miss for anything a premiere of Germany's greatest filmmaker." Goebbels smiled at Thea. "I believe you wrote the story yourself, my dear? Soon we may have to keep your stories of people flying on rockets to the Moon a secret, eh? Enemies of the fatherland might get ideas."

"Now that you are here, Herr *Gauleiter*, we may begin," Lang said, anxious to avoid a political discussion.

He nodded to Oberth, who waved to the technicians below.

"Let the countdown commence!" an excited alto voice blared from loudspeakers placed in trees along the perimeter of the plaza. "*Noch zehn Sekunden!*"

Searchlights crisscrossed the rocket and the crowd, crowd and rocket.

"*Zehn, neun...*"

Von Braun approached Willy and Johannes.

"Eight, seven..."

The crowd, not sure what the rocket had in store for them, fell back, then surged forward.

"*Sechs, fünf...*"

Dornberger, flanked by his two aides, shook Johannes's hand. Something in the older man's bearing, a hint of the *Reichswehr*, caught Willy's eye.

"Four, three..."

Von Braun joined them. He smiled an irresistible smile backlit by a searchlight that seemed to follow him wherever he went.

"*Zwei, eins...*"

The balcony quartet leaned out from their perch as far as they dared, to almost float in space.

"*Jetzt!*"

White sparks erupted from under the rocket. The crowd gasped.

"*Start-Rakete ausgebrannt! Vollgas auf Mittel-Rakete!*"

Orange and yellow particles zigged and zagged among the four fins. They popped and crackled, reflected in the faces of those closest to the spectacle. Von Braun's and Dornberger's respiration quickened, but the sparks subsided and blinked out.

The rocket had never left the ground.

The fire marshals relaxed.

"Pathetic," Lang mumbled on his balcony, loud enough for Oberth to hear.

"*Verwunderlich!*" von Braun laughed with Dornberger.

"*Meine Damen und Herren*, our exciting preshow is over!" the loudspeaker announced. "Ticket holders may now proceed into the foyer for the breathtaking premiere of *Woman in the Moon!*"

Berliners filed through theater doors.

Bereft of sightseers, the tall rocket, its lower third singed and blackened by the small explosives, was encircled only by true believers, who saw in its silver-bullet Platonic form a transcendent future.

Chapter 3

"Market Losses Reach New Level"

—Harrisburg Telegraph

Roswell, New Mexico
Tuesday, December 30, 1930

Two day workers tramped along an unpaved road about a quarter mile outside the small town of Roswell. They were covered from head to shoe in a thin layer of dull gray dirt.

A cream-colored Ford Model A pulled up beside them, and its passenger window rolled down.

"Ve are looking fur de Eden Valley," said a thin face behind green-lensed aviator sunglasses. "It's not on map. Can you help, please?"

The driver, a fat man with a double chin, kept his eyes straight ahead.

"Sure, mister," said the taller worker. "Just keep going where you're going, and at the crossroads take a hard right on One Horse Road. You'll see Eden Valley soon enough."

"Zank you."

The car sped away, trailing a yellow dust cloud.

"You don't approve of furreners, do ya?" said the shorter worker in the yellow swirl.

"I respect folk's privacy. If they'd been invited by the professor, they woulda known the way." The tall man spit some tobacco, and they tramped on. "Besides, the professor and his crew are up to something behind those cottonwood trees. And I'm pretty sure they don't want anyone knowing what it is."

The two workers crossed a road and continued on their way.

Ten minutes later a lone motorcyclist roared past. The shorter man, waving another dirt cloud away, happened to notice long brown curls poking out between the rider's black helmet and leather jacket.

* * *

In Eden Valley, three rickety Ford trucks rattled along in single file across a barren prairie floor. The lead truck towed a two-wheeled farm wagon, its cargo draped in heavy blankets.

They pulled up in a clearing among the dry shrubs, where Robert Goddard's rocket testing tower stood sixty feet above the dirt, secured by guy wires anchored in concrete slabs.

The vehicles' occupants climbed out and began unloading their equipment. The winter morning air stung their cheeks. The six men sported berets or straw hats and jackets.

"Easy with her," Goddard said.

It took two men to lift the thirty-three-pound, eleven-foot-long slender cylinder from the farm wagon.

"Right, doc," said one of the men.

Professor Robert Goddard loved his handiwork, from glistening nose cone to flaring stabilizer vanes; he loved its tanks and tubing. He'd had one quadrant painted Chinese red. Goddard was bald, with dark eyebrows and intense eyes in a gentle sphere of a head. The inventor's body was stooped over with age, his chest thin and hollow, racked from tuberculosis. The desert air was good for him. He and his wife, Esther, had moved from the East Coast to Mescalero Ranch for his health and his work.

Crew readied the rocket in the tower. A workman played out electric cable from the rear of a truck as it drove slowly from the tower a thousand feet to the control shelter, which they'd buttressed with sandbags. Two others assembled the controls.

Standing beside Esther, the professor supervised his assistants, bowlegged Henry Sachs and careful Larry, who fed gasoline into the tanks. This was followed by liquid oxygen, called "lox," which they kept in a thermos. Henry had made the move out west with the Goddards. Larry studied engineering at a local college. Young and enthusiastic, he'd become the professor's confidante.

"If the combustion chamber holds," Goddard said, "we might do well today."

"Any word from the government?" Larry asked, at his task.

"None at all. There's no public money for experiments nowadays, but"—Goddard held up a finger and smiled—"but in no case should we allow ourselves to be deterred. Test by test, step by step, until one day we may travel where we want in space, cost what it may. In the meantime, thank God for Guggenheim."

"May his money last," Esther intoned. "We received another letter from overseas this morning." Esther had wavy hair and a sturdy build under her warm coat, and she saw that the news irritated her husband. "What should I say in return?"

"Let me think about it," he replied. "I certainly wouldn't mention what we're doing today to that nosey German, Oberth."

Esther nodded. She considered Oberth a brilliant mathematician as well as an overweening pest.

After a final check-over, they all piled into the third truck and drove over uneven ground to the control shelter, scaring off a jackrabbit.

About six hundred yards away, the double-chinned driver and his partner with green sunglasses lay hidden in the shrubs. They'd found their way to Eden Valley and Goddard. The fat man looked through field binoculars at the launch tower and spoke in German while the other took notes.

Standing on the shelter's roof, the professor observed his rocket through a telescope. When its pressure-generated tanks had built up to two hundred pounds, he said quietly, "Fire the igniter, Larry."

Larry pressed control-key number one, and flame shot out of the rocket's base. Goddard brought the second pressure gauge up on the fuel tank. The rocket strained at its cables. At 225 pounds, an automatic release allowed her to rise from the tower slowly until she shot up.

"One thousand feet and still climbing!" Larry shouted.

But the professor saw the rocket slanting. Henry timed her with a stopwatch. Larry observed its red quadrant and recorded its rotation; another technician with a telescope registered its time position.

With a shrill whistle, the projectile crashed down seconds later, about half a mile away.

"Its parachute didn't work," Goddard said to Esther. "Something must have jammed."

"I'd say the apex of the flight was about two thousan' feet," Henry reported, "and goin' about five hundred miles an hour."

Goddard went with the others to retrieve the remnants.

"First we have to reconfigure that parachute release," he told them, "then we better start retesting our gyroscopic controls."

"Hey, doc." Henry pointed southwest. "Who's that over there?"

They saw two men hurrying to a car.

"Think they're spies?" asked Larry.

"Could be," Goddard said. "Let's go after them."

Their overloaded truck rumbled slowly forward, however, while the Germans in a more powerful vehicle plowed back onto the road with a good lead. The fat man lost sight of the Americans, but his thin-faced companion with green sunglasses pivoted and squinted hard at a motorcycle that had come into view behind them.

"Mach schnell!" he cried.

The double-chinned man pressed the accelerator down to the floor; through the rear window his partner saw the cycle close.

About two hundred yards behind them, the rider removed a revolver from a side holster as the bike hit eighty miles per hour.

The thin-faced man leaned out, aimed, and fired his Luger twice as the rider swerved right to left. The biker fired and the car's left rear tire exploded. The automobile zigzagged into the prairie and skidded sideways to a stop.

The fat driver climbed out and the motorcyclist slowed before putting two bullets through his chest. The thin-faced man threw himself to the ground, tried to roll away, and screamed when the motorcycle wheels sped over him, crushing his calves.

His cries of agony stopped short—his green glasses shattered, pierced by a bullet through his eye.

The rider put the Harley-Davidson on its kickstand and took off her helmet in order to rummage through the car. The dead men couldn't see that the cyclist was a woman with a pale face who gathered up their notes and passports. She stowed them in her vehicle's rear compartment.

Back astride her bike, she pulled at a brown curl, tossed a hand grenade into their Model A, then peeled out and away.

Still more than a mile behind, Goddard cried, "Look at that!"

A fireball had erupted where the spies had been heading.

The professor reported the whole incident to a local sheriff, but it remained a mystery for years to come.

From that day on, however, Goddard became even more secretive, for he knew what only a few others scattered across the globe suspected: the country that solved the problems and harnessed the fearsome power of the fledgling rocket would dominate the world.

Chapter 4

"Chancellor Von Papen Lifts Ban on Nazi Party Paramilitary Group—Over 400,000 Strong"

—*The Times,* London

Berlin, Germany
Wednesday, June 22, 1932

A thick morning fog north of the city caused the few automobilists on the road to drive slowly.

A black sedan, yellow headlights on, turned off the main thoroughfare onto an unpaved side path. A few hundred meters later it stopped with a jerk, brakes squeaking. Its yellow beams illuminated a weathered wooden sign nailed to a post that read, through dripping water: RAKETENFLUGPLATZ BERLIN.

Four men dressed in civilian greatcoats stepped out of the vehicle and proceeded silently on foot across a barren field spotted with clumps of dwarf trees and derelict shacks.

"Our agents continue to have bad luck in New Mexico," Colonel Karl Becker said to Captain Walter Dornberger as they crossed a rivulet. "That American professor Goddard seems to have guardian angels who protect his work from prying eyes."

"Herr Colonel, I have good news on that subject. Lucky for us, the Americans are stupid. While they protect the man, his patents are easily bought for a pittance. As we speak they are being translated and analyzed."

"*Gut!* When one door is closed, another is opened." They passed a large mound of gravel. "Now let us see what these young madmen of the Berlin Rocket Club have to show us."

Becker, Dornberger, and their two officers marched into the fog.

About 150 meters away, beyond the marshes, three shabbier dressed fellows struggled to detach from a car roof their four-meter-long pencil-thin rocket.

"Hurry!" urged Johannes Winkler. "They will be here any minute."

"Don't rush me," said Willy Ley.

"Friends, let's not bicker," said Wernher von Braun, who wore the white, dirty long-coat of a workman. "They are probably near even if we cannot see them."

"Who is going to do the talking?" Johannes panicked.

Their mentor, Herr Oberth, had returned home to teach.

"We will play it by ear," said Wernher.

Johannes whispered, "They're here!" when the four men emerged from the ground mists, the bronze buttons on their greatcoats wet and sparkling.

"I'm glad we found you in this pea soup!" Becker called out.

He had brown eyes and a cleft chin. His head of short-cropped auburn and gray hair was uncovered, and he looked at the young men paternally.

The two groups faced each other in semicircles and introductions were made. Dornberger announced that he had recently been appointed to the ballistics council of the German Army, responsible for the development of secret weapons. Becker was his superior. "I said goodbye to my old department, the Wa Prüf 11. To be honest, Colonel Becker and I—we are presently in search of talent."

"We are honored," Wernher spoke in his best upper-class cadence, "that such distinguished guests from the ballistics section would attend one of our club's test launches." He had a high voice, but instead of sounding girlish, it made him seem more intelligent to others.

So Wernher will lead. Willy was relieved.

It was not the army's first visit, yet it promised to be their last if things didn't go well. Their rocket club needed cash badly.

"Tell me," Colonel Becker inquired, "how did you get your start?"

"We formed our little society several years ago," Wernher said in an easy manner, "after many good drinks in the back room of a very bad restaurant. The Golden Scepter, in Breslau, on July 5, 1927—I know the exact day because each year we celebrate the anniversary."

"We are committed to spreading the idea of space flight," said Willy. "Wait a few moments please and we will show you."

They excused themselves to make final adjustments to their rocket.

Dornberger, in his thirties, and Becker, in his fifties, traded amused glances.

Minutes later, the rocket blasted off.

Seconds later, flames shot through a crack in its cylinder. The projectile traveled horizontally rather than vertically and came to a fiery crash less than two kilometers away.

"A pitiful display!" Becker scolded them. "You would do better to concentrate on scientific data rather than fire these toys. Captain Dornberger and I are interested in rocketry, but there are a number of obvious and glaring defects in your organization."

The officers saw that the three young men were embarrassed but the visitors did nothing to hide their disappointment. Willy and Johannes hung back, leaving Wernher to absorb the brunt of the colonel's words.

"You must strive to advance with more scientific thoroughness. On the occasions Captain Dornberger has paid you a visit, he has reported on boys at play. Now I have seen it with my own eyes. What we want are serious people. What we want to know is fuel consumption per second, what mixture is best, how to deal with extreme temperatures, what types of injection, combustion chamber shape, and exhaust nozzles yield the best performance. We are most concerned with a properly functioning propulsion unit."

"I must agree with the colonel," Dornberger barked. "Your operation is flimsy. With this kind of rinky-dink setup, how can you measure your propellant consumption or your combustion pressure?"

"Gentlemen," Wernher replied calmly, "we would be pleased to satisfy each of your demands if you would only be so good enough to purchase for us the necessary instruments."

"Ha!" Becker made his laughter sharp. "Bluster is fine in its place, yet there is far too much showmanship in your group's theatrics. We may be pleased by your gumption, but if you want our guidance, you will also have to stop wasting energy on publicity articles in newspapers about fantastic stunts."

"Gentlemen, you must not blame us for our approach. We have to use a certain amount of showmanship to keep our place going. As you can see for yourself, this forsaken spot and our meager tools—well, it's not much to look at."

"True." Dornberger lit an Atikah cigarette. "Yet it is just this weakness for publicity that makes it difficult for us to do business with you. If we are going to make something of military value, it will have to be done under the strictest secrecy."

"Of course."

The colonel glanced at Dornberger, who nodded.

"Very well," Becker decided. "We will consider giving your group an opportunity to continue with more adequate means—if you will work behind the fence of an army post. No more newspapers. No more stunts."

Becker and his two officers withdrew.

"Herr von Braun," Dornberger said before joining them, "why not discuss our offer with your associates? You have five minutes."

The three young men retreated behind one of the shacks and they, too, lit cigarettes.

The fog was lifting, and a hazy sun shone through it in spots.

"I have a dread of ignorant bureaucrats," Johannes began. "They will terribly hinder the free development of our brainchild."

"*Ja*," said Willy. "Once we go behind that fence, the army will choke us with their red tape. And what about Hitler? What if he gets hold of the army?"

"Hitler?" asked Wernher. "Hindenburg will trounce him."

"How can you be so sure?" Johannes blinked and rubbed his eye.

"I am not sure. But if we do not move forward, we will never get anywhere. This won't be a marriage, after all. It will be a business arrangement. The real question is, how can we milk this cash cow most effectively so they get what they want—and we get what we want."

"Wernher is perhaps right," Johannes said, rubbing his other eye. "The others didn't even show up today, and our experiments are now too expensive for any organization except a millionaires' club."

"Or the army, I suppose." Willy sighed. "Wernher, your attitude is too *Deutsche Adels Gesellschaft*. Convenient for you, but nobody else..."

Out of earshot, Becker asked, "Do you really think this young man can help us build a liquid-fuel rocket suitable for mass production?"

"I do." Dornberger took a drag on his Atikah. "When I come here, I am struck pleasantly by this von Braun's energy and his shrewdness. His knowledge is astonishing, though I admit far too theoretical. While the others make wild boasts, he lays bare the difficulties. In this respect he is a refreshing change; he is a realist and of superior character. If they agree, I will send him back to school and train him properly."

Becker nodded. "Perhaps we should invite only this von Braun into our good graces?"

"An excellent idea, Herr Colonel." Dornberger clicked his heels.

Five minutes elapsed, and the last wisps of fog burned away.

The two groups faced each other once more, in the sun. Wernher opened his mouth to speak, but Dornberger cut him off. "We have a different proposal. Herr von Braun will join us. We will bring in you others when our important work has progressed."

"I would rather not leave my friends." Wernher exhaled smoke through his nose.

"You will not leave them." Becker took the young man by the arm and led him away. "They will join you—later."

Dornberger and the two soldiers followed, watched by Willy and Johannes, who weren't sure what to do or say.

Two ravens fluttered out from the sunlight to perch atop a nearby tall fence. They watched the officers and the young man walk away.

"If you cannot be a whole body unto yourself," Becker said to Wernher, "why not join such a whole by serving as a mighty limb. That is wisdom from Schiller."

One of the ravens cawed. It had a powerful beak to tear flesh from bone, and its claws gripped the rotting wood like iron.

* * *

The following Saturday, Willy called on the von Braun family at their home in a lush park southeast of the Brandenburg Gate.

Wernher, dressed for dinner in a black evening jacket and pressed pants, greeted Willy at the door. He guided him through their luxurious rooms, by stained glass portraits of folklore heroes and art deco furnishings. Willy commented on it all with familiarity and expertise.

During an elegant repast, Baron Magnus Freiherr von Braun sat at the head of a long gilded mahogany table. His wife, Emmy von Quistorp, severe in manner and regard, her blonde hair in a bun and a pearl necklace round her rosy neck, reigned at the opposite end. Like their son, they were dressed formally. To the baron's right dined twenty-year-old Wernher and his friend; to the baron's left, his youngest son, thirteen-year-old Magnus Jr. His eldest, Sigismund, was not at home that day.

"Donc, c'est officiel, père," Wernher announced. *"Notre petite societé de la fusée va faire partie de l'Armée."*

"Et bien, mon fils, tout ça me semble un peu soudain," said the baron, who had a long, aquiline nose.

"All this French is spoiling my appetite," Willy said in German. "I cannot translate and eat."

"The key is not to translate," Wernher said, wolfing down some boiled cabbage. "At each dinner we speak another language—French,

English, Portuguese—so they become second nature. Anyway, I said to my father that our rocket club has become part of the army. Officially." He addressed his mother. *"Maintenant, chère mère, notre travail avancera plus rapidement."*

Emmy glanced at her husband in a manner that sought his support.

The baron placed his silver mother-of-pearl fork and knife carefully to either side of his plate and spoke in German, out of politeness to Willy. "Wernher, do you realize Hitler may soon be elected chancellor and that he will control the army of which you speak? At every turn he outsmarts the government."

"Hitler will not last." Wernher pierced a Brussels sprout with his fork. "Besides, has he not promised peace while he rebuilds the country?"

His father stiffened.

"Son, I have heard that an art gallery in Munich has recently acquired a large painting of Adolf Hitler in which he is plated in shining armor. Let me tell you something: men who wear armor intend to go to war."

"That is my fear also," said Willy.

"Well, if we are going to war," Wernher said, "we shall have to win it. *Nous serons les vainqueurs!*"

Chapter 5

"Hitler Made Chancellor of Germany but Coalition Cabinet Limits Power; Centrists Hold Balance in Reichstag"

—*The San Francisco Chronicle*

Nakhabino, Union of Soviet Socialist Republics
Thursday, August 17, 1933

"Put that book down!" commanded Mikhail Klavdievich Glushko. "How can you stomach such vile propaganda?"

Sergei Pavlovich Korolev, stretched out on a fallen tree, raised his eyes from his novel and laughed. He thought it a good joke, for in truth they were both reading *Red Star*, whose young revolutionary is carried off by aliens to a Marxist paradise on Mars. There, to the young rocketeers' delight, their countryman experiences the abolition of money (they had little), advanced technology (their dream), and free love (why not?).

"Has our guest arrived?" Sergei Pavlovich asked, putting his book into a satchel.

"Yes."

Glushko had slicked-back hair, an ironed cotton shirt, tailored pants, and he nodded sideways at a tall elderly man in a forest clearing surrounded by an admiring group of GIRD members. The elderly man held a tin trumpet to his ear to hear their questions and compliments.

The legend: Konstantin Tsiolkovsky! thought Korolev.

In contrast to Glushko, Korolev appeared to have slept in his clothes. Yet it was he who had persuaded the revered father of Russian rocketry to come and witness the launch of GIRD-09.

"You had better go greet him," Glushko advised. "Introduce yourself. He may not remember you."

"Yes, yes." Korolev stumbled to his feet. "You're right."

He overcame his lingering shyness and loped over, with Glushko, his chief engineer, right behind.

"The basic drive to reach for the Sun," Tsiolkovsky was saying, "to shed the cables of gravity, has been a dream of mine ever since as a young man I read Jules Verne. I would wander the streets of Moscow late at night trying to figure out how to make his fantasies a reality."

"Dobriy den, Kamrad!" Korolev shook the old man's hand firmly and spoke into his hearing aid. "I am Sergei Pavlovich Korolev, director of the *Gruppa izucheniya reaktivnogo dvizheniya*—GIRD."

"Of course you are," said Tsiolkovsky, and Sergei saw recognition in the old man's clear eyes. "In the years since we last met, your GIRD has come a long way."

"I agree with Lenin," Korolev said. "We are a backward country, and only the real applications of technology can save us. We must master the highest technology—or be crushed!" He gestured toward the silver projectile being prepared by GIRD members. "Your work has been my inspiration."

"The modern age is a difficult business, young man." Tsiolkovsky still held onto the young man's hand and peered into his face and dark eyes—Korolev had the confident shoulders of a bull. "It will require knowledge, willpower, and many years—perhaps a lifetime of failures and difficulties."

"I am not afraid of difficulties. To be honest, we've already had our share."

Korolev led his guest to a small stage that had been constructed not far from the access road so he might say a few words to the engineers and enthusiasts: a grand total of three women and seven men in

Lenin-style leather caps and labor shirts with rolled-up sleeves in the cool evening air.

"My dear fellow workers," Tsiolkovsky said. "There is no end to life and to the improvement of mankind—today you are to launch a small rocket..."

After his short speech, they moved to a concrete dugout. Only Korolev and engineer Efremov remained in the launch area some fifty meters away. Efremov stepped onto a high wooden box to double-check the jellied petroleum in the combustion chamber, while Korolev fueled the two-and-a-half-meter-long four-finned rocket.

At 20:10 he lit the fuse and ran with Efremov back to the dugout, where he switched on the ignition.

"Launch!" Korolev shouted.

"There is contact!" GIRD member Kruglova turned a handle.

Efremov jerked a long launch rope that rotated a cock that allowed liquid oxygen into the combustion chamber.

Tsiolkovsky, trumpet to his ear, heard a sharp *bang!*

The engine growled and the rocket raised itself up.

Everyone crowded around the dugout's single slit window.

"Forward—to Mars!" they shouted.

The rocket accelerated into the gray sky. At about four hundred meters up, it stalled, flattened out, and dove into the forest.

Efremov and Kruglova sprinted into the woods to dig for remnants. Minutes later they returned.

"A gas puncture in the flange was the culprit," Efremov said.

They made vodka toasts to their first successful launch.

"Long live interplanetary travel!"

"Soviet rockets must conquer space!"

Tsiolkovsky bid them adieu and was chauffeured back to Moscow.

Korolev, glass in hand, sought out his friend. "Here, read this," he said, shoving into Glushko's open palm a short manuscript. "'Rocket Flight in Stratosphere,' by Sergei Pavlovich Korolev. Me. Perhaps it will help you improve upon your natural ineptitude."

"So," Glushko smiled. "The little boy who ventured out of his lonely attic has become a rocketman today."

"Both of us. Do you think our revered guest enjoyed himself?"

"How could he not? There were tears in his eyes. I saw him wipe them away myself."

* * *

Everyone had walked or hitched a ride back to the train station but Glushko. Korolev had a date with his childhood sweetheart, Lyalya.

The only movement in the dark forest were light branches blown by a strong breeze.

In the dugout, Glushko rechecked the altitude reading with a flashlight. He swiveled to the right and saw a young woman in drab clothes with her arms crossed.

"Yóbanny v rot!" he exclaimed. "Who the hell are you?"

She pulled out a folder from within her jacket and threw it on the ground.

"What the hell is that?"

"Detailed plans of the American Robert Goddard's discoveries." She had a soothing voice.

"We don't need it," retorted Glushko, resentful. "The Germans might be copying him like mad, but not GIRD."

"Then don't use it."

"Hold on." He stopped her with a smooth hand. "Why come to us? We are not soldiers."

"Not yet, Mikhail Klavdievich Glushko. But your Revolutionary Military Council has recently formed a reaction propulsion institute. With a little nudge from Tsiolkovsky, they will see the value of GIRD's work. You and Sergei Pavlovich Korolev are going to be in the military aircraft business. And soon."

Glushko judged her European features beautiful, with a touch of the Semitic. Her brown, curly hair was unusually long. Though he had no fear of women, he thought he'd better mind his manners.

"You are a Jew?" he asked. "Why are you doing this? The Party does not exactly look on your people with love in their eyes."

"In exchange for that folder, six hundred families are on their way to Palestine. They will be able to leave this communist shithole."

She brushed past him.

Glushko hesitated, then picked up the dossier.

It contained a report Goddard had written for the American Acting Secretary of the Navy, test flight results and military applications for his rockets, translated into Russian.

Glushko thought he would show it to his friend Korolev.

Or perhaps not.

Chapter 6

"German Troops Enter Rhineland; Hitler Proposes to Re-Enter League of Nations—On Conditions"

—*Evening Standard,* London

Kummersdorf West, Germany
Friday, December 11, 1936

The violence of the explosion sent shards of steel and aluminum whistling through the thin winter air. Von Braun made a run for the line of fir trees, where Dornberger, recently promoted to the rank of major, had already taken shelter. Jagged metal fragments stuck deep into the bark only inches above their heads. They looked at each other in disbelief—and laughed.

"What fools we have been!" Major Dornberger roared.

They returned to the launch area and found their control room burning, its planks and metal sheets twisted into a splintered mess. Searchlights meant to track the rocket had malfunctioned when cords carrying their juice had burst into flames.

Johannes Winkler, somehow unharmed, stumbled over to them, his lab coat singed and blackened. They grabbed him by the arms and made their way over hard ground to the nursing station.

In their efforts to realize more formidable weapons at Kummersdorf West, the German Army's experimental firing station, Dornberger, von Braun, and their growing team had two buildings with offices, a design and measurement room, a workshop, and a test stand for liquid-propellant rocket development. Money flowed easily to their secret projects.

At midnight in the cafeteria, where only a few others snacked, they deliberated head-to-head. The enthusiastic duo had already drawn up an ambitious schedule of experiments during hours of lively discussions that often endured late into the night.

"It is obvious to me," Dornberger said.

"Yes." Von Braun nodded curtly. "We are going to need more space, bags and bags of reichsmarks, and many more people. Qualified people."

"And above all—security."

A phone rang on one of the long white tables.

A tired lieutenant answered it, listened, and relayed a message to the room: "Dr. Wahmke says he is about to mix hydrogen peroxide and alcohol. He's going to feed them into a rocket chamber through a single valve and ignite it."

"Has Dr. Wahmke gone crazy?" Dornberger leapt up and the other technicians ceased snacking. "No safeguards have been installed yet!"

"*Ja*, that is why he called." The lieutenant hung up. "The doctor wants help to be sent right away if we hear a loud bang."

Von Braun shrugged. "There is no stopping him. That maniac is obsessed with mixing propellants before combustion."

Dornberger rushed to the door but was lurched sideways when a blast rocked the building.

He, von Braun, and the others made their way through the wreckage to a testing room. Among the lead pipes dripping water, they could find nothing of Wahmke and his three colleagues except, oddly, two cigarette butts still smoldering in the ruins.

* * *

Perhaps due to its high rate of fiery accidents, Johannes Winkler quit the rocket society, and the army, not long afterward. His talents would be missed. Going over their dwindling list of qualified personnel, Dornberger and Becker also learned that an early member of the society,

Rudolf Nebel, had recently been dismissed from the Schutzstaffel for being mentally unstable.

"Can you imagine the SS kicking anyone out because they think he is deranged?" Dornberger asked Colonel Becker. "That is hard to believe."

"You can replace Winkler with Dieter," Becker pointed out.

Dornberger looked over Dieter's file. An engineer from good schools who spent his spare days as an honorary *Sturmabteilung*. He'd signed up early with the Nazi Party.

"Arthur Dieter," Major Dornberger said aloud. "I will take up his eligibility and qualifications with von Braun…"

* * *

Willy Ley, alone in his apartment living room, folded in two the forged letter he'd written on company stationery that allowed his legal departure from Germany and put it into his wallet.

He switched off the lights and looked out the window. Turbulent night winds blew the snow in every direction at once.

Carrying only his favorite books and his treatises on rocketry, along with some clothes shoved into an old green suitcase, he descended a circular staircase and took a tram to the Anhalter Bahnhof station. There he caught a late train to Paris.

What I am doing is right, Ley reassured himself as he crossed the frontier into France.

He wanted to put a lot of water between himself and the Nazis, their storm troopers, the army, the Brownshirts, and Hitler. Ley saw Germany headed toward disaster. He planned to make his way to the United States, where he hoped to be free and safe—unless his former associates succeeded in their plans to build the most long-range, most terrifying weapons the world had ever seen.

In which case it wouldn't matter.

No one would survive.

Chapter 7

"Roosevelt Urges 'Concerted Action' for Peace—League Committee Condemns Japan"

—*The New York Times*

Peenemünde Army Research Center, Germany
Friday, February 18, 1938

A passenger train rolled through the countryside. A woman with brown curly hair saw through her window cows grazing in pastures, a sight that became more frequent as the pine forests thinned out.

She had worked on a kibbutz in Palestine. Her fluency in German, Hebrew, English, and Arabic had brought her to the attention of a secret organization. She knew little of engineering and physics, but her ability to blend in with several cultures, as well as her physical abilities, honed through long training, made her a natural. She knew when someone told the truth and when they lied, so she had been turned into a spy.

The young lady and those on their way to Peenemünde had to pass through a military checkpoint at Damerow. Guards in heavy overcoats examined her documents and her special *Sondergenehmigung*, printed on watermarked paper.

Forty-five minutes later, the train stopped at Zempin, a town on a strip of land barely wide enough to hold its own against the Baltic Sea. She could make out the faraway Swedish coast despite an early morning mist. Under her ankle-length winter coat, she wore a plain cream blouse and a floral-patterned skirt down to her calves. The young lady showed her *Zusatz*, an orange card, to an inspector.

She was returning to her job after a day off spent with friends from the facility. They were known as the "wallpaper girls," because they processed large sheets of technical drawings.

The train chugged minutes later into Zinnowitz, a former resort taken over by the rocket team. Deboarding, she observed many men in army and air force uniforms going about their daily tasks. She counted them and would remember their numbers.

The young lady followed a crowd of day workers from the Federal Station into the smaller wooden structure of the Plant Terminal for the transfer. There were no ticket windows here, only a large sign in emphatic lettering: WHAT YOU SEE, WHAT YOU HEAR, WHEN YOU LEAVE—LEAVE IT HERE!

More guards and a last checkpoint. A sergeant with a ruddy face scrutinized her *Vorläufige Genehmigung* on white vellum.

A red-and-yellow train pulled into the station, a Berlin commuter-style S-Bahn. It had large windows, comfortable seating, automatic double doors, and elegant finishing touches. It ran on a single track straight to the factory gates, the same route she'd taken six days a week for the last month.

"Why does the train not go faster?" asked a young man, new to the place.

An engineer she recognized, an older man, wearing a brown suit and hat, answered, "It's rather embarrassing, but somebody slipped up. The voltage of the rectifier stations does not match the train motors. It is too late and too expensive to change. We are stuck with it!"

Thicker clusters of pine trees crowded both sides of the commuter car, and the young woman let the *clink, clink, clink* of metal wheels on steel tracks calm her nerves.

They passed about fifty men building wooden barracks behind a chain-link fence.

For the prison workers to come, she thought. *Planning for the future.*

They reached the "suburbs" next, solid brick structures two or three stories high, where the heads of departments, engineers, and scientists lived with their families.

The train then rolled through the open iron portal of the Peenemünde Research Facility, where multiple tracks branched off to larger buildings hidden beneath camouflaged netting. The car clanked noisily over junctions until they stopped at the westernmost extremity of the long sand spit.

Employees filed out.

The young lady sashayed in her flower skirt with the other girls toward their assigned building. They chatted and passed many who had the letters HAP, Heeresanstalt Peenemünde, sewn onto their jacket shoulders. Besides those of the Wehrmacht, Luftwaffe, and local flak units, she noted officers from SS detachments and sailors from patrol vessels.

The army controlled Peenemünde East; the Luftwaffe, Peenemünde West.

Inside a large, airy hall, the wallpaper girls curtsied to their director, Dr. Paul Schroeder, and took their places at a long measurement table. Side by side with about twenty women in frocks, she would spend the day poring over blueprints, using a slide ruler to fill in correct numbers.

Normally her access would have been severely limited—badges of different shapes and colors strictly controlled where one could go and which gates would be opened—but, smart and pretty, the young woman was mobile. She'd become Schroeder's adjunct to several plant departments, whose young, unmarried men enjoyed flirting with her.

Soon I will visit the office.

"There he is again—*Seppl!*" one of the younger girls giggled, pointing out the window.

They swiveled to see the commander of the camp, Major Walter Dornberger, striding by in his Bavarian-style leather *Seppl-Hosen*. He often exhibited the traditional outfit when off duty, much to the women's delight.

"Do not be distracted by the major's spectacular legs!" Schroeder wagged his finger at the *Messfrauen*.

The spy smiled with the others but kept her eyes on *Seppl*, who had stopped to speak with a man in civilian clothes. She recognized him as the plant's technical director, Wernher von Braun.

After a brief exchange, they parted ways.

She had gleaned, through discreet questioning, that von Braun's own mother had recommended this remote site when he'd mentioned their need for unprecedented secrecy. The Air Ministry had split the cost with the army—several hundred million reichsmarks for the land—and a government official had been sent in a high-powered car with the proper authority to purchase the roughly twenty square kilometers from the city. All this, less than two years before.

Government money had flooded in. The plant had landed on Hitler's priority list, which meant it could gobble up raw materials and men as needed. Dr. Schroeder's superior had a copy of that priority list, and the young woman had photographed it late one night.

She'd noted, despite the plant's importance to the *Führer*, that its politics were oddly neutral. Strong views on the state or Nazism were largely absent from conversations. The "super engineers," as they called themselves, were "out of the world," obsessed with their work. She'd probed during lunches in the canteen or on outings, yet discussions would always lapse into valves, relay contacts, mixers, or other technical matters. They would even talk excitedly about interplanetary travel and intercontinental mail delivered via rocket.

They are fooling themselves. That Seppl knows it.

She sensed that von Braun believed himself half man, half lion, an object of veneration to himself and others, especially to women, the driving force of the factory, beloved and charismatic. They even had nicknames for him: "Sunny Boy" or "the Merry Heathen."

The spy made a notation on the technical drawing. She wished she'd been sent to kill him, wished her mission might cripple Germany's nascent rocket program.

But her organization didn't want that.

* * *

While the *Messfrauen* toiled, von Braun headed toward the Development Works. He absently recalculated how long a trip to Mars would take and admired the two big concrete sheds of the Preproduction Works.

His long leather raincoat tightly cinched, he crossed paths with those from the Harbor Station and with those on their way to the Oxygen Generating Plant. He stopped once or twice for a brief word with supervisors. He always emphasized to them the importance of personal communication over memos.

He looked up at the sky, a deep blue studded with white clouds, then quickened his pace to arrive on time for his weekly directors' meeting in the Development Building, his mind sharp. Sitting to his right, Dornberger was now in military garb, his peaked cap on the rectangular pinewood table. Most of the other fifteen serious faces were civilians; among them, Helmut Gröttrup, flight control; Dr. Walter Thiel, deputy director and engines; Dr. Kurt Debus, firing; and Arthur Dieter, fuel research and statistics. Dornberger had gone over Dieter's file with von Braun years before, and the technical director had not objected to the statistician's zealous politics.

The assembled quickly went over several items on the agenda. A stenographer took notes.

Von Braun asked, "How are our competitors doing?"

"We continue to intercept Goddard's mail," reported Debus, who doubled as intelligence liaison. He had jet-black hair and a raised dueling scar that snaked from below his lower lip up his right cheek. "He receives considerable support from the Guggenheim Foundation, as well as the Carnegie Institute. Fortunately for us, not a single branch of the American military takes him seriously. They think he is a…loon."

Dieter chuckled, and Debus flipped to the next page of his report.

"Our military attaché to the United States, von Boetticher, has submitted a four-page report to the Abwehr. Goddard has had little success since his rocket obtained an altitude of two-thousand four-hundred meters."

"And the Russians?"

"In almost total disarray. Their internal squabbling has derailed any meaningful work."

"Although the American is not adequately funded," Dornberger said, looking at each of them in turn, "we must not forget that we are in a race to create the first large liquid-fuel rocket. Tomorrow his navy might recognize its importance and give him millions. In all of your work it is essential to remember this state of affairs if we are to remain on the *Führer*'s priority list."

"I could not agree more," said Dieter. "We are already about halfway through the first three hundred million reichsmarks and without a true success."

"That may explain why," Gröttrup sighed, "my order for pencil sharpeners was rejected."

Several of the fifteen laughed.

"My poor Helmut, here is a solution: even the cheapest budget bureau official cannot suspect that an 'appliance for milling wooden dowels of ten millimeters in diameter as per sample' is a pencil sharpener. I humbly suggest you follow my lead, and surely your supplies will miraculously appear."

"Gentlemen, it is our duty and the hour to advance," said von Braun. "Dieter is right on both counts. The A-2 and A-3 rockets have not been total failures, yet the moment has come for the Aggregate-4. This one has to be an unequivocal success. It should have a payload of 1 ton. Our calculations have shown that if traveling at a maximum of 5,400 kilometers per hour at an elevation of 45 degrees, upon entering practically airless space, the rocket would achieve a range of about 280 kilometers. With a diameter of 1.5 meters the rocket would have to be over 13 meters long."

"To achieve these goals," said Dornberger, "we will have to modify our subsonic and supersonic wind tunnels from pressure feeding to pump feeding. We will also have to fashion a new kind of lighter and stronger fuel tank."

Dr. Thiel observed, "For the moment, I know of no existent pump that can handle liquid oxygen at minus 185 degrees Celsius."

"We can start with the motor"—Von Braun sidestepped the problem—"and concentrate on the other components later."

"We will need the best mixture ratio," Thiel spoke louder. "We will have to decide upon the ideal shape to be given my motor—and soon."

Thiel was arrogant and difficult, but von Braun and Dornberger rated him highly. He had a pale complexion and dark eyes behind black-rimmed glasses.

"I estimate my motor will weigh in at about twenty-five tons. The other departments will have to snap to it if we are to meet the schedule."

Heads swiveled toward Dornberger. "We will work together as usual," he said. "If there are problems, come to me or the technical director, and we will find a solution."

"Yes, this is correct," said von Braun. "We must keep up a steady stream of communications from top to bottom, bottom to top."

Major Dornberger stood. "It is settled. We will put the technical requirements into a formal document and everyone can comment. Thank you, gentlemen."

* * *

Friday evening, cold and foggy, they held a costume party in the officer's hall to celebrate the first German landing on Mars, which they estimated would occur in sixty years.

Von Braun shuffled into the room as an older version of himself, long white beard and white wig, his face wrinkled.

"I have returned from the Red Planet!" he exclaimed to the forty or so guests.

"Sunny Boy, why are you so pessimistic?" cried Dieter, glass in hand. He was wearing a pilot's outfit modified for space travel with oxygen canisters on his back. "You will surely look much younger when you take your first space trip."

"You are probably right." Von Braun slapped him on the shoulder.

He accepted a martini from a waiter in a white-tie tuxedo. A few of his engineers were dressed as green Martians or red Venusians. Some of the plant's chorale group had come as the Nibelungen: Siegfried, with armor; Kriemhild, with long black robes, too much mascara, and a crown made in one of the metal shops; Gunther; Hagen Tronje; and a pantomime green dragon.

After a few beers, the Nibelungen recited the opening verses of the saga, to not a little heckling:

Uns wird in alten Erzählungen viel Wunderbares berichtet,
von rühmenswerten Helden, großer Kampfesmühe,
von Freuden, Festen, von Weinen und von Klagen;
von den Kämpfen kühner Helden könnt ihr nun Wunderbares erzählen hören.

They then sang snippets from Wagner's *Ring* cycle, with others joining in, while increasingly tipsy guests in the adjacent hall drank toasts of bourbon and whiskey.

The young lady with brown curls had borrowed some clothes and come as a farm girl. Other *Messfrauen* had transformed themselves into mermaids. Local girls from the village, typists and secretaries, frolicked as noble ladies.

Wernher asked the young farm girl to dance, and they moved with the others in costume to the rhythms of a slow American tune played by the center's jazz ensemble. He remarked to himself that the farm girl seemed unusually mature and invulnerable to his charms.

When the song ended, he left her to chat with Irmgard, to the annoyance of Helmut Gröttrup, her husband. Irmgard had come as Brunhilde, armed with shield and sword. Helmut had chosen not to wear a costume.

The farm girl mingled, forgotten by the technical director, slowly making her way to a door that led to a suite of offices. Security was light.

"We must reach infinite space," she heard Debus confide to Dornberger, "and for this we need to attain unheard of, undreamt of speeds!"

The two men wobbled. Their crimson faces complemented their burgundy capes. Debus's wife, Gay, danced in the other room, where Dieter chatted intently with one of the younger technicians.

Amidst the revelry, the farm girl slipped through the office door unnoticed.

"What we want to do is build big rockets," Dornberger agreed and emptied his glass of sherry. "Big, big rockets—and space stations to circle the Earth at hundreds of kilometers!"

After searching through four rooms, she located the safe.

"I have been thinking." Wernher joined Debus and Dornberger. "What about atomic energy? It might get us to Mars in a flash!"

She opened the safe, but the files weren't inside.

Moving to the desk and reaching underneath, she touched a concealed compartment. Inside were confidential memoranda, schedules, and financial papers. Some information she committed to memory. Other plans and drawings she photographed with a small camera she'd hidden in her purse.

Von Braun, Dornberger, and Debus raised their voices and glasses to belt out a song of triumph, *Die Wacht am Rhein*, "Dear fatherland, no fear be thine…"

Six days later the young lady with brown curls, the spy, was back in Palestine.

Chapter 8

"Stalin Wütet Weiter (Stalin Rages On)"

—*Völkischer Beobachter*
(*National/Folkish Observer,* Nazi Party newspaper)

Moscow, Union of Soviet Socialist Republics
Monday, June 27, 1938

Kseniya Maximilianovna Vincentini hurried through the streets. At a crossing, her eyes searched the crowds and trolleys for hostile agents. Seven of her husband's colleagues had already been arrested.

Kseniya Maximilianovna, or "Lyalya," had married Sergei Pavlovich Korolev four years ago, and they'd been happy at first. She had been considered one of the great beauties of Odessa, sky-blue eyes and thick eyelashes. Korolev had admired her slender figure and long blonde hair.

In the humid evening heat she crossed another busy intersection.

Was that fellow looking at me?

Almost home.

Korolev had recently become more anxious, angrier. Since they'd moved to Moscow, his work on stratosphere aircraft at RNII had consumed him. Lyalya, a surgeon working long hours, had concluded that they'd married too young. She'd been on the brink of leaving him when their friends began disappearing. Langemak. Kleimenov. Tupolev. Glushko.

She couldn't abandon her husband.

What if they've already taken him?

Lyalya ran the rest of the way.

* * *

Only a few blocks from their three-room apartment on the fifth floor, Korolev purchased a gramophone record in a small store. He'd sold a state bond, unbeknownst to Lyalya, to pay cash for it.

That night, he and his wife listened to the record's folk songs. They held hands solemnly on their red velvet sofa, a leftover from their Odessa apartment. Because he expected the inevitable, Korolev had on his military outfit with two diamonds on the epaulettes. He was thirty-one years old, and the despair of the melodies "Snowstorm" and "There Stood a Birch Tree" matched his own.

A loud knock.

In the entryway, when Korolev opened the front door, a hall light with a cracked shade shone on four men.

"Comrade senior engineer Korolev—you will come with us," ordered one of the two uniformed agents of the NKVD. Two "witnesses," mandated by the People's Commissariat for Internal Affairs, looked bored.

"We have a warrant." The agent, of medium height, athletic, broken nose, shoved a piece of paper at Korolev.

Scrawled writing and an official stamp. *Warrant Number 129*. Signed by Zhukovsky.

"What is this?" Lyalya came to his side. "You cannot arrest my husband—he has done nothing wrong!"

"You will only make it worse if you resist," droned the second NKVD man.

The married couple were told to sit. With the two witnesses making a show of observing, the secret policemen opened a wardrobe and a desk and threw the family's few belongings onto the floor. They searched through their linen, their books, even under a sketch on a drawing board. Lyalya asked them politely to conduct their search more quietly, for their toddler slept.

The secret police confiscated the most banal objects—two candlesticks made from World War I brass shells, vacation photos—as well as financial records and money.

It took hours.

"Read this and sign, comrade," commanded the first agent at last.

Korolev examined their thorough report and mumbled, "It is not right what you have done. Why have you sealed my study? Why are you taking my wallet?"

"Make a note," said the NKVD man to his second. "Comrade S. P. Korolev declares that the sealing of his office and withdrawal of money to be wrongfully conducted."

"Grab your coat and shoes—and sign. Let's go," the second man ordered. He had a large birthmark on his left cheek.

At 6:00 a.m. Korolev signed. He put on a gray scarf and his black leather jacket. He forgot to put on his socks and slipped bare feet into black shoes.

"Can I not at least pack him a change of clothes?" Lyalya pleaded.

Korolev embraced her and she made a movement to follow them out, but one of the witnesses barred her way with his arm. "It is not provided for," he said.

Through a stairwell window, she watched the four men put her husband into a gray car and drive off. She dropped to her knees in their ransacked apartment and made painful moans, which mingled in her ears with the sound of a passing street trolley. Sergei had wanted to live on the top floor to be closer to the sky.

But he is no more. Disappeared, like the others...

She crawled into their daughter's room, where three-year-old Natasha hadn't stirred despite the commotion. Lyalya collapsed by her bedside and sobbed.

* * *

They took Korolev in the dark to Lefortovo, a three-story building of yellow brick, where he was interrogated, beaten, and confined to a small cell, its walls, floor, and ceiling painted black.

A month later, Korolev, prisoner number 1442, still couldn't understand why he'd been arrested. He went over the previous year's events in his mind. The government had established a reaction propulsion division, where he'd been given a desk in the design hall. When he'd disagreed with others about the direction of research, he'd been demoted from group chief to senior engineer.

Not a fact in my favor.

He'd had nothing to eat or drink for two days. He'd been put in solitary, where a rat kept him company. The rodent enjoyed the damp, coming and going through a gash in the concrete. A bare electric bulb shone always.

To stay sane, Korolev did stretching exercises and recited aloud passages he remembered from the books he'd written. He replayed favorite films in his mind and went on believing his arrest to be a mistake.

A week later, he sent a third letter to Stalin. Korolev had never met the general secretary but had great confidence in his sense of justice. Writing in elegant cursive, Sergei Pavlovich heard loud tractor engines revving in the inner courtyard. He'd remarked that the authorities ran the engines to cover up the screams of tortured prisoners and the rifle shots of execution squads in the basement.

"Comrade, today is your trial!" Shouted words and the clunk of a great lock being tumbled. The metal door swung open and two large guards loomed in the gap. "Come!"

They dragged Korolev to the basement, through a long corridor, and into a room barely large enough for the three men sitting at an ornately carved wooden table, on which were several glasses and an earthen water jug. The two guards pushed Korolev into a chair to face them. The trio wore cheap suits. With no change of clothes, Korolev wore the uniform from the night he'd been taken.

So it's going to be a secret trial, he thought.

"I, presiding president of the tribune, Comrade Vassily Ulrich, declare this session of the court open," said the man in the middle. "You are Comrade Sergei Pavlovich Korolev, senior engineer at the Reaktivni Nauchno-Isledovatelski Institut?"

"Yes."

"Do you take exception to the composition of this Court of the State Prosecution?"

"Yes."

One of the large guards moved between the prisoner and his judge and slapped the prisoner hard in the face, first with the front of his hand, then with the back.

"No."

"Prisoner 1442, having declined the services of counsel for defense, we shall proceed," Ulrich went on, and the guard returned to his position. Korolev thought that Ulrich had a fat face sitting on a stiff collar. "In the case of Comrade S. P. Korolev, accused of crimes covered by article 237 of the Criminal Code of the RSFSR, we present the following evidence."

"May I have a glass of water?" Korolev asked.

The second guard smashed him in the head with the water jug, which shattered on impact. Korolev fought to remain conscious in his wet clothes. The figures at the table blurred into an indistinct mass.

"Comrade S. P. Korolev…enemy of…people," he heard. "General Secretary…reliable reports from intelligence agents…German Army has…research…that outstrips our own. Several Soviet engineers and scientists are selling state secrets to these Germans."

"That is a lie." Sergei shook his head.

"You do not agree with the accusations?"

"No."

"None of you *svolochi* has ever committed a crime!" Ulrich shouted. "Yet three of your own colleagues have already sworn to me that you are a member of a Trotskyist anti-Soviet sabotage organization. Therefore, for espionage and for deliberately slowing research on key defense projects at the institute, with an aim to delay their deployment as Red Army armament, this court sentences Comrade S. P. Korolev to ten years' hard labor."

"I would beg the court to consider my young age…" Sergei Pavlovich managed. "I would beg the court to consider my devotion to the

Communist Party and Soviet government, despite your baseless accusations. I would beg the court to let me carry on my important work in aircraft design—so we are not overrun by the emissaries of Satan..."

The guard did not strike him, and the three men briefly conferred.

When Ulrich turned back, Korolev saw that his judge's fat face showed no pity. "Having found S. P. Korolev guilty of the criminal actions provided for in the Criminal Code, Clause 58, points 7 and 17, we further sentence you to a removal of political rights for a term of five years, and a complete sequestration of all personal belongings and property. Go! Bring in the next prisoner."

The two large guards yanked Korolev from his chair and pushed him back through the basement corridor. Over the grind of tractor motors, he heard a condemned man exclaim, "Long live Comrade Stalin!"

Followed by the cracks of multiple rifles firing.

* * *

In the terrible heat of an overcrowded freight car, Korolev and his fellow political prisoners starved. It seemed to them an interminable journey to the east. The weak or elderly died off. When the slow-moving train stopped at junctions, soldiers tossed the corpses outside.

The freight car's two windows were barred, but during the long hours, resourceful inmates came up with a way to smuggle out messages. Sergei followed their lead and procured a tiny piece of *samokrutkas*, a thin tissue used to roll cigarettes. On it he wrote in shorthand with a pencil stub to tell his family that he was alive but being sent away. He inserted his message into a triangular envelope made of the same tobacco paper and sealed it with a moist breadcrumb. He addressed the makeshift letter to his Moscow apartment, hoping Lyalya hadn't been evicted.

He attached a thick bread crust with threads pulled out of a towel so the wind wouldn't carry it aloft. Between the crust and the envelope, he inserted a five-ruble banknote on which he wrote: "Please paste a stamp and drop into a letter box."

He said a prayer, stuck his bruised hand through the metal bars, and let fly his desperate note.

* * *

Days later their train delivered them to the Siberian wastes. Korolev and the others were shown their cots in one of ten double tents at the Kolyma gulag. They were then shoved into a large wooden mess room. At long tables, convicts consumed thin soup and mashed flour out of metal bowls.

Heads swiveled in Korolev's direction. A man in quilted trousers and a sailor's jacket got up and looked at him. "Sergei Pavlovich?" he asked. "It is you. Welcome to the realm of Hades. Do you not recognize me?"

Several of Korolev's former colleagues—Kleimenov, Erikovich, Langemak—embraced him. He cried to see so many smiles on faces scarred by months in the gulag. He ate hungrily with many of the best minds in Soviet aircraft technology.

He asked, consuming his broth, "How is it possible you are all here?"

"It's insanity, but at least we are together," said Kleimenov, a tall fellow who had thinned much since Korolev saw him last.

"Did you confess?" Langemak asked.

"Did you?"

"Enough!" shouted a guard by the tent flap.

The famished men resumed their dinner and explained only in whispers the horrors that awaited Korolev the following dawn.

ACT II

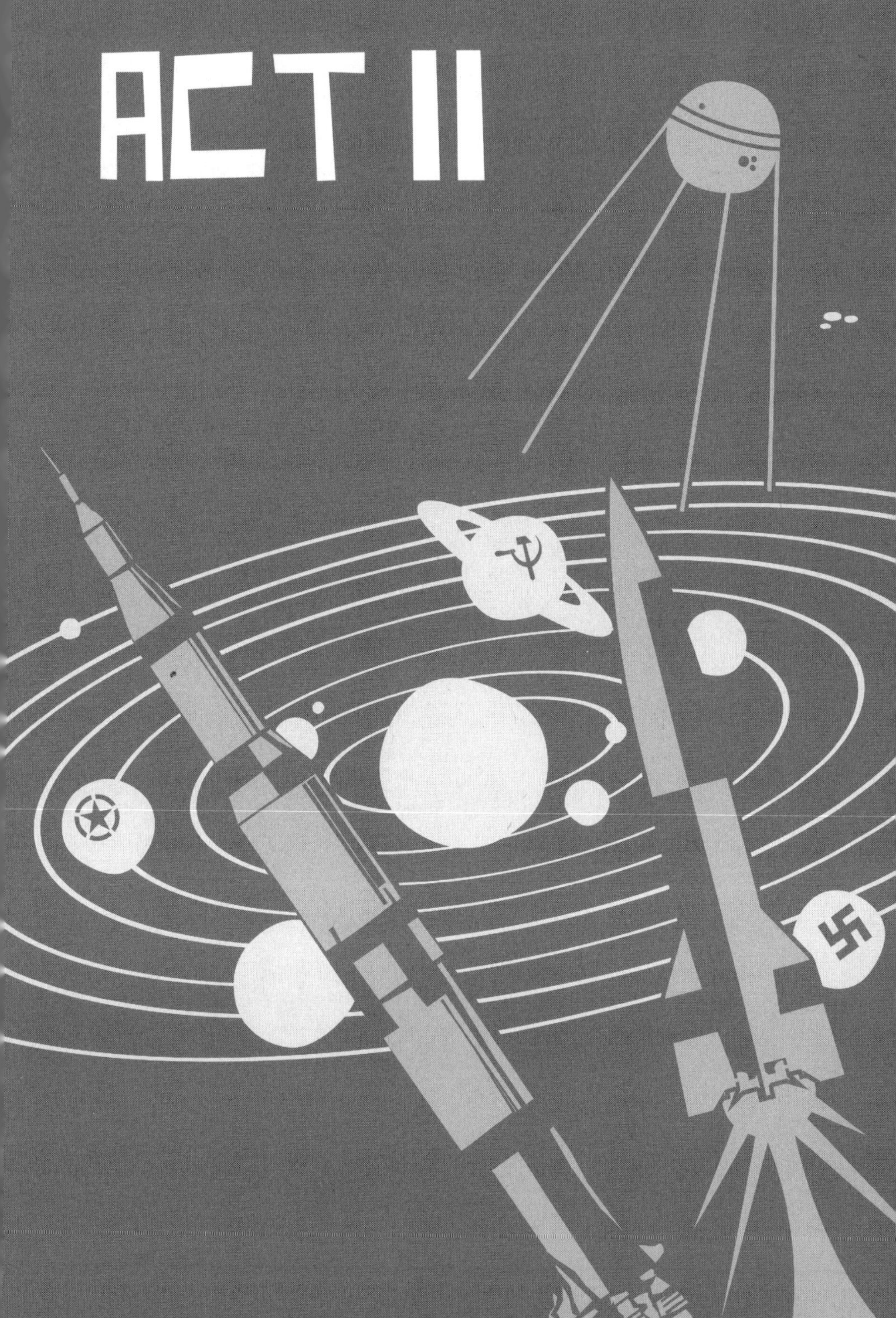

Chapter 9

"Hitler Seizes Austria"

—Los Angeles Examiner

Peenemünde Army Research Center, Germany
Tuesday, January 17, 1939

At 10:30 a.m. a car called for *Oberstleutnant* Walter Dornberger, who uncharacteristically had spent the night outside the facility. Von Braun was already seated in the back, wrapped tightly in his trench coat.

"*Guten morgen*," he said when his boss climbed in.

"*Ja*, I heard you had news on our missing *Messfrau*?" Dornberger asked.

"A mistaken rumor," von Braun grunted. "It has been over a year, so who knows, maybe she eloped."

"We will wind down the investigation quietly. The last thing we want to do is alarm the SS and have them come snooping around our operation."

Their car stopped at a snow-trimmed checkpoint.

"They certainly will not object to the increased security." Wernher peered out his window at heavily armed guards. "*Auf Schritt und Tritt... keine Maus kam rein und raus...*"

"It does not matter," Dornberger said. "They will use any excuse to force their way in, I am afraid. Becker and I and you—all of us—need to keep this a strictly army operation."

Their car was waved through.

Dornberger admired the natural beauty of their camp. Although his responsibilities kept him busy from dawn till dusk, he enjoyed the facility's congenial company. It seemed a long holiday in many respects. They all said so. The rigid class structure, with a clear chain of command, reassured them. The saluting, the singing, even the window cleaning had become part of a routine that made them feel like a big family.

"Dr. Schroeder's calculations are a problem," von Braun said, changing the subject. "He is too slow and too cautious."

"I would think caution is a good thing when calculating chemical explosions."

"You would think wrong. Tests will bear out the numbers. Replace him."

Dornberger nodded. "What about Steinhoff? He holds the world record for distance in gliders and an honorary Luftwaffe rank of flight captain. He's a real Nazi."

"Sounds like a fun guy. Hire him."

Their vehicle passed through two inner gates.

At the Administration Building they jumped out and walked the last few hundred yards, past the Materials Test Building and the Tool Workshop, toward a long, low building of red brick. Their colleagues hurried by them in a variety of civilian attire, from smart business suits to official-issue leather coats, with their triangular HBP badges; laborers in ragged overalls spoke in their native tongues.

Dornberger numbered these laborers in the thousands; they did the facility's digging, fetching, and carrying, the pulling and pushing. Foreigners. He made a mental note to look into their food budget, for he'd received complaints of hunger. However, he judged his permissive attitude toward the brothel in the work camp, where two reichsmarks bought a girl, vodka, and a few cigarettes, to be liberal in the extreme.

Dieter, at some distance, spotted the duo and cried out, "What do you think you are doing, Herr Technical Director?"

Neither von Braun nor Dornberger broke their stride, but the technical director called back, "To what are you referring, my dear Arthur?"

Dieter jogged up to them. His red face nearly matched his red hair. "Herr Technical Director, you cannot surprise me and my whole department by casually stating that three ordinary aircraft gyros can be used to indicate a rocket's position. You must consult me first on such matters!"

"But, Arthur, a solution boldly asserted is half proven! *Nicht wahr?*"

Wernher slapped Arthur on the back and left him behind to stew.

Dornberger glanced sidelong at his protégé. Wernher had come a long way since his days in the rocket society. As technical director of the Heeresversuchsanstalt, the young man managed hundreds of subordinates, from janitors to professors, with a sure hand that often astonished the career army officer.

Von Braun had become a grown man of strong build, with broad shoulders and a firm handshake, easy movements and a boyish smile, a fine balance of body and mind; indeed, he radiated good nature and exhibited a surprising knowledge of many things, which, for Dornberger, bespoke of a superior education. Von Braun also had a remarkable gift for leaving behind the problems of his office to enjoy a leisure hour or two of hunting or flying.

I chose and trained him well, Dornberger thought.

They ambled through well-tended gardens of planted daisies and roses yet to bloom, framed by soaring pine trees, and entered a brick building that housed the rocket plant's showpiece: a well-crafted wind tunnel able to simulate flight parameters.

Together, they crossed a wide sunlit entrance hall to the reception room, where Dr. Kurt Debus waited for them beneath a quotation engraved in the wall: TECHNICIANS, PHYSICISTS, AND ENGINEERS ARE AMONG THE PIONEERS OF THE WORLD.

Von Braun joked, "Are those fellows in the hangar still sticking to their ten o'clock siestas? Whenever I come to the test stand, they seem to be having a break. Have they been converting the alcohol to schnapps again?"

Debus snorted. "No, they gave up schnapps and naps since you did not send those comfortable couches you promised."

"This is not funny," Dornberger said. "One man went blind and another died from alcohol poisoning. This ridiculous news has come to the attention of Nazi Party HQ at Swinemünde. Now they are taking an interest, which is just—"

"Don't worry," Wernher interrupted. "I've already thought of something. Have the dead man brought here. We will nail his body to the main gate and leave it there for three days as a warning. They will think we are even more ruthless than they are. They will leave us alone after that."

Dornberger nodded. "Good idea."

The trio inspected the premises, checking schedules. They had to shout to be heard over the shrill hiss of air streaming at high speed through the measuring section, which vied with the roar of rocket motors being tested nearby.

Upon exiting the building, Debus lowered his voice. "Herr Technical Director, I think I have a solution to your little problem of landing on Mars."

Wernher's blue eyes lit up, but Dornberger snapped, "Gentlemen, we must concentrate on the coming war. It is not an occasion for idle fantasies. We need results. After all, we cannot expect the foolish behavior of our adversaries to last forever. And army money that was once plentiful is drying up!"

Dornberger's adjutant, Max Magirius, ran toward them waving an envelope. "*Oberstleutnant*, a telegram from Berlin!"

Dornberger tore open the envelope and read. "Speak of the devil. Gentlemen, prepare yourselves." He raised his eyes to theirs. "Playtime is over. *Er will unseren Fortschritt sehen*—the *Führer* demands a presentation. He arrives in a fortnight."

Chapter 10

"1,327 Cops Called Out to Guard Nazis in Rally at Madison Square Garden"

—*Daily News,* New York

Tel Aviv, British Mandate of Palestine
Monday, February 20, 1939

At dawn a bus transporting the *Ha-Po'el,* a sham sports organization, drove south of the city and parked at the dunes. Sixty Jewish athletes filed out in shorts or khaki pants, white cotton shirts, long or short sleeves. They carried tan backpacks. Lookouts were posted and the façade dropped.

For the first hour, as the winter sun rose, fifty-five men and five women ran up and down the sand, the men carrying rifles and grenades, the women carrying first-aid packs, canteens, and stretchers. Only two women were allowed to carry weapons and to receive weapons instruction.

Armed with a handgun, the young woman with brown curly hair had to expend the last of her strength to clamber up the cold, shifting ridges.

Can't fall behind the boys, she thought. *Not now.*

It didn't seem unfair to her that she was carrying more weight than her male counterparts or that, after the men had completed their exercises, she and the four other women would pour tea for them and tidy up.

At mid-morning, the temperature was a cool sixty degrees and the full platoon stood at attention on a windy plateau facing a ramshackle shower cabin.

Major-General Charles Wingate emerged, naked, except for a bathing cap and an alarm clock strapped to his right wrist. Not one face betrayed surprise. They were part of the *Haganah* and he was their British officer, their *hayedid*, albeit an eccentric one. He'd been given permission to train them.

The alarm clock rang shrilly.

"Jolly good! Bang on time!" Captain Wingate shouted, switching it off. "I should like you to shoot well in target practice, to lob your grenades with consummate accuracy, and to become proficient in ambush techniques. Today! When you are back in your groups, I shall hand out assignments. That's all. Dismissed!"

Standing with left leg forward, the young woman with brown curly hair aimed her Mosin-Nagant bolt-action rifle and fired repeatedly at several glass bottles fifty yards away. She was wearing a button-down shirt with its long sleeves rolled up and its tails tucked into her tan shorts; her legs, bare and shapely, were a distraction to the men, but she ignored the leers and comments. She reloaded, dug in her boots and pulled the trigger.

"Good shooting, Rachel," said Wingate.

He requested a private moment that noonday break. Her shirt was stained by then, with grease and splashed tea, while the Captain's uniform was clean and his beard trimmed. They were sitting beneath a palm tree.

"Tell me about yourself," Wingate requested. "It's very rare to see women in combat positions. Those men I choose for the Special Night Squads are instructed to kill without compunction. You already do that. Yes. And except for your short, ugly eyelashes, you are beautiful. I have something in mind for you. Intelligence sources indicate that the Nazis are working on something secret, perhaps related to rockets, which you already know about. That chap Himmler is involved. We want you to follow him. He and his associates."

"And may I ask, sir, if the information I learn will be sent back to London?"

"That is none of your business, young lady."

Chapter 11

"Hitler in Defiant Nuremberg Speech Pledges Aid to Sudetens; Threatens Czechs"

—*The New York Times*

Peenemünde Army Research Center, Germany
Thursday, March 23, 1939

Dornberger, von Braun, Debus, Thiel, Dieter, and ten others huddled beneath charcoal-gray clouds in a cold downpour, sheathed in long black raincoats. Drenched pines dripped water onto soggy ground.

"Alles Gute zum Geburtstag," Arthur congratulated Wernher. "May I be so impolite as to ask how old you are?"

"Twenty-seven." Von Braun kept his eyes on the road. "But I feel older."

They'd been told that Hitler, Becker, Göring, and their entourage had passed through the perimeter gates. They would soon arrive at the Assembly Building. Von Braun's eyes searched the mists. The visit had already been put off twice, and the delays had caused more problems.

"You realize his interests are limited to weapon potentials?" Dornberger warned von Braun again.

A midnight-blue Mercedes-Benz sedan slowly crawled out of the torrents, followed by a motorcade of dark vehicles.

"Ja." Wernher had grown tired of the reminders.

"Gut," Dornberger said. "So I must urge you again, by all means do not bring up the subject of spaceflight."

An adjutant leaped from the passenger seat of the Mercedes and opened the rear door for Chancellor Adolf Hitler, who stepped out of the back seat.

As the other cars pulled up, support staff opened more doors for military officials and dignitaries: Luftwaffe Field Marshal Hermann Göring; General Becker, Dornberger's commanding officer; *Generalfeldmarschall* von Brauchitsch, who had backed Becker and Dornberger from the beginning; *Reichsleiter* Martin Bormann; and Deputy *Führer* Rudolph Hess. They splashed briskly through the mud to exchange greetings and introductions.

Dornberger and von Braun noticed that Hitler appeared to have his mind elsewhere. Field Marshal Göring, on the other hand, smiled at them like a little boy who had been let into a candy store and been told he could have whatever he wanted. His military uniform, studded with brightly colored medals, peeked out from between the lapels of his trench coat, and he twirled a gold-and-white baton. Hitler wore no decorations, only a shirt and tie under his leather long-coat. On his head a peaked cap with a red visor protected him from the rain.

"What have you to show us?" Göring asked Becker while shaking Dornberger's hand eagerly. "I have been looking forward to this day!"

"We have prepared a few demonstrations." Becker spoke dryly. "*Oberstleutnant* Dornberger, along with our technical director, Herr von Braun, and Dr. Thiel, in charge of engine design, will be your guides."

"Excellent!"

Göring glanced at Hitler with the eyes of an adoring son. He and the group followed him toward the brick building, led by the rocket specialists.

"Aggregates-3 and -5 are for research purposes only," Dornberger explained. "Our first rocket with a warhead will be the Aggregate-4, which is already at an advanced stage of planning."

Hitler nodded his head to the sound of their encouraging results, but his glum expression alarmed Dornberger.

Von Braun was repulsed by the chancellor's snub nose and brittle black mustache, his thin lips and tanned face. He remarked that Hitler gazed sickly at something far away, as if Dornberger's clinical language bored him.

In the great hall of the Assembly Building's Werke Sud, they gathered round a cutaway model of the Aggregate-3, whose related components had been color coded.

"Fantastic!" Göring exclaimed.

"This is the kind of intricate machinery I like," Hitler said.

Von Brauchitsch gave Dornberger and von Braun an encouraging wink.

As agreed, von Braun segued into an energetic explanation of the twenty-one-foot rocket. His enthusiasm was contagious, and Hitler peered through slits in the rocket's thin sheet-metal skin to examine its pipes, valves, tanks, and resplendent motor.

"These are the batteries," von Braun pointed out. "They supply the necessary electrical power for operation of the control system and instrumentation. Underneath is the gyro-stabilized platform and three damping gyroscopes, which control the servomotors. Here is a small motion-picture camera to photograph the readings of those instruments during flight."

"How do you recover the film?" Hitler asked as he studied the instruments.

"After reaching maximum altitude, a parachute is ejected automatically. The rocket falls into the ocean, where it floats, and we can pick up the camera."

The rain pelted the walls of the building; Dornberger thought he heard an animal howling, a wolf, or the wind.

Dr. Thiel took his turn to speak of the tools for measuring surface temperature and chamber pressure, and the radio receiver that cut off the engine if it received an emergency signal from the ground.

"What is its rate of thrust?" Hitler asked.

"The rocket develops one and a half tons of thrust for a period of forty-five seconds."

The chancellor relapsed into silence.

Dornberger and von Braun glanced at each other nervously.

The chancellor's support staff talked among themselves, only feigning interest in the model, while Göring grinned at the doctor.

At the door of the Assembly Hall, Hitler abruptly asked von Braun: "I still don't know what makes a liquid-propellant rocket fly. Why do you need two tanks and two different propellants?"

Von Braun managed to conceal his astonishment. He realized the chancellor had not been briefed and knew nothing about rocket propulsion. "The rocket of course will work in the absence of air," he said. "It does not use the atmosphere's oxygen for combustion, as would any other engine in an automobile or aircraft engine. The rocket carries its own oxygen in an oxidizer tank."

"But why is that?" Hitler persisted. "Why not use gasoline or diesel fuel and some kind of carburetor system that uses the oxygen in the air it flies through?"

"That type of engine—a pulse jet—is limited to the relatively low trajectories of a missile and can be shot down by flak artillery or fighter aircraft," von Braun clarified. "The main advantage of rocket propulsion is that the missile travels at a very high speed and at a very high altitude, which should make it impossible to stop."

Despites his best efforts, von Braun saw Hitler's interest wane.

"And of course the greater the initial speed," he spoke more rapidly, "the farther the missile will go. In order to attain those high speeds, the rocket must carry and burn propellants much heavier than its own dry weight."

"What kind of payload can it carry?"

"Substantial warheads can be built."

Becker leaned in. "As I mentioned to you some days ago, Herr Hitler, we have fully developed plans for an Aggregate-4 rocket which will soon be capable of sending one ton of explosives over a distance of three hundred kilometers."

"But how long will it take to develop such a missile?" Hitler asked impatiently.

"With our present level of effort and with our *present* budgetary support," Dornberger said—and Becker shot him an angry look—"it will take considerable time."

"We shall have to find you more money!" Göring exclaimed. "Perhaps the Luftwaffe can help."

"Whatever you do, do not ask Becker for advice," Hitler snapped. "He cannot even handle his own present duties."

Göring laughed, along with several other officers.

Dr. Thiel led them out of the building. Becker stayed behind, motionless.

They marched through the heavy drizzle and thickening mud to an exterior test stand. Dornberger again thought he heard a wild animal growling and crying from among the pines.

The rocket specialists hoped the static firing of the A-3's vertically suspended 1,500-kilogram motor would impress the lethargic chancellor.

He and Göring stood at the front of the group, only a few feet away from the motor but protected by an armor-plated log wall. They plugged their ears with cotton. They saw a pale-blue jet of gas and heard a deafening roar. The narrow stream generated supersonic shock waves in bright colors.

Göring slapped his thigh and laughed again. After the static fire quieted, he declared, "Soon we will all be traveling by rocket!" He grabbed Dornberger by the shoulders and hugged him. "Quite fantastic. Colossal! We will transport huge payloads. For weapons, the sky's the limit! We must have one of your splendid rockets to fire at the first Nuremberg victory rally."

Dornberger could hardly believe his ears, yet Hitler's silence troubled him more.

* * *

At lunch the chancellor seemed more relaxed. At the center of a U-shaped table, he ate his vegetarian meal of mixed greens and drank his habitual glass of Fachingen mineral water. Hess and Bormann flanked him; the rocketeers faced them. Despite the long visit, they had no idea if their work would receive the funds so desperately needed to keep the Aggregate-4 on schedule.

"I met your friend Hermann Oberth in Munich," Hitler said, "and he spoke to me about rockets to the Moon. Absurd. What I need are practical weapons in plentiful supply."

He glared at Becker, who had been banished to a seat at the end of the table.

Dornberger wondered what Becker had done or failed to do to provoke Hitler. He'd already noted that the present officers and hangers-on demonstrated servile, uncritical, nearly infantile behavior toward their leader. Göring in particular was visibly excited, even agitated, whenever the *Führer* condescended to address him.

Von Braun, chewing his broccoli, wanted to defend Oberth and hold forth on spaceflight, but a sign from his boss told him not to take the bait.

"Spaceflight is definitely a long way off," Dornberger said diplomatically.

Hitler appeared satisfied.

Von Braun swallowed a mouthful of potatoes in their skins and helped himself to a second serving of green peas.

Hitler emptied his third glass of mineral water and pronounced, *"Es war doch gewaltig!"*

"Yes, it *has* been fantastic," Göring agreed. "Stupendous!"

They posed for a group photo in the lingering wet weather.

On their way back to the motorcade, Hitler again surprised von Braun: "What kind of impact effect would the A-4 have?" he asked.

"Our bird will hit the ground at a speed of over one thousand meters per second," the technical director replied quickly. "The shattering force of its impact will multiply its destructive capacity to great effect."

"Herr Technical Director, I do not accept this," Hitler reflected, head bowed and hands clenched in the small of his back. "It seems to me that as a consequence of the high-impact velocity, you will surely need an extraordinarily sensitive fuse so the warhead will explode precisely upon impact. Otherwise, your warhead will bury itself in the ground and its explosive force will merely throw up a lot of dirt."

"I will order a study to be made right away!" Von Braun had to admit to himself that it was a test worth making.

The rocketeers each thanked the *Führer* for coming.

Göring slapped each of them on the back in turn. "I cannot wait for our next visit!"

Becker lagged behind and was driven away in his chauffeured vehicle, alone.

Von Braun and the others watched the motorcade drive off through another downpour.

"Should we be pleased?" Dr. Thiel asked, his tiny eyes half open.

"I cannot say with certainty," Dornberger replied.

"You know," Dieter spoke his first words of the day, "after he annexed Austria, *der Führer* had his father's village obliterated, razed to the ground. He turned it into an army training area."

The men trudged back to their jobs through the mud.

Chapter 12

"L'angleterre et la France Sont Entrées en Guerre Avec l'Allemagne (England and France Declare War on Germany)"

—*Journal du Loiret,* "le plus ancien journal de France"
(the oldest newspaper of France)

London, England
Friday, November 10, 1939

With black umbrella in black-gloved hand, Dr. Reginald Victor Jones strolled past the plaque on 54 Broadway, which read, MINIMAX FIRE EXTINGUISHER COMPANY, and through the rear entrance of 21 Queen Anne's Gate.

Above the street-level shops, in the vestibule outside his third-floor suite, R. V. Jones deposited his umbrella in a red basket. Because he was chief of Air Scientific Intelligence, Section 6, or MI6, he'd been provided with a secretary, Ms. Daisy Mowat, who looked up from her typewriter with fingers still typing and said, "Your old master is waiting."

"You're late, isn't that so?" remarked Lord Cherwell from a chair in Jones's private office. His hands were on his knees and he looked quite symmetrical, parallel black shoes on polished parquet floor.

Jones hung his mackintosh on a coatrack. "I'm sorry, couldn't be avoided." He entered and closed the door behind him. "I had to go the long way. Emergency defense measures in the street."

Hitler had invaded Poland on September 1. France and England declared war on Germany two days later. The Second World War had begun.

"Here's a present for you." Jones opened a desk drawer and handed his visitor a small yellow parcel.

Lord Cherwell had recruited Jones, a promising student of average height and pale complexion, after his physics exams at Oxford. Jones had a habit of appearing extremely concentrated, something Cherwell, his professor at the time, had liked right away. Jones's eyebrows and deep eyes, under a crop of wavy dark-brown hair, often formed a single expression of utter diligence.

Cherwell studied the parcel's contents as Jones explained, "Our naval attaché in Oslo was told to alter the preamble of the BBC news if he wanted information. Something about German scientific and technical developments—"

"Hence its title, 'the Oslo Report.'"

"Dutifully, they broadcast, '*Hallo, hier ist London.*' This package came through the letterbox the following morning. Anonymously, of course."

The older man, dressed in a dark-gray tailored suit, leafed slowly through the last of its seven pages, then leaned back in his wicker chair. His father had been German, and Lord Cherwell, scientific advisor to Churchill and head of S Branch, had a faint accent.

"Any idea who sent it?" he asked.

"Not exactly, no. Personally, I believe it was written by a malcontent in the German High Command. A rare anti-Nazi. Although the letter has something of a Jules Verne ring to it, I thought you'd find it contains rather detailed, rather interesting material."

"Possibly." Lord Cherwell handed the parcel back.

Jones considered Lord Cherwell to be a temperamental, high-strung, though superbly intelligent man. Indeed, hardly anyone dared disagree with him.

"It also came with this." Jones placed a small box on his desk and removed from it a sealed glass tube. "A new kind of proximity fuse, most likely. Made at a place called Peenemünde, where they are apparently conducting experimental work with long-range rockets and pilotless aircraft. An isolated island off the Baltic coast."

"Hmm...yes." Lord Cherwell leaned forward. "I believe our ambassador to Russia might have mentioned it, but work out there seems to have stalled."

"That's strange. I received a report on a couple of adventurous Finns who sailed close enough to hear explosions and the roar of engines. Indeed I once dined with the German military attaché, a von Boetticher. He talked more than usual, maybe he'd had too much to drink, until I asked about rockets. At which point he turned the discussion quickly and so definitely that I felt I'd been cut off."

"It's obviously a plant." Lord Cherwell reestablished his symmetrical position.

"Excuse me?"

"Whoever sent these letters knew they would pique our interest. They wish to waste our valuable resources. No one man could possibly know about all of these developments in such minutiae."

"But some of the information is genuine; I've already verified—"

"Oldest trick in the book. Mix some genuine with a preponderance of fake."

"And what of Hitler's speech in which he raved about some kind of secret weapon?"

"Your German needs work," Cherwell admonished him. "You and the other idiots mistranslated. Hitler meant *striking force*; his Luftwaffe bombers, not secret weapons."

"There are a number of weapons listed, of which a few, I insist, must be considered seriously. Bacterial warfare, new gases, flame weapons, aerial torpedoes, these long-range rockets—"

"Don't be a bloody fool! Rockets will never be a threat."

"What about this tube?"

"Have it analyzed." Lord Cherwell got to his feet and put on his coat. "I will do this for you: I'll pass the report around, and I'll put a copy of it in our correspondence with Professor von Kármán. But I certainly cannot go to the cabinet with a lot of half-baked material and no visual proof."

"Yes, sir," Jones conceded; the MI6 man had argued as much as was prudent. "I can't say I blame you."

A few days later Ms. Mowat informed R. V. Jones that the Oslo Report was being disregarded by the ministries, which, according to their secretaries, did not even deign to keep their copies.

During a supper, with little appetite, Jones made his distress known to his wife and told her that the war was going to be long and bloody.

Chapter 13

"Russia Signs Pact to Aid Germany, to Force 'Peace' on Allies—Warns France and Britain"

—*The Indianapolis Star*

Kolyma Gulag, Union of Soviet Socialist Republics
Friday, April 26, 1940

Korolev and over a hundred ragged, ghostly souls toiled outside the gold mines, digging and pushing wheelbarrows. From dawn to sunset, they worked. They cut down trees, sixteen a day.

Korolev rinsed gold by hand in a *butar* with water from the Kolyma River. His shoes had disintegrated on the hard gravel road. To replace the soles, he'd fashioned a *chuni*, footwear made out of old jackets and discarded boots. Mornings, he wrapped his feet with rope mesh for warmth. He and his fellow inmates were starving; Korolev had scurvy.

Every week, a few died.

Korolev avoided brawls and sexual assaults, yet guards and fellow convicts beat him regularly.

As he pushed a loaded wheelbarrow up a frosty hill, Langemak maneuvered his conveyance parallel to Korolev's. They both stank of sweat and dirt. They couldn't bathe at the camp, which only had hand basins to wash. They could never clean their underwear, and each had lice.

"Glushko is the one who denounced you," Langemak said.

Korolev filed away the fact.

"He did it to shorten his own prison sentence." Langemak's tone was conciliatory. "Andrei Kostikov denounced him."

"What does it matter? We are all slaves."

They stopped at one of the fires the prisoners maintained against the cold. Korolev suspected Langemak himself had denounced him. Kleimenov, too. All three of his former assistants. The trial prosecutor had mentioned several, not one. He hardly cared.

"We are made to build roads, bridges, and dig—what kind of work is that for us? But let us not lose hope. Russia has something better in store for us. I, for one, am sure we will be useful to the motherland one day."

Langemak rubbed his calloused hands together. He saw that the camp had hardened his friend's character without perverting his spirit.

At the end of their long day, they were marched along a path through a minefield and a gate of barbed wire, past the gatehouse and the guard barracks, to their tents. Not far from Korolev's cot snored a violent man, imprisoned for robbery and several murders. He had a habit of stealing Korolev's food and punching him in the stomach.

In a light-blue dusk, Kleimenov and Langemak were lined up and shot.

At breakfast, Korolev heard that Marshal Mikhail Tukhachevsky, the sponsor of his own rocket group, had been executed for collaborating with the Germans.

A snowstorm swept in from the Arctic Ocean and temperatures fell to minus thirty degrees. Because they had only a small stove and, for insulation, snow heaped against thin tent walls, twenty-seven prisoners froze to death during the night.

Korolev hugged close to the others to survive.

Chapter 14

"Churchill Asserts Allies Hold the Advantage at Sea and in Man Power—Says Hitler Must Yield"

—The Washington Post

Peenemünde Army Research Center, Germany
Friday, June 7, 1940

Von Braun, Dieter, and Thiel watched the A-5 rocket rise up from launchpad VII. A scaled-down test model for the A-4, it hesitated, tilted slightly, then lifted off. Its burn formed an elegant elongated oval until it vanished into a low cloud.

The three engineers expected their work to be more integral than ever to the war effort, since Norway and Denmark, as well as Belgium and France, had capitulated, yet they'd heard no official word.

An earsplitting atonal howl warned the rocketeers, and they threw themselves to the ground. The missile struck about a kilometer away and threw up a giant splash of dirt.

"Well, we have at least solved once again the thorny problem of getting the A-5 off the ground." Von Braun brushed himself off. "Now if we could only control it for more than a few seconds…"

"Something odd happened," Thiel said while the quartet walked over to the control room building.

"We just blew up half a million reichsmarks, that's pretty odd," Dieter noted. "We could have divined the same more accurately with a tool the price of a small motorcycle."

"You are no doubt correct," Wernher admitted. "But until we can improve our telemetry equipment, keep quiet about it."

A black sedan cut them off. A glum-faced Dornberger and Becker clambered out. Dieter and Thiel politely moved away, but not too far off, in case they were needed.

Von Braun spoke first, to alleviate what he sensed was bad news. "I'll be damned if Herr Hitler wasn't absolutely right. We'll have to develop a new fusing system. Without it, our rockets will explode underground."

It seemed to him that General Becker's body had shrunk so much that his military coat and cap were several sizes too large for him.

"A message has just arrived from headquarters," Dornberger said angrily. "That same Hitler has had a dream—which has told him that none of our rockets will ever reach England. He believes they could unleash a deluge of ice meteors that would devastate all of Europe. In short, we are to be taken off the priority list."

"We are our own worst enemy," Becker moaned.

"I have to agree," Dornberger said and lost his temper. "We are an inefficient jumble of competing ministries! Overworked bureaucrats, political crackpots, rival military branches, secret police—all of whose damned intrigues are impeding our important work!"

Von Braun tried to calm him. "We cannot let this get under our skin. After all, we are not shut down, only slowed down."

"Snap out of it!" Dornberger shouted at him. "The budget will be cut in half! Our steel allotment will be reduced and our manpower stolen away. Wernher, for once your good nature is misplaced. We are off the list. Our essential building projects will not be finished—or not even started!"

"Sir—"

"In short, we are going to fight this war in a completely stupid, idiotic, asinine way." Dornberger slammed his fist into an open palm. "Let's not kid ourselves. We may be the best at what we do, but it is over!"

Von Braun waved to Dieter. "Arthur, tell them!"

The short red-haired man, content to be called upon, ran back to them. "Gentlemen, I have calculated that our bombers are shot down after an average of five to six flights over London. If one carries a total of six to eight tons of bombs, the crew and equipment will have cost about thirty times the price of an A-4, or around thirty-eight thousand reichsmarks. It is obvious to anyone with a brain that the A-4 comes off best. It is a much better buy, so eventually—"

"More figures?" Dornberger stared at his subordinate. "Today, Arthur, I see that you and our naïve technical director are hopeless dreamers!"

"I have been mistaken in my estimate of you and your work," Becker said, his face swollen with worry. "Herr Dieter, I am not even sure your math is correct."

He returned to the car and was driven away.

Berlin, Germany
Saturday, June 8, 1940

After dining, General Becker retreated to the study of his country estate. He was followed by two Gestapo officers in long leather trench coats despite the warmth of the evening, who took up positions on either side of the velvet-draped doors. Three *Sturmbannführers* patrolled outside the study's shuttered windows, which faced a manicured garden.

The SS officer in charge waited outside the study. He had given Becker five minutes.

Seconds later, he and his men heard a muffled shot and the thud of a falling body.

Chapter 15

“Германия Объявляет Войну России (Germany Declares War on USSR)”

—*Pravda,* Moscow

Magadan, Union of Soviet Socialist Republics
Sunday, December 21, 1941

Korolev dragged himself through a watery bog of sticks and brambles. He was bleeding from his gums and a deep gash in his head. He needed to catch a train but had lost his sense of direction. He crawled aimlessly over the ground, his face no longer able to feel the cold, his mind still searching for reasons…

Fate has been against me since they let me go…

A few weeks before at the Kolyma gulag, Korolev’s jaw had been broken and several teeth knocked out during one of the beatings. After days in a foul-smelling tent that passed for a doctor’s ward, he’d received an official letter summoning him back to Moscow for a reinvestigation of his case.

His fellow inmates had collected clothing for him—a new hat and felt boots—so he might walk to the nearest town and find transportation before winter set in. But the port city of Magadan was over 150 kilometers away, and he had only a few rubles.

“You’ll never make it!” a guard had laughed.

The indifferent authorities and the doctor with a filthy coat assumed Korolev would collapse and die on the road. They let him go, not caring if he survived. News had come to the gulag of Japan's attack on America and an expansion of the war. Nazi hordes threatened Mother Russia. Everyone expected the worst.

One dead prisoner more or less made little difference to the camp administrator.

During his second day on the road, Korolev had flagged down a truck. The driver had taken him to town in exchange for his sweater and overcoat, a decision Korolev regretted the first freezing day in Magadan. There, he'd learned the last ship for the season had already set sail and was far out in the Okhotsk Sea.

He would have to take the train to Moscow, which meant more rubles. He worked as a laborer and a shoe repairman during the early snows. He snuck into an army barracks to sleep late at night.

He didn't eat for two days to save money.

The big storms came and Korolev was discovered by an angry sentinel, who threw him out the gate into a six-foot-high snowbank. His skin burned.

To avoid freezing in his flimsy rags, he'd stumbled along the only path cleared of snow, his arms folded to his chest, head down in the dark.

He came upon a still-warm loaf of bread lying in the street.

A gift?

He ate until he got hiccups.

He slept in a crawlspace under an elevated building.

When he awoke, his clothes had frozen to the ground.

He boarded a train. Near Khabarovsk, a nosy conductor had taken a long look at Korolev. Fearing a contagion of some kind, train officials treated him roughly, knocking his head into a steel frame before kicking him off at the next station.

On the platform, villagers had taken Korolev for a dangerous and destitute enemy of the state, obliging him to flee into the nearby countryside.

I must see Natasha, he kept thinking to himself as he crawled. *I must…*

He lifted his head. Though blood from his wounds had caked around his eyes, he saw a rapidly flowing river. In spots water bubbled up from an underground source. The picturesque marsh soothed him. Korolev rolled onto his back and took in the sky for what seemed to him like hours.

Peace. If I do not die…

He breathed heavily, aware of a presence, two strong hands pulling him backward through sparse grass. The earth beneath him alternated cold and warm.

"I'll make you better, sonny."

The gravelly voice of an old man.

Korolev thought he detected compassion in his tone, a frequency he hadn't heard in years. He felt himself being propped up against a tree. In the thick branches above, a cuckoo called.

"Don't worry, sonny. I'll be back…"

The kindly voice trailed off.

Korolev tried to focus. He saw a butterfly with green-and-yellow wings flapping before him. He sensed a pattern in its flight.

The butterfly blinked away, and Korolev saw the old man return. He shuffled forth in a typical gray peasant's shirt and pants, with a brown leather satchel slung across his chest. He was bald with thick lips and a large nose. The old man's thin, gentle eyes and toothless mouth smiled at him.

He reached into his satchel and said, "This will help, sonny."

He put a shriveled hand into Korolev's mouth and rubbed a stinging substance onto his gums and his forehead. The bleeding stopped.

The peasant gave him an aromatic paste to eat.

They sat together for a long time, silent.

When Korolev got to his knees with difficulty and looked at the old man, the old man nodded.

The engineer limped off in the direction of the train station.

The conductor honored his ticket. Korolev's health was no longer suspect.

After days on the lurching locomotive, Korolev walked out of Kazansky station and made his way through the snowy streets of Moscow.

The contrast with the vast, empty east could not have been greater, and he had to fight through several waves of panic. Soldiers, tanks, and noisy military vehicles bustled everywhere among a fretful populace. Newspaper headlines loudly declared that the Nazis had marched to within nineteen miles of the city but were being driven back.

Korolev arrived at the address indicated on his official summons, Radio Ulitsa. He showed his letter to a sentry at the small entrance door. The six-story concrete building, with its many windows, looked more like an apartment complex than a minimum-security NKVD penal institution.

The prison warden, a colonel, studied Korolev.

"You don't look so good," he said.

Korolev thought the officer's bright blue uniform seemed immaculately clean and pressed.

"I am innocent," he stammered.

"My dear man, we know you are not guilty of anything in particular." The colonel rang a bell. "We know who you are, after all. If you can help get Tupolev's bombers in the air…"

Two guards took hold of Korolev's arms.

"Your sentence has been commuted to eight years in our *sharaga*," the colonel continued as they led Korolev down a hallway. "I am Kutepov, but you can call me Patriarch. You will work. We need incarcerated aviation designers such as yourself to develop military aircraft. You may have noticed we are at war."

Korolev listened, but he understood little.

The colonel pushed open a door.

"Allow me to introduce you to the head of our special group, Chief Designer Glushko!"

Korolev eyed his former friend and vaguely remembered his betrayal.

"My dear Sergei Pavlovich!" Glushko beamed. "Welcome to Central Construction Bureau 29. You have your mother to thank for the transfer. I hear she is most persistent and clever. For her sake, I sincerely hope that I won't have to ask the Patriarch to line you up against a wall and have you shot."

Chapter 16

"Hitler, Mussolini Join Japan in World War Upon America"

—Buffalo Evening News

Berlin, Germany
Tuesday, January 6, 1942

A government-chauffeured Mercedes rounded the corner of the Voss-Strasse and drove through a monumental double gate. Haj Amin al-Husseini, Grand Mufti of Jerusalem, president of the Supreme Muslim Council and of the Arab Higher Committee for Palestine, slid out of the car and was escorted through the New Reich Chancellery's Court of Honor.

Two SS guards flanked its exterior staircase, as did larger-than-life statues of nude muscular men. One of the belligerent statues held a torch, the other, in a fist at the end of an outstretched arm, a sword.

Inside, the Grand Mufti mounted a second staircase.

Another staff member walked him down the long Mosaic Hall, beneath eagles clutching swastikas, which led to the Marble Gallery and its tapestries designed to impress visiting dignitaries.

The Grand Mufti passed between two guards with carbines flanking a recessed door framed by marble and into the chancellor's private office.

Adolf Hitler and Heinrich Himmler greeted al-Husseini, a short man, dressed simply in a long black robe that descended to his ankles, above black patent-leather shoes. He wore a traditional headdress, a red tarboosh wrapped with a large white cloth into a turban. His face, like Himmler's, was meek, even humble.

"I wish to thank you for this great honor," the Mufti spoke formally to Hitler. "I have been treated with such respect during my stay in Berlin, and I have been overwhelmed by the miracles you have wrought. Indeed I wish to express to you, *Führer* of the Greater German Reich, the admiration of the entire Arab world. You have our deepest gratitude for the sympathy you have always shown for the Arab and especially the Palestinian."

"Had the Arabs won the Battle of Tours, the world would be Muhammadan today," Hitler said and paced. "Yours is a religion that believes in spreading the faith by the sword and in subjugating all nations to that faith. The Germanic peoples would have become heirs to your religion. Such a creed would have been perfectly suited to the Germanic temperament then, as it is today. However, in the long run, the Arabs would not have been able to contend with our harsher climate and conditions. They would not have been able to keep down our more vigorous ancestors. Ultimately, not Arabs but Islamicized Germans would have commanded the Muhammadan empire."

The Grand Mufti didn't balk at Hitler's idiosyncratic history lesson. He replied, "Arab and German have the same natural enemies: the Englander and the Jew."

"Jawohl."

They adjourned to the sitting partition of the long office, where a servant filled their cups with afternoon tea on a round table.

"Germany stands for uncompromising war against the Jews." Hitler paced once more. "Our policy has already been implemented in Poland. In Russia, wherever there is a German soldier, there are no more Jews. Naturally we are in absolute opposition to a Jewish national home in Palestine." He looked al-Husseini in the eye. "Germany will furnish positive and practical aid to those Arabs involved in the same crusade. Let me assure you, Germany's objective is the total destruction of the Jewish element residing in the Arab sphere. I say this to you, my friend, as the most authoritative spokesman for the Arab world."

"*Mein Führer*," Himmler said, "His Excellency has promised to recruit one hundred thousand Muslims to fight for Germany."

"Excellent!" Hitler exclaimed and sat down.

"All we ask is a free hand to eradicate every last Jew from Palestine," said the Grand Mufti, "and the greater Arab world."

"Under Eichmann, a special *Einsatzgruppe* has already been formed with this intention," Himmler assured him.

The Germans sipped their tea on matching silver-gray and yellow cushioned chairs, the Grand Mufti on a wood-trimmed floral couch.

"*Mein Führer*, may I ask if you would make a formal statement and declare to the world Germany's full support of the Arabs."

Hitler popped up again. Framed by a portrait of Bismarck hanging over the fireplace, he replied, "The Jews are already yours. The German armies will, in the course of this great struggle, reach the southern exit from Caucasia. Once Germany has forced open the road to Iran and Iraq through Rostov, it will be the *end* of the British world empire. At that moment, I will give the Arab world the assurance that its hour of liberation has arrived."

"It is my absolute view that everything will come to pass as you have indicated." The Grand Mufti paused and glanced at Himmler. "However, I wonder if it would not be possible, secretly at least, for the Arab High Committee to enter into an agreement with Germany."

Hitler smiled. "My friend, I have just given you that secret agreement."

Talk turned to a toxin that could effectively poison Tel Aviv's water system; although they intended to target Jews, they accepted the inevitable collateral deaths of many Arabs.

"*Mein Führer*, Your Excellency," Himmler announced, "I have something important to show you."

He stepped to the door and whispered something to one of the guards.

A slim, athletic SS man appeared, his light blond hair streaked with gray and brushed straight back. His restless brown eyes scanned the room. Himmler's subordinate projected an iciness that outsplendored the ranking SS officer. He had the confident comportment of a cavalryman. Under his left arm, he carried several rolled-up blueprints.

"Gentlemen, allow me to introduce *Brigadeführer* Hans Kammler." Himmler sounded like the proud father of a favorite son. "He is the agent of our desires. Once he is given orders, he carries them through with an obstinacy rare even for the SS."

The Grand Mufti laughed, and Kammler spread his blueprints on the map table.

"As supervisor of all SS construction," Himmler said, adjusting his glasses, "*Brigadeführer* Kammler has been working on a plan for increased efficiency in the disposal of the subhumans. We will reveal these plans as part of our Night and Fog directive to the General Staff at the Wannsee conference next month. But I wanted to share them with you both—today."

The three men leaned over the technical drawings of crematoriums, and Kammler explained, "*Mein Führer*, our ultimate goal is to design these camps to be Germany's central institution. They will be the training ground for the masterly conduct of the new superman. In this great occupation, he will reveal his true nature..."

* * *

In an empty apartment on the wide Wilhelmstrasse, the woman with brown curly hair and her handler had binoculars trained on the Reich Chancellery. She'd transitioned from the Haganah into the Plugot Mahatz, or "strike companies." She was a fist at the end of the Palmach's extended arm, the Zionist's newly formed commando group. They were preparing for the inevitable British withdrawal and the Axis invasion of Palestine.

They knew that Himmler was meeting with al-Husseini and Hitler. The latter's personal standard flew over the building to signal his presence. The SS guard had also increased its number to about forty.

"They are sure taking their time," remarked her handler, a youth of twenty-one.

"They have much to discuss."

As the sun set, they spotted Himmler, the Grand Mufti, and an unknown SS officer in the courtyard.

After farewells, the Grand Mufti was driven away.

"I don't see why you are allowed to hunt the Arab," she said, "and I am not allowed to put a bullet through Himmler's head."

"Rachel, your intelligence reports on the Abwehr"—her handler checked his pistol—"are much more useful than his corpse."

Rachel pulled at a curl of her brown hair.

Her handler and his associates would fail. She could sense it.

She looked through her binoculars again at Himmler and the unknown officer.

As they strolled down the Wilhelmstrasse, she asked herself, *New boy, how dangerous are you?*

Chapter 17

"Terror Reigns as Nazis Attack Jews; Thousands Slaughtered in Conquered Soviet Areas; Boy, 14, Hired as Killer"

—*Journal Every Evening,* Delaware

Los Angeles, California
Wednesday, February 25, 1942

It dropped out of the midnight sky at an impossibly steep angle about a hundred miles off the Pacific coast. Nearly invisible, it skimmed above the ocean's waves, heading toward the lights of the city at over a thousand miles per hour. When tracking devices pelted its exterior skin twenty miles from shore, it slowed, as if confused.

The craft made landfall at Point Dume and banked south for Santa Monica, skirting the beaches. When it passed over an electrical plant, workers on the night shift sensed its presence and jerked up their heads.

"What the hell is that?" asked a man in overalls.

"Way too big for a Jap reconnaissance plane," said another. "Nazi?"

"It's as big as a battleship! Gotta be over five hundred…no, seven hundred feet long."

The ship didn't seem to mind being studied. It moved slowly and low in the sky. As far as they could see, it consisted of a black hull, wide and flat, without windows, portholes, hatches, or seams. The night shift got a good, long look.

No propellers or exterior motors.

Silent.

"It ain't got wings or fins," said a watchman with a pilot's license. "No stabilizers. Not Kraut. It ain't bombin' us…"

When it had almost completely passed over them, they saw to its rear three vertical openings, each about fifty feet long, which pulsated like red-orange shark gills. The night shift became aware of a faint odor, like an overheated transformer. They felt a slight hum in their chests.

"I'm callin' somebody," said their supervisor.

"Who?"

"I dunno—the air warden!"

The military's regional controller ordered a blackout of the whole area at 2:15 a.m., from Los Angeles to the Mexican border, and as far north as the San Joaquin Valley. The order automatically triggered the warning system. Antiaircraft batteries went to Green Alert.

At 3:06 a.m., the mysterious flying ship reappeared *behind* the coastal guns, so the Fourth Antiaircraft Command opened fire. Caught in the glare of searchlights from both Palos Verdes and Malibu, the huge ship was a sitting duck, and clouds of exploding shells temporarily obscured it from view. Yet the ship kept on its steady route northeast, unperturbed and untouched by the massive barrage.

Fighter planes took off in swarms but, guns blazing, arrived too late. The object had vanished. For three hours they searched at every altitude and found nothing.

Chapter 18

"Air Battle Rages Over Los Angeles, Army Says Alarm Real"

—Los Angeles Examiner

Peenemünde Army Research Center, Germany
Saturday, October 3, 1942

"These flying ships buzzing your launches are from another planet, or even another solar system," said Hermann Oberth in his thick Transylvanian accent. "They may have been sent to conduct systematic long-range investigations: first of men, then animals, vegetation—and, now, your rockets."

"Your Martian friends are showing more interest than our own *Führer*," said armaments minister Albert Speer, leaning casually against a wall.

"Gentlemen," Dornberger said and clapped his hands, "the hour has come to change all that. If all goes well, you will certainly be paying more attention to our A-4."

He'd arrived too late to prevent Oberth from lecturing the *Oberst*'s important guests. The lot of them, Luftwaffe and navy generals, had crowded into the underground Control Center, where along its perimeter crew and senior propulsion guidance engineers read manometers, frequency gauges, ammeters, and other illuminated instrumentation.

"Dr. Thiel is in charge of the launch. He has a schedule that has to be followed to the second! So let us please proceed to our designated areas."

Dornberger, von Braun, Dieter, the military officials, and honorary guests proceeded two by two down an underground tunnel adjacent to the viewing platforms.

Debus and Dr. Thiel stayed behind to monitor preparations.

"Well, teacher, I hope 'good luck lies in odd numbers,'" von Braun quoted Shakespeare to Oberth. "This is our third try. We have been in financial purgatory, under tremendous pressure. We are low on everything from raw materials to qualified engineers. We need a viable product, yet so many things can go wrong that—"

"Nonsense! I have an automobile with eight cylinders and a lawnmower with one. The automobile starts whenever I turn the key, but the lawnmower gives me endless trouble."

They took a staircase to the roof of the Measurement House, which would provide their guests a panoramic view of Prüfstand VII. The A-4 missile stood forty-five feet tall, painted a black-and-white checkerboard pattern. Its pinnacle reached high above workers on the ground conducting last-minute checks. Two umbilical cables connected it to instruments in the Control Center and to the test stand's electric power supply. A stream of evanescent vapor, evaporating liquid oxygen, trailed off its side, like someone breathing in the cold.

"Teacher, what do you think of our little joke?" Wernher directed Oberth's gaze to the upper portion of the A-4, where the logo from *Frau im Mond* had been painted: a young lady sitting astride a crescent Moon.

"It is apt," said Oberth. "What was a hollow tube is manifested before us."

Ernst Rees, long arms and long legs, sidled over and asked, "What are *they* doing here?"

The new engineer had his eyes fixed on two men in SS garb atop the Assembly Workshop, their binoculars trained on the rocket.

"That is Himmler and *Brigadeführer* Hans Kammler," Speer said from behind Rees. "They are as interested in your project as I."

"Peenemünde war stärker als die SS," said von Braun.

He'd been informed late that morning that Dornberger had been obliged to grant them access. Their presence could only be proprietary, yet von Braun calculated that they could outpower the SS.

He looked up at the clear, cloudless sky and noted, as he often did, the natural beauty of their location, which contrasted dramatically with their industrial wonders. The calm, sparkling Baltic Sea against thc base's loudspeakers, sharp and loud. He listened proudly to the technical chatter of his experienced, high-functioning control staff, measurement officers, and engineer in charge of the power supply.

"Wernher, snap out of it!" Dornberger whispered. "And keep your fingers crossed. It must come off or else we are in terrible trouble. Perhaps done for."

"Of course, *Oberst.* I can feel our baby is anxious to be released."

Dornberger picked up a black phone from a portable command post and gave the order.

All other telephonic conversations ceased.

"X minus three..." Debus said from the Control Center over the loudspeakers.

Three long minutes, Dornberger thought.

He saw periscopes built into the thick roof of the center turn toward the launch site.

Crews withdrew working platforms from the rocket, then retreated to their assigned shelters.

"X minus one..."

Hundreds of workers streamed outside Peenemünde's more remote buildings to catch sight of the missile launch. The thousands of foreign laborers had been locked within their barracks for their own "safety."

Dornberger gritted his teeth, trying not to think of the many attempts they'd had to cancel at this stage because of some technical failure.

"Ten, nine, eight...*Zündung eins...*!"

Inside the Control Center, a propulsion engineer triggered the first of three main switches.

Outside, a cloud of smoke puffed from the base of the rocket.

White sparks shot through the churning gray exhaust.

"Preliminary stage. *Vorstufe…*" Debus droned.

Second switch.

Zigzagging scintillas coalesced into a clear flame, a shrieking jet of red and yellow combustion gases. More smoke coughed out. A violent wind expelled cables, stray fragments of wood, and tufts of grass from the launch area.

"Rocket instrumentation switched over to internal batteries."

Nothing can go wrong here! Dornberger prayed.

"Hauptstufe!" Debus said.

Last lever.

Dieter willed the turbopump at 4,000 revolutions per minute and 540 horsepower to do its job.

Thirty-three gallons of alcohol and oxygen per second flowing into the combustion chamber…

Thrust power—*What power!*—increased to twenty-five tons.

Von Braun and Dornberger saw their A-4 ballistic missile, under considerable strain, rise up.

Two ground cords dropped away.

"Rocket has lifted!"

Officials fixed their eyes on the missile ascending from the thick green forest into a light-blue sky. A flame almost as long as the rocket darted from its stern.

"Sonic velocity."

Will it explode? Dornberger asked himself, then risked a glance at his guests gathered on the rooftop—each was mesmerized.

"Twenty-nine, thirty, thirty-one…" Debus counted off the flight seconds.

No detonation. Thank God.

Supersonic speed has been achieved, Dieter said to himself, *a first for a liquid-propelled rocket.*

"Mach 2!"

A trail of white appeared.

"An explosion!" shouted one of the generals.

"Nonsense!" shouted another. "That is the oxygen venting."

Prevailing winds blew the exhaust contrail into a white zigzag.

"Look, student," Oberth said to von Braun. "Odin blesses your rocket with his lightning."

Rees stared at Himmler and Kammler, neither of whom said a word.

The rocket was only a glowing dot.

"54...*Brenschluss!*"

End of burn! thought von Braun. *We did it, if all ends well.*

The gas jet disappeared. The missile climbed too far for their eyes to follow. Only instruments would monitor its progress from this point.

"296 seconds. The rocket has plunged into the Baltic Sea. From his Messerschmitt aircraft, Dr. Steinhoff will now locate the rocket by the green dye released automatically on impact. That is all."

The loudspeakers cut off with an audible clunk.

Dieter boasted to Rees, "I calculate that our baby smacked into the water with the impact energy of fifty express-train engines."

Hats were thrown off rooftops. Military men and high officials appeared pleased to Dornberger.

"It has brushed the edge of space," he said to Speer and wiped away a tear. "That is what counts. I have worked ten years for this day. A great weight has fallen from my shoulders."

"I haven't been so excited since I was a schoolboy," said Speer.

"This is something only Germans could achieve," Oberth joined in. "I feel like a composer who wrote a symphony long ago and has finally heard it played."

* * *

That evening at the elegant Schwabes Hotel, Peenemünde officials and officers, their honored guests and civilians, held a gala soirée to celebrate their success.

Himmler and Kammler stayed for the event.

Drinks proliferated, and Speer bumped into von Braun.

"I want to congratulate you, personally, for your concern for your work," the armaments minister said. "I will not forget to mention it to the *Führer*."

"Can you also keep out the SS?" von Braun asked pointedly.

"That I cannot guarantee."

Dinner was served amidst lively and loud conversation from one end of the banquet hall to the other. The finest vintages seized from France were sampled and drained. Dining on embossed china, fine silverware in hand, they observed elaborate protocols during their successive courses. A line of waiters in black tuxedos, white shirts, and bow ties, marched in a solemn procession among the tables. The first ladled soup into Italianate bowls; the second placed a potato on each gold-encrusted plate; a third laid out long strips of beef; a fourth, vegetable greens, to von Braun's delight; a fifth drizzled gravy over the delicacies; the last poured exactly thirty centiliters of red Bordeaux into silver goblets.

When Dornberger got up to speak at the head table, where von Braun, Oberth, Speer, and several others were seated, the hall fell silent. Medals pinned to uniforms glistened in electric lights.

"Do you realize what we accomplished today?" the *Oberst* asked in a loud voice. "This afternoon, the spaceship was born! Success! But I warn you, our headaches are just beginning..." Many of the attendees laughed uproariously. Two or three glanced at Himmler a few tables away, who sampled his wine, expressionless. "No, our problems are by no means over, for our rocket must now become a weapon of war. It is our duty to perfect the A-4, for it must strike fear into our enemies." Suddenly feeling foolish for his honesty, he quickly concluded, "Our rocket group must—launch, launch, *launch!*"

He lifted his fists into the air, and the large hall erupted into shouting and cheers.

Afterward, Himmler and Kammler made their way through the revelry to Dornberger's side.

"Herr *Oberst*, congratulations," Himmler said. "An extraordinary feat."

"Thank you, *Reichsführer*."

"Yes, congratulations, Herr *Oberst*," said Kammler. "But surely, given your location on the Baltic Sea, you are well aware that on clear days your white contrails can be seen in the sky as far away as Sweden. Foreign agents are no doubt already alerted to your work. Sooner or later the keen eye of an Allied airborne camera will pinpoint your base."

"Yes, that is true. We have no illusions about what will follow. Rest assured, we have taken every necessary precaution to—"

"Have you?" Himmler asked, his eyes half hidden behind round glasses. "The SS would take much better precautions. Good night, gentlemen, good night."

The two SS officers walked away and Dornberger turned to Speer, who shrugged.

Von Braun snuck off to flirt with Irmgard Gröttrup, for he'd heard a rumor that she'd argued earlier with her husband, Helmut.

"If it isn't the *fröhlicher Heide*," Irmgard greeted him using his "Merry Heathen" epithet.

"The stallions of my family have been Merry Heathens since 1285," he gloated.

Wagging tongues would say the two left the banquet together.

* * *

That same night, two Polish prisoners at Peenemünde entered a heavily guarded area of the installation on latrine duty and passed by a shed with its door ajar.

While one watched for patrols, the other quickly backtracked and poked his head inside, where he spotted a torpedo-shaped object with wings, but no cockpit for a pilot.

They resumed their path before anyone noticed their indiscretion.

Chapter 19

"Battle for Stalingrad Goes on With Unabated Fury"

—*Coventry Evening Telegraph,* England

London, England
Thursday, November 12, 1942

Duncan Sandys and his father-in-law, Winston Churchill, met in the cabinet room of 10 Downing Street. They took cushioned mahogany chairs on the warmer side of a solid oak table. Flames crackled and embers glowed orange in a marble fireplace, to stave off fall's dark evening.

"Reports from Denmark, Sweden, Norway, and Poland are sketchy, but they form a pattern," Sandys said. "They indicate two basic possibilities: long-range guns or long-range rockets. *Wunderwaffen.* Local fishermen have seen strange objects with flaming tails streak across the night sky above the Danish islands. These last phenomena seem to emanate from a tiny German spit of land, called Usedom."

On the far side of the oak table were Churchill's two-man science team, Lord Cherwell and R. V. Jones, chief of science branch at MI6. There had been disturbing rumors since the Oslo Report, which they were reconsidering over scotch, cognac, and whiskey.

Jones thought "Sands" the picture of the rising aristocratic English politician: tall, broad shouldered, well dressed, with wavy red hair and a dashing smile. That Sands walked with a distinguished limp and was married to Churchill's daughter, Diana, made him all the more attractive to quite a few upper-class women.

Sands was a parvenu, however, in the realm of science. While Churchill didn't play favorites, he had appointed Sands chairman of an investigative war cabinet committee on German secret weapons, on special assignment. When the PM had informed Lord Cherwell of this fact, Jones had witnessed what he could only describe as a "womanly" reaction.

Jealousy?

The appointment had also complicated Jones's job, for it had hardened the Professor's position into one of uncompromising antipathy. If Sands was receptive to the idea of missiles, the Prof was in rigid opposition.

Sands opened a wall map affixed to the room's cream-and-gold paneling. "Here," he said, pointing to a spot on the extreme north of Germany. "We know there's something going on *here* at Peenemünde. The SS have stepped up security measures in the area and thrown a cordon around this spot in particular."

"Hmm," Churchill grunted. His cigar had burned out. "Prof, what does S Branch say?"

The Prof produced from his pocket, with a satisfied air, one of his famous graphs. It was the moment Jones had anticipated with dread. The Prof was invaluable because the PM wouldn't listen to any other scientist, but his illustrations, in Jones's estimation, oversimplified the facts.

Churchill took the graphic handed to him and studied it, while the Prof delivered his verdict: "Hitler would be justified in sending to a concentration camp whoever advised him to persist in either such project, long-range guns or crackpot rocketry. The construction of a long-range rocket, in particular, would be so difficult that it's inconceivable the Germans would divert precious manpower and material from the manufacturing of bombers, which are far more effective than any rocket could ever be."

Churchill looked up from the graph and relit his cigar. The conversation was over in his mind, for he considered the Prof nearly always right.

"But the Jerries are going to want to come up with something big," Sands said what Jones was thinking. "Last summer they had their victories in southern Russia and North Africa, but they're bogged down in Stalingrad now. Rommel has been driven back, so they'll want something decisive."

"I don't know if you've noticed, sir," Jones addressed the Prof, "but the Nazis are not the most rational people."

"Rational or not, it would never work. The technology required simply doesn't exist. Long-range military rockets are feasible only if they are propelled by solid fuels—like the American JATOs. These fanciful missiles would have to be of enormous size and therefore totally impractical, as my graph indicates."

The PM fidgeted, but Sands went on. "Sir, I would like to show you something."

He removed a black-and-white photograph from a folder, and Jones realized that Sands's appointment did come with one singular advantage: the son-in-law appeared oblivious to his father-in-law's impatience.

"This was recently taken over the island of Usedom, by one of our reconnaissance units."

Churchill and the others studied the grainy image under a desk lamp with a fluted shade. Because it had been taken from several thousand feet up, Sands held a magnifying glass over the photo to enlarge an object in a clearing that resembled a long white torpedo.

"Interesting," the PM mumbled, "but not proof."

"Exactly," said the Prof. "It's probably a giant hoax designed to distract our war effort from more important military targets. You may take thousands of aerial photographs, but you will be uncovering nothing but ingenious dummies. If that were an accurate picture, it would mean the Germans had succeeded in putting a four-thousand-horsepower turbine into something approaching a twenty-inch space. Lunacy. It simply can't be done."

"Jones, have you more to say?" the PM asked.

Churchill also had faith in the MI6 man, who had solved several knotty problems in the last few years.

"Yes, sir, I do," Jones replied. "In addition to the disturbing and frequent reports of a long-range weapon capable of bombarding England from the continent, the Polish underground has two eyewitnesses of some sort of pilotless flying torpedo. It is being worked on in the exact same area Sands indicated—in what we think is a secret base at Peenemünde."

Churchill lit another match and held it to his cigar, puffing and thinking.

Jones sipped his cognac and studied the PM. In Jones's view, Churchill embodied the solution for which the population had asked: a politician who would tell them the stark truth. He was a Victorian through and through, a learned, pampered snob, but honest and stoic. On his lapel was a "thumbs-up" pin, for he was also, except for periodic bouts of severe depression, unflinchingly optimistic.

"Peenemünde is the place to watch," Churchill announced.

Lord Cherwell frowned; he would've preferred to forget the whole thing.

Jones took a breath; he would've preferred a more aggressive strategy.

"We need to know everything we can about that base and what the 'Natsis' are doing there," Churchill said, using his particular pronunciation of the word. "Thank you, gentlemen."

"Good evening, sir." Sands returned his photograph to its folder.

After the trio left the cabinet room, Churchill smoked his cigar and contemplated the two pairs of Corinthian columns by the cabinet room's entryway.

Chapter 20

"French Africa Is Invaded by America—
Rommel Trapped by New Army"

—*Sunday Pictorial,* England

Moscow, Union of Soviet Socialist Republics
Friday, January 8, 1943

Glushko, Korolev's friend and betrayer, was using the war, even his own arrest, to his advantage. He'd matured into an elegant man, with delicate features and soft, sensuous Asiatic eyes. He took great pride in his appearance. He had handmade suits sewn from imported black-market fabrics and his shirts cut and starched in the latest styles of their Western allies.

Korolev's clothes remained ragged and discolored by yellow soup. His black hair was thin and unkempt, and his thick fingers were stained with nicotine. His cheeks were sunken, his eyes listless. However, he'd gained weight eating three solid meals a day. Two weeks in the prison's medical facility had provided him dentures, though they'd failed to mend his jaw.

The two men loitered one night within Central Design Bureau 29, at a double row of drafting tables lit by single bulbs under green shades in a long, otherwise dark room.

"I haven't heard from my wife or child in years," Korolev said. "Not even a letter."

Glushko was weary and replied absently while studying a technical drawing on one of the tables. "Sergei Pavlovich, you must know by now that your wife denounced you to survive. She had to defend her science thesis at the academy. What did you expect?"

He proceeded to the next table. Korolev didn't react. His eyes went from Glushko to their *popka*, who had to monitor them wherever they went. Korolev doubted his rifle was loaded. The unstated agreement between guards and prisoners held that the latter would follow the rules, while the former would be as polite as possible.

"My daughter's name is…Natasha," Korolev said. "I no longer know what she looks—"

"Do not take it badly," Glushko scolded while examining another drawing. "It was nothing personal."

Korolev leaned on the edge of a drawing table. "Why did you do it, Mikhail Klavdievich? Why did you denounce others?"

"Why did I denounce *you*?" Glushko corrected and moved to the next board. He bent over a sketch of the RD-1, a four-chambered liquid-propelled jet engine. "Expediency. Maybe I feared for my life and my own family. I received eight years and wanted less. I am not proud of it. Maybe I am even a little ashamed."

Korolev hadn't denounced anyone, but he didn't care to judge. "My strength is gone. I want to help kill Germans, to beat them back, but…"

"Get up," Glushko said. "Get up!"

Automatically, Korolev obeyed.

"*Your* work on *my* jet engine has helped generate thrust for the Peshka dive bomber." Glushko thrust a finger at the drawings. "Together, we have increased its speed by eighty kilometers an hour. Stalin is pleased. At least that is what I am told."

"What of it?" Korolev's eyes drifted. "Today we are solving differential equations, but tomorrow we may be back in a gulag. Beaten. Murdered. The goddess of justice is—"

"Sergei Pavlovich." Glushko grasped him by the shoulders. "You have worked through many nights on endless sheets of calculations and drawings. So I am naming you manager of engine installation development in my Group Number 5." He let him go. "Perhaps after we have crushed these foreign invaders, we can return to our beloved rockets."

Glushko held a schematic up to a light.

"But if your work here does not surpass the Americans'," he added, "and their jet-assisted planes, the Patriarch will still have you shot. And no one will ever know. Not even your daughter."

When he looked again at Korolev, Glushko wasn't sure if he saw a faint sign of life, even anger.

But the light flickered and went out.

Chapter 21

"Stalingrad Reds Hurl Nazis Back"

—New York Journal-American

Hirschberg, Germany
Sunday, January 10, 1943

Magnus thought Wernher might strike their elder brother, Sigismund. They were supposed to be hunting pheasant but were instead arguing bitterly. Their father and mother, who usually acted as restraints to their bickering, were bird-watching elsewhere in the woods with their young niece Maria. A thick wet mist obscured the sun.

"You will corrupt poor Magnus absolutely!" Sigismund shouted at Wernher. He was on leave from the Vatican, where he held the post of Germany's Legation Secretary to the Holy See. He'd returned to his family's country estate in a hurry after hearing of Wernher's plans for their younger brother. "When you are not dreaming of landing on Mars or some other godforsaken planet," Sigismund's voice rose, "you are plotting the destruction of mankind!"

"And you know nothing of destruction and corruption?" Wernher shouted back. "You are wallowing in the filth of the most disgusting church in the history of the world!"

He raised his gun and fired at a rabbit, missing by several meters.

The three brothers had grabbed their weapons and set out after a hearty family lunch, but the prospect of twenty-four-year-old Magnus quitting the Technische Universität München to work at Peenemünde had become a cause for recriminations and long-festering accusations.

"Nice shot," Sigismund taunted. "While I have my finger on the pulse of the entire planet and I'm doing everything I can for peace—you cavort nonchalantly with our country's most irresponsible war-making scum."

Wernher threw away his gun. He clenched his fists and took a step toward his older brother.

"Yes, *scum!*" Sigismund insisted. "Every one of them! If you cannot see that, you are being deliberately blind."

"You may not have noticed, but we are at war," Wernher hissed. "And I, for one, would like to win it."

His lips trembled; he was a big man, but Sigismund was his equal. Both of them had their blond hair slicked back. Both of them had been raised to believe that they were right and everyone else wrong. Both of them were convinced that they knew what was best for their baby brother.

Magnus dared not say a word. He wanted to join Wernher at the rocket facility, to participate in that exciting adventure, but would bow to his elders' decision. Of the three siblings, his face formed the most perfect oval.

"And what if they are all crazy?" Wernher went on. "Do you think Stalin is a nice guy? He will dismantle your precious Jesuit organization, have your cardinals lined up against a wall—and shoot them in the head!" He snapped his fingers. "Like that!"

The two of them rolled onto the ground and clawed at each other in the snow. Magnus wasn't sure what to do and, looking up, was relieved to spot his father walking briskly toward them.

"Wernher! Sigismund!" the baron bellowed, binoculars in hand. "What has gotten into you? Stop it this instant!"

Their mother hung back, embarrassed, with one arm protectively around Maria.

At the sound of their father's voice, the two brothers clambered to their feet and brushed the leaves off their tweed hunting suits and thick pants; their knee-high black boots were caked with mud and slush, and Wernher's face bled from two scratches. They hung their heads but remained fuming and petulant.

"We will discuss your reprehensible behavior before dinner—in private," the baron said. "Get back to the house."

Fourteen-year-old Maria Luise von Quistorp watched her first cousin Wernher march away and saw he was the more furious. She liked and admired him for it. She had already noticed that men were often angry and immature and needed to be looked after.

Peenemünde Army Research Center, Germany
Wednesday, May 26, 1943

Dornberger had persuaded Speer to attend another launch at Peenemünde, a competition between the A-4 and the flying bomb. The flying bomb was something the Luftwaffe had been developing. The winner of the contest would have a good chance of re-obtaining the sacrosanct high-priority designation.

In what von Braun considered a dangerous move, Dornberger had invited *Reichsführer* Himmler and Hans Kammler to the competition. The latter had already made several surprise appearances at the research base. Kammler wanted to know everything about their work, and often showed up in von Braun's office unannounced to ingratiate himself or bully the technical director.

Von Braun saw that Dornberger would have been happy to use either man—Speer or Himmler—as a conduit back to the *Führer* and high-priority status. When Himmler had invited von Braun to join the SS, Dornberger had pointed out that for purely political reasons his technical director had better accept the offer. Von Braun had agreed without much reflection, anything to advance their cause, and was given the honorary rank of *Hauptsturmführer.*

"You are a kind of double agent," Dornberger had joked.

So it came to pass that fine spring day that von Braun wore his black dress SS uniform, with its crimson swastika armband, in the company of

Dornberger, Speer, Grand Admiral Dönitz, a Luftwaffe field marshal, an armaments chieftain, and assorted luminaries, all gathered once again on the roof of the Measurement House. Himmler and Kammler had arrived together and watched the contest with interest.

"Two nothing in your favor!" Speer clapped Dornberger on the back.

The pilotless flying bombs, missiles with wings, were having bad luck. A couple of them had crashed, while the A-4 had performed well.

"These demonstrations have finally convinced me of the rocket's complete reliability," Speer announced even before the event had concluded.

Dornberger and von Braun assumed the armaments minister's sudden about-face had something to do with the destruction of the Wehrmacht's Sixth Army at Stalingrad.

"You will hear from me," Speer went on. "I will arrange a meeting with the *Führer*, and you can present your complete plans directly to him."

"We could have done that eighteen months ago!" Dornberger let the words slip out. "All that time has been wasted, Herr Minister."

Speer ignored the remark and descended the staircase with Dönitz, as Himmler sidled up. Von Braun had tried to understand what made the *Reichsführer* one of the most feared and hated men in Germany, yet the SS chief looked to him nothing more than a meek elementary school teacher of average intelligence.

"If the *Führer* decides to give your project his full support," Himmler said to Dornberger, "your work will cease to be the army's concern. The rocket will become a concern of the German *people*. In that case, it will be up to the SS to protect this entire base against sabotage and treason."

"I seem to be saying this often these days, Herr *Reichsführer*: Peenemünde is an *army* establishment," Dornberger replied evenly. He'd got what he wanted from Speer and no longer needed the SS. "In an army establishment the army alone is responsible for security. I should, however, welcome your continued enforcement of the prohibited zone around our base and a tightening up of security measures in northern Usedom and the adjacent mainland."

"We will talk to the police commissioner for Stettin and make necessary arrangements." Himmler's thin lips barely moved when he spoke. "*Danke schön, Oberst.* You have carried the day."

It was an ungracious concession, von Braun noted.

Chapter 22

"Le Desastre Germano-Italien en Tunise—Capitulation des Troupes Allemandes (German-Italian Disaster in Tunisia—Surrender of German Troops)"

—*Le Petit Marocain,* Morocco

Książ Castle, the German Empire
Thursday, June 10, 1943

A chauffeured black Mercedes-Benz Type 320, flanked by four SS storm troopers on motorcycles, delivered Viktor Schomberger to Książ Castle. Its weathered limestone walls had been built on a jagged promontory overlooking a deep ravine.

An ox-like man with a thick rectangular beard, dressed in a crumpled tweed suit, Schomberger sighed heavily upon exiting the vehicle. It had been a long drive from Austria. *Brigadeführer* Hans Kammler greeted him impatiently on the steps of the thirteenth-century fortress.

"From one castle to another!" Kammler exclaimed. "But I believe you'll find our Schloss Fürstenstein more fascinating than the Schloss Schönbrunn."

Schomberger would have preferred to go on a long hike in the surrounding forest.

Instead he followed Kammler and his chief of staff, Bernard von Ploetz, who could have been Kammler's twin, through large baroque double doors, down a gilded hall, and into a ballroom occupied by secretaries, typists, and draftsmen. The ornate ballroom had been converted into their headquarters.

"All of this is made possible by the backing of Siemens's Schlesische Werkstätten Dr. Fürstenau & Co. and the Allgemeine Elektricitäts-Gesellschaft," Kammler gloated. "Certain work is done aboveground. More important work is being done below. You will see."

Schomberger nodded, but his thoughts, stimulated by the forests nearby, wandered back to years before.

He'd dwelled by a clear-running creek for hours, entranced by its waters.

How is the trout able to swim upstream without effort in a complete mockery of gravity?

He had detached his consciousness, a trick he'd discovered as a child during one of his long reveries, and sent it into the water.

The trees take communion from the clouds, the clouds from the trees.

Kammler motioned Schomberger over to a reinforced steel door, guarded by two troopers. "I will show you!"

A third storm trooper approached with keys on a hoop; he took one and unlocked several iron bolts.

Von Ploetz switched on overhead lights, and the trio proceeded down a gradually sloping tunnel.

They descended steep, narrow stairs built into the rock.

"There are many abandoned coal mine shafts here," Kammler said, "but we have found much older passages."

A blast shook the walls.

"More digging."

Schomberger estimated they were perhaps ten stories underground when the tunnel leveled off and widened. They walked side by side, their way lit by industrial lights connected by long cables along the stony ceiling.

At a junction, Kammler paused and von Ploetz directed his flashlight down a dark tunnel. There was no one.

Schomberger sensed a presence, feminine, hiding in the shadows, but chose to keep silent.

An elevator took them deeper underground.

Its doors opened on a kind of vestibule where more tunnels branched off.

Facing them was a steel barricade more than fifteen meters high and twenty meters wide, guarded by three more storm troopers.

"Herr Schomberger," Kammler said, "behind this wall is the reason you were brought here. The reason why Germany will win the war."

They stepped through a smaller door, embedded within the larger one, and into an immense underground hangar. A squad of troopers, armed with rifles, lined walls covered with a thick rubber matting.

At one end of the hangar, technicians in white coats attended to the remains of a strange object on a raised platform. To Schomberger, it resembled two equally sized saucers, about four meters across, one placed on top of the other. Spotlights built into the high ceiling illuminated the craft, revealing a large hole in its upper half. Parts of the lower half were also missing, as if someone had taken a large hammer to it.

I am far from the forest.

"Interesting?" Kammler asked, rubbing his hands together.

"Yes." Schomberger had heard rumors about such machines.

It cannot be of this world. A ship, a flying ship.

In an odd way, it was familiar to him, although he'd never seen so elegant an exterior.

"Our SS archaeologists dug it up near Nuremberg, where local legend had long said something was buried. We had been looking for a vehicle of this type for years, our third actually, thanks to some…shall we say, top-secret information."

He signaled to a bald man in a white lab coat. "Herr Neugebauer, you may begin."

Von Ploetz led them behind a thick concrete wall in a corner. Other technicians already in place looked through a thick pane of glass at animals and reptiles in cages being placed at the base of the craft—lizards, rats, frogs, snails, even insects, as well as a plate of eggs and raw meat.

Schomberger saw three men in ragged clothes, prisoners, positioned among the menagerie an arm's length from the vehicle.

The top saucer began to spin slowly in the opposite direction of the one spinning beneath. A pale-blue light appeared between the two halves.

Schomberger sensed a vibration, like the humming of hundreds of bees in a sealed bottle.

The ship levitated a few centimeters off the ground. The rats ran erratically in their cages. One of the prisoners bent over, clutching his stomach.

"Something is wrong," Schomberger protested.

"Don't stop!" Kammler ordered.

Schomberger felt like his feet were sinking into the floor. The air around the ship warped, distorting his view.

The second prisoner shrieked and twisted. Blood spurted from his mouth and nose. The third prisoner leapt from the platform and made it about halfway to the door before a sharp crack rang out and he sprawled forward.

The first prisoner, holding his stomach, stumbled closer to the vehicle—and vanished.

The technicians gasped. Von Ploetz's mouth hung open.

"Desist!" Kammler cried.

The craft descended back to the platform.

The prisoner reappeared, erect and dazed, a meter from where he'd stood before.

Schomberger smelled a sweet odor wafting through the air as the animals and reptiles were collected, a few of which appeared to be unwell. Crew hosed the area with a liquid that resembled a brine.

"The *Führer* himself has informed me that *you* are the man destined to help us understand the energy causing these anomalies," Kammler said to Schomberger. "The Reichsforschungsrat in Berlin has validated your theories on energy and a vortex propulsion motor. We should have more—"

"How did you start its motor?" Schomberger asked.

"Start it?" Kammler laughed nervously. "There is no motor. As far as we can tell, it is always on. It has been on for hundreds of years or more. We only stimulate it with a magnetic charge in order—"

An SS guard ran up to Kammler. "*Brigadeführer*, one of the prisoners has escaped!"

"Escaped? Impossible!"

They followed a trail of blood to the hangar door. Outside, the guards lay dead and the trail vanished. Someone had done the impossible—had helped the wounded prisoner to flee.

"Search every tunnel!" Kammler cried. "They cannot have gone far. Use the dogs!"

"Jawohl!" the storm troopers ran off.

At that moment Schomberger understood that he would stay and conduct research on the craft, which the SS would try and duplicate. They wanted a fleet of them, for it was and had been a warcraft.

That is their goal and my curse.

He also understood someone else lurked in the tunnels almost at will, someone important.

He would send out his consciousness to find her.

Chapter 23

"Churchill and Roosevelt Work in Close Contact; Churchill Predicts Huge Allied Drive in 1943"

—*El Paso Herald Post*

London, England
Tuesday, June 29, 1943

"Among the more colorful rumors are that the Germans will be firing huge tanks of poison gas, or red death (whatever that is), in order to annihilate every inhabitant of Great Britain." Foreign Secretary Anthony Eden was reading from a memo in his hand. He and other members of the war cabinet had been summoned for what they knew to be a critical meeting in an underground complex built beneath the New Public Offices in Westminster, behind Whitehall. They were trading stories until the PM should arrive. "Another, it seems, is that those mysterious structures on the French coast are actually refrigerating apparatus designed to stop our air force by forming ice clouds over England. Even better, they will somehow build artificial icebergs in the channel to block our invasion fleet."

The right honorable Major Clement Attlee chuckled.

The room's green door, fitted with an observation slit, swung open. From the narrow passage outside, the PM waddled in. He beamed at them, a sure sign to Attlee that their leader was in a feisty mood and meant to disarm them. Churchill took his customary seat in a wooden chair at the head of an angular U-shaped table fitted with blue baize cloth.

The ceiling of his cabinet war room had been painted red, the walls off-white. A black fan affixed to the wall behind the PM swirled slowly between detailed maps of Fortress Europe. Low-wattage lights gave the scene a hazy look.

Churchill had called for a full session of his Defense Committee to discuss rocketry. He glared at them, from Attlee to Stafford Cripps, to the three chiefs of staff and other important people, ministers, academics, and scientists. On one side of the table was Mr. Anthony Eden, shoulder to shoulder with the PM's trusted advisor, Lord Cherwell; on the other side, his son-in-law Duncan Sandys shuffled some papers.

R. V. Jones had been seated in "no-man's-land," or the "Siege Perilous," at the foot of the table, in the gap of the U, facing the PM.

"You've read the papers," Churchill growled. "This is a time of frustrating confusion in our investigation, a period of groping in the dark, of trying to lay foundations in a swamp. But I'm counting on you, all of you, to distinguish fact from fiction, fantasy, or foolishness."

"Let's dive in," Lord Cherwell said. "I will play *advocatus diaboli* and present the arguments against."

Jones saw Churchill wince. Though the latter loved language, he was a disciplined writer and judged gratuitous displays of Latin pretentious in the extreme.

"As for the objects photographed at Peenemünde," continued Lord Cherwell, "they are either torpedoes or wooden dummies, as I've always maintained, deliberately painted white to show up easily. I must insist that the whole thing is a hoax to distract our attention from more formidable weapons: for example, a pilotless aircraft. If we focus on these phantom rockets, we will most certainly overlook the much larger, much more tangible danger."

Churchill grunted, tapping his cigar on its ashtray. "There's one man here whose views I particularly want to hear." He looked into the gap. "Dr. Jones, now I want the truth!"

All eyes turned toward the MI6 man. The PM had set the stage for him, and Jones assumed his part in a confident voice. "While I do not think there is a likelihood of a heavy attack for some months," he said, "I do feel that the evidence for the existence of the rockets is stronger than when I presented it to you only months ago. Just six days ago, as Lord Cherwell knows, reconnaissance photos revealed four small airplanes yet without tails and which left behind them a curious trail of dark streaks as they rose above the airfield. In fact—"

"Stop!" Churchill called out and leaned toward Lord Cherwell. "Do you hear? That's a weighty point against you. Remember, it was you who introduced Jones to me!"

"Those may well be inflated barrage balloons," Lord Cherwell replied calmly.

"May I ask," Jones was equally calm, "why the German Army finds it necessary to transport barrage balloons on heavy-duty railroad tracks?"

"At the end of the war, when we know the full story, we shall find that the rocket was simply a mare's nest."

"If it is a hoax, and if I may continue, I would ask the assembled, what would be the result of this hoax if it were successful? Almost certainly, we would attack Peenemünde. It is as though we, in trying to mislead the Germans, had set out some dummy weapons at Farnborough for them to photograph. If the Germans were then to attack Farnborough and destroy that facility, even if for the wrong reasons, we should think it a very silly hoax indeed."

Lord Cherwell managed a rueful smile and said, "Yes, Mr. Jones, but how do we know Peenemünde is the equivalent of Farnborough?"

"Using Enigma," Jones replied, "we have recently come across an important list at MI6, a circular, concerning petrol coupons. The petty officer who signed this list addressed it to several establishments in what seems to be, in our estimation, an order of precedence, starting with Rechlin." He coughed. "Rechlin, as you know, is the nearest equivalent in Germany to our aircraft establishment at Farnborough. Second on that priority list is Peenemünde. Peenemünde is *second*, ahead of several other *verified* military establishments, whose importance is well known to us. Therefore we must logically conclude that Peenemünde is a real establishment—a very real military establishment—which exists most likely for the creation of secret weapons. The *Wunderwaffen*."

"Yes, but what about the question of fuel," asked an emaciated academic from Cambridge. "Lord Cherwell and I simply cannot see how a solid fuel could power a rocket of that size, not even using cordite."

"That is eminently true." Lord Cherwell folded his hands on the table. "The Germans do not have a sufficiently powerful propellant to launch any kind of meaningful rocket."

The PM bit his cigar, but Jones took up the gauntlet once more. "Gentlemen, to answer that same question at MI6, we adopted a commonsense approach. We asked ourselves how great a velocity was required and whether any known fuels contained the needed amount of energy to propel a rocket the required range. Then it was a simple matter of consulting the available physical and chemical tables, where it was clear that there are indeed many combinations of fuel which would be suitable. One could use liquid oxygen or nitric acid as one constituent, and an organic fuel, such as petrol or alcohol as the other. Therefore, in principle, with ample time and resources, the rocket could be made. Indeed Robert Goddard, the American scientist, has been using liquid oxygen for some years."

"Ah, yes." The academic retreated into a theoretical reverie. "Liquid fuel…"

"Reply?" Churchill glared at Lord Cherwell, who did not care to reply.

"Where our 'experts' have been repeatedly wrong in their analyses," Jones went on, "was in assuming that the Germans were trying to make an enormously enlarged version of a schoolboy rocket. But their model, we are pretty sure, is nothing of the sort. Whatever they are working on, and we shall find out soon in all of the details—it is like nothing we've seen before."

"Well, what do you recommend?" Churchill now addressed his Defense Committee. "Where do we stand?"

Major Sommerfeld, a technical advisor with curly short hair and a mustache, said, "Our estimates are that fifty to one hundred of these rocket bombs would suffice to destroy London. They will be so laid out as to methodically decimate most of Britain's largest cities during the winter. A single rocket could cause up to four thousand casualties, killed and injured."

"That is a long jump from nonexistent to total annihilation." Churchill puffed his cigar.

"I do not believe a single rocket, even if exists, could cause four thousand casualties," Lord Cherwell rallied. "However, I have checked with the Ministry of Production, and, to protect the populace, we would be required to provide another one hundred thousand Morrison shelters for London *if* we pursue this line of thought. I am compelled to point out that this would mean scrapping two entire battleships to provide steel for the shelters. That would be a strategic blunder of some consequence."

"The alternative prospect," said Eden, "is to undertake a wholesale evacuation of Metropolitan London. Quite difficult, if not impossible."

"The issue, as I see it"—Churchill relit his cigar—"is not in the realm of yes or no, but of more or less. Will these rockets launch sooner or later, in a month or a year? Will they cause a citywide catastrophe? Let us lose no wagers on wild-goose chases."

"What really matters is not the experts' opinions," Jones said, crossing his arms, "but what the Germans are actually doing. Just because we have only now thought of liquid fuels, there is no reason to assume their rockets are either more or less imminent than before our argument started. Yet there is no cause for panic."

"Panic!" The PM chewed his cigar. "Who is panicking?"

A knock on the door preceded a domestic, who entered and placed Churchill's four o'clock whiskey and soda next to his ashtray, then departed.

"It seems to me, sir, that some of us around this table are getting pretty near panic," Jones said and glanced at Major Sommerfeld. "Allowing for inaccuracies that often occur in intelligence gathering, we nevertheless have formed a coherent picture that we should contemplate coolly. The Germans have been conducting an extensive research into long-range rockets at Peenemünde. Their experiments have naturally encountered difficulties, which may still be holding up production. But it is not without precedent for the Germans to have succeeded where we have doubted. If they have succeeded, and it looks like they have, we may be sure that Hitler will press the rockets into service at the earliest possible moment—though I maintain that this moment is probably some months ahead."

Churchill spotted Jan Smuts, arrayed in his military uniform with belt and decorations. "Now, Field Marshal, you have heard the arguments—tell us what you think!"

Smuts had a sagacious face and a trimmed white goatee that came to an elegant point at his Adam's apple. "The evidence may not be conclusive," he said, "but I think a jury would convict."

"The arguments were nicely balanced," Eden said. He gave Jones a well-earned nod of recognition.

"Good," said the PM. "What we have to do is prevent the Natsis from putting into action large quantities of rockets before the cross-channel invasion."

"We must attack Peenemünde at once," said Stafford Cripps.

"Peenemünde is far beyond the range of targets currently being attacked," Smuts pointed out. "It will be a dangerous and costly raid."

"There are arguments for and against bombing," said Jones. "Despite our curiosity to watch the development of the trials, MI6 is prepared to take the risk of a raid. However, we should be aware that if the raid is not completely successful, we may, to our detriment, force them to simply shift their operations elsewhere."

"The earliest date for a large-scale attack, in view of the short nights, won't be until mid-August," Smuts said. "We will target the bigger buildings and installations."

"It is of more importance to target the housing estates," Sandys spoke up. "The scientists and engineers, the brains of the operation. Destruction of the physical facilities will not be enough. The only effective way to stop their work, for good, is to kill as many scientists as possible."

"That's not so," Jones countered. "The essential scientific work has most likely been finished. The main objective should be to smash up the research and manufacturing facilities."

"Enough discussion for now," Churchill said. "Work out the details with Bomber Command and inform me of your decisions. Peenemünde should be attacked at the first favorable opportunity on the *heaviest* possible scale. It should be utterly destroyed, every last timber blown asunder. This will be a British operation. The Americans will not be fully informed. That is my burden.

"Surprise should be the keynote. We should catch them napping."

Chapter 24

"Eisenhower Strikes! Allied Troops Storm Shores of Sicily"

—Chicago Daily Tribune

Plock, the German Empire
Wednesday, July 14, 1943

Von Braun gazed out the Heinkel He 111's cockpit window onto a thick white fog that blanketed the Vistula River below them. It was early afternoon. That morning he and Dornberger had been summoned by Speer for an audience at the *Führer*'s headquarters.

Their constant requests for top priority had reached Hitler's ears at last.

"This weather worries me," von Braun said to Dieter, who piloted the plane.

He glanced at his watch again. The wireless operator to his right put out another call to nearby airfields and meteorological stations to find out how far the fog extended eastward.

Von Braun returned to the plane's midsection, where Dornberger had organized their support material: film canisters of the October 1942 flight, wooden scale models, colored sectional drawings, organizational plans, a manual for field units, drawings of trajectory curves.

"You are nervous, Wernher. This is unlike you. I suggest you improve your state of mind."

"Who knows what mood he will be in? The Eastern Front is collapsing. Things aren't going too well and he knows it."

"Does he? Even so, we are offering him a solution. We have to be careful not to overplay our hand, but it is simple: The Luftwaffe is losing control of the skies. We have an alternative."

"*Ja*, as agreed."

They were still of one mind, although there had been tension between them, even arguments the last few months. Von Braun felt increasingly exposed in their dealings with the SS.

Dornberger pressed: "Do not refer to the rockets as *Wunderwaffen.* If we fall into the propaganda trap Goebbels has set for us, we are done for."

"Ja, ja…"

Von Braun was tired of it. He retreated to the cockpit and saw the fog melting away. The thick forests of East Prussia stretched over the horizon, interrupted only by glittering lakes and oddly peaceful meadows.

Half an hour later Dieter set the plane down on a muddy field at Rastenburg. A gray four-door car waited for them with its engine idling. Dieter stayed. Von Braun and Dornberger piled into the spacious back seat, film canisters and material under their arms.

Their chauffeur threw the vehicle into second gear and gunned it from wet grass to dirt road, leaving deep ruts in the soil.

Wernher thought ahead to their second meeting with the *Führer*, tapping his fingers on the armrest. He told himself he would be speaking only to a man, though a strange one.

Pumped full of mescaline, opiates, barbiturates, amphetamines, and God knows what else.

Tongues had been wagging. He'd heard that Hitler achieved an orgasm only if a young woman, naked, squatted over his face and urinated or defecated on him.

He forced himself to concentrate. He would provide the voice for their silent film, not more than a decade after he'd watched, mesmerized, *Frau im Mond.*

He'd been so young, a child.

Now what am I?

But introspection was not natural to him. His aristocratic bearing and bloodline discouraged it. Ordinarily his heritage made him feel somewhat superior.

Not today.

He continued to drum his fingers.

Dornberger stared ahead, stone-faced, his fears like those pumping through the Third Reich. Germany was in trouble, though hardly anyone dared say it aloud.

The driver braked at the first guardhouse of Sperrkreis 3, third ring of the Wolf's Lair.

Their progress slowed as they penetrated deeper into Hitler's iron-clad security zone, which spiraled into tightening concentric circles.

Despite his long experience, Dornberger ground his teeth. So much was at stake. The career army officer, newly promoted to *Generalmajor*, nevertheless admired the facility's protective armor, well engineered and weaponized, surrounded by land mines.

They drove past camouflaged buildings with thick concrete foundations buried deep in moist earth. The Wolfsschanze was a massive fortress of security posts, barbed-wire fences, gun emplacements, and flak cannon positioned on bunker roofs.

At the second Sperrkreis the driver showed their papers and passes again.

The last checkpoint was Sperrkreis 1.

They were searched from top to bottom and their film canisters inspected. Soldiers examined the vehicle's interior and knelt down with flashlights to examine its undercarriage.

They passed through a gate flanked by armored tanks.

Dornberger frowned at the presence of SS *Begleitkommando* troops, regiment strength, which here replaced those of his beloved Wehrmacht.

Heavily armed soldiers escorted them on foot to a clearing among oak trees, the heart of the *Führer*'s headquarters. Von Braun observed another featureless low bunker, its windows facing north to avoid direct sunlight, marked "13."

They entered a larger concrete building and were told to wait in an alcove. It was not yet the appointed hour, so an assistant took their presentation materials into an adjoining room. A secretary asked if they preferred tea or coffee; Hitler was behind schedule.

Dornberger had expected worse—cancellation—so they made small talk and sipped their hot drinks.

More than two hours ticked by, during which Wernher silently rehearsed his speech.

Long after five o'clock, Dornberger's face was pale. He rechecked the projection room to make sure the models had been set up correctly.

The door flew open and a voice called out, "The *Führer!*"

Hitler entered wearing a black cape over his hunched shoulders and stooped back, followed by Field Marshal Keitel, Generals Jodl and Buhle, Speer, Goebbels, and several adjutants.

Von Braun was relieved to see neither Himmler nor Kammler among them.

"*Mein Führer,*" Dornberger said, "our technical director, Herr von Braun, whom you've met before, will begin by narrating our film of the A-4 rocket taken October last. We will then go over the other materials."

Hitler wore a gray tunic and black trousers under his cape. His skin was an unhealthy yellow, tinged with dark-green veins, the flesh of his hands like melted butter. He looked at Dornberger with pitted eyes, nodded joylessly, and took his place at the front of the projection room.

The others occupied seats in three rows of chairs.

Lights were dimmed, the projector switched on, and von Braun began his narrative, standing to the side of the screen. Dornberger was relieved to see his technical director vanquish his nerves and enthrall their official audience with his boyish enthusiasm. He provided context and even humor to accompany the moving images of the great gates of the Assembly Hall sliding open and their rocket's dramatic appearance and flight.

The live-action portion was followed by an animated segment that illustrated the missile's trajectory, speed, height, and range.

The film closed with the end titles: *"Wir haben es doch geschafft!"*

"Yes, we have made it after all!" von Braun reiterated.

An awkward silence followed.

While a stenographer scribbled, no one dared say a word before the *Führer*'s verdict.

Lights were switched back on and curtains drawn back.

Their *Führer* rose and paced.

The *Generalmajor*'s stomach contracted.

Hitler came to a stop before von Braun and said, "I thank you, young man. Why was it I could not believe earlier in the success of your work?"

The room relaxed, and Dornberger stood to outline details concerning the rocket's motorized batteries and delivery dates.

When the *Generalmajor* was finished, Hitler's lips moved and his eyes stared from deep within dry sockets; he looked to von Braun like a man taking dictation. "If we'd had these rockets in 1939, we would never have had this idiotic conflict. From now on Europe and the world will be too small to contain wars. Humanity will not be able to endure such weapons."

They examined the models and charts, and Dornberger introduced their plans for a multistage rocket.

"The A-4 can decide the war," Hitler declared. "What encouragement it will be to the home front when it strikes the English! It is the decisive weapon." He turned to Speer, who had a discreet smile on his face. "And you say it can be produced with relatively small resources? Albert, you must push production of the A-4 as hard as you can. Labor and materials must be supplied instantly!" He turned to Dornberger. "I was about to sign a decree for the tank program. But now I'm changing it around so your rocket is on a par with tank production." He said to the group, "In this project we can use only Germans. God help us if the enemy finds out about this business."

"Very good, *Mein Führer*," said Speer. "It will be done immediately! The rocket will be designated *kriegswichtig*."

"What an all-inspiring murder weapon!" Goebbels's wide mouth dominated his narrow face. "When the first of these missiles screams down on London, panic will break out! It will force England to her knees and smash the global criminal conspiracy. If we could only show this film in every cinema in Germany, I would not have to make another speech or write another word—the most hard-boiled pessimist could not doubt our victory."

"You can only smash terror with counterterror!" Hitler pounded his fist on a table. "Anything else is rubbish. But before the rocket is put into action, I want a stock of five thousand to be ready for wholesale commitment. Your A-9 and A-10 should also have top priority! What we need is a ten-ton warhead and a production rate of two thousand rockets a month!"

Speer looked to Dornberger, who said, "*Mein Führer*, I am truly sorry, but in the immediate future a ten-ton warhead is not possible. Perhaps five years from now, if we can find enough fuel."

The *Generalmajor* saw a sudden shift in Hitler's eyes and braced himself.

"But what I want is annihilation—an *annihilating* effect!"

"*Mein Führer*, when we started our development work, we were not thinking of an all-annihilating effect. We—"

"*You*? No, *you* didn't think of it—*that* I know—but *I* did!"

"*Mein Führer*, no one can get more out of one ton of explosives than it is capable of giving."

As quickly, Hitler conceded the point. "If we cannot deliver ten tons, we will make up for it in sheer numbers."

General Jodl pushed a document across the table, and the stenographer placed pen and ink at the ready. Hitler pulled a pair of cheap spectacles from his pocket. His hand trembled as he scrawled an illegible signature, with a flourish, across three copies of an order that put the army in charge of the launchings, a directive they'd agreed upon beforehand.

Speer whispered in Hitler's ear.

"Yes, arrange this at once," Hitler said. "I will sign the document in person."

He grabbed von Braun's hand.

"Alexander the Great conquered a vast empire at twenty-three; Napoleon won a brilliant victory at thirty," he said. "Most ordinary people waste their younger years—but you...you have created a technical wonder at Peenemünde, a technical breakthrough which will change the face of the future. *Professor* von Braun, I congratulate you on your success."

He cupped Dornberger's hand with his two clammy hands. "I assure you that Peenemünde will always enjoy my favor. I do not revoke that... despite our difficulties."

The *Generalmajor* remarked that the man who had shouted at him moments before seemed to be holding back tears.

* * *

Two weeks later, von Braun received a large framed diploma with Hitler's signature. He had his secretary, Hannelore Bannasch, hang it in a place of honor on the wall of his office at Peenemünde, near a family portrait.

The document made official his honorific title: Professor of the Third Reich.

Chapter 25

"Japan Loses 7 Ships, 49 Planes to U.S. Fliers in Solomon's Fight; Allies Speed Advance in Sicily"

—*The New York Times*

Buckinghamshire, England
Tuesday, August 17, 1943

Royal Air Force Bomber Command was hidden among red-roofed brick buildings in the village of Walters Ash. Encircled by a green forest, a white manor house served as the officers' mess. A tunnel led to a Romanesque village church that masked the fire station.

In the underground Operations Block, beneath a motto reading *Non Sibi*, the advisory staff formed up around Air Chief Marshal Arthur Harris, who stroked his white mustache on his ghastly white face. They were strained and somewhat squashed between oversized sawhorse bulletin boards thumb-tacked over with maps and typed memos.

"Weather?" asked Harris.

"Clear full moon," the radio squawked. "No clouds over the islands of the north. Clear weather for the return trip and landing."

Harris picked up the phone. "Put me through to all group commanders."

Proper connections were made via several thousand kilometers of telephone cables to outposts throughout southern England.

"Hello, are you all there?" he asked. "Operation Hydra is on. Repeat: Operation Hydra is on. Targets as planned. All aircraft are to operate—maximum effort. Full instructions to follow in one hour's time."

Wyton, England

Air Commodore Don Bennett escorted Duncan Sandys and R. V. Jones across a wet, verdant field to the main hut. Recently appointed commander of the new Pathfinder Force, Bennett worried they would be late that afternoon for Group Captain Searby's squadron briefing. Sandys's limp was slowing them down.

Two airmen came up behind them and Jones couldn't help overhearing them.

"That's a good thing I haven't been off ground for a week," said one whom Jones thought a navigator.

"That's all right for you, but I had a party tonight," said another whom Jones thought a pilot.

"It's a code Goodwood."

"Anything but the Big City and I'm all right."

The long room inside the main hut was already packed with airmen sitting in rows at small wooden desks. Bennett led Jones and Sandys to two folding chairs at the front, to the side, so they would have a good view. Bennett remained standing.

Many crew of 83 Squadron sported roll-necked pullovers against the chill, caps on the back of their heads. They smoked cigarettes in an air of excitement and speculation. They could plainly see service policemen hanging about, which meant increased security, and more than the usual number of wing commanders, which meant importance.

A black curtain covered the far wall.

"The gold braid is thick 'n here," someone said.

"Yes. Something very big is up."

At the sound of an ostentatious locking of the door, conversation ceased.

Group Captain John Searby and his two deputies entered from a side door and the men stood.

"Sit down, please," Searby said.

A thirty-year-old Lincolnshire man, Searby was well known to Jones and never failed to impress him. The Master Bomber had flown over fifty operations, and his eyes, beneath thick black brows, seemed to be on permanent lookout for enemy fighters. Weeks ago, he'd been called to Pathfinder headquarters for a special briefing. Speedy preparations had followed.

An officer pulled back the black curtain to reveal a large map of Europe. Colored ribbons ran from bases in England to a target in Germany.

"Operation Hydra is on," Searby announced. "From intelligence sources and subsequent photo-reconnaissance sorties, it's been established that highly secret work is taking place at an experimental station on the Baltic coast—here." He indicated the target with a pointer. "Right here, at Peenemünde. We believe they're developing a new form of radar that will be lethal to your bombers."

"Radar" had been substituted for "rockets" by Sandys and his department, backed by MI6. Bomber crews didn't need to know about classified *Wunderwaffen.*

"Because of this threat, detailed plans have been drawn up and will be carried out tonight. Lads, it will be a precision attack. We've chosen tonight because we'll have a bright full moon to help you drop your bombs from eight thousand feet."

Jones wasn't surprised by the reaction—whistles, groans, catcalls, murmuring—and didn't blame them. Peenemünde presented a target of unusually miniscule proportions—these men usually bombed large cities—and a full moon would most definitely favor the German night fighters.

"I would like to stress at this juncture the lightness of local flak at your target," Searby sought to reassure them. "You'll also use Windows to confound their radar. To keep the German fighters off your back, a spoof raid of Mosquitos is planned for Berlin, which should delay counterattacks. Lads, I know you've never heard of Peenemünde, but intelligence assures us that this mission is vitally important."

The room calmed while an aide placed a small wooden table in the center aisle. Two others brought in a projector and a screen for the slide show.

"The first aiming point for Number 3 and Number 4 Groups will be a housing estate." Searby indicated with his pointer tiny homes grouped together in an aerial photo.

It was immediately evident to the crews that many of their bombs destined for scientists would also be falling on women and children.

They'll be trying to kill only a few people out of thousands, Jones thought. *And they know it.*

"It's unfortunate, but essential, that the top Nazi scientists be killed," Searby said. "It's no good destroying laboratories and workshops if the scientists survive to start it all over again."

"That's all right, guvnah," said a less-squeamish gunner from the back row. "How 'bout a prize to any arse-end-charlie who comes back with a pair of steel-rimmed spectacles hanging from his undercarriage?"

"The second aiming point is the production works, for Number 1 Group," Searby went on. "The third and last aiming point will be the experimental works, for Number 5 and 6 Groups. My Pathfinders will use parachute flares to illuminate the area. Radar-guided blind marker and visual marker aircraft will drop colored target-indicator flares on the three aiming points."

The overhead lights were switched on.

"We're sending all we've got," Searby concluded. "Over four thousand men in over three hundred Lancs. More than two hundred Halifaxes and fifty-four Stirlings. The distance to target and back is about one thousand two hundred and fifty miles. Your actual flying time should be about seven hours, so you'll need to conserve fuel. Lads, it's going to be a highly explosive raid. Over fifteen hundred tons of bombs and two hundred and fifty tons of incendiaries. Your job is to blow Peenemünde to bits. Any questions?"

No questions—only thoughts of a full moon and enemy fighters.

A weatherman gave his report, followed by a signals man. The crews took notes.

"Good luck to you—and flatten it," said Master Bomber Searby.

The men of Squadron 86 headed toward a door being unlocked by one of the service policemen.

Jones nodded to Sands, and they were about to leave when Bennett shouted, "Hold on, lads! There's just one more thing."

Everyone turned back, more than a few grumbling.

"We've just now received a personal message from Air Chief Marshal Harris," Searby said. "The message is as follows: 'If Operation Hydra fails to completely destroy its target, it will be repeated the next night and on the following nights, regardless, within practicable limits of casualties and planes gone down.'" He paused. "You know what this means, lads. Our failure could have a major impact on the outcome of the war—so my life and yours are not to be considered in the destruction of the target. All right then, get cracking."

Jones and Sandys noted the absence of the usual banter and horse-play on the airfield. Small open trucks transported crews—in flight jackets and warm pants, with suspenders, sheepskin boots, and inflatable life-belts—to pick up their parachutes and gear, then drove them to their planes.

Daylight faded and a purple sky framed a flight surgeon handing out wakey-wakey pills to those men who had flown the night before.

"I can't believe this is happening to us at the end of such a lovely day," remarked a bomb aimer.

One or two of the crewmen, most of whom were barely twenty, had difficulty putting cigarettes to their mouths. Their hands trembled.

"Nerves?" the MI6 man asked.

"Most likely."

Retreating to a safe distance, they watched the last of the high-octane petrol being pumped into the bombers. Pilots and their six-man crews climbed into their Lancs. Led by Searby in *William*, his Master Bomber aircraft, a Pathfinder Lanc, planes lined up on the runway.

"Switches off," said an aircraft hand.

"Switches off," Searby confirmed from the cockpit.

"Inner tanks on."

"Inner tanks on."

"Brakes on and pressure up."

"Okay, brakes on and pressure up."

"Undercarriage locked?"

"Undercarriage locked."

"Prepare to start up," Searby called to the flight engineer.

"Okay, ready to start up."

Engines were primed, and he put his hand on the throttle. His crew worked the switches and booster coils.

"Contact—starboard outer."

The four great Merlin engines sparked to life, each making a sound like a hawk's cry, and propellers turned.

"Chocks away!" called a ground crewman.

"Chocks away."

The crew inside *William* said their prayers, if so inclined.

"Hello, control," Searby radioed. "May we take off, please? Over."

"Okay, take off," replied control. "Listen out."

"Flaps thirty, radiators closed. Lock throttles. Prepare to take off. Okay behind, rear gunner?"

"Okay behind."

"Full power."

"Full power," the copilot confirmed.

Across the southern swath of England, on nearly forty airfields, over two thousand motors ripped on during that same quarter hour.

Pilots slammed their windows shut and pushed open their throttles.

"Climbing power!"

"Climbing power."

"Wheels. Flaps. Cruising power."

Sandys and Jones waved goodbye along with ground crews and WAAFs, as one heavy bomber after another ascended into the sky.

* * *

No. 3 Group aircraft arrived first, a gathering of Stirlings, at the rendezvous above the town of Croomer. Crews grinned and V-signed each other from their cockpits and turrets.

About midway to the Danish coast at exactly zero minus two hours, the balance of aircraft converged from their various bases. Planes extinguished their navigational lights and straightened up on course, cruising at about 210 miles per hour into a clear, bright night at 18,000 feet.

At 10:00 p.m., Master Bomber Searby led the way in *William* across the cold North Sea.

Behind him the formidable air armada stretched two miles across, twenty miles long, eight thousand feet thick, a roaring, concentrated wave of steel and explosives.

Chapter 26

"Russians Winning Kharkov Fight—Germans Losing 10,000 Men a Day"

—*Daily Express,* London

Peenemünde Army Research Center, Germany
Tuesday, August 17, 1943

Dornberger and von Braun loafed in the Hearth Room of the Officer's Club in the company of Dieter and Hanna Reitsch, a petite woman with blonde hair and blue eyes, a wide, flat nose, and a photogenic smile. Wernher thought Hanna irresistible because she was pretty and vain, and a popular test pilot. They reminisced about their days at the advanced gliding school.

"And now you are flying Messerschmitt Komets," von Braun remarked between sips of his martini.

"And you are building rockets to Mars." Reitsch laughed. "Who could have predicted what wonders National Socialism would do for us?"

She toasted the *Führer,* who had officially, at last, redesignated their secret rocket facility high priority.

The club's large windows were opened wide toward the west. Dornberger stretched his legs under a glass table. He was pleased with the colors of the room, its handsome furniture and paneled walls, its sturdy brass chandeliers. He approved of the fresh flowers and oil paintings, which he'd chosen himself, of German heroes.

He was even more pleased with the matériel cascading into their base.

"Tomorrow should be another day of blazing sun," Dieter said. "Good weather for testing the Maikäfer."

"*Ja*," agreed Hanna. She would be piloting the usually pilotless flying bomb to identify a persistent flaw in the design. "I would love a fresh, cooling thunderstorm afterward."

Wernher escorted Hanna to the door. She was staying in the visitor's quarters at the Luftwaffe experimental station three miles away. When air-raid sirens howled, he said, "Never mind that. The English airmen often gather over the Baltic before flying south to Berlin."

She shuddered.

"You must find a way to obliterate London, Wernher."

"Never fear." He kissed her cheek. "Good luck tomorrow."

Hanna slid into the back seat of her car and tapped the chauffeur's shoulder.

They drove off and the alarms died down.

Von Braun, Dornberger, and Dieter returned to their residences, not far from the administrative headquarters, and slept fast, comforted by the warm breeze blowing in from the sea.

* * *

Thousands of feet above and only a few kilometers distant, Luftwaffe night fighters had fallen for the ruse and hotly pursued the Mosquitoes of Eight Group.

At 10:56 p.m., the four million people of Berlin ran to that city's shelters and its defenders filled the sky with flares.

Eight hundred kilometers to the east, at Air Force Operations Headquarters, Chief of Air Staff Colonel-General Hans Jeschonnek signaled, "All night fighters to Berlin!"

* * *

Near the Dutch coast the flying armada of nearly six hundred bombers began their descent to eight thousand feet in a luminous night sky.

They made landfall to the north of Romo, an uninhabited island in the Wadden Sea. Searby saw two seals on a beach, their black shiny skin reflecting the light of the full moon ahead.

Twenty miles out from the Danish coast, the bombers released Window, their anti-radar flak, dropping two bundles per minute. Searby had memorized every prominent feature that could help them on their way. He worried mostly about the island of Sylt a few miles to the south, home to a night fighter airfield.

They dipped so low over the Baltic upon crossing Denmark's mainland that they could clearly see whitecaps on the sea.

Searby took a deep breath as *William* passed quickly above several small islands and their whitewashed farmhouses.

They skirted Rügen to avoid flak.

We're standing out like a toilet in the desert, he thought.

Shortly before midnight, the first wave of bombers made their approach over the narrow peninsula upon whose northern tip was their target: Peenemünde.

Searby saw the base was nearly undefended, lifeless and drab. He thought the landscape resembled the profile of a man with the back of his head being blown off.

They encountered no searchlights or flak, only light antiaircraft fire and a few belching smoke canisters, a tardy reaction to what those below assumed to be planes on their way to a more distant destination. The smoke came far too late to hide anything except the edges of several lakes.

Searby circled his *William* over the area, taking careful note of landmarks adjacent to the three aiming points. He then turned out to sea and climbed to five thousand feet to take up a position just off visible land. He switched on his voice radio.

"Ready...drop red flares!" he ordered his Deputy Master Bombers.

William circled round again.

His Pathfinder Force dropped the first group of four yellow target markers over the scientists' housing estate.

At 12:17 p.m., Searby ordered the first wave of nearly two hundred heavy bombers to attack.

"Fighters?" queried Ray Gibson in his squad commander Lanc.

"No activity," his midgunner replied.

"Seven thousand feet and holding."

"We're on target," reported his flight engineer. "Clear, good visibility."

His six-person crew was sweating out their first run.

"One minute to target," reported his aimer, bombsight to his left, triggers to his twin 7.7mm guns above.

"Bomb doors open."

"Fifty seconds…forty seconds."

"Lots of flak now."

"I see it," said Gibson.

The first wave of bombers remained in tight formation.

"Yellow TIs straight ahead."

"Good show," said Gibson. "There's the sky marker."

"Thirty seconds."

The Lancs flew dead level.

"Twenty seconds."

"Steady…hold it…"

"Bombs gone!"

The same shouted words echoed through the first wave, and their crews felt the thuds of exploding bombs on the ground.

* * *

The first deadly punch fell on workers in the Polish and Russian labor camp, more than a mile south of the intended target. Wooden huts and barracks erupted in splinters and flames. Sturdier buildings of light brick shattered or collapsed inward.

"Co się dzieje?" cried a prisoner who stumbled outside clutching a wounded shoulder.

"Mamy zrobić dla!" cried another, just before they both were blown to bits.

Direct hits burst planks, but the barracks remained locked. Men inside kicked at the doors and screamed. Hissing incendiaries transformed those who broke outside into flailing torches.

Survivors clawed at a high chain-link fence at the periphery topped with barbed wire. Guards, unsure what to do, threatened to shoot. SS men, without orders to release them, waved the prisoners back, then loosed Doberman pinschers, who tore at their burning flesh. When more laborers ran at the gates and a few squeezed through, the guards opened fire with their machine guns and splattered more gore across the camp.

* * *

Searby flew his *William* directly over the markers and saw they were off point. He radioed the remaining pilots of the first wave, but the whole target area roiled in confusion. Tremendous fires swept over the land, and gray-orange smoke billowed up in a hundred spots.

Their payloads released, the first wave of Lancs dove and slithered to avoid the increased flak. Pilots slammed their throttles wide open to put their engines in a high pitch. As they banked sharply homeward, their crews saw walls of flames spreading below.

"Bang on, skip!" said the flight engineer. "We hit 'em bang on!"

"That's how it's done, lads!" shouted Gibson.

He put his plane's nose down and got out of there in a hurry.

The second wave prepared to attack its target…

* * *

Half asleep in his bed, Dornberger thought the din was a result of late-night experiments—until he vaguely realized, *Too many explosions for a test.* He sat up fully awake when he recognized the sound of antiaircraft guns firing from their elevated positions.

He looked out a window and saw the 37mm gun of the harbor blasting away at what seemed like a multicolored string of pearls in the night sky.

A violent quake threw him from the bed and blew out windowpanes on the ground floor. He staggered to his feet and checked himself. No injuries. He nearly leapt downstairs in his pajamas, threw on an overcoat, and grabbed his cigar case. He switched off the outside light. Loud, sharp bangs nearby hurt his ears.

He ran outside and saw ceramic tiles sliding down roofs and shattering on the ground. Another detonation and half of the house next door collapsed. A shock wave rolled over him—*boom, boom, boom!*—intermingled with the hiss of phosphorus and incendiary bombs.

He moved toward the closest shelter, but painful stabs from the broken tiles pierced his thin slippers. He stopped, transfixed by the spectacle.

Colors arranged by the Gods of Life and Death. An Apocalypse.

A cloud of pink mist enveloped him. A fine white sand that smelled like sugar settled on his shoulders.

He saw von Braun running toward him and quit his reverie. His technical director had on pants and a shirt, dress shoes, but no socks.

"I suppose you forgot all about me!" Dornberger shouted above the noise.

"Nein!" Wernher shouted back. "I was coming to get you."

"Ten to one, our gunners were too keen and brought this down on us!"

"*Nein, nein!* They are really after us. Come on!"

They were knocked to the ground. Bombs and incendiaries blasted cement fragments hundreds of feet into the air. Sirens wailed.

They jumped back to their feet and raced with others to the main-office shelter.

Dornberger rang the bell and a thick steel door opened. Frau Zanssen appeared, the shelter guardian, three children clinging to her legs.

Inside the gray cement room Dornberger called the command post and lit a cigar. A crowd of frightened people in various states of undress met his eyes.

"Report!" he barked.

"At about twelve fifteen a hidden wave of bombers arrived," the chief warden replied, "coming from Rügen. The first bombs fell on the labor camps. Telephone lines to the preproduction works and camp—knocked out. The last message from the settlement was seven bomb hits. No damage to the test stands so far—but it's an all-out raid!"

* * *

The second wave of over a hundred Lancasters flew toward their more difficult targets: two assembly buildings, each less than three hundred yards long. Searby ordered red markers of Seven Squadron dropped over them and called for height and speed. His Master Bomber brought the second wave to the main base. Great sticks of mile-long incendiaries crisscrossed the target indicators.

"Bombs gone!"

An inferno—green and blue eruptions at a rate surpassing Searby's ability to count.

"Threepenny bit and two and six!" he heard over the radio. "That got 'em!"

Eight minutes later the second wave tore homeward, but Searby couldn't tell if the structures below had been touched.

* * *

In the sky over Berlin two hundred night fighters converged. Göring ordered fifty day fighters into the fray. In the confusion Messerschmitts and Focke-Wulfs attacked each other. Flak defenses and heavy antiaircraft guns opened fire on everything within range.

It didn't take long for the three-man fighter crews and solo pilots to note that the small number of target indicators and bombs signaled a decoy operation. The Mosquitoes had vanished, but they could see to the north the sky over Peenemünde, only a twenty-minute flight away, sparkling with bright flashes of color.

Orders were to stay put, but older pilots decided to act on their own. Twenty fighters broke off, heading in a hurry toward the Baltic coast, a flat-out, full-throttle extended dive from their higher elevations.

They could soon make out enemy bombers flying unusually low and radioed the control rooms: "*Negative in 6,000 Meter; keine dicken Autos. Dicke Autos greifen in 1,500 bis 2,000 Meters an.*"

* * *

"The Measurement House is on fire. The Assembly Workshop is ablaze and—"

"I'm coming over to you at once," Dornberger shouted over the phone to his chief warden.

12:35 a.m.

An adjutant handed him his riding boots.

Von Braun yanked open the steel door and they both ran into the suffocating smoke and destruction.

Great fires soared, and Dornberger realized that the bombers had adjusted their targeting. Dark gray fumes stung their eyes. On the crossroads, thermite incendiaries shone a dazzling white. Bright flames flicked in and out of the Construction Bureau's tangled window frames. Glowing sparks spiraled upward.

"Take over the bureau," the *Generalmajor* ordered, pointing toward the building. "Try to restrict the fires to the top floor. Get a hose from the fire brigade. If you cannot put a halt to it, grab all the important papers and drawings out of the big safe! I'm going to the Measurements House and the settlement!"

"Right!" von Braun replied and they ran their separate ways, throwing themselves down as bombs blew up around them, then resuming course.

* * *

A gunner spotted five enemy fighters diving at several Lancs.

"They're sitting ducks!" a captain exclaimed. "Rear gunner, can you hear me?"

"I hear you, skipper. The Crickets are back! Someone's caught it."

Out his cockpit window Searby saw Lancasters and Halifaxes in trouble. If the fighters came in large numbers, they would not survive. He also noted patchy low clouds and thick smoke over the next target area. The third wave might easily overshoot the experimental works.

The crew of the *William* had already made six runs over the peninsula. Navigator and flight engineer crowded with Searby into the front of the plane, keeping track as best they could of developments on the ground while ignoring the strain of flying over a defended target for more than forty minutes. Perspiration drenched their faces, burned their eyes, and ran down their backs under their flight jackets. Urine soaked their crotches and thighs.

"Let's go!" the navigator shouted.

"We need one final run," the bomb aimer said.

"We've got a bandit on our tail!" the rear gunner announced.

The mid-upper gunner brought down the older-model Bf 110 with a good burst.

The third wave encountered stiff opposition at fifty minutes after "H" hour.

Searby saw a Lanc's fuel tank get hit between its two engines and catch fire. Another bomber exploded in midair, a fragment of its wing missing *William* by yards.

Three men in parachutes trailed behind.

Five more bombers corkscrewed down.

"Dive port!" Searby heard a pilot order evasive action over the radio.

"God bless and keep you, mother McCrea!" an Australian pilot shouted.

Searby tried to exercise control amidst the carnage, but it was an impossible job.

"Make a steady run," he radioed to anyone listening. "Keep the target in view—and bomb the greens."

An aircraft flying ahead was transformed into a fireball. Two more bombers went down. Long, slow flashes in the dark-blue sky.

Surviving craft slalomed through exploding wreckage. Parachutes sprinkled the night.

Bodies without parachutes tumbled out of broken up planes.

The last bombers navigated a reenergized flak gauntlet, where bursting shells sent shards of razor-sharp steel through fuselages and flesh.

The third wave finished its last run—Searby shouted, "Set course for Mando Island—we're going home!"

The remaining Lancs sped into the night, trying to put as much distance between them and the smaller fighters, which, low on fuel, could not follow.

* * *

Von Braun made his way to the Construction Bureau skirting craters and dodging pieces of hot twisted metal.

When the all-clear signal sounded, his watch confirmed that it had been about an hour since the first bombs fell though the attack seemed to have lasted all night. The sky was red, bright as day, lit by flames. Men emerged from cover, a few groaning in pain. A last bomb exploded in the sea, spouting a water fountain twenty meters high.

As he loped along, his face covered with sweat and black soot, two ravens flew overhead and cawed.

"Everywhere it's fire!" cried a woman emerging from between two demolished trucks.

Though her face was stained like his and her hair singed, von Braun recognized Hannelore.

"Come!" he shouted and grabbed her hand.

She let him lead her into the burning entrails of the bureau's front hallway.

"Professor, where are you taking me?"

He pulled her through a pool of blood, where a shorn-off leg extended from a boot.

She screamed and, to her astonishment, von Braun turned and reached down between her breasts. He pulled out a key attached to her necklace.

"You are the only one—the cabinet safe!" he exclaimed. "We must save our drawings."

He led her up a short flight of stairs into what had been a rear room. One wall was gone and the floor ablaze. Their backs to the remaining walls, they reached the second floor, where doors had been shot out of the building or lay splintered on the floor. The roof was knocked off, its gable ready to fall. The third story had disappeared.

He yanked Hannelore down a hallway, counting, "*Eins, zwei, drei, vier, fünf…*"

He stopped before an empty door frame—"Here!"

Small fires burned, but they edged their way in. Half of the room was open to the night.

For a horrible moment von Braun thought their work lost, until Hannelore pointed: "There it is!"

Beneath wooden beams was the large overturned strongbox, blown open, its contents intact.

"Quickly!" said von Braun, and they scooped up an armload of papers.

They made several trips up and down the stairs with the bundles while suffering mild burns.

Wernher found others nearby and ordered them to help. They threw drawers full of plans out of windows to the ground, where Hannelore gathered them up in the heat.

Wernher spotted a soldier, whom he told to guard their valuable documents.

When the first rockets fall on London, he thought as he went to find Dornberger, *I will feel no remorse.*

Dornberger hurried along a beach road of the settlement where many homes were on fire.

"*Mein schönes Peenemünde*," he lamented.

He made his way to Dr. Thiel's home. He needed to consult with the doctor on damages and was relieved to find his house had not been hit. He called for the professor on the ground floor.

No answer.

He called again, and a soldier ran up to him.

"What is it?" Dornberger snapped. "Do you have something to report?"

"Only that Dr. Thiel and his family have been killed."

"What are you talking about? We are standing right here!"

"I regret to inform you that they fled their home and took shelter in a slit trench," the soldier said through blackened lips. "The trench received a direct hit."

Dornberger dismissed the soldier. The loss of his chief engine technician was going to be hard to bear.

We will have our revenge.

Grantham, England
Wednesday, August 18, 1943

In St. Vincent's Hall, Air Commodore Ralph Cochrane stood before a fatigued squadron. Cochrane was accompanied by his squadron commander and the navigation officer for the debriefing.

6:00 a.m.

The last aircraft had landed seven minutes before, after a total flight time of eight hours and forty minutes.

Once again Jones and Sandys had motored in as observers.

"The bulk of the force landed by 04.27," said Cochrane, who had a narrow face and hazel eyes. "The third and last wave was caught in the moonlight and suffered great damage. I'm sorry to say we lost 29 out of 200. All together, we lost 40 aircraft and probably 270 crewmen. But it could have been much worse."

Jones was sorry for those killed, but he knew perhaps better than anyone how important it had been to knock out the rockets—if they did.

"Consequently, we consider Operation Hydra a success," Cochrane went on. "We consider the base dealt with. A return visit to Peenemünde will not be necessary."

Jones saw the relief on their faces. Their job was done. Aerial reconnaissance would assess the damage over the next few days.

"That's all. Dismissed."

Crews filed out.

A few managed to find a spot in the mess hall kitchen to drink four-finger shots of scotch and whiskey poured into water glasses.

"An excellent prang that was," said Officer Fitzgerald of 207 Squadron, "well and truly, I'm sure."

Chapter 27

"Roosevelt Says Allies Will End 'Gangsterism' in World; Mountbatten to Command in Southeast Asia"

—*The New York Times*

Peenemünde Army Research Center, Germany
Thursday, August 19, 1943

Dornberger and von Braun strolled down the main avenue. Teams of repair workers walking in the opposite direction split into two streams to flow by them. Each day since the raid, the duo had toured their rocket facility to assess damages and prioritize. They'd laughed at the sight of Dieter, naked, washing himself in a barrel of beer because the pumping station had been destroyed.

They'd surveyed the destroyed design office, senior officer's mess, and the steam power plant, whose large supply of coal was still burning. They'd been pleased to note that not a single item of scientific importance had been touched. The wind tunnel had survived intact, and the workshop was only scratched.

The first rescue parties had arrived from the towns of Wolgast, Anklam, Greifswald, and Swinemünde. Hundreds of civilians and soldiers labored to restore communication links and roads. The wounded had either been evacuated or taken to an expanded medical station.

Von Braun unrolled a blueprint. He wore civilian clothes and a light jacket; the *Generalmajor* was in uniform. They looked from the blueprint to the mostly destroyed office block.

"We must continue to maintain the look of devastation," Dornberger said. "The British must think they were successful."

"Of course."

"We will refurbish only essential buildings under camouflage. Burnt timbers will be laid across the roofs; craters should be left in roads."

"Let us hope our rockets hit their targets with more accuracy than the British hit theirs."

Von Braun rolled up the blueprint, and they recommenced their tour.

"Because so many foreign laborers were killed, we will say publicly that the British bombers meant to hit the barracks."

"I have been thinking: Rees and Debus can fill in temporarily for our dead friend, Dr. Thiel, until Wolfgang Sänger is transferred from the Wehrmacht; they say he's brilliant. Together, they may—"

Kammler and his chief of staff, Bernard von Ploetz, arrived at a quick march, more blueprints under their arms.

"You are ahead of schedule, *Brigadeführer*," Dornberger remarked.

"Of course." Kammler headed toward an annex of the design building. "And we must *act* quickly! *Kommen Sie mit mir*."

Dornberger and von Braun traded wary looks before following the SS men.

In the atrium, secretaries were gathering up scattered papers to refile them. Workmen replaced windows.

Kammler shut an undamaged door behind them in a vacant room and bolted it.

"London radio reports your work will be delayed by a minimum of three months," he said.

"Less," Dornberger said.

"We will see. Yesterday at a meeting with Himmler and Speer, the *Führer* reiterated his demand for twenty thousand rockets—which must be ready for launch by next year."

Kammler waited for their reactions.

Von Braun said nothing, but Dornberger scowled. "Impossible. Were you not outside with the rest of us? It will take us at least one month to fully recover. And we have not yet solved—"

"Perhaps. But I am on your side." Kammler removed a piece of paper from his breast pocket and unfolded it. "This order I am holding allows me to transplant your manufacturing center to the Mittelwerk in the Harz Mountains near Nordhausen. At that factory, I will put at your disposal thousands of foreign laborers. The *Führer* has ruled that all available manpower will be used for rocket production. *Generalmajor*, this new facility will be impregnable."

Dornberger took the order and read it.

"How is this possible?" He looked at Kammler. "Even the SS has not created a shield that can stop a five-hundred-pound bomb."

Kammler nodded to von Ploetz, who wiped away dust and debris from a table, then unrolled one of the blueprints on it.

"Look here," Kammler said. "We have already excavated two long tunnels. We will expand them. You will have the space you need and more—underground. The bombs will no longer be able to touch you."

Von Ploetz spread out two more blueprints on top of the first.

"The development team will be dispatched to a cavern blasted into a cliff in Austria, here," Kammler pointed. Von Braun noted that the back of Kammler's hand was almost skeletal. "An important inland rocket test range will be established here, in Blizna."

They studied the drawings, running their fingers along the penciled lines. They saw the thickness of the mountain's protective rock.

Von Braun glanced at Dornberger, who gave an almost imperceptible nod, and said, "I cannot say absolutely at this point, but your plan appears to have merit."

"*Gut*." Kammler clicked his heels. "I am pleased you both concur. *Generalmajor,* Herr Professor, please see to it that necessary preparations are made. There can be no delay in manufacturing our V-2 rockets."

"V-2?" Dornberger was perplexed. "I am not familiar with this new designation."

"Of course not. You have not been told. Goebbels coined it for the public: 'V' for vengeance. The flying bomb is designated V-1. Your rocket is Vergeltungswaffe-2. You should both be proud. The German people are thirsting for vengeance—and you will get it for them."

The *Brigadeführer* rolled up his blueprints and handed them to von Ploetz, who unbolted the door. They both Sieg Heiled and quit the room.

"Kammler is mad," said von Braun.

"He is arrogant. Unfortunately the British bombing has played right into his hands. We must be careful or the SS will wrest every control from our hands."

"Which we have known."

"I will nevertheless take it up with the *Oberkommando der Wehrmacht*."

"You can stall. Speer may still be of some help."

"Speer is a fool. He does not yet realize Kammler is being groomed to replace him."

* * *

Less than a week later, Kammler was in Nordhausen to oversee the arrival of the first one hundred foreign laborers at the Mittelwerk. Russian, French, and Polish men in striped garments climbed out of the trucks and were assigned places on the rocket construction assembly line.

SS guards eyed the ragged laborers with a detached, sadistic air. Everyone had to perform to expectations, and the *Unterscharführers* were not about to let the subhumans disappoint them. Camp Dora was not yet ready, so the prisoners would sleep in the same mountain tunnels where they worked.

Kammler thought of the engineers and scientists at Peenemünde. He wanted their rockets.

He also thought with pleasure of the results he'd forced out of Schomberger at the castle. The inventor had improved control of the saucer's propulsion system, and his implosion machines would soon be capable of producing light, heat, and mechanical motion with only air and water as fuel.

Kammler wanted to be the locus of the *Wunderwaffen.*

He would then eclipse the *Reichsführer.*

As for the foolish Allies…

They won't stand a chance. He watched the slave laborers filing into the mountain. *They will never know what hit them.*

Chapter 28

“Germans Murder 700,000 Jews in Poland—Travelling Gas Chambers”

—*Daily Telegraph,* London

Głogów, the German Empire
Thursday, November 18, 1943

Rachel pulled hard at a brown curl. For two hours she'd been waiting inside an abandoned windmill, its ribs and tattered spokes creaking in the midnight wind. Her eyes scanned the western horizon. She'd eaten only a slice of stale bread that day.

When Rachel saw the code flashed from just beyond the field, she responded with her torch.

A minute later her Palmach handler came up the stairs. This one was older, with a black mustache, in a bomber jacket, worn pants and worn boots. She assumed he'd been sleeping in the woods for the last few days, like her, but she'd been doing it longer.

“Is there another way out?” he asked.

She inclined her head to the right, where he saw a second staircase framed by dark timbers.

“You worry too much,” she said. “The patrols don't come here at night. Not usually. My motorcycle is well hidden.”

“Sorry for the long wait.” He sat cross-legged on the floor and drank from a leather pouch. “We had to fight to get in. We lost two.” He offered his pouch to Rachel, who declined. "Did your man say anything more about what they're up to underneath the castle?"

"No. Whatever they're doing, it killed him quickly."

"Your report mentioned secret experiments..." The spy paused to pull a chunk of cheese out of his satchel, which he also offered.

She accepted and said, "They brought in a man he didn't recognize, a large man from Austria. Some sort of inventor. The SS has a big operation going. Work has increased since his arrival. Nearly every week they are testing a craft of an unusual kind, often with human guinea pigs."

The Palmach man took notes with a pencil and pad. Rachel described the craft in as much detail as she could, having risked several trips through the caves.

"I've also seen monks, Tibetans maybe, coming and going, which makes some sort of sense. The prisoner I rescued said he'd seen several very old drawings, on parchment, called *vi-māna*. I looked it up in the town's library."

"You shouldn't be seen there. *Vi-māna*, what is that?"

"Flying machines from Indian Sanskrit texts. What of the death camps?" she asked, changing the subject.

He stopped writing. "We are nearly helpless. We've carried out small operations, but the Allies ignore our requests to bomb the railways. This cannot be a war to save the Jews."

"It's not just Jews."

He wasn't going to argue, so she added, "I'd rather be killing Nazis."

"Don't worry. The Russians are taking care of that."

Rachel took another bite of cheese. "They're trying to break away from gravity. This is what I think."

"The Russians?"

"No, you idiot. The Nazis. The SS. They believe the Vedic texts, and this large Austrian man is helping them. God help us if they succeed."

"Let me know if they do." Her handler was dismissive. He rose and slung his satchel over a shoulder. "The usual way."

He and his superiors had come to view Rachel with suspicion. She'd started out as a deadly spy, but her reports had become strange, her tone, haughty; her clothes were ragged. They doubted she'd last much longer.

From her window she watched him disappear into a thicket.

Silence again, except for croaking frogs.

And a presence.

She jumped to her feet and took a defensive position, pointing her rifle into the darkness of one, then the other staircase.

"Be not afraid, Rachel," said a voice.

The presence seemed to have changed locations—she swung her rifle toward the window and called out, "Who are you?"

"An old friend." The voice came from behind the walls. *"Time to remember."*

"How did—"

Rachel felt sleepy.

Gas.

She sunk to her knees and saw herself from above, curled up on the floor.

A shadow crept over her body. The blackness sprouted great wings, which fanned out and engulfed the walls of her hideout.

I'm upside down, tossed beneath a roiling ocean. Can't breathe. Serpentine monsters a hundred meters long coil by. Red-and-yellow luminescent eyes stare at me from black depths. I look up and see a strong hand reaching out, above the cresting waves. I extend my arm, I stretch with all my heart, yet I cannot reach it...

Chapter 29

"Hitler Abandons Smolensk—Most Disastrous Defeat Suffered by German Army"

—The Johnstown Tribune

Moscow, Union of Soviet Socialist Republics
Friday, November 19, 1943

In his thick winter jacket, Sergei Pavlovich Korolev descended three steps into the sunken perimeter outside their production and design building. Facing him was a high iron fence. On its three horizontal black bars hung hundreds of daggerlike icicles; the setting sun shone through them to create a jeweled prism effect on the enclosure.

Mikhail Klavdievich Glushko kept a sharp eye on Korolev from the doorway.

The on-duty sentry allowed a small figure in a light-green coat through the iron gate.

"Papa, papa, papa!" the little girl cried.

"Natashka."

Korolev picked her up and hugged her. He held her at arm's length. She had her father's dark eyes and her mother's soft, pale cheeks. He hugged her to him again, and his voice cracked, "My darling black-eyed Natashka."

Glushko had arranged the reunion. His position gave him certain advantages. The two men, forced to cohabitate for so long and so intensely, had begun to call each by their first names. Glushko had come to realize that if he wanted Korolev to build suitable vessels for his engines, he needed to restore his will to live.

"Papa, papa," Natasha pleaded. "Will you not come home?"

Korolev lowered her and brushed some snow from a pink bow in her reddish-brown hair.

"I will come home as soon as I can. I am working here now, so Mother Russia can win the war."

Natasha was eight and talkative. He listened to her tell him how silly school was and what she preferred to eat. She looked up and down the alley and asked, "But Papa—you are a pilot. How can the planes land in this place?"

"You are right," he laughed. "In fact it is easy to land here but not so easy to take off."

The sentry guard smiled at his wordplay, but Natasha didn't understand.

"Where is your mother?" her father asked.

He'd received a letter from Lyalya at last, but her tone had been solemn. The war, his absence…

"She could not come. I walked here by myself. Mama gave me money for the tram."

"Natashka, you must not go out by yourself. Tell your mother—I forbid it."

He kneeled down and began making a snowman for his daughter.

Glushko observed Korolev's revived spirits and knew they would soon be able to test the RU-1 jet launchers on the Pe-2. It would perform to expectations, and the work of his potentially brilliant colleague would improve.

He would continue to feed him emotionally.

Not too little.

Not too much.

Chapter 30

"Entschlossen und Hart: Demaskiertes England (Determined and Stubborn: England Unmasked)"

—*Das Reich,* Berlin

Peenemünde Army Research Center, Germany
Monday, November 22, 1943

The vast research base had a deserted, forlorn air. Only half- or completely destroyed buildings were visible to reconnaissance planes. A few civilians walked its broad snow-lined streets. Enormous camouflage nets hid utilities and workshops. Though about half its personnel had been shipped out to work in places too small or remote to bomb, Peenemünde had been reborn as a pure research facility.

Its remaining chief engineers often lounged in the untouched Officer's Club. Within the bay of its Hearth Room, between the carved transoms of its four windows, Heinrich Himmler reclined in a burgundy armchair, legs crossed. He wore his dress uniform of white wool, shoulder boards with oaks, and pleated pockets. Kammler idled behind him, also in dress uniform, glass of champagne in hand. Seven or eight SS officers at their right kept warm around the fireplace. To their left, posed in various positions of interest, were Dornberger, von Braun, Dieter, Debus—and the technical director's brother Magnus von Braun, who was now employed as a chemical engineer at the rocket facility.

"You are lucky you have been bombed only once," said the bespectacled Himmler. "The city of Kassel has been the object of a concentrated bombing campaign. At least twenty thousand good, loyal Germans have perished, and the flames are still burning. So you see, gentlemen, the rocket is long overdue."

"It would have been ready much earlier, *Reichsführer*, if not for unavoidable delays," Debus said obsequiously.

"You refer to manpower. Raw resources," said Kammler. "Thanks to us, you presently have that required manpower."

"Consequently *Brigadeführer* Kammler has been named commissioner of the SS building office," Himmler announced, "in order to take charge of the Ministry of Munitions's special V-2 project. He will instill *order* in the thirteen committees."

"So he will be in charge of the rubbish," Magnus quipped, playing on the word *Ausschuss*, which could mean "committee" or "garbage" depending on the context.

No one thought it funny enough to laugh.

Instead Dornberger pushed his chin into his neck and glared at them, red-faced. The embodiment of two hundred years of Prussian military tradition, he looked down on the SS upstarts from a great height. "The efficiency of our army program has already been *vitiated* by the introduction of these special committees," he said. "What is the point of splitting the program still further by appointing a commissioner? Please do not think you are one of us just because the emaciated inmates of your vile concentration camps are digging caves, and you are their judge and god. The rocket has been and always will be under army jurisdiction."

Himmler glared at him and Kammler murmured—"You are fortunate, *Generalmajor*, that today it is one way. Tomorrow, almost certainly it will be another."

Von Braun smoked his cigarette and had to admit to himself that Kammler could demonstrate sufficient powers of self-control if needed.

For his part Dornberger imagined how it would feel to slam his fist into the *Brigadeführer*'s light-boned face.

"Gentlemen, thank you for your hospitality." Himmler rose and led his SS contingent out of the room.

"You had better watch yourself." Von Braun sipped his martini.

"*Ja*," Dieter seconded.

Debus also thought the *Generalmajor* had overstepped his bounds.

"No, Herr Professor. I am in no danger." Dornberger placed his hand on von Braun's shoulder. "They will not fight the army head-on. No, it is *you* who may be their next target."

"You must be joking."

But Magnus could see the *Generalmajor* was not.

Chapter 31

"Allies, Germans Vie for 'Secret' Weapons Antidote Supremacy: Nazis Concentrate on Rocket Bombs, 'Death Rays,' Atom-Smasher, Noiseless Aircraft Ridiculed"

—*The Tennessean*

London, England
Friday, December 3, 1943

"They have increased their camouflage and left damaged buildings unrepaired," R. V. Jones said to Churchill. He'd been summoned once more to the cozy cabinet room of 10 Downing Street. "The Germans are hoping that we won't notice, but our aerial photography analysts have confirmed that Peenemünde is up and running."

Churchill made an unhappy sound.

"Consequently, MI6 has intensified its photographic efforts, which has revealed something like the measles popping up all over northern France. This is work of an unexplained nature—what we're calling 'ski' sites—which I feel are almost certainly launching pads for the pilotless bombs."

"That is as I predicted," said Lord Cherwell, who smacked his lips on a mint.

"However, transcripts of conversations between two German generals captured at El Alamein hint strongly at *rockets*," Jones emphasized.

"Apparently, one of the imprisoned officers said, and I quote: 'Wait until next year—that's when the fun will start.' Agents from Luxembourg also tell of a rocket being developed. Our American friend Professor von Kármán at Caltech has provided an analysis on the German program. He believes they are working on rockets and *have been* for several years." He glared at the Professor. "He wonders why England is so complacent."

Churchill lit his cigar while Sandys took his turn. "For the last six months evidence has continued to accumulate from many sources," he said. "They say the Nazis are preparing an attack on England, evidence which would seem to be in line with what the two German generals divulged. My committee believes that it is entirely possible that a premature and short-lived attack might be made imminently, while the main attack of pilotless bombs and rockets will be attempted after the New Year."

Churchill bent over to take off his black oxford shoes and said, "Thank you, gentlemen."

Jones was amused to see that his task was made easier thanks to custom zippers instead of laces.

"Sands," said the PM, straightening, "I'm expanding Bodyline into Crossbow, code name for the new Anglo-American collaboration against the Natsi secret weapons program. The urgent question, which I expect you to answer, is what will become of our Overlord plans if we are hit by a massive bombardment? I cannot allow that. What if these rockets cause a panic in the streets? That, too, I cannot allow."

"It's difficult to say."

"Every effort to avoid a panic should be made," the Prof sidestepped. "Any information in connection with our bombing targets should be kept top secret. In the press we can refer to them as 'military objectives' though...we will be heightening the mystery."

The PM bent over again and pulled off embroidered socks to expose two white feet. To Jones's amazement, he then pulled out a second pair of socks from beneath his chair, sequestered there beforehand no doubt by his personal valet.

Resoled in silk slippers, Churchill straightened again and took a puff of his cigar. "I prefer mystery to the alternative. Crossbow debuts with America's Ninth Air Force. Mr. Jones, I will suggest that its first bombing target be those damn ski sites."

Chapter 32

"Himmler Takes Goering's Post as No. 2 Nazi"

—*The Ogden Standard Examiner*

Peenemünde Army Research Center, Germany
Tuesday, February 22, 1944

At the controls of his blue Messerschmitt 108 Taifun, von Braun had a bumpy ride with poor visibility due to whirling snow. Ice had formed on the ribbed cockpit windows. Nevertheless, he found the single-prop plane a refuge from long meetings with suppliers in far-flung sectors of a vast corporation known as the German Empire.

The decentralization of his work was not to his liking, but he kept at it diligently. He wanted his rockets to fly. He wanted to win the war.

The Taifun touched down on Peenemünde's small landing field in darkness, three hours late. Upon entering his office, he asked Hannelore to order coffee and sandwiches from the mess and to tell his department chiefs to join him for an all-night session. He needed to brief them on technical problems raised at the Mittelwerk factory during his most recent visit.

"Yes, Herr Professor, right away," she said and handed him a telephone message. "This came in two hours ago."

Reichsführer Himmler wanted to see him. "Urgent."

After only an hour's sleep, von Braun climbed back into the cockpit wearing his black SS *Sturmbannführer* uniform. He was wary and annoyed at being called on such short notice, though he liked the intrigue. A good game of cat and mouse.

If Dornberger was right, Himmler had laid a trap for him.

He kept his Taifun at a low altitude because of prevailing weather in the North Rhine-Westphalia region and to avoid chance encounters with Allied bombers or stray night fighters.

He navigated through dark Alme Valley as night became dawn.

He jumped from his plane onto a cold, muddy landing field and ducked into a waiting heated Grosser Mercedes six-seat touring car.

They're rolling out the red carpet. Better be careful...

The driver accelerated down a smooth country road toward Wewelsburg Castle.

The automobile came to a stop in a courtyard of paving stones. Medieval towers flanked a covered entranceway of arced wooden doors. Inside, a young blonde SS *Untersturmführer* escorted von Braun with exaggerated hospitality on a quick tour of the imposing triangular edifice. He showed his visitor a circular crypt and the large auditorium. They walked down a hallway of the classroom wing, where von Braun heard snatches of various lectures. SS marriage consecrations were held in an ornate chapel.

"Herr *Reichsführer*'s private collection of weapons is displayed here and in other rooms." His guide gestured at a wall full of swords and daggers affixed to oak paneling.

Stepping over one of the many swastikas inlaid in the tiled floor, they climbed the north tower past carved pilasters.

"The axis here is the actual *Mittelpunkt der Welt*," the *Untersturmführer* proclaimed. "Soon we will make here an eternal flame to mark this center of the world. A fitting symbol, do you not agree?"

"Of course. Most fitting."

The tour came to an end in an unrestored wing of the castle, a shabby corridor lined with small rooms containing tables covered in blueprints. His guide knocked on an old wooden door and opened it.

"Please go in, Herr Professor. *Reichsführer* Himmler is waiting."

"Thank you."

He took a chair opposite the *Reichsführer*, who kept his head bowed while leafing through some paperwork on his desk.

A petty tactic by a petty man, thought von Braun.

He took the opportunity to make a study of the small office and saw evidence of the archaeological digs carried out by the SS: ancient tablets with swastikas, stelae with arcane symbols, and, on the walls, more swords, maces, and daggers.

After signing a document, Himmler looked up at his visitor. The light from a desk lamp afforded von Braun a good view of blue eyes behind glasses that wished to convey the idea of a benign interrogation. A trimmed and blackened mustache floated above thin lips, in contrast to a pale face. He wore his standard black SS uniform.

"Where is *Brigadeführer* Kammler?" von Braun asked. "I thought he would be here."

"He is in Lower Silesia, on assignment. I thought it better for the two of us to meet in private. Herr Professor, before we speak I am obliged to swear you to secrecy. Do you swear?"

Von Braun understood the stratagem, but swore.

"I hope you realize your A-4 rocket has ceased to be a toy," Himmler said. "The whole of the German people are eagerly awaiting the mystery weapon. Yet you are handicapped by a lot of army red tape and endless business. Why not join your little production to the SS and help me in my invaluable work? I could clear up that mess for you. No one has such ready access to the *Führer* as I. Not even Speer. I can promise you vastly more effective support than those hidebound career generals."

"Herr *Reichsführer*, thank you for your concern, but I could not ask for a better superior than *Generalmajor* Dornberger. Such delays we are experiencing are due to technical troubles and not red tape." He added, perhaps in response to Himmler's receding chin or his flaccid, wrinkled neck, "You know, our A-4 is rather like a little flower. To flourish, our baby needs sunshine, a well-proportioned quantity of fertilizer, and a gentle gardener. What I fear you are planning is a big SS jet of liquid shit."

He thought that Himmler's smile became contemptuous at its corners.

"You do not seem to fully comprehend the situation, Herr Professor." Himmler revealed two rows of dry white teeth. "Need I remind you that you are a member of the SS. I have given you an honorary title, but your uniform makes you at least answerable to me. Do you even know what the runes on your uniform signify?"

"I had supposed them to be bolts of parallel lightning."

"Not at all. They are magical signs, symbolic of power and victory. While the Wehrmacht uses conventional means to defeat our opponents, my loyal corps and I are embarked on a more important quest. The terror we sow is only the superficial wave of a mighty underground current." He leaned forward. "The world is sick. Only Germany dares to find a remedy. Whether ten thousand or ten million workers collapse from exhaustion while digging tunnels or making your rockets interests me only in so far as it advances our remedy. But we Germans are a kind people," he softened his tone, "so we will also adopt a decent attitude toward these human animals and subhuman *Juden*. I hope you understand, Herr Professor. Killing is difficult, yet it is therefore good and justified. It purifies us and, at our core, we remain civilized."

Von Braun leaned back in his chair, amazed.

"We in the SS have altered many world events," Himmler said and also leaned back, "though only a few are aware of it. We use our *will* to manipulate unspeakable powers."

"Permit me to say, Herr *Reichsführer*, that despite these awesome powers, we are manifestly losing this war."

"Traitorous words." Himmler's expression didn't change. "Yet I forgive you, because you are a man of vision. Your rockets could not have been made by one lacking faith. So I repeat my request to join us. Sign your civilian scientists and engineers over to Kammler. Herr Professor, even your rocketry is little compared to the legendary feats of old, nor to those secrets in Kammler's more *essential* arsenal."

Here, von Braun thought he heard something new.

"I will have to think it over," he said. "It is not a decision to be taken lightly."

"Then be quick. I may have to demand an immediate investigation into the manpower tied up in the V-2 program. It is certainly not making as much progress as the V-1. There may be sabotage afoot. Goodbye, Herr Professor."

He pressed a button on the side of his desk and resumed his paperwork.

The *Untersturmführer* returned and escorted von Braun to a waiting car.

Back at the controls of his plane, halfway home, von Braun decided Himmler was bluffing.

* * *

A month later, after yet another long and contentious business trip, von Braun was asleep by midnight. He was not alone.

A loud knocking downstairs on his house door awakened them both.

In silk pajamas he cracked open the door and saw three uniformed SS officers of equal height standing in the hallway. The middle one, a *Gruppenführer*, had a mole near his left eye.

"Professor von Braun?" the moleman asked politely.

"*Ja*, that is me. What could it be at this absurd hour?"

"You will please put on suitable clothes and accompany us to police headquarters in Stettin."

"What on earth for?"

"You must make an important statement there."

Von Braun swung open the door. "You have roused me out of my sleep for that? Surely it could have waited till morning!"

"We have our orders, Herr Professor," added the *Obersturmführer* to the moleman's left. "They cannot be altered. You must accompany us to Stettin."

"You are arresting me?"

He glanced upstairs at his bedroom door, but the lady stayed put. Neither wished to be discovered with the other.

"By no means are we arresting you," the moleman corrected him. "Rather, we have express orders to take you into protective custody."

"So now we are talking in euphemisms?" von Braun snapped. "Call it what you will. In any case, I won't be long."

"*Danke schön*, Herr Professor. We will wait here."

Von Braun dressed quickly, making a sign that conveyed silence to his guest. She could slip away afterward. While packing a small suitcase, his hands trembled.

He'd underestimated Himmler.

Outside his house, two black sedans idled in the cold. Pine trees beyond them swayed in the wind. The moleman held open the first car's back door.

Von Braun was surprised to see the vehicle's interior already crowded with his brother Magnus, Dieter, and Helmut Gröttrup. No one said a word. Wernher looked away. Sigismund would be furious with him.

The moleman slammed the door and slithered into the front seat by the driver.

As they drove off, von Braun said, "You know, tomorrow is my birthday."

"I know," said Magnus. "Thirty-two."

Dieter smiled wanly, and Gröttrup declined to comment.

I am their way past the granite wall of the army. Von Braun stared out the window at passing dark shapes. *I am so stupid...*

He lit a cigarette.

It wouldn't be the first time Himmler and his thugs lined up and shot the brains behind a key operation.

Work would go on without him. Dornberger, he noted, was not among them.

What is his role in all of this? We are all so stupid—to fight over a weapon, to hinder our victory. Stupid and provincial.

The four men remained silent for the rest of their long drive to the port city.

At police headquarters, von Braun said, "Magnus, do you not recognize this building? Father served as police chief here during the unrest, some...twenty odd years ago."

No specific charges were placed against them. After some formalities and paperwork, the four were "lodged" in the headquarters' holding cells on the top floor.

SS guards locked their doors and left them in limbo to contemplate their fate.

Chapter 33

"Germans Seize Control of Hungary"

—*The Marion Star*

Wünsdorf, Germany
Thursday, March 23, 1944

Dornberger faced *Generalfeldmarschall* Keitel in the latter's windowless underground office of Maybach I, Oberkommando des Heeres. "Who is the informer?" he asked. "These charges can only be the result of calculated malice. Do they even come from someone with the first idea of what's involved?"

"The charges are so serious that arrest had to follow!" Keitel yelled back, straight and rigid at his wide desk. "Your men are very likely to lose their lives. How people in their position could have indulged in such dangerous and ridiculous talk truly surpasses my understanding."

"What talk is this? Can't I know?"

Dornberger had been awakened hours ago by a telephone call and had traveled most of the day, following a chain of command that had led to the field marshal.

"Of course you may know! Your colleagues made the ridiculous statement that it has never been their intention to make the rocket a weapon of war. They say they worked under pressure only from yourself but that the whole business of development was a ruse, a way to obtain funding for their experiments and the confirmation of their theories. In short, Professor von Braun and the others maintained at a recent party that their object all along has been *space travel!* What kind of talk is this? I am flabbergasted! Have you no control over these men?"

Of course you are flabbergasted—you are an idiot! thought Dornberger, but he said, "They are dreamers. In fact, it's contagious—we all know the rocket has a future beyond the war."

"But what counts now is winning that war!"

"Who do you think we are? We want to win the war as much as any German—more!"

"Don't your engineers and scientists realize the SS has spies everywhere?"

"Of course they do—we all do—but at a certain point, they no longer care."

Both men paused.

Dornberger remained at attention, yet he judged Keitel's baggy pale-blue eyes to be indicative of a weak personality.

"Let me be clear," Dornberger said. "I can vouch for Professor von Braun, his brother, and Dieter. Gröttrup, I do not know so well. In his case, I should have to hear in more detail what he is accused of."

The field marshal's expression changed to astonishment. "You would vouch for these men with your own life? Their words are sabotage. They could be shot—and you along with them."

"Of course! If men under my command committed sabotage, I ought to be arrested, too. And need I remind you that these arrests will be *ruinous* for the whole project? The rocket is due to come into service very soon, and we have not yet resolved its latest troubles. Without our technical director, we will no doubt be in for a catastrophe."

"Well, I cannot do anything about it. Don't you see? I am vulnerable; I am being watched. All of my actions are noted. If I protest, Himmler will take over absolutely; he will rule Germany and the army will crumble."

"Sir, with all due respect, service and civilian staff at Peenemünde nevertheless come under military law. They are subject to *military* jurisdiction. These men should be taken out of the Gestapo's hands at once and transferred to military detention, where we can deal with them according to our own bylaws."

"You are truly mad." Keitel slumped in his chair. "I cannot interfere in the middle of an investigation. The best I can do is to detail an observer from counterintelligence for the hearings. He will report directly to me." His eyes became furtive. "You really think these men will be a vital loss to the war effort, do you?"

"Herr *Generalfeldmarschall,* I wish to put on record that if these arrests stand—and God forbid they are shot—that completion will be problematic in the extreme. Indeed, employment of the rocket in the field will have to be postponed indefinitely—yes, indefinitely! It will surely be the end."

Keitel picked up a phone.

After talk with intermediaries, he said, "Himmler declines to see you. He has requested that you apply to the SS security office in Berlin and ask for General Kaltenbrunner."

Dornberger felt the blow in his gut. His beloved army was losing yet another battle to the SS.

Berlin, Germany
Friday, March 24, 1944

At precisely 11:00 a.m. in the Reich Main Security Office, Dornberger ascended a pockmarked staircase three steps at a time. Still furious, he couldn't help notice the once palatial building had been battered by bombs. He navigated a hallway of crumbling marble and scattered debris.

On a landing, one of the grand windows had been blown in. He strode by workers carrying wooden planks. If he hadn't been so angry, he might have buttoned his coat against the cold blowing in through large holes in the wall.

General Kaltenbrunner had been called away, so he'd been directed to the office of SS General Müller, a smallish man with cracked lips and gray-blue eyes that scrutinized his visitor with malice.

"So you are Dornberger," Müller said. "I've heard a great deal about you. I take it you have come to talk about this business. Please sit down."

"Yes, sir," Dornberger replied in a crisp tone. "I am demanding that the *Sicherheitsdienst* release the gentlemen so surprisingly arrested. I should like to specify their importance for—"

"I beg your pardon. In the first place, the gentlemen have not been 'arrested.' They are being held in protective custody for questioning by the police commissioner. Secondly, the SD had absolutely nothing to do with it." He sneered. "As a *Generalmajor* on the active list, you should know the difference between the SD and the Gestapo!"

"Sir, I have never in my life come into close contact with either, so I would not know the trivial differences between competing bureaucracies. As far as I am concerned the Gestapo, the SD, and the police are the same. The last two days I have had my fill of both and their vocabulary calisthenics. 'Arrest' or 'questioning' or an invitation to a waltz with Himmler is all the same to me. My men must be set free—immediately!"

Müller scoffed, "You are an interesting case yourself, *Generalmajor.* Did you know what a fat file of evidence we have against you right here, down the hall?"

"Indeed. Why not arrest me now? I extended the same invitation to the *Generalfeldmarschall.* Well, I will tell you why you dare not touch me. Because you know as well as I that we need the so-called *Wunderwaffen.* For that reason I will walk freely from this office with your order to release my invaluable civilian colleagues."

"I disagree." Müller pulled a small red notebook from a drawer and opened it. "Are you aware that *Sturmbannführer* Wernher von Braun met privately with Himmler not so long ago? On February 22, to be exact." He saw that his news rattled Dornberger. "Why do you think they spoke? And at Wewelsburg Castle, no less."

"I can only surmise that the *Reichsführer* tried once more to take the rocket from us and that these arrests—"

"But why did Professor von Braun keep this meeting from you? You must ask yourself this question. He is SS. You are not."

"Because—"

"We have nothing more to discuss." Müller dropped the notebook back in the drawer and slammed it shut. "The fate of these men and your program is not my affair. Indeed, I fear your rocket is faltering due to endless technical problems; personally I would not be surprised if the *Führer* pulls the plug on the entire wasteful affair."

Dornberger left the damaged building with his head down. He shivered now in the bitter cold. He had one more card to play, and if he succeeded in freeing them, he would ask about the visit to Wewelsburg Castle. He thought it strange that von Braun hadn't mentioned it to his superior officer…

Stettin, Germany
Saturday, March 25, 1944

Von Braun had endured three fairly miserable days at police headquarters. He hadn't been tortured or interrogated, however, and his driver had even been allowed to bring him flowers and gifts for his birthday.

Lying back on his prison bed, he peered through the bars on his cell window at an afternoon sky.

Well, at least I am losing a few kilos.

A slight wooden frame supported the old mattress on which he lay. The large building consisted mainly of solid bricks. He'd noted upon entering that over the archway a stony Prussian knight was skewering a serpentine dragon.

How did I *end up on the wrong end of a lance?* he asked himself.

He worried about his parents. They would wonder why he'd disappeared.

And Maria.

His days of reflection often touched upon his cousin. This surprised him. Intelligent and lovely, she occupied the edges of his idle thoughts, yet they might never see each other again.

Thinking of the fairer sex…

At a recent cocktail party he'd flirted with a short, curvaceous woman and had told her of his plans to fly to Mars.

I drank too much. An SS informer? Perhaps it would be more appropriate to settle down.

He tapped on the wall and his brother Magnus tapped back. They'd established a code. Of course he felt a little guilty on his younger brother's behalf.

I will have to make it up to him, and send a note of apology to Sigismund, when we are—if *we are—released.*

And still no sign of Dornberger…

Chapter 34

"Silver Balls Floating in Air Nazis' Newest War Device"

—The Chicago Tribune

Northwest of Portsmouth, England
Tuesday, March 28, 1944

A solitary silver-and-black automobile drove at a high speed along a winding country lane. On its way to Southwick House, it took a long left curve and splashed through a wide puddle. That early morning marked the fifth day of intermittent rain, and the surrounding fields and clumps of Scots pines were heavy with water.

Women's Auxiliary Air Force corporal Irene Kaye was at the wheel. In the back seat, Eisenhower and Churchill brooded on breakneck preparations for Operation Overlord.

"We dropped over four thousand tons of bombs on Crossbow targets in northern France last month," the PM reported. "But not a soul can tell me how effective the damn bombardment was."

"Well, let's hope—" Eisenhower hesitated in midsentence as Kaye pulled the Daimler off the road in front of a closed Victorian-era pub. "Why are we stopping?"

"Just a little cloak-and-dagger, Ike. You'll see."

The PM imagined that if Ike had his way, he would be living a quiet life in the country. A career military man, the general hated war and hated the Germans more for waging it.

"Ah, here they are," Churchill remarked as another car pulled up.

Two men in long gray raincoats clambered out of the second car and into the Daimler to occupy jump seats opposite Churchill and Eisenhower.

"General," said the PM, "I'd like to introduce you to Duncan Sandys, my son-in-law and chairman of our special defense committee. And Reginald Jones, director of science intelligence at MI6. I asked them here to discuss, away from prying eyes, what you saw and what others have been seeing."

Eisenhower nodded and the two men nodded back.

"Tell me about the rockets first," he said. "Are they a danger to Overlord?"

"Not as yet, sir," Jones replied. "Six months ago I set a watch on two companies of the German Air Signals Experimental Regiment, the Fourteenth and the Fifteenth. Their movement may give us advance knowledge of what the Germans have in mind."

"And?"

"We recently learned Fourteenth Company has decamped to the Baltic coast where it has strung out its detachments, including one on a small island north of Peenemünde called Greifswalder Oie."

"So the rockets will be tested and launched from that region, near the island?"

"It would seem so."

"Any idea when or what the range is?"

"The range is the subject of some debate." Jones shot a wary glance at Sandys. "But I would estimate 250 to 300 hundred miles. They wouldn't be going to all this trouble if they couldn't hit London. Fortunately, I believe we still have a few months before a full-scale attack."

"It would seem they're having production problems," Sandys said.

"That means we have to get over there"—Churchill lit his cigar—"and clear them out in a hurry."

"When we're ready and not before," Eisenhower cautioned. "Now what about the other, uh, ships? My intelligence reports don't think they're German. What about yours?"

"We don't think so either," Jones said. "Mainly because we've learned the Germans are pursuing their own inquiries. The latest incident on our side allegedly involves an RAF reconnaissance plane returning from a mission in France. Flying near the coastline, in the same general vicinity as you were, sir, he was intercepted by a strange metallic object. This object matched his aircraft's course and speed for several minutes, until it hit a terrific rate and disappeared."

"It's an epidemic," Ike observed. "It's also advanced technology. Its origins don't matter as much right now as who they might be working with, if anyone."

"I believe there are two phenomena at least," Sandys said. "The craft that instigated the scare on your West Coast. As well as the so-called 'Foo Fighters' and—"

"I want somebody in charge of all this," Ike interrupted. "I want it to be independent; I want it to be civilian; I want it to be some top scientists, American and British. I want answers soon and recommendations sooner."

"I agree. Their names will be kept secret." Churchill looked at Jones and Sandys. "You will both see to that. And not a word to the Prof about this. I don't need him to tell me it couldn't happen, because it most definitely is."

"The other thing—the public," Ike said.

"We can't have trouble there." The PM smoked his cigar. "We already have the rockets to attend to. Nothing in the papers, nothing in the press, a complete void everywhere. Knowledge of their existence would raise too many questions which could, possibly, destroy the public's belief in the church and its confidence in government. I cannot allow that. As for the rockets..."

"As for the rockets and Overlord, gentlemen," said Jones, "it's a matter of who strikes first—and how hard."

Chapter 35

"Now Bulgaria, Then Rumania— Formal Occupation by the Germans Near"

—*Daily Express,* London

Stettin, Germany
Wednesday, April 5, 1944

Von Braun had counted fourteen days since his confinement when, without warning, the large locks on his door were thrown back and two guards dressed in shiny black Gestapo uniforms entered.

"Get up, Professor!"

Wernher rose stiffly from his prison cot.

"Make yourself presentable, Professor!"

Von Braun wasn't sure why the second guard was speaking to him rather loudly, considering the short distance between them.

"It is the day of your trial!"

They permitted their prisoner to straighten his clothes and put on a tie. He walked the hallway between them, down several flights of stairs, and into a makeshift courtroom adorned with two heraldic black flags and staffed by three SS officers at a table. Oddly, the fear that had plagued von Braun of late dissipated even as his situation visibly worsened.

The SS man whom von Braun assumed was the prosecuting officer stood up and told him to sit. The guards took up positions by the door.

"Professor Wernher von Braun," the prosecutor began in a flat voice. "You are accused of jeopardizing and preventing efficient work on a vital element of the war effort. You have been heard to make statements to the effect that you regret the A-4 will be used as a weapon of war."

His mind raced. Though not what he'd expected, he was, in a perverse way, amused. If Germany were to lose the war, a real possibility, and if he survived, this whole sordid ordeal might work to his advantage in the eyes of the conquerors.

"It is also a fact that you keep in constant readiness a private airplane. Its evident purpose being to take you and top-secret rocket data to England."

Absurd, but difficult to disprove.

"Moreover, at a recent party, you were heard to say, and I quote, 'Where else are we to get funds for our work if not from the army? War has to serve science.' That is treason, is it not, to defraud the military?"

The door flew open and Dornberger strode in past the guards. His adjutant Max Magirius trailed him, a black attaché case under his arm. They stopped next to von Braun but didn't look at him. Dornberger clicked his heels and said in a confident voice, "I wish to present to the court a document, if I may."

The prosecuting officer could not refuse him. "Please approach."

Magirius took from his attaché case a single piece of stiff paper covered with overlapping stamps and signatures, took three steps forward, handed it to the prosecutor, and took three steps back.

The prosecutor read it carefully, then pursed his red lips and ordered, "Release Professor von Braun. He is free to go."

Outside the building moments later, an elated von Braun almost fell over the front steps. "And the others?" he asked.

"They will be released soon." Dornberger appeared to be pleased with himself. "A 'misunderstanding,' they said."

"Tell me about this document, which had such a magical effect."

"Let us say we experienced another example of the *Führer* principle," Dornberger replied as the trio jumbled into his staff car. "For once, in our favor. You might want to thank our friend Albert Speer."

Any misgivings von Braun had about Dornberger—his resentment at becoming a pawn in his superior's games with the SS, and his seeming neglect—vanished from his mind. For his part, Dornberger said nothing about his technical director's tête-à-tête with Himmler. It could wait.

"I think we need a drink!" he said instead and reached into a picnic basket on the floor of the car to produce a bottle of calvados du Domfrontais.

"This is what got me into trouble in the first place," von Braun laughed.

"Let us drink to our rocket, and to winning the war!"

"That's the irony, I suppose." Von Braun relished the taste. "I want to win this blasted war as much as those blinkered morons."

Chapter 36

"Der Gefährlichste Feind—Der Krieg und die Juden (The Most Dangerous Enemy—The War and the Jews)"

—*Das Reich,* Berlin

Nordhausen, Germany
Monday, May 15, 1944

The SS guards at the Mittelwerk had become more savage, the constant inspections and beatings more scrupulous and arbitrary. A hungry Russian named Pete whispered that it was because spies had infiltrated the underground factory dressed as German officers. A Pole passed on a rumor that thousands of Allied soldiers had parachuted in. An inmate with a bloody open sore under his eye said Hitler had been poisoned.

On an overcast morning, five staff cars crept through the gates.

Those few prisoners allowed outside the caves glanced at the disembarking visitors.

"Civilians. The assholes in charge," Ivor whispered to Jan the Czech; they both carried sixty-pound bags of cement on their backs.

Jan risked another glance at Hans Kammler escorting his guests through the main archway.

"The chief shit is giving them *le Grand Tour.*"

Within a long tunnel, several of the visitors covered their ears. The noise was deafening. Quite a few of the prisoners had gone mad or suffered from frayed nerves due to the constant roar of machines, explosions, and pickaxes striking hard rock. The bell of a locomotive clanged.

"We will soon be producing nine hundred of your rockets a week!" Kammler shouted to Albin Sawatzki, a Mittelwerk director.

By their side was the camp's *Obersturmführer*.

Behind them walked Dieter, von Braun, and his brother Magnus, who had been assigned to oversee turbopump production inside the underground factory. The latter wore a long black raincoat, cinched at the waist. Although Sigismund and their parents had been outraged by the Gestapo's arrogance, rocketeering still provided the family's best option. Germany was in decline, so Magnus stayed put.

Kammler guided them deeper into the factory's innards while describing its operations. They had ample room to proceed abreast in the main corridor, which averaged more than ten meters wide and high.

"We have forty-six parallel tunnels," the *Brigadeführer* boasted above the din. "About 220 meters long, some of which are dug for manufacturing purposes. Railway lines link the two main lines to outside services."

A first visit for some, it offered an opportunity to see how work was being accomplished far from Peenemünde. Dieter, in charge of the Technical Division, had already made dozens of trips. He often stayed on the premises for a week or more.

It was von Braun's fifth trip.

After a quick look around, on a prearranged signal, he, Magnus, and Dieter split off from the group. Kammler spotted them hurrying away. Annoyed, he chose not to say anything in front of the other supervisors. The SS had promised them autonomy, in theory, if not in practice, though no one had ever dared venture into the factory without armed escorts.

"This way," Dieter said.

He and the two brothers ducked into one of the connecting passageways.

Slave laborers in gray striped pants and shirts toiled on various parts of the A-4 rockets in long assembly lines. One or two of them turned in the trio's direction. SS guards, *Unterscharführers*, studied the interlopers but made no move to stop them. Wernher, walking down the line, was sickened by the conditions but concealed his feelings.

An essential aspect of war. These things are tolerable.

The vagaries inflicted on the lower classes and his enemies were not his responsibility.

The real question is—are they doing the work properly?

He and his two companions worried more about their own reputations, their own fates, which were linked to the performance of the rockets. The first three missiles had been shipped out of the tunnels on the first day of the New Year and had not flown as expected. More problems had arisen. Afraid of sabotage, they had initiated this fact-finding mission to see for themselves how the A-4s were being manufactured.

Neither von Braun nor Dornberger had any faith in the SS reports.

The trio rounded a corner and gagged. The stench of filth choked them. Two prisoners were relieving themselves into latrines, big barrels cut in half with planks across their tops, placed at the end of each row of sleeping cots.

The visitors took out white handkerchiefs to cover their noses and mouths.

Magnus turned away, but von Braun and Dieter saw an SS guard walk over and, with a loud laugh and perhaps for their benefit, shove a prisoner off the board into a barrel full of shit. They heard a sickening splash and coughing; the other SS men laughed. When the prisoner tried to climb out, the guard hit him on the head with a truncheon and he fell back in with another splash accompanied by even greater laughter.

Dieter and the brothers moved on. Beyond the sleeping tunnel, they encountered another assembly area. Von Braun directed their attention at a laborer who had climbed onto a rocket shell to install cabling. He had neglected to remove his wooden clogs and was being careless where he stepped.

Magnus sprang onto the platform and dragged the man off by the seat of his pants.

"You there—out of here!" Magnus scolded him. "You are committing sabotage!"

The prisoner removed his cap and bowed his head.

"You should never step with your shoe on this! Don't you realize, *Dummkopf*, that you were squashing a servomotor? It is worth twice more than you!"

Magnus slapped his face.

"What is your name?"

"Yves Michel," the prisoner answered with a French accent.

An SS guard approached, not sure what to make of these civilians in suits butting into his business.

"Guard, make sure this man is punished—fifteen lashes!" Magnus told him in an authoritative voice. "And make sure they learn how to do their work without damaging the machinery—this is *your* responsibility!"

"Jawohl!" The guard prodded the prisoner with his rifle—*"Schnell!"*—and they disappeared down an adjoining tunnel.

Von Braun lit a cigarette. "You were a little hard on the poor Frenchman."

"It is not the moment for softness," Dieter said.

Von Braun was amused by his colleagues' sweet yet severe nature.

In a long, cold corridor they came across several inmates running with heavy sacks of rocks on their shoulders, while SS guards and *Unterführer-Anwärters* casually beat them on their head and shoulders with rods and stiff sticks. The trio watched their routine of running, carrying, and beatings, then returning for another sack. They thought the process worked reasonably well, for the rocks accumulated quickly in a neat pile.

After inspecting more assembly areas, the trio retraced their steps, comparing their observations.

"This way—a shortcut," Dieter said.

A smaller passageway led them to an intersection where nine or ten prisoners hanging by their necks blocked their path. A few swung slowly in a breeze coming from somewhere deep within the mountain. The dead had been stripped of their trousers and shoes; they swayed a meter above puddles of their own urine. The Germans had to push through the corpses to advance; Magnus recoiled when a pee-soaked leg brushed against his face.

"You are civilians?" asked a guard from the shadows on the other side. A bloody naked body was propped up next to him; its dead hands held a headless chicken.

"*Ja*, we are from—" Dieter began.

"I don't care where you're from or why you're here, but you should know…this is a bad place."

Wernher nodded sympathetically. He couldn't make out the guard's face, but he didn't seem more than twenty; he had an odd blue complexion.

"The Russians, they're the worst. We hate them and they hate us. Nobody ever helps them and they never help anybody. We beat the shit out of them, but they fight back like rabid wolves. They steal anything they can from anyone. The only thing that matters to them is other Russians. And survival. My name is Olaf. Do you have a cigarette?"

Magnus gave him one and lit it.

"But let me tell you, not one of those dirty shit Bolsheviks will get out of here alive." Olaf inhaled the smoke deeply. "I swear it."

"It is war," Magnus said.

"It is hell."

Dieter led the two brothers past the guard to one of the main tunnels. They mounted a scaffold for a better view. As far as their eyes could see and their ears could hear, men and metal meshed noisily to the sound of a thousand engines.

"Mein Bruder, schau nur, das sind tausend Leichen," Magnus said.

"Closer to ten thousand dead," von Braun corrected him.

A few kilometers away, Rachel prepared her sniper rifle. She had stolen a truck and was waiting on an isolated dirt road not far from where Kammler would soon pass by in an open car. She planned to shoot him, despite orders. She'd followed him on several trips to the slave labor camp and had seen enough. Her handlers "appreciated" her reports but had forbidden her from taking action.

The end cannot come soon enough, she thought in her tears. *I will kill that bastard now.*

She pulled at a brown curl.

I'll kill him and everyone with him. And then I might go and kill some more.

On the passenger seat was a grenade belt.

Minutes ticked by.

Come, said the voice from the mill.

She leapt out to investigate, nerves taut—*Where are you*?

Come into the forest of signs.

Two deer watched her disappear into a dark thicket.

Chapter 37

"L'evacuation Obligatoire Des Enfants de 6 a 14 Ans (Mandatory Evacuation for Children Aged 6 to 14)"

—*Le Journal,* Paris

Hampshire, England
Sunday, June 4, 1944

Weather.

Ike had received reports of high winds and high seas. Variable low clouds and limited visibility.

He'd therefore delayed the invasion of France.

Meanwhile two hundred thousand troops waited for their orders. They were crowded into tents, barracks, and huts, killing time. Hundreds of thousands more men and women in support roles also waited. Unprecedented quantities of supplies and munitions had been moved into the assembly area over jammed roads and railway lines. An armada filled the harbors of Plymouth, Portsmouth, and Portland, holding its breath…

Waiting for good weather.

So Ike could give the command.

Late Sunday night, slanting rain and howling winds buffeted the white colonnaded porch of Southwick House. Inside its former library, converted into a command post, Eisenhower could hear the shutters outside rattled violently by a gale-force tempest. He chain-smoked his

Lucky Strikes in a pale-blue easy chair. His sore throat and cigs caused him to cough frequently.

Damn bad habits, he thought and rubbed his eyes, annoyed that one of them was infected.

Across the room from Eisenhower sat Air Chief Marshal Sir Arthur Tedder and Lieutenant General Walter Bedell Smith, his chief of staff. Each with a case of nerves. To their right, in three overlapping rows of overstuffed club sofas and davenports, lounged Trafford Leigh-Mallory, Bernard Montgomery, Bertram Ramsay, and their chiefs of staff. Churchill was sandwiched between Lord Cherwell and Jones on one of the more ornate settees.

"Must I repeat how much I look forward to urinating on Natsi soil?" the PM declared.

His effort to lighten the mood failed.

The weather looked bad, and they were in danger of losing the month's full moon.

A Wren wearing a dark-blue outfit delivered a tray of steaming coffee to fend off the cold. The library's fireplace gave off little heat, though its shadows danced merrily enough on the lacquered wooden floor. Jones could hear the operations center down the hall—one of the nerve centers of SHAEF, Supreme Headquarters Allied Expeditionary Force—typewriters and Teletypes clattering, low chatter and ringing telephones.

"Where in blasted hell are they?" General Montgomery asked in exasperation. "They're *late!*"

Ike retained a pained but solemn attitude, took the carafe, and poured himself a mug.

The others sipped stale tea from porcelain cups.

"Well, let's don't make any mistakes in a hurry," he mumbled.

9:30 p.m.

"I hate to go over this again," Tedder said, "but what are the odds the Germans might lay down some sort of radioactive barrier along our invasion route?"

"Very little," Lord Cherwell replied.

"What about those rockets?"

The PM looked to Jones, who said, "Their weapons are not ready. Yet I must also point out that the landings are nearly sure to provoke Hitler into ordering an immediate bombardment regardless of their state of readiness. The Prof and I predict the German counterattack may very well arrive on D-day plus seven."

The library's French doors swung open to exhibit an unlikely pair: Captain James Martin Stagg, SHAEF's unusually tall chief meteorologist, and his deputy, Colonel Donald Yates. Stagg's auburn hair lay flat, and his drenched suit hung onto a bony frame; Yates, also dripping, appeared more dapper with a Clark Gable mustache.

"Well, Stagg, what do you have for us?" Ike barked. "Don't keep us waiting."

"In short, even though the weather is mostly horrible," said Stagg, excited, "visibility should improve and winds should decrease. There is a glimmer of hope for tonight—and tomorrow morning we predict a period of relatively fine weather heretofore completely unexpected. It should hold out for thirty-six hours in our ports."

"What will the weather be over the French coast?" Montgomery asked.

"To answer that would make me a guesser, not a meteorologist."

"If Operation Overlord is to proceed on June 6," Ramsay said, "I must issue a provisional alert to my forces within the next half hour."

"Let's take a quick poll," Ike said.

"It's chancy," Leigh-Mallory said.

"I agree," said Tedder.

"Monty." Ike turned to the general. "Do you see any reason why we should not go on Tuesday?"

Montgomery announced in a loud voice, "No. I say—*go!*"

"I'm quite positive we must give the order, too. I don't like it, but there it is. Just how long can we hang this operation out on the end of a limb—and let it hang there? We'll go."

The room's faces, even if worried at the edges, brightened a little.

"Let's see how Corporal Hitler likes it when the fight is taken to his front door."

9:45 p.m.

The generals and their aides fairly bolted from the command post to flash out preset coded messages that would set their war machine asail.

Another signal was relayed to the Combined Chiefs of Staff: "Halcyon plus five finally and definitely confirmed."

Ike couldn't sleep amidst winds and storms, nor did anyone in his orbit. Each of them agonized in their own way about the upcoming monumental effort.

3:30 a.m.

Eisenhower took his place in the Operations Room. Updated reports were shuttled in from ships every ten minutes and posted on a wall-sized painted map of the entire European coastline, from Norway to Spain.

"Freedom itself means nothing unless there is faith," Eisenhower said to those nearest him, and he confirmed his order.

The landing would carry on as planned.

Pas de Calais, France

In the radio room of the German Fifteenth Army, a fresh-faced intelligence officer tuned in as he did every night to the BBC broadcast. They knew the British were sending coded messages to the French Resistance.

"Blessent mon coeur d'une langueur monotone," he heard the English announcer say.

The officer walked down the hall to give his report.

"The invasion of France is imminent," he said.

"How can you be so sure?" asked his ranking officer.

"They have broadcast parts of the same poem previously. They finished the phrase today. The invasion is imminent. It fits the pattern."

The ranking officer's jaw clenched. He thought of himself as older and more experienced.

"Do not be so naïve!" he snapped. "Do you think the enemy would be stupid enough to announce their arrival over the radio?"

The West Country, England
Tuesday, June 6, 1944

A young girl and boy stopped their backyard game of catch and turned their faces upward. In the morning sky flew more airplanes than they'd ever seen, making the loudest noise they'd ever heard. It seemed to them as if every plane in the world was soaring over the water to where their mother had told them the villainous men kept their slaves.

The United States

Citizens flocked to their churches that morning. Bells tolled, stores closed, and Broadway shows and sporting events across the country were canceled.

"Almighty God, our sons, pride of our Nation, this day have set upon a mighty endeavor," Roosevelt prayed on national radio that evening, "a struggle to preserve our Republic, our religion, and our civilization, and to set free a suffering humanity."

Nordhausen, Germany

Word of the invasion penetrated even the darkest places. Within the Dora concentration camp, a secret radio played quietly.

"The Americans have landed. Their air force has command of the skies. The Maquis has sprung into action"—they could barely murmur to each other the tidings without weeping.

Their SS overlords, strangely, took no notice.

"The Allies have prepared for everything," a Frenchman, no more than a skeleton, told a Pole. "They will hold firm. You have no idea the amount of matériel they have amassed..."

On the assembly line of the Mittelwerk, many workers did not react at all. Death had already taken hold of them and would not let go.

Chapter 38

"Invasion! Allies Land in France, Smash Ahead; Fleet, Planes, Chutists Battling Nazis"

—*The Philadelphia Inquirer*

Carentan, France
Monday, June 12, 1944

Chemical warfare troops patrolled the shores with Geiger counters. Soldiers had battled off gore-soaked beaches, and Allied divisions were coiled for the big breakout.

"Nothing but zero," said Sergeant Nicholas of the "Hellfire Boys."

They registered no traces of radioactivity, no sign of the *Wunderwaffen*.

The code word for the wonder weapons would *not* be flashed.

Château de Martinvast, France

At 9:00 p.m. in the *Abteilung* command post, *Oberst* Max Wachtel, commander of Flak Regiment 155(W), read a decoded message.

"*Gut*," he told his officers. "You may give the orders for launch."

They hurried to their tasks.

The *Oberst* hoped their magnificent wonder weapons would make the Allies think twice about their prospects.

London, England
Sunday, June 18, 1944

The Prof was right, Jones thought.

He was walking briskly through Saint James Park on his way to a luncheon appointment. More or less as Lord Cherwell had predicted, pilotless buzz bombs had begun to fall on London. Only four the first day, over a hundred since. His friends and the newspapers maintained that the winter blitz of 1940 had been a mild strain on the nerves compared to the sound of an approaching flying bomb.

The waiting *was the worst.*

Anticipating the moment its motor would cut off automatically—then its silent fall into the city.

Jones could see the lake.

At least no rockets as of yet, only a buzzing…

He stopped beneath a lamppost. There really was a buzzing in the sky.

Others in the park also stopped short. They looked up and at each other.

The unspoken question—*What should we do?*—ricocheted between them.

The buzzing grew louder.

Jones saw a gentleman in a high black hat and topcoat deliberately step under a wide oak tree.

The buzzing stopped.

Oh, no…

A deafening roar shook them, throwing several to the ground.

It had come from nearby, perhaps Birdcage Walk.

Jones and others on their feet ran toward the source.

At what had been the Guards Chapel, he froze. Its stone roof was caved in. Its exterior walls, crumbling. The surrounding trees were barren.

Their foliage floated gently in the air.

A direct hit.

A bishop faced the chapel's center aisle, on the threshold of twisted ruins. He'd been untouched, protected by a portico. Votive candles in a semicircle around him still flickered in the breeze. At his feet, his congregation lay dead or dying, crushed beneath tons of debris.

Jones joined the first emergency workers. He scrambled between gaps in the altar walls to administer morphine and first aid, helped by guardsmen from the barracks digging out survivors.

What if the rockets arrive now?

Chapter 39

“Hitler Speaks: ‘Officers Tried to Murder Me’— 1 A.M. Broadcast: ‘Plotters Will Be Crushed’”

—*Daily Mail,* London

Peenemünde Army Research Center, Germany
Friday, July 21, 1944

Dornberger stared blankly at a mountain of papers on his oak desk, many of them contradictory memos from Kammler. Von Braun, Debus, and Dieter quietly stepped into his office.

“Is it true?” Dieter asked.

“Yes. They tried to kill Hitler,” Dornberger muttered. “What is worse, they failed. The army is in disgrace. The SS, triumphant.”

“We are in trouble.” Von Braun was matter of fact.

Dornberger gulped his coffee. “On Himmler’s request,” he said, “Kammler has been given provisional supervision of the A-4 program. Our baby. We have only weeks before our rockets must be made ready, troops trained. The fight for control is over. They have won.”

“The consequences for us are plain,” Debus said. “We will send to the front a missile far short of what it could be.”

“That is completely inconsequential to Kammler and his SS.”

“Kammler hates our project.” Von Braun lit a cigarette. “But he loves power.”

His mind wandered back to the Mittelwerk and the foreign laborers, and he reconfirmed to himself that in times of war, a man has to support his country regardless of whether he agrees with government policy. They were losing, and their rockets were not yet deployed.

Besides, I'm helpless to change—

"My own role has been reduced to the supervision and the training of launch troops," Dornberger sighed. He opened a drawer and took out a bottle of schnapps.

"We cannot jump ship," von Braun said. "We must stick to the helm and make sure the A-4 works as well as it can. We should even try to help Kammler. I will."

Dornberger hung his head over his glass.

"So will I," said Dieter, his hazel eyes alert. "We must do everything we can."

Debus agreed.

Chapter 40

"Robot Toll 2,752; London Worst Hit—Rocket-Bomb Attacks on N.Y. Held Possible; Buzz-Bomb Facts Issued by Churchill"

—*The Stars and Stripes,*
Daily Newspaper of the U.S. Armed Forces, London Edition

Kent, England
Saturday, July 22, 1944

At about 2,500 feet up and approximately 300 yards behind it, Wing Commander Roland "Bee" Beamont fired a short round from his four cannons. The V-1 erupted in a brilliant ball of flame and smoke that knocked his Tempest fighter sideways. But Bee was used to shooting down buzz bombs, with twenty-eight kills, and was well out of harm's way.

His fighter climbed to fifteen thousand feet.

He scanned the skies and scratched his bulbous nose. A yellow silk scarf prevented a high collar from chaffing his neck. Acting commander of the 150th, he didn't want to let a single doodlebug through. His Tempest wing had seen fewer of them since the AA guns had been moved to the coast, yet—

Bee heard a familiar high-pitched whine.

He banked to the left and spotted a V-1 chugging along below him, not too far ahead. Its single impulse-duct raised engine belched flame, pushing it to a little less than four hundred miles per hour.

Bee put his fighter into a controlled dive and pressed the top switch for his outboard cannon. Nothing.

Ammunition gone.

He pressed the center button for all four cannons.

Empty.

He pushed the throttle into override and his Tempest leapt forward, engines screaming.

No one's going for six on my watch.

Bee thanked God and his ground crew for his aircraft's increased speed; even its camouflage paint job had been scraped off and its metal surfaces burnished to reduce drag.

He caught up to the buzz bomb in seconds and flew alongside of it carefully to avoid the flames from its pulse jet. He looked down and saw their two shadows passing quickly over country fields and the infrequent house or barn.

Better to chance it.

He flew abreast and abeam of it, then gently inserted the tip of his wing underneath the buzz bomb's. By executing a slight roll, he allowed his boundary layer airflow to lift the doodlebug's wing—and tip it over, toppling its gyro mechanism.

It spiraled out of control.

Banking the other way, he saw the hapless craft twisting downward until it crashed into a field and exploded in a giant spray of dirt.

Bee swept the area once again and, low on fuel, headed back to base.

If more flying bombs were spotted on radar, other fighters on patrol would do the job.

Chapter 41

"Fly-Bombs: Full Story of Great Victory—Allied Planes Dropped 100,000 Tons on Buzz-Bomb Sites"

—*The Evening News*, London

Hook of Holland, the German Empire
Friday, September 8, 1944

A launch train of ten railcars, several camouflaged with piles of hay, pulled up to the designated coordinates in the Haagsche Bosch, and hundreds of men jumped to their tasks. Powerful tractors hauled the V-2 rocket from the train's flatbed car along a precut path through a thick wood.

Dornberger looked at his watch. Servicing and launch would take four to six hours, but they were on schedule.

"Just think, sir, in not so long your years of dedicated work will pay off," gushed his battery commander. He'd been a delivery boy before the war and was in awe of the *Generalmajor*.

"And in the nick of time!" barked Dornberger, who had forgotten his subordinate's name. He'd barely slept for two days.

He observed the launch crew backing up the *Meillerwagen* to a small portable platform made of welded steel. In minutes the forty-six-foot-long rocket was upright, and soldiers swarmed over the gantries. Dornberger thought they appeared grotesquely outdated in their drab uniforms compared to his rocket's streamlined modernity. He moved closer as they bolted the V-2's fragile carbon-graphite exhaust rudders into place and commenced fueling.

Dornberger wished von Braun could have come, but Kammler had forbidden it.

The *Generalmajor* nodded to the battery commander, who opened his A-4 manual.

"Listen everybody!" the ex–delivery boy cried. The launch crew lined up before him and he read from the book: "In an age of guided missiles, a sky ship in the universe, long a dream of mankind, may someday fascinate our century. But today you must master a weapon still unknown because it is classified top secret."

He stopped to show those closest to him an illustration of bosomy girls in bathing suits and negligees frolicking in the snow around an erect rocket.

"Remember," he read, "every miss will help the enemy and endanger the lives of you and your comrades. So you must verify everything operates perfectly to ensure the missile hits its target. *You* are proud members of the long-range rocket squad!"

"I would like to add something," Dornberger announced. "After months of waiting, the hour has come for us to open fire. As we launch our rocket today, and in the future, let us always bear in mind the destruction and the suffering wrought by the enemy's terror bombing. Soldiers! *Führer* and fatherland look to us. They expect our crusade to be an overwhelming success. When our attack begins, our thoughts will linger fondly and faithfully upon our native German soil." He raised his voice and the others joined in: "Long live our Germany! Long live our fatherland! Long live our *Führer!*"

Moments later, within an armored *Feuerleitpanzer*, the battery commander peered through a wide slit at the launch site 150 meters away and ordered, *"Schlüssel auf Schießen!"*

"Ist auf Schießen, Klarlampe leuchtet!" responded a soldier at the propulsion controls.

Dornberger, though he was next to him, could barely hear his last words over the rushing howl of engines outside.

"Hauptstufe!"

Fuel pumps and steam turbines wailed. The earth trembled beneath them, pummeled by twenty-five tons of thrust.

With a slow then a tremendous whoosh, their V-2 shot into the atmosphere.

Tears ran down Dornberger's cheeks.

London, England

In the venerable lounge of the Saint Ermin's Hotel, R. V. Jones and physicist Charles Frank drank stiff drinks.

"Look at this." Frank pointed to a sprawling headline in the *Daily Mail*. "'The Battle of London Is Over!' You might've prevented this. I can't understand why they didn't ask you to speak at the press conference."

"I do," Jones said, but he didn't want to talk politics. "Anyway, we've been told to cease planning precautionary measures for the V-1. The chiefs of staff are positive we're in no further danger. Crossbow air attacks on suspected rocket transportation systems and storage depots are being halted."

They leaned back into their deep-red plush armchairs with their brandies.

A loud double bang jolted them forward again.

They looked at each other and blurted out, "That's the first one!"

After quick calls from a hotel phone, they hailed a cab.

A second rocket had fallen in Epping, but their driver took them to closer Chiswick.

They leaped from their cab into a drizzling rain and saw firemen and hospital workers helping the wounded. Neighbors with torn clothes milled about a large crater in shock. Others were trying to reach those trapped in a crumpled building.

Jones counted at least ten homes blown to pieces; many civilians had to have been killed.

"What happened?" asked a woman without shoes in a tattered dress and apron.

"I didn't hear anything," replied an older man. "Just a great gush of air and—*boom!*—a whirlwind. Like a peel of thunder, it was. Blew me at least thirty yards cross the playing field."

"We'll be lucky to find a rivet," Frank remarked.

"Call in the teams and have them thoroughly check each site."

Frank left to find a functioning phone, while Jones surveyed the missile's destruction. The bombed-out scene was a familiar sight in London, but how would they stop this latest threat?

Jones's heart was beating too fast.

Peenemünde Army Research Center, Germany
Saturday, September 9, 1944

Hannelore Bannasch charged through the door of her boss's office with the afternoon newspaper in her hands. "I am sorry, Herr Professor," she said. "But look!"

She flattened the front page on his desk so he could read the headline in large black letters: *"Vergeltunswaffe-2 Gegen London im Einsatz!"*

Von Braun smiled.

"You already knew?" Hannelore realized.

"Of course I already knew."

Word spread throughout the base. Magnus and his assistant ran from their laboratory down the road to his brother's office. Dieter, Debus, Rees, and other engineers and supervisors streamed in, talking and cramming the hallways.

Von Braun popped a cork from a bottle of champagne and said loudly, "This is not the final payoff! Our baby is still not fully developed, despite the exaggerated propaganda."

They cheered. He admired the city of Shakespeare but loved Germany more.

"The best is yet to come!"

"Fantastic," Dieter exclaimed. "So welcome after so much bad news."

Kammler, often at the camp on business, sauntered in with a few hangers-on. "Professor, your rocket is a success." He permitted himself a wan grin. "The *Führer* is most pleased. He has accelerated production yet again."

"Thank you for the good news, Herr *Brigadeführer.* We can now reverse the tide of the war, *ja*?"

"Naturally. If you only knew how close we are to doing even more than that."

He and his cronies filed out.

Von Braun swallowed a few energy pills. He and Dornberger had a pretty good idea what Kammler meant. They'd made inquiries and had received discreet answers indicating *Wunderwaffen* far in advance of their own. However, the rocketmen seriously doubted the SS projects would ever make any real headway.

Meanwhile, those in his office, the anteroom, the corridor beyond, and throughout the facility celebrated.

Chapter 42

"The V-2 Rocket Comes to Southern England—'Comets' that Dive from 70 Miles"

—*Daily Herald,* London

Hook of Holland, the German Empire
Tuesday, November 7, 1944

A German battery team, accomplished and smooth in their mechanical routine, prepared their V-2. As they toiled, the embers of a smoldering half-extinguished cigarette wafted unseen into a fuel line that had been mistakenly left open.

The rocket burst with a decimating clang and a thundering blow that instantly transformed its crew into a multiheaded fireball of melting flesh, which tottered to and fro before collapsing into a pile of soldered bones.

A few kilometers away, Battery 444, on Site 47 N of Waterpartij, launched their V-2 without a hitch.

London, England

Two clerks, their workday over, walked side by side on their way to the Tube station on Lower Road. Each of them had an afternoon paper tucked under their arm and they could've been twins, dressed in identical bowler hats, long black woolen coats, and black shoes with black laces. The sidewalk jostled with people going home or weaving their way to sundry destinations under wrought-iron lampposts.

"Gas main explosion?" said one clerk. "Not on your life. Definitely one of those weapons they've been going on about."

"I read they're calling the stretch between Calais and Cherbourg the 'rocket-gun coast,'" said the other clerk. "With the V-1, you could hear it coming. Not no more. Comes out of thin air. Pure chance. Young or old, any class of person, doesn't make the slightest difference. No point worrying about it. Are you worried?"

"I ain't worried. If London can take it, I can take it."

* * *

To the north of Lower Road, Mrs. Peters shopped at a street market, then popped into a pub for a glass of stout on the corner of East India Dock Road and Cotton Street. Pedestrians outside the establishment heard the whiplike crack of a compression wave. They squinted at a brilliant flash of white. When the warhead exploded, some were blown over by a gale of rubble and shattered glass that broke one person's arm and slashed bodies and faces. Those still standing saw the pub vanish completely and an all-mighty bright light rise up into the sky.

Mrs. Peters landed on her back three blocks away, blown out of her flower-patterned dress and red coat, nude except for one tattered sock. Body parts of her fellow patrons, limbs, torsos, and heads, rained down over several city blocks.

A Woolworths department store full of holiday shoppers was next, obliterated by a V-2.

Survivors at New Cross Gate lay metal sheets over more than a hundred corpses, but couldn't staunch the blood streaming out from under them.

In a house on Roman Road, a four-year-old girl with red hair sat on the lap of her ten-year-old sister, who also had red hair and was reading a book. When the younger child happened to look out the window, she spotted a long, thin white streak coming down from the sky. *A shooting star*, she thought. There was a loud bang, and a yellow mass of flame lit up that part of the city and her home. Their living-room wall collapsed in a heap of bricks and plaster; doors and windows imploded, and her older sister fainted to the tilting floor, her red hair splayed in dust.

After pulling his two daughters from the rubble, alive, their father rushed them outside, where he hid their eyes from the gory remains of a horse-drawn milk carriage and its roundsmen who were littered up and down the road.

* * *

Two days later, on Hazelhurst Road, a drab morning hung on workers going to their jobs. A block of air punched them down. They rose to their knees within an expanding brownish-black cloud of debris.

"Where is Granddad?" a woman shrieked. She clung to her husband and their three small children in a crater. They'd been inside but were now outside; half of their house was gone.

"I'm over here!" her grandfather shouted. "But I can't find my trousers!" Wearing only the top half of his woolly pajamas, he cleared away some rubble.

An elderly couple next door, asleep in their brass bed, had been blown straight through their roof and landed in a garden two houses away, safe and sound.

* * *

In his wool felt homburg hat and dark-gray overcoat, Winston Churchill led a group of officials on an inspection of damages in another neighborhood. He separated himself from the others in protective helmets for a closer look at the ruins. Umbrella in hand, his back to the reporters. An old woman farther up the block, however, could see tears running down the prime minister's pudgy face.

"You see, he really cares!" she pointed and shouted to bystanders loitering in the cold.

The PM retreated to his car, but fellow Londoners yelled encouragement. "Give it 'em back! Let 'em have it, too!"

Standing between the open door and his car's interior, he replied in a loud voice, "The tears of London are bitter. But we will do our duty. We will repay this debt ten—or twentyfold!"

He flashed a sign with his fingers, V for victory, and ducked into the vehicle, which drove away.

* * *

Back on Lower Road, the same two clerks in their bowler hats climbed steep steps from the Tube station on their way to work, morning newspapers tucked under their arms.

"The V-2s aren't just falling here," said one. "Antwerp, Norwich, Paris, and other places; they're falling there, too."

"Yes," said the other. "They might evacuate all London. Afraid of a panic, though I don't think anyone's in a panic. I heard you have a pretty good chance of not being hit. Only one in fifty thousand is getting it."

"I'll take those odds," said the clerk, and they vanished into a gray mist.

Chapter 43

"Fourth Term for F.D.R.—Blow to Isolationists"

—*The Sun News-Pictorial,* Melbourne, Australia

Wapakoneta, Ohio
Friday, November 24, 1944

On the porch of the Armstrong residence, a light-blue two-story wooden house on the corner, Neil waited for his father, Stephen, to return home. The slender teenager peered through the darkness in a cold sweat. His father had a bad temper, but Neil had to get his permission before going on an overnight fishing trip with two friends. His mother had said so. The solitude and the stars increased his terror. Stephen didn't always drink, but the late hour increased the odds.

Neil spotted his father's car at the far end of the street. His stomach ached, but he had to stick it out. His father's job kept him away from home for long periods. If Neil missed this opportunity, he wouldn't get another.

The black Packard jerked into the driveway and stopped a few inches short of the garage door. Stephen climbed out and slammed the car shut behind him. He came round the side of the house and onto the porch in a brown disheveled suit.

"Dad, could I—"

"Not now, son."

"But Dad, the other guys—"

His sentence was cut short by a backhand slap to the face.

"I said not now, goddamn it!"

Neil staggered.

"I don't want to repeat myself, understand?"

He swore angrily, hazy words to his son whose face stung like hell. Neil wheeled about and nearly fell down the steps into the wide, empty street.

"And straighten up, for chrissake!" his father yelled after him.

The teenager straightened up.

Chapter 44

"Reds Plunge Beyond Warsaw—Shattered German Armies Retreat on 250-Mile Front"

—*The Topeka Daily Capital*

Bydgoszcz, Poland
Thursday, January 25, 1945

At noon in his field tent, Marshal Georgy Zhukov of the Soviet Red Army was handed a phone by one of his adjuncts.

"Yes, Comrade Stalin?"

"Comrade Zhukov, let us discuss your next move."

The sound of distant guns was too far away to disturb them.

"Since the enemy is demoralized and incapable of serious resistance, I will push the attack and advance to the Oder," Zhukov said in a sharp tone that impressed his officers. "The main objective is Kustrin, where we will seize a bridgehead. My right wing will then turn north-northwest against the East Pomeranian groupings to—"

"This cannot be done at present," Stalin cut him off. "You must wait until the Second Belorussian Front completes its operations in East Prussia and regroups its forces on the Vistula."

"Our advance on Berlin will—"

"Peenemünde," Stalin interrupted again.

Zhukov was grateful his Supreme Commander couldn't see his annoyed expression. The marshal had heard about the secret research facility, but it had never been a military objective.

"You will join with Rokossovsky and smash our enemies. Then you must go to Peenemünde in great haste," Stalin ordered. "I am sending engineer Sergei Pavlovich Korolev to meet you there."

"Comrade Stalin, the German prisoners of war we parachuted into that area have reported nothing. Only one radioed back anything of interest before he was caught. In my opinion, the base is already abandoned, stripped of anything worthy of your interest."

"Stalin disagrees," Stalin said. "Our spies in Cambridge report English intelligence services have begun Operation Backfire. They will try to reverse-engineer a V-2 rocket. Their armies are determined to reach Peenemünde before me. Stalin cannot permit this to happen. Do you understand, Comrade Zhukov?"

"Yes, Comrade Stalin," the marshal said, and the line went dead.

Zhukov called an emergency meeting. He and his general staff made plans for a lightning strike across Germany—straight for Peenemünde.

Chapter 45

"Die Tieferen Ursachen—War Dieser Krieg zu Vermeiden? (The Deeper Causes—Was this War Avoidable?)"

—*Das Reich,* Berlin

Peenemünde Army Research Center, Germany
Monday, February 12, 1945

On a windy winter day, von Braun circulated discreetly among his most trusted colleagues. He whispered an hour and a place to his chosen men—Debus, Rees, a few others.

Each of them made excuses to go out that moonless evening. Von Braun, bundled in a heavy coat, walked quickly along the main avenue beneath a row of human corpses hanging from tall trees, their bodies at odd angles, pushed by hard winds. He'd been informed of their impending execution—they'd talked openly of abandoning the base—but he'd been powerless to countermand Kammler. His SS men had posted a placard above each cadaver: "I WAS TOO COWARDLY TO DEFEND THE HOMELAND."

Wernher, with loyal Hannelore in the passenger seat, drove his sedan from the carpool out the gates, past the abandoned buzz bomb launchpads, and through the forest between Zempin and Zinnowitz. With one hand on the wheel, he swallowed a couple of green-and-red energy pills.

He'd chosen the Hotel Inselhof because it would be deserted during the off-season. He and his coconspirators were relieved to find the summer resort's iron stove functioning. A waitress delivered warm cognacs in the parlor, where Dieter, Rees, and Debus took up positions by draped windows; Hannelore perched on a wooden stool with her pad of paper and a sharpened pencil. Magnus von Braun and Helmut Gröttrup occupied a yellow love seat.

"Germany has lost the war," von Braun said, standing on the parlor's tiled floor. "Friends, I am sorry to say it, but we must face facts. We all know it is true, and we must be frank."

Gröttrup, Rees, and Magnus were sanguine. Debus's face sagged at the corners, and Dieter looked glum.

"Let's not have any illusions. If our rocket had received better treatment, if we had been left alone, perhaps things would be different. We could not have labored harder, but our efforts to help win the war have failed. Now our most sacred responsibility is to preserve our work."

"May I ask why *Generalmajor* Dornberger is not here?" Dieter asked.

"Do not be so naïve!" Debus snapped. "If he were here, he would have to order himself to be shot."

"Of course, Arthur, I have already spoken with the *Generalmajor*," Wernher said and sipped his cognac. "We can trust him and, believe me, he is sympathetic to our plight. He is one of us. And so we must come to the crux of it: Germany has lost two world wars in my rather young life. Next time I want to be on the winning side."

"The American side," Magnus said.

"Yes." He took another sip. "We will put it to an open vote. Both sides, east and west, are going to be pressing hard. We will need to stick together. We have to act as a group to keep our knowledge intact. If we do, we will have a much better chance of surviving what is probably going to be a bloody aftermath."

"It might be wise to separate ourselves from Peenemünde," ventured Gröttrup, whose narrow face always struck von Braun as a curious combination of courage and cowardice. "Both sides will surely say the plant was under direct command of the SS. Everyone captured alive will be killed. I heard so over the Russian radio."

"Fool!" Debus snapped again. "You cannot believe what they say. Germany will be partitioned after the war. I heard *this* news on radio broadcasts from the Swiss, French, and British. Surely they are more trustworthy." He addressed von Braun. "We will need to get to one of the Western zones."

"I have to make a confession," Gröttrup said. "A message was already smuggled to me from a member of a Soviet technical commission; they want to reconstitute the V-2 production line. They have no long-range rocket specialists…" He said in a more resolute tone, "The future belongs to the socialists. Capitalism is a horrible evil. I vote for seeking out the Russians first."

"Why?" Dieter exclaimed, his red eyebrows raised. "Are you mad?"

"One vote for Russia." Von Braun nodded to Hannelore, who scribbled on her pad.

"Listen, friends." Magnus placed his glass of cognac on a small table. "Our brother Sigismund was stationed at the German Embassy to the Vatican when the American Fifth Army took Rome. He's been with the Americans for a while and has been treated most respectfully. Sigismund has told me a lot about American ways—he's been there, you know—and he says it is the place for us to build our Moon rockets. If it were up to me, the Americans would have already taken Berlin."

"One vote for America," Wernher said.

Hannelore made a notation.

The winds blew at the windows, whistling through cracks in the casements. Debus parted the curtains with the back of his hand and checked outside. Magnus went to the parlor door and opened it a crack; he made an all-clear sign to the others before shutting it again.

"We despise the French." Debus moved from the window to the stove and rubbed his hands for warmth. "I, for one, am mortally afraid of the Soviets. I do not believe the British can afford us, so that leaves the Americans."

"Another, if somewhat cynical, vote for the Americans." Wernher nodded again to Hannelore.

Dieter and Rees also voiced their preference for the United States.

"I appreciate your idealism, Helmut," von Braun said. "Yet the tide is overwhelmingly for the Americans. You know, we fired our missiles against the West, but it is the Russians who will take revenge. Will you reconsider?"

"No," Gröttrup replied. "My mind is made up."

"Then I must ask you to leave the room. We assume you will mention nothing of this to anyone."

"Of course not."

After Gröttrup had quit the parlor, von Braun lit a cigarette. He collapsed into a stuffed red chair, crossed his legs, and inhaled deeply. Hannelore stoked the stove.

"One thing is certain," Rees said. "When the clock strikes, we must be mobile."

"We will be," von Braun said.

"When will we make our move?" Debus asked, lighting his own cigarette.

"When the time is right."

Wernher swallowed a blue pill with the last of his cognac.

Hannelore crumpled her tally into a ball and threw the wadded paper into the fire.

The others knew the Merry Heathen was bluffing. No one could be sure. They took comfort, however, as they had for the last several years, in his unfailing bluster and optimism. If they hadn't been so anxious, they would have toasted their new venture. But the howling gale and the memory of the ghastly corpses back home ruled out trivial gestures.

Each took to their bed that night in varying states of fear.

Chapter 46

"The Big Three Meeting Again to Make Plans for the World—Yalta Parley Ends"

—*The New York Times*

Książ Castle, the German Empire
Wednesday, February 14, 1945

Kammler and Viktor Schomberger examined the inventor's drawings, which had been placed on an eighteenth-century French table in the great hall of the castle. Behind them, Kammler's toadies idled between two baroque fireplaces.

Schomberger glanced sideways at his jailer.

He is unnatural.

The woodsman couldn't understand why Kammler was ceaselessly promoted.

What kind of organization would do that?

"Snap out of it!" Kammler barked.

"I don't sleep well here." Schomberger stroked his beard.

"That is no excuse! Do you think I sleep more than one or two hours? Well, I don't!" Kammler slammed his palm on the drawings. "Your work is nearly done. You claim the Haunebu II will attain an altitude of 15,000 meters and a forward speed as great as 2,200 kilometers per hour—is this correct? Tell me."

"Yes. In theory," said Schomberger. "But the pilot's nervous system has been often disturbed in operation. They've experienced severe headaches accompanied by a metallic taste in the mouth. Some of the subjects, and one or two scientists, have died from the more serious side effects."

"Small matters. Listen, Herr Schomberger," Kammler said. "*Der Führer* will bring about the determination of the war in the next three weeks."

"By political means?" Schomberger couldn't see how anyone could have faith in prototypes alone.

"*Nein*," Kammler snorted. "The new retaliation weapons and air discs will give us a respite. On this table"—he caressed the drawing with his hands—"if I deliver a finished flying disc in a fortnight, equipped with a ray cannon, it will create mass hysteria in the ranks of our enemies—complete panic! Our troops will look into the sky and forget any fear. They will *believe* again!"

Schomberger's head drooped.

Monstrous.

"It will fly," he murmured, "but it has yet to be fully tested. Far from—"

"We will test it—tomorrow morning!" Kammler headed out of the room, followed by his coterie.

Schomberger rolled up his drawings, and his thoughts returned to the spy in the hills, the fairy nymph. When he sent out his mind, he would often find her meditating. She led a monk-like existence, but she wasn't like him. She was a warrior.

He had great faith in the female sprite and wondered if she would order an air strike to kill them all.

* * *

Since the second visitation, Rachel had known who she was. She'd never been afraid of death, but any lingering doubts had been stripped away. She no longer pulled at her hair. Subsequent and successive painful visions had shocked her into remembrance. The revelations hadn't come as a complete surprise. Even before that night, she'd had vague memories of an angel who had touched her philtrum before birth.

In her dirty clothes, she lived from the small game she hunted and ate berries, even bark. She spoke infrequently to anyone, except the Polish resistance or the even rarer Palmach agent. During their comings and goings, she'd learned that Patton's Third Army had been hobbled by intrigue and conflicting information and that Hitler's operation to occupy Hungary had resulted in the deportation of that country's Jews to Auschwitz.

One morning she watched and waited, but with a different purpose, a larger one, beyond the ken of her handlers. SS guards had scoured the area and nearby forest, but they couldn't see her. She was up in an old tree, invisible to them.

She looked through her binoculars. *Obergruppenführer* Kammler stood between the blockhouse and a gray disc ship spinning slowly within a circle of concrete pillars inlaid with ceramic tiles, whose formation reminded her of Stonehenge. Rachel estimated the saucer was about twelve meters wide. The forest ranger Viktor Schomberger, along with scientists and engineers, milled about, taking notes.

She'd met Viktor's electric mind on a few occasions. She'd asked him to explain his work in plain language, and he'd obliged. Neither of them had any fear of the other. They both appreciated the stakes and played no games. She knew he would never speak of her to anyone.

The disc craft rose rapidly, three, four hundred meters into the hazy sky, pulsing with a blue-white luminescent glow. Rachel held her breath.

It will be as before, but different.

Kammler shouted something and the saucer flew to its left. He shouted again and it moved to the right. It hovered, faltered, but did not fall. It made no sound.

When it came back to earth with a slight bump, she saw Kammler smiling and patting an engineer on the back.

He's going to kill him. He's going to kill them all.

SS storm troopers lined up along a long slit in the ground. Guards swarmed out of the blockhouse and herded the surprised workers, engineers, and scientists toward the trench. They were forced to stand with their backs to the slit's edge and face the forest. Rachel could see them gesticulating in protest.

Kammler strode over, pulled Schomberger out of the group, and raised his hand. When he swung it down, bullets erupted from a machine gun hidden among the trees, and bullets ripped through the others. The impacts knocked their bodies backward into the trench. The invisible gunner strafed the line until each had fallen. SS *Oberscharführer*s and Kammler walked up and down using their handguns to finish them off. Their shots echoed in the valley.

Rachel saw Viktor fall to his knees, sobbing. She saw his electric body above the scene. She saw Kammler amused at what he perceived to be his weakness.

Weakness. There can be no *weakness. Hans Kammler is a small boy led to a cellar by his father, a policeman. The boy strips and bends over a wooden chair. His father thrashes him mercilessly and counts softly. He urges his naked child to count with him and to be cheerful. He is truly sad if the child cannot be cheerful. Every day before breakfast the ritual in the cellar is repeated without reason, without fail. The boy's mother allows it to happen. She must be cheerful, too.*

Storm troopers doused the corpses in petrol and lit them on fire. Lowering her binoculars, Rachel could see their spirits mingling above before their departures, could see the myriad lives that had led the men to their brutal ends. She couldn't understand it fully, but she was shown the vision stream by an unseen hand.

Refocusing her field glasses upon Kammler, she saw him staring in her direction. Illuminated from behind by the roaring flames, half hidden by black smoke, he appeared to be grinning at her. In his altered state, he'd found her.

She smiled back.

Chapter 47

"Resistance Crumbling—The Great Push to the Rhine Goes On Unchecked"

—*The Times,* London

Peenemünde Army Research Center, Germany
Thursday, February 15, 1945

Von Braun picked a path through the bomb-scarred avenue that led to the Preproduction Workhouse. Another coworker judged treasonous hung from a lamppost, his eyes bloody. He passed by a tenacious Wehrmacht sergeant instructing civilian engineers in close-order drills, rifle and bayonet. They'd been ordered to defend the research facility against the approaching Red Army. He rounded a building and collided with a boy carrying a thick folder.

"Sorry, Herr Professor!" stammered the boy, who looked about fourteen.

He ran off and von Braun continued. Around him swirled a simulation of organized work, a frenzy of activity for activity's sake. Superiors gave commands to subordinates, who passed them on to their subordinates.

A sham. The next few days will decide it.

In the workhouse, von Braun joined Dornberger and Dieter at a drawing board beneath a high ceiling supported by steel girders. The two broke off their examination of a scale model Taifun antiaircraft missile.

"Ah, Professor Sunny Boy," Dornberger greeted him. "Do you know, yesterday alone I received exactly 123 Teletype orders from our good friend Kammler. Scores of them, and each contradictory. Most of them meaningless, all of them a complete waste of my time."

"I received two or three myself."

They moved to a small office, where Hannelore had already drawn the curtains, and stood before the same group who had voted for America, along with several more supervisors. Von Braun in gray-black suit and tie; Dornberger, in his standard military outfit. Civilian garb for the others.

"Gentlemen, as you know, the Soviet Army is approaching," von Braun said. "The result is chaos. Even this morning a colonel ordered me to help defend our holy soil and another colonel directed me to oversee an immediate evacuation."

"Five promise death by firing squad if we move," Dornberger said, "and six make it clear that if we do not move, we will also be shot."

"What are we to do?" Rees asked.

"We have only two important conflicting orders. One from Kammler telling us to go south. One from the army telling us to stay put and defend the base. Kammler controls the base. We will follow his directive."

"This is right," von Braun said.

"Kammler has ordered the relocation of the most important defense projects into central Germany. That suits us, for now."

There was murmuring, and Rees started, "What if they—"

"We will go as an organization," von Braun cut him off. "This is important. We will carry our administration and structural chain of command straight across Germany. It will not be a rout. We will go to the area of Nordhausen near the Mittelwerk." He addressed Dieter. "You have the tally ready?"

"*Ja*, Herr Professor. I have broken it down to six groupings. Among them: A-4 development and modification, 1,940 workers; Wasserfall development, 1,220 workers; Taifun development, 135. A total of 4,325 personnel to be evacuated. A big job."

"We have the problem of who will go and in what order," said Dornberger. "Top priority must be assigned to those whose efforts are required to maintain production at the Mittelwerk factory. Second, those engaged in problems related to increasing the missile's range and improving accuracy."

"Every department must work day and night," Wernher added. "Planning for spare parts for trucks, travel authorizations—"

"Herr Professor, may I say something, please?" Hannelore asked. "I am afraid the army will never let us pass out of the camp."

Von Braun grinned. "As luck would have it, a recent shipment of stationery, which was meant to identify Peenemünde personnel as a branch of the SS, was badly mangled at the printer. Instead of reading '*BZBV Heer*,' it now reads '*VzbV*'—the initials of a nonexistent organization."

"So?" Debus asked impatiently. "What good does that do us?"

"We saw an opportunity where you see nothing," Dornberger answered. "We quickly invented an agency with those exact initials, '*VzbV*,' to stand for *Vorhaben zur besonderen Verwendung*—a top-secret undertaking ordered to central Germany by Himmler himself."

Von Braun nodded to Dieter, who handed him a tan briefcase.

"Our most trusted staff have already painted those initials on vehicles, trucks, boxes, you name it." He pulled out of the briefcase armbands emblazoned with the initials and tossed them onto the table. "These are yours. Sew them onto your shirts and jackets, anything which could be checked by the army."

"It might work." Debus smirked.

"It *will* work."

During the next two days they prepared their escape. Von Braun concentrated his considerable charm on some and bullied others. He used his SS rank of *Sturmbannführer* to forge commands, which Hannelore mixed in with real ones. He sweet-talked doubters, cajoled the slow, and threatened the obstinate. No one could resist.

Dornberger oversaw the military side of things until he left for Berlin to take care of business there.

They both remarked upon Kammler's strange absence from Peenemünde. They wondered if he was watching from afar.

* * *

The first trucks and overloaded vehicles pulled out before dawn on the third day, carrying over five hundred technicians and their families. Von Braun and Magnus stowed themselves in the back seat of the lead car, a black four-door Hanomag Sturm limousine, driven by a young man with bad acne.

Soldiers at the gate examined their paperwork, studied the acronym *VzbV*, which had been stenciled on everything in sight, and let the convoy pass.

They made slow but steady progress toward Nordhausen. With the Russian front only about twenty kilometers to the east, they could hear the big guns.

Wernher thought of Dornberger in Berlin.

Is it my imagination or have I done something to shake his trust?

At twilight, they skirted Eberswalde, a city on the railroad line some kilometers north of Berlin.

At a roadblock, a Wehrmacht major shot out of a striped red, white, and black sentry box and approached the lead vehicle. Soldiers armed with machine guns protected the barrier arm behind him.

"Where do you think you are going?" shouted the small, solidly built man.

Von Braun clambered out of the car and shouted back, "Who do you think *you* are to question me?"

"My instructions are clear: civilian traffic is forbidden in the area!"

"Can't you read?" Von Braun pointed to his armband. "We are not civilians!"

"Read?" the major growled. "Those initials mean nothing to me!"

"Really? Is that so? You know, I am not responsible for your appalling ignorance. You have heard of the V-2 rocket? My convoy is carrying the many components needed to manufacture it. *My* directives come straight from *Reichsführer* Himmler. Our only hope to secure ultimate victory is contained in our trucks."

The major hesitated.

"*Ja*. Ultimate victory," von Braun repeated. "You would do well not to doubt it." He moved to an inch of his opponent's face, teeth flashing. "*Nicht wahr? Nicht wahr?* Watch yourself!"

"Er, what do you call your group?"

"We are the Project for Special Dispositions."

The major flipped open a notebook and made a long, precise entry. He then pivoted and signaled stiffly to his men, one of whom lifted up the barrier arm.

Von Braun climbed back into the car, and his long column of vehicles drove through.

Minutes later, they were winding over difficult terrain. Von Braun gazed through one back-seat window; Magnus, the other.

The sky darkened as the convoy drove by moonlight past devastated cities. Each of the brothers kept silent. The effects of heavy bombing were always worse near railroad stations. Trains were scarce and the ones they saw, overcrowded.

When the convoy crossed paths with a long single file of foreign laborers heading eastward in the pitch black, their pimply driver stopped and spoke with one of the guards, a young man not more than seventeen who had lost his map. Their driver indicated the right road, and the forlorn skeletons in striped work clothes marched on. Dieter and a few others jumped from their trucks and jeered at the slaves. Someone from the convoy threw a rock at them.

The von Brauns arrived at their hotel after midnight, a hundred kilometers from Nordhausen, and checked in. They rated their accommodations inferior, their fellow civilian guests haggard and sullen, but they slept well in their shared feather bed.

Others of the convoy found rooms in surrounding villages but had to scrounge for food at that late hour.

They pulled out at dawn.

An hour later the convoy encountered hordes of refugees from East Prussia fleeing westward. For several kilometers the convoy vehicles paralleled two long lines of frightened old men and women, bent over, pushing wheelbarrows piled high with their belongings and children. Young mothers, who to Magnus looked starving, trudged through the snowdrifts.

We have utterly failed, he thought. *And for what?*

At checkpoint after checkpoint, his brother blustered their way through, sometimes using Dornberger's authority, sometimes forged or real Gestapo orders. They all felt some measure of relief with each kilometer they traveled toward the Allies, away from the vengeful Soviets. Sunlight faded.

After talking his way past another sentry box, Wernher climbed back into the car and declared, "The machinery is crumbling but has not broken."

"I do not know if we should be proud or horrified."

Wernher swallowed a handful of green pills. Magnus had seen him take dozens during their journey.

They covered another hundred kilometers. Magnus snored.

To remain invisible to enemy planes overhead, their limousine was traveling with its four headlights turned off.

Just south of Halberstadt, Wernher closed his eyes...

A glider with eight wings, aloft...

Confused, he jerked himself semi-awake, not sure how much time had elapsed, interrupted by a vague sense of alarm—

The sound of tires on the road—gone!

He saw their young driver's head nestled on the steering wheel, asleep—

Flying through the air at a terrific speed—

Wernher threw up his arms to protect himself just before their vehicle smashed into a railroad siding. Steel and iron crunched, dirt sprayed, and they flipped over. The hood snapped off and Wernher was thrown violently to the side. Its rear windshield shattered inward and the front doors blew open. Something sharp stabbed Wernher's left shoulder—he cried out in pain.

The shattered limousine rolled to a stop.

Wernher rammed open the back door with his good shoulder and pulled Magnus from the wreckage. He squinted into the night, trying to find their driver—when the car's motor exploded.

About twenty meters beyond the burning hulk, he discovered the young man, his head cracked bloody wide open on a rock.

Wernher pulled his brother farther away from the flames onto an embankment, then blacked out.

Dieter and Hannelore scrambled down the hill toward the glowing blaze. They'd noticed minutes before that von Braun's vehicle had been driving too fast.

Upon finding the brothers, they administered first aid. Magnus came to, but Wernher's face was battered, his left arm mangled.

"Do what you can!" Arthur shouted to Hannelore. "I will be back in a hurry."

He struggled up the hill. Before driving off to find an ambulance, he glanced down at the trio, illuminated by the crackling fire, and wondered if any of them would survive.

Chapter 48

"Russians Advance Nearer Dresden—Reds 90 Miles Southeast of Berlin, 15 Miles from Stettin"

—*Cumberland Evening Times*

Bleicherode, Germany
Monday, February 19, 1945

Von Braun regained consciousness in a plain white room. Weak winter sunlight slanted through a lead window to brighten the foot of his white bedsheet. The glare hurt his eyes. His head throbbed and his body ached. A thick white cast encased his upper torso and his entire left arm, bent and suspended by a harness.

I have been cared for…hospital.

Something else…

To avoid the blinding light of the white sheets, he shifted his eyes to the far side of the room and its shadows.

Someone sitting there. A single eye staring…

"Your arm is broken in two places," the eye said.

A familiar voice…

"Your shoulder was shattered, but pieced back together by the good doctor."

"*Obergruppenführer* Kammler," Wernher said. "May I ask where I am?"

The eye rose up and stepped into the light.

"Bleicherode." Kammler looked out the window and mused, "I am uncomfortable in a town named after a Jew. We will have to find another name for it after the war." He took a small mirror and a comb from a nightstand and handed them to von Braun. "Here. Clean yourself up."

In the mirror, the technical director saw several cuts on his face already patched and a large gash over his lips stitched shut. He ran the comb through his blond hair.

"May I ask how Magnus is?"

"Much better than you. Barely a scratch."

Kammler moved a frail wooden chair next to the bed, which creaked under his weight.

"Thank you for seeing to our—"

"Do not bother with niceties." Kammler leaned close. His breath smelled of chocolate and nicotine. "We are far beyond this hypocrisy. I came to tell you in person: I know what you and Dornberger and your tight little clan are doing. I know what you have planned. You follow my orders only when they are to your liking."

Wernher's eyes darted to his visitor's holstered Luger. Kammler pretended not to notice.

"As for me, I have my own plans," he said, leaning back. The chair creaked again, and he put his scuffed black boots on the bed. "As it happens, my plans may coincide with yours."

Their eyes met. Something went unsaid. Wernher shifted his weight, jostled his encased arm, and bolts of excruciating pain shot through him.

"*Gut*." Kammler grinned upon their silent pact. "While you recover, you will please make me a complete list of the weapons in progress, detailing performance, delivery dates, and potentials. Most of your group has already arrived at Nordhausen—but I am sorry to say they are in a state of complete confusion! Halfheartedly, they try to set up for business. You must therefore get out of here quickly—and you must whip them into shape. I give you two days." He paused and, as if to explain, added, "I have no confidence in that idiot, Dornberger."

Wernher adjusted himself again, uncomfortably, trying not to touch Kammler's dirty boots with his bare feet under the sheet.

"Here." Kammler pulled a small metal pillbox from his black SS jacket. "Take a few."

He poured water from a clay pitcher into a glass, and von Braun swallowed three red ones.

Kammler jumped up, knocking his chair into the wall. "We will still snatch victory from the flames!" he cried. "We have to!"

Startled, von Braun said, "Of course we'll do everything—"

"Do not shit me with platitudes!" Kammler shrieked. "I could kill you all! I have ordered von Ploetz to follow ten paces behind me at all times with a machine pistol. If the situation becomes hopeless, he will fire a burst into my head—so don't think I will hesitate one second to have you and your precious shit friends thrown up against a wall and shot."

Kammler's chest heaved.

"We are Germans..." Wernher searched for the right words. "We are in this together. I want to win as much as you. Even now."

"*Gut.*" Kammler's breathing slowed. "We can still make use of one another."

Von Braun realized that he and his colleagues would have to be even more careful than planned to avoid being murdered by the SS.

Kammler went out the door, where his footsteps were doubled in the hallway by those of von Ploetz, his potential executioner.

Chapter 49

"Yanks 19 Miles from Rhine at Cologne—Two-Army Drive Cracks Nazi Defenses"

—*The Lowell Sun*

Cologne, Germany
Thursday, March 8, 1945

Cologne had been bombed into rubble and silence, except for sporadic mortar shots and sniper gunfire. Not far from the blackened cathedral, an old yellow house, one of the few still intact, had been commandeered by the Third Armored Division.

Major Bruce Staftoy and Major Calvin Cory drank lukewarm coffee in the house's dining room. It was their first respite in a week of trailing behind tanks and infantry. They gulped the foul liquid to stay awake; they had work to do.

Only a fortnight before, Staftoy had reported for duty as Rocket Section Chief, under the recently formed Combined Intelligence Objectives Subcommittee, or CIOS. At his first meeting in London with Major Cory, a V-2 had exploded a block away. The force of the detonation had thrown both men to the ground and blown the window drapes straight out from the wall. They'd brushed themselves off and Cory, a short man with a pockmarked face, had informed Staftoy they were "going in"—into Germany—to find the scientists and engineers who had built the V-2 rockets.

"The V-2s are still in action, and over five hundred civilians got theirs from our own bombers." Staftoy leaned his chair back against floral wallpaper.

He and Cory looked out of place in the feminine décor, dirty faces and "Ike" field jackets, worn pants tucked into grimy boots.

"It's war." Cory took another gulp.

A noisy motorcycle pulled up in the street.

"Anyway, they'll clear out the Krauts from The Hague soon enough."

A knock on the door.

"Come in." Cory lit a cigarette.

A private pushed his goggles up to reveal more of his muddy face, saluted, and handed Cory a fragment of worn paper.

"What is it?" Staftoy asked.

"A list, sir."

"Where'd you get it?"

"Uh..."

"Spit it out."

"Sir, a Polish laboratory technician discovered it, not far from here... stuck on the inside of a toilet bowl."

Cory put down the paper.

"They musta tried to get rid of it," Staftoy said.

He walked over and took the scrap. It had a few names, two complete, three partial.

"Shouldn't you be wearing gloves or something?" Cory asked.

Staftoy had a high rectangular forehead and round black glasses and would've preferred to be smoking his pipe, but he'd lost it when their jeep had hit a pothole the day before.

"There's more." The private reached into a tan leather knapsack flung across his chest and emptied the contents of its side pocket, about three dozen more scraps, onto the table. "The toilet must have flushed wrong or clogged...or something."

Staftoy took a seat and started laying the fragments side by side.

"Thank you, Private. Good work." Cory dismissed him.

"Get me that lamp over there," said Staftoy.

An hour later they had pieced together most of the papers to reveal the positions and responsibilities of key German rocket personnel. It was information they'd been hoping to find.

Cory read aloud the name at the top of their reconstituted list: "Professor Wernher von Braun."

* * *

Twelve days later the First Army captured Ludendorff Bridge, and the Third Armored Division received new orders. Combat commands moved out first.

Far in the rear of the column, Majors Staftoy and Cory bumped along in the back of their vehicle, jostled between trucks and heavy vehicles. Staftoy had radioed back their find, which they called the "Black List," and their search had been given a code name: Overcast.

"The Brits have pinpointed Nordhausen as the most likely place to find them," Cory said, consulting a map on his knees. "Patton is hell-bound across the south."

Their jeep lurched sideways.

"Hey, watch out!"

"I'm not sure I like the idea of recruiting Nazi rocket scientists," said Staftoy, who'd borrowed a pipe from an enlisted man and was smoking it.

"It's not just them." Cory stowed the map in his satchel. "They're going after experts in ammunition, artillery, chemicals...even Heinies who know about metallurgy. You were in the meetings—it's a game. We're supposed to shorten the war against the Japs and deny their know-how to the Bolsheviks."

"You see it as basketball, don't you?" Staftoy said between puffs. "If we don't find these bastards, if we miss the hoop, we give the Soviets a chance to get the bastards on the rebound."

"That's right."

They jeeped it across the Rhine on a pontoon bridge.

"And into the maelstrom we go..."

Chapter 50

"Hitler Says No Surrender"

—*The Stars and Stripes*, London Edition

Nordhausen, Germany
Sunday, April 1, 1945

Von Braun and Dornberger lit cigarettes outside their midsized hotel in the village square.

"Of course you will still come with us," von Braun said under his breath and took a drag.

"Not just me. I am quietly posting an army detachment not far from our destination. We may need them."

They would ignore Kammler's dismissal of the *Generalmajor* but follow his order to evacuate 450 of their scientists and engineers to the lower Alps near Oberammergau. They would be heavily guarded by the SS.

"We are his hostages and his bargaining chips," von Braun said.

"The game is not only his. It's our move at present. Is Arthur ready?"

Dornberger had to trust his technical director. The latter's silence on the subject of his secret meeting with Himmler could mean many things, but the *Generalmajor* had concluded that von Braun had no ulterior plans and certainly no love for the SS.

For his part, von Braun was relying on their old comradeship, or at least a simulacrum of it. Dornberger had listened intently to his description of Kammler's visit to the hospital and his cryptic remarks.

Von Braun looked at his watch. "He should be inside."

The hotel lobby swarmed with armed SS, confused and menacing as their world collapsed. Von Braun spotted Dieter leaning against a painted wooden column. Somehow he'd located a barber, and his red hair was freshly coifed.

He opened his mouth to speak, but Dornberger told him, "Wait in the restaurant."

A quarter of an hour later the trio huddled at a secluded table. An elderly woman with an apron served their drinks and remarked, "How nice to see the hotel full of life again," before returning to the kitchen.

"You are no doubt aware of the unwelcome presence of these SS," von Braun said to Dieter. "Frankly, I am unhappy with this intrusion into our business. Regardless of what is happening to Germany, we are the bearers of an entire engineering science—and I am afraid Kammler's men may develop a severe case of nerves. Kammler himself is displaying every sign of an imminent nervous breakdown. They may destroy us and everything we have accomplished."

Arthur nodded.

"How did you get here?" Dornberger asked.

"In one of the trucks from the convoy, but I am low on gas."

"You will need to find two or three more trucks and commandeer plenty more gas."

"Rather than let our work be destroyed, we have conceived a little plan." Von Braun leaned closer. "Kammler has ordered us to the Alps. No equipment can be taken, but you will gather our classified material together, all of it, and store it somewhere in these mountains until it can be used again."

"But where?" Arthur asked. "You are talking about something like fifteen tons of documents, over sixty thousand drawings—"

"Quiet down," snapped Dornberger.

An SS-*Oberscharführer* took a quick look at them before joining friends at another table.

Dieter drained his glass of schnapps.

"Probably the best idea is an old mine or cave, something of that sort," von Braun said. "There is no time to lose."

Dornberger pulled a small packet from his coat pocket and handed it to Dieter. "I have made out a letter of safe conduct stating your mission is top secret. With it, you can obtain materials and men. After that, you are on your own."

"I understand." Dieter slid the packet inside his suit jacket.

The following morning Dieter was gone and they moved out.

Dornberger chose a surreptitious route for his soldiers, one which would throw off Kammler and his Gestapo informers.

Von Braun, Debus, Rees, and key supervisors boarded a special train. The strain showed on Rees, who had developed a cold and cleared his throat constantly. The rest of their team had been divided into groups and left to travel as they could, each with their SS overseer.

The sleek "Vengeance Express" chugged out of Nordhausen at nightfall and rolled through the countryside. The brothers von Braun enjoyed its unexpectedly splendid accommodations and dining car stocked with fine wines.

Once again, the Merry Heathen put on a cheerful front. He shut out worries, the pain from his crippled arm, fears for his parents and Maria.

Two days after the Peenemünde gang moved out, Allied bombers flattened Nordhausen.

Chapter 51

"V-E Day Is at Hand—But V-2 Pictures Remind Us of London's Grim Ordeal"

—*Hampstead and Highgate Express,* London

Eschenrode, Germany
Wednesday, April 11, 1945

Task Force Welborn of the Third Armored Division wound its way over the Harz Mountains, tons of heavy vehicles on a thin road with a sheer drop.

Miles ahead of Staftoy and Cory, Sherman tanks rumbled in single column toward the valley hamlet of Eschenrode. Intelligence had reported six companies of SS troops there, led by a fanatical officer, dug in behind big guns on a clear, warm day. Beyond Eschenrode was Nordhausen, their target, but they'd have to clear out the enemy first.

The task force called in P-47 Thunderbolts to soften up the village with strafing and bombs, but it was well fortified.

Two American tanks roared into town, firing one after the other, and blew storm troopers and their machine-gun nest to pieces. Another tank burned on a side street, hit by a camouflaged Panzer. An infantryman kneeled and fired bazooka shells that turned the Panzer into scrap. He ran up the street and fired again, bringing down the wall of a house. German troops stumbled out and were cut down by submachine-gun fire, their blood spraying a stone wall behind them.

A *Hauptsturmführer* aimed at a GI from six feet, but his gun jammed and the American lunged forward, grunting, and slashed his razor-sharp bayonet across the *Hauptsturmführer*'s throat. The SS man fell. The GI stepped over another SS body, but the German was playing possum and tried to stab him in the groin. The American knocked the knife away and drove his bayonet through his enemy's chest, pinning him to the ground. He twisted his weapon until the SS man's eyes glazed over; then he lurched to a corner and vomited up his morning coffee and K ration.

Houses with white flags harbored SS zealots armed with grenade launchers. They were killed along with the inhabitants, women and children and elders. Savage combat waged into a third hour. GIs swallowed methamphetamines. SS men ingested handfuls of Pervitin, tablets they called "tank chocolate," and remained euphoric even if shot in the guts.

Company F of the Thirty-Sixth Armored Infantry Regiment led the attack, and several of its forward scouts reported the same SS commander directing his troops. He seemed to be everywhere, screaming at his men, threatening, urging them on.

"I swear the guy is crazy," muttered one scout into his radio. "He's enjoying himself."

Brigadier General Truman Boudinot, in light khaki trousers and tunic, had a good view of the action from an elevated point about a thousand yards from the town.

"I want that SS bastard captured," he said to his man on the ground.

"Yes, sir!"

"That SS Heinie wants a real bloodbath, so it's up to you and our boys to give hell! Got it?"

"Yes, sir!"

Minutes later his man on the ground was shot through the heart, but his pals kept up a relentless artillery fire that battered and subdued their enemies at last.

Task Force Welborn mopped up house to house. They killed and wounded or captured what was left of the SS divisions—except the crazed SS commander, who eluded them.

Climbing out of his Sherman, Corporal Irwin, a gunner, barely twenty, saw the hamlet had been transformed into a butcher shop. Its narrow streets were drenched in blood and gore. He walked over a wide human carpet of ripped-up corpses that stretched the length of town. He blinked at prisoners being herded into trucks, at those wandering among ruins or staring out from the shell of a building. So horrible were their gaping wounds, he thought they'd be better off dead.

Back on the road to Nordhausen, at dusk, General Boudinot sniffed the air and said to his lieutenant, "Something stinks. And it's in front of us, not behind."

His Combat Command B drove under a pink dawn to Nordhausen, with little opposition. Its two task forces, the northern and southern assault elements, converged on Camp Dora and the source of the smell: hundreds of half-naked putrefied cadavers lying in the morning sun.

A preliminary search revealed hundreds more in the barracks. Infantrymen wrenched open barricaded doors and windows to allow air in, and the sun's rays revealed grotesque heaps of stinking men. One soldier saw an eye blink at him from deep inside a stack of naked bodies.

Private Alders stared in disbelief at the skeletons who stared back from the floor, their mouths filled with dirt and straw. Corporal Luceno stumbled upon a stash of human limbs under a staircase that led to offices with paperwork stacked in neat trays.

Most of the SS guards had fled, but about one hundred stragglers were rounded up. They swore and cursed at their former victims. The American soldiers opened fire with machine guns on the Germans, killing them all.

Staftoy climbed out of his jeep. He'd studied psychology, had intended to be state certified in Pennsylvania, but had volunteered for the service instead.

"Now I get it," he said to Cory.

"Get what?"

"Why those Krauts were fighting tooth and nail, with no hope of victory."

Cory looked at him.

"Shame," Staftoy said. "A few weeks ago, they were the Master Race, the super SS bastards."

A ragged assortment of bones tottered toward him.

"Il y a quelque chose…fantastique…" it rasped through cracked, bloody lips. *"Fantastique! Sous la montagne, important. C'est…tres important!"*

Staftoy caught the dying man in his arms. Cory called for a medic; then they headed for the mountain.

Deep inside the main tunnel of the Mittelwerk, they discovered V-1 and V-2 parts arranged in seemingly endless orderly rows.

"It's a scene right out of *Flash Gordon*," Cory said.

Cross tunnels overflowed with precision machinery and tools; telephone, ventilating, and lighting systems still functioned. Seven fully assembled rockets lay on flatbed railroad cars.

"Looks like they abandoned the place in perfect working order," Staftoy said.

"I'll send word. This is going to be big."

Cory went off to wire military intelligence headquarters in Paris. Paris would notify army ordnance units.

Staftoy encountered several laborers at work, their minds gone. He discovered corpses stuffed into corners. He counted a hundred before he stopped counting. Some had been left in place to die of starvation or illness; others had been shot in the head or hung.

He kept counting the V-2s. They'd been asked to find one hundred.

* * *

A few days later Cory had news. "Technical Intelligence just sent back word. A large part of the land we just conquered is going to be handed over to the Reds," he told Staftoy. "And soon. Weeks. Son of a bitch!"

They walked down a station platform as the first supply train pulled out of Nordhausen bound for Antwerp, forty freight cars jammed with rocket parts.

"We better hop to it." Staftoy puffed on his pipe. "When the Reds arrive, I want them to find this grave already looted."

"Apparently Patton and his Third Army rolled into a similar setup in the Arnstadt-Wechmar-Ohrdruf triangle. A huge underground base, miles long, three stories high. They were looking for the big bombs. Their orders are to dismantle and go on their merry way. There's something else out there, eastward."

The train's caboose rumbled past.

Over the last few days they'd helped in the care and burial of over five thousand former slaves. They'd seen with their own eyes what had been only rumors before.

"I'm not a violent man. I'm not," Cory said. "But I want to kill every last one of them, you know what I mean? They've ceased to be men to me. They're nothing but brute beasts—and we're their slaughterers. 'And the Lord shall visit the iniquity of the fathers on the children and the children's children, to the third and the fourth generation.' That's what they deserve."

"Amen, brother." Staftoy watched the train round a long bend. "But we're gonna save the unholy rocketmen."

Chapter 52

"Patton Nearly Severs Reich—Tanks Roar Toward Junction with Reds"

—*Ohio State Journal*

Adolf-Hitler-Pass, Germany
Monday, April 30, 1945

Delicate white flakes fell on the Haus Ingeburg, a becalmed mountain inn sheltered by thousands of pine trees already heavy with snow, their peaks set against a black-blue evening sky. White hills ran up to the stately, pale resort, which had a top story of exposed wood under a slanted roof.

Von Braun and Dornberger walked the perimeter of the inn's large indoor swimming pool on their regular after-dinner promenade. They smiled at colleagues in the water and admired the beautiful outdoors through spotless floor-to-ceiling windows. They'd dined on fine pheasant delivered by a commissary down the road and cooked by top-notch chefs. They joked that Wolfgang Sänger, who had so ably replaced Thiel, was actually putting on weight. Although they heard frequent reports and hourly rumors of the battles raging around them, the war felt far away.

Magnus sidled up to them. "Arthur has arrived."

In the hotel lobby, two SS "protectors" guarded the doorway. They spotted their redheaded colleague at the long polished reception desk.

"Success?" Dornberger asked quietly.

"*Ja.*"

"I will introduce you to Corporal Seidlitz," said Magnus. "He's in charge of the rooms."

Wernher added, "Try to ignore the fact that at any moment we could all be lined up and shot."

Dieter thought his boss might be tipsy, but he followed his eyes to the other side of the lobby, where *Obergruppenführer* Kammler was carousing at a low table with von Ploetz. He saw an amused smile on Kammler's face.

Have they been watching us?

"Professor!" Kammler shouted across the room. "Join us!"

Von Braun tried to appear confident as he strolled across the cut marble floor to their booth.

Dornberger, Dieter, and Magnus quit the lobby.

Kammler kicked out a chair.

"Shouldn't von Ploetz be behind you?" Von Braun accepted an offered glass.

"Shouldn't that idiot Dornberger be on the Russian front?" Kammler snorted. "But Herr Professor…we are drinking."

Von Braun had never seen Kammler gassed, or his face and high forehead dirty and bloodstained, his blond hair matted, his uniform torn. Von Ploetz was in a similar state of disarray.

"We have been discussing various ways to escape," Kammler slurred. "We have discussed…the merits of burning our uniforms. We could put on civilian clothes and enter a monastery. We could pose as monks. The idea has merit, do you not agree, von Ploetz?"

Von Ploetz nodded while pouring himself another glass of vermouth.

Kammler puckered his lips. "The monastery would be a perfect hideout and…there would be plenty to drink. We might even…manage the commercial end of their operation. You know, you could really make a bundle, eh, Professor?"

Von Braun would have laughed, but the machine pistol in Kammler's right hand, resting on his right thigh, worried him.

"Well, there would be a spiritual side, which—"

"What are *your* plans? Seriously, how is your broken shoulder? Are you being well taken care of? I sincerely hope so. You must resume your essential work. Your Arthur Dieter has done his job, has he not?"

"A good doctor has adjusted my cast." Von Braun didn't flinch. "I am no longer in pain. I have been taking in the beautiful surroundings. You should, too. You should clean yourselves up."

"We cannot. No time. I have my own affairs to arrange. Listen, Professor. I have to leave for an indeterminate period. I am turning over local command to Major Stark."

He and von Ploetz loomed up and emptied their glasses.

"Now we must move on. We must be realistic!" Kammler exclaimed. "It is a new world! What would you say if I proposed to fly your men to Tirol, where General Patton's intelligence men could pick you up? They could smuggle you to Trieste and America, to fight communism to… smash it over and over!"

He extended his arm in an energetic "Heil Hitler!"

They wobbled out of the hotel's double doors laughing.

* * *

The evening afterward, in a thickly carpeted recreation room that doubled as the lounge, the German rocketeers chatted after another fine dinner. The snow had stopped, and a thousand stars spread across the night sky. Rees coughed and observed the constellations, while von Braun recounted again his conversation with Kammler to Dornberger and several others seated in cream-colored chairs with tufted backs.

"I still don't know what to make of it," he confessed. "It reminds me of something Willy Ley used to say about when there is no way out—a Russian resorts to vodka, a Frenchman finds a woman, and we Germans resort to magic."

"I'll be damned if he finds a way to fly us anywhere," Dornberger said. "There is no more military force left."

"Well, I for one am glad we still have Kammler's gang around us," said Dieter. "I heard a horde of Moroccans with a nasty reputation for cutting people's throats are moving up the pass. It will not be long before they find us."

"Nonsense. Conjecture, because the French Army is near. The Americans are closer." Dornberger stretched his legs and pushed his chin into his neck. "My friends, I have enjoyed these days of quiet meditation and repose. Do you recall how we began? Our long and perilous journey? It fills me with happiness and immense gratitude when I think of—"

"Shh!" Debus hissed from nearby.

He and others were gathered round a large radio from which came a long roll of military drums, followed by the first notes of Bruckner's Seventh Symphony.

Dornberger and Von Braun joined them.

A high-pitched voice announced, "The German wireless will now broadcast serious, important news for the German people..."

Three more drumrolls.

"It is reported from headquarters that our *Führer*, Adolf Hitler, fighting to the last breath against Bolshevism, fell for Germany this afternoon in his operational headquarters in the Reich Chancellery. Grand Admiral Doenitz, his successor, will now speak to the German people."

A tear slipped down Dieter's cheek; Debus rubbed his scar.

Admiral Doenitz came on the air. "German men and women, soldiers of the armed forces. Our *Führer*, Adolf Hitler, has fallen. In the deepest sorrow and respect bow the German people. His life has been one of service and sacrifice for Germany. His activity in the fight against the storm of Bolshevism concerned not only Europe but the entire civilized world. It is my first task to save Germany from destruction by the advancing Bolshevist enemy. For this aim alone, the military struggle continues. As far and for so long as achievement of this aim is impeded by the British and the Americans, we shall be forced to carry on our defensive fight against them as well. If we do all that is in our power, God will not forsake us after so much suffering and sacrifice."

Bruckner's symphony swelled up; the rocketeers dispersed. Dornberger and Dieter drifted to the windows. A few resumed their games of chess or their books.

Von Braun lifted a martini with his good hand. "Well, Magnus, my friends, my colleagues," he drained his glass. "Hitler is dead…but the service is excellent."

Chapter 53

"Hitler Dead—U-Boat Chief Claims He's New Fuehrer, Tells Huns to Fight On"

—*Daily Mirror,* London

Książ Castle, the German Empire
Wednesday, May 2, 1945

Kammler ran from room to room in the underground labyrinth to make sure his storm troopers were emptying every file cabinet and desk drawer into railcars. He dashed into an open courtyard, followed by von Ploetz, to verify that the railcars' contents were feeding a bright bonfire. Amidst the disintegration of the German armies, Kammler was following Field Marshal Keitel's order to destroy everything, even the prototype discs.

Atop the bonfire, two charred corpses burned, too, local workers who had tried to make off with secret plans. The partisans would spot the black smoke in the early morning sky, but Kammler didn't care. The Polish resistance knew the castle to be a site of military importance, and they would come.

"Is the plane ready? Has the prisoner been prepared?" Kammler asked. "My orders for the one disc to be dismantled and stowed, the drawings—all has been loaded up?"

Von Ploetz nodded.

Gunfire. About two kilometers away.

When Kammler and von Ploetz emerged upstairs in the great hall of the castle, the rifle shots sounded closer.

"How many?" he barked.

"We think about two hundred," replied his *Obersturmbannführer*, who'd taken a position by an open window.

Boom!

They saw the castle gates tossed high into the air.

Resistance fighters ran through the gap amidst gunfire and took cover behind brickwork and parked trucks. The remnants of Kammler's SS division returned fire. One man fell, shot through the chest.

"We can hold out for maybe fifteen minutes," said the *Obersturmbannführer*.

Kammler drew his machine pistol. "Come with me!"

He swung the door open and charged out, his SS men close behind. The partisans fell back, three wounded. Kammler laughed and killed an older man with a bullet in the throat.

"Meine Ehre heißt Treue!" cried his *Obersturmbannführer* before a machine-gun blast took off half his head.

The partisans regrouped. Storm troopers dropped to the left and right of Kammler. Pistol fire grazed his temple. Standing a few feet behind him, von Ploetz took aim as he'd been ordered to do.

Instinctively, Kammler spun and shot his chief of staff in the face.

Von Ploetz crumpled at his feet, blood gushing from a hole in his cheek. Kammler twisted and squealed at his SS men crouching behind a burnt vehicle. "You saw! The traitor was about to shoot me in the back!" He laughed shrilly. Buckshot shredded another storm trooper. "You cover me—I am going back for reinforcements!"

He sprinted inside, deserting his men. As he opened a steel door with a key, large glass panes shattered on either side of the entryway. He vaulted down the stairs and raced down a tunnel. At a barred portal to an unmarked room he saw that his prisoner had vanished.

Her!

She'd grabbed Schomberger from under his nose. Kammler cursed, but he couldn't delay.

Outside the tunnels in a valley, an open-top car waited for him. He jumped into the back and they sped away.

His driver chose a country lane to avoid the main road.

With a few moments to think, Kammler concluded that even without Schomberger, his planeload of prototype parts and blueprints constituted a storehouse of valuable research. His ticket to safety and a new life.

They arrived at a deserted landing field west of Schweidnitz, where an enormous Junkers Ju 390 idled in the distance. With the yellow-and-blue markings of Sweden, it would be allowed to pass through Allied airspace. The pilot, seeing the car arrive with its passenger, threw several switches and six propellers turned. Kammler leaned forward, about to shout instructions, when the car hit a bump and lurched him sideways just as something shattered their windshield.

An audible rifle crack followed, and Kammler threw himself to the floor of the vehicle. His driver swerved, and he peeked out to see a lone motorcyclist racing from a grove of trees on a path to intercept them. Her braided hair was tied back, and she wore no helmet.

The copilot saw her, too, and opened fire from the fuselage door. Kammler removed several stick grenades from a side compartment and lobbed one after another at the cyclist.

She was forced into a slide.

The copilot peeled off several more shots, and Kammler gleefully cried, "She is pinned down!"

She swung a rifle from her back and fired. The copilot retreated into the plane.

Bumping along, Kammler tossed another grenade. She rolled left and shot again, killing his driver. The car skidded and Kammler leapt out.

The copilot reappeared and fired repeatedly to cover Kammler's dash to the plane. A sudden barrage from the cockpit made her scramble behind her cycle.

Kammler bolted up the steps, and the copilot slammed the fuselage door shut.

The plane accelerated down the runway.

She fired at the rising craft, but it escaped without serious damage.

Damn it, Rachel thought. She had defied the voice and failed. *He's going to be hard to track.*

Chapter 54

"Doenitz, New Fuehrer, Says: We Fight On—Wehrmacht Ordered to Maintain Discipline"

—*News Chronicle,* Late London Edition

Adolf-Hitler-Pass, Germany
Wednesday, May 2, 1945

During coffee and toast, von Braun and Dornberger heard that locals had spotted the American Army on the Austrian side of the Tyrol. The French were advancing from the northwest, Bavaria.

Von Braun had spoken frankly to Major Stark. By morning his SS contingent, having received no orders to shoot the engineers, had disappeared. Not all of them left peacefully. One SS man fled to a nearby town, shot his wife and four children, set their bodies on fire with mattresses, then blew his brains out in front of the villagers.

Wernher and Walter went looking for Magnus. They strolled past civilians on the stone veranda basking in the sun. Magnus saw them coming. "I will say it for you: I am the youngest, I speak the best English—and I am the most expendable."

Dornberger laughed and von Braun confessed, "Yes, it's true. So please be good enough to find the Americans and tell them we are pleased to surrender."

* * *

Private First Class Fredrik T. Schneikert popped up from his trench and spotted a lone civilian emerging from a noonday fog. He was pedaling toward him on a squeaky bicycle.

"Roll up your flaps—cover me," he told his three sentry buddies.

The four of them formed a small part of the Forty-Fourth Infantry Division's anti-tank platoon.

Although a white handkerchief fluttered from the bicycle's handlebars, Schneikert removed the safety lever of his M1 rifle before climbing out of the culvert. He leveled his gun, and the bicyclist stopped on the damp road at a respectful distance.

"Komm vorwärts mit den Händen oben!" Schneikert ordered in German.

Surprised to hear his own language spoken, the civilian raised his hands and walked slowly forward, trying to look as unthreatening as possible. Schneikert saw that the blond man sported a spotless blue-gray ankle-length leather coat over a white silk shirt and a dark-blue tie. Too well dressed, too proper to be army or run-of-the-mill civilian.

"My name is Magnus von Braun," the civvy said in passable English. "My brother invented the V-2. He and many men responsible for the V-2 are in a hotel not far from here. We want to surrender to the Americans."

Schneikert called down to his buddies. "Hey, I've got a nut here. A real big-time operator!"

"Yeah, sounds nutty all right," came back the verdict.

Schneikert scratched his temple under his steel helmet and shouted back to Magnus, "They think you're nuts, too!"

"Nevertheless, I would like to see General Eisenhower as soon as possible!"

"Now I know you've got a screw loose!" Schneikert called down to his buddies again, keeping his rifle on the stranger: "Shit for birds. What do I do with him?"

* * *

At about two that rainy afternoon, Magnus returned to the Haus Ingeburg. He spoke with his brother and Dornberger, seated on a sofa. Debus loitered behind them.

"I have safe-conduct passes, and they want us for further questioning," Magnus said. "It is all arranged. I spoke with a Captain Stewart, and he gave me passes for three cars. They are evidently afraid of an ambush, so they will meet us at the bottom of the mountain."

"Do they understand we are from the Peenemünde research facility?" Wernher asked.

"The first men I ran into didn't know a thing." Magnus enjoyed being the center of attention for once. "But they phoned their headquarters, and those men seemed to have specific instructions to be looking for us."

"You see," Wernher said to Dornberger and Debus, "it is as I predicted. They are as anxious to find us as we are to find them."

An hour later, six men and their drivers crammed into three field-gray sedans jammed with personal belongings and what proof they had of their claims to have invented the V-2 rocket.

The cars drove down the mountain path between densely wooded slopes. Fog gave way to afternoon clouds, low and thick.

"We are all that remain of the greatest engineering adventure in the modern era," Wernher said to Dornberger in the back seat of the lead car.

Wernher's left-hand suit pocket held an ample supply of pills, and he swallowed one.

The major general didn't reply. The German Army had lost. He grew more somber as they drew closer to the victors.

Debus, Dieter, Rees, and Magnus, in the second and third cars, didn't talk much. Rees blew his nose. The only constant sound came from the splashing rain and their vehicles' rubber tires on the macadam.

At the foot of the mountain, Wernher saw heavily armed GIs waiting by two jeeps. Water dripped from their helmets.

The gray sedans stopped a distance away. A soldier walked over slowly. He examined their passes, then stuck his head through the lead car's driver window and asked a question in English.

Wernher answered that they had no weapons, and the GI motioned with his hand to follow.

* * *

They reached the town of Reutte after dark. Their convoy halted in front of a Bavarian-style chateau of white plaster with a second-floor balcony of carved wood and flower boxes.

One of the armed soldiers jumped from his jeep and ushered the group of six into a large, dim hall.

At one end of a table covered with papers, a single candle illuminated the broad face of an officer. He had a prominent chin and blue eyes.

"We would like to be taken to General Eisenhower as soon as possible," Magnus repeated.

"Ike's a little busy. I'm Captain Stewart. Just who the hell are you?"

"As I've mentioned, we are the men responsible for making the V-2 rocket."

Von Braun nodded in agreement; Dornberger glowered at the American.

Stewart studied them for a moment.

"Oh yeah?" he said. "Prove it."

"We have several tons of documentation hidden in the Harz Mountains. Our colleague here, Arthur Dieter"—Dieter stepped forward—"he can lead your men to the exact spot. If you are fast, you may retrieve this before the Bolsheviks."

That got the American's attention, Wernher thought.

"We also have papers and some proof in the cars."

Stewart ordered the GIs to keep it quiet and to put the Germans into a holding room under guard. Others were told to retrieve the vehicles' contents.

Then he made a call.

Counter Intelligence Corps personnel, speaking fluent German, questioned the group for the next two hours. The *Generalmajor* explained how to open the crates safely to avoid the booby traps and preserve the documents.

The Germans were then escorted to small, dirty rooms on the second and third floors. Compelled by the others, Magnus complained to an

American soldier about their untidy accommodations, beds not freshly made, and no light by which to groom themselves.

"Hey, Mac, there's still a war on," the corporal drawled. "And, oh yeah, you assholes started it!"

In the hall below, Stewart phoned CIC headquarters in Paris.

"Screen them for being Nazis? What the hell for?" he shouted into the receiver. "What if they're Hitler's brothers? It's besides the point. You know as well as I their knowledge is valuable for military and national reasons." He paused and listened. "Yeah, yeah, it could be egg in our beer. Yeah, all right, yeah. I'll find out if they are who they say they are. I'll do it—but get Staftoy or someone competent over to that cave and get those papers—pronto!"

* * *

The next morning, von Braun and his companions were shown into a spacious dining room and treated to their first American breakfast. Dieter and Debus, favorably impressed, devoured fresh eggs and slathered butter on toast.

"I have not seen white bread for years," Rees remarked.

Wernher, eyeing the GIs and CIC men eating at the long tables, said, "They did not kick us in the mouth or anything..."

Dornberger sipped real coffee with eyes downcast, while Magnus crunched on dry cereal. His brother elbowed him and indicated a sergeant a few seats away pouring milk onto his Cheerioats. Enlightened, Magnus did the same.

Word spread fast. With the blessing of his CIC superiors, Stewart took the group of six outside after breakfast, into the cold air and slushy snow, to pose for photos. He'd verified their identities.

Magnus introduced Private Schneikert to his brother, who boasted, "I'll bet zat I'm in der United States before you."

"I'll take that bet," Schneikert said.

"Sir, I'm from the Seventh Army's *Beachhead News*," a reporter in uniform introduced himself. "Can you tell us about your role in the invention of the V-2 rocket?"

"I can tell you zat if we vere given two more years, the V-2 could have won ze war for Germany," von Braun calculated. "If we had been able to increase our production to two hundred per day and improve ze gyroscope for pinpoint accuracy—"

"What about the concentration camps where they made your rockets?"

Wernher smiled and said, "I'm sorry, my English isn't zat good…"

He stepped away from the reporter to pose with Dornberger and Magnus in the bright sun, his arm horizontal in its cast. Their hair slicked back, each had an almost crazed smile frozen on their faces. With his good hand Wernher coolly smoked an American cigarette. Flashbulbs popped, and a 16mm movie camera rolled.

Cornelius Ryan, on loan from Patton's Third Army, had traveled all night to be there and took notes not destined for publication. He saw that the elder von Braun's expression held not the slightest trace of remorse or shame, yet Ryan appreciated the show.

"We're celebrating now," Wernher blustered, "but I bet they vill toss telephone books at our heads ven we reach New York."

Two of the Americans laughed, and the army reporter resumed his line of questioning: "Do you think your invention will help or hinder the free world?"

"Zat question I can answer. Our rocket is surely ze greatest achievement of the war. Nothing can match it. You vould be foolish not to let us help you."

He posed for more photos.

Ryan confided to Captain Stewart: "Well—if you haven't captured the greatest scientist of the Third Reich, you've certainly got its greatest liar."

Chapter 55

"Сталин Сообщает, Что Армия Вторглась В Берлин—Центр Германского Империализма (Stalin Reports Army Has Invaded Berlin—Center of Germany's Imperialism)"

—*Pravda,* Moscow

Peenemünde Army Research Center, Germany
Saturday, May 5, 1945

Zhukov's Red Army stormed in and obliterated the handful of soldiers defending Peenemünde. Advance troops of the Second Belorussian Front, blind with drink, broke into a house and pulled off the dress of a woman; when her husband tried to fight them off, they shot him repeatedly and stabbed her to death.

A day later, Sergei Pavlovich Korolev drove onto the base. He'd been commissioned a colonel and made responsible for future long-range ballistic missile development.

"Amnesty!" Glushko had told him. "Our good work has freed us."

Korolev had smiled and asked, "No more secrets between us?"

"My dear friend, there will always be secrets between us. We are men, not beasts."

Korolev climbed out of his armored car, and a captain saluted him. "Colonel Korolev," he said, "I regret to say we can find nothing of consequence. The place has been cleaned out."

Korolev strode past him and down the main street. He found his intelligence team inspecting an abandoned launchpad.

"Report!" he ordered.

"Colonel Korolev," a major answered, "we have located the technical director's house, but not a single intact rocket. Most of the base has been dynamited or otherwise rendered useless. We estimate that seventy-five percent of the complex has been destroyed."

Korolev followed the major through the debris. They stepped over the body of a young German whose legs had been blown off, and turned onto a tree-lined street.

Korolev dismissed the officer and entered von Braun's home.

He took off his cap; his hair underneath was gray at the temples. He'd survived the war and shed his prisoner's skin; with more success had come more responsibility and means. He felt closer to his old self; he felt good in action but missed Natasha and decided to send for his daughter and wife.

He took note of the house's superior accommodations, four bathrooms and two dining rooms, a study. He decided to commandeer von Braun's former domicile for the days it would take to grill Helmut Gröttrup and the other Nazi engineers they'd taken into custody. At night, he would continue to teach himself English and German.

In the small library Korolev noticed a notebook lying open on a side table. A name was written in red ink on a flyleaf. He picked it up and read, "Yuriy Vasilievich Kondratyuk," the name of a Soviet engineer who had disappeared in the fighting near Kaluga.

Astonished, he scanned its bloodstained pages, recalling Kondratyuk's theory of lunar orbit rendezvous, then slid the valuable item into his coat pocket.

On the second floor, he lay down on his back atop a snow-white feather bed. He saw himself reflected above in a large gilded mirror.

"This is not at all bad," he said aloud. He pulled out a cigar from his breast pocket and lit it. "These fascist beasts knew how to live."

Chapter 56

"The War in Europe Is Ended! Surrender Is Unconditional"

—The New York Times

Dörnten, Germany
Monday, May 21, 1945

Majors Staftoy and Cory tore through the Harz Mountains on a breakneck mission. Their celebration of Germany's surrender had been brief. The international scramble for the biggest consolation prizes had entered its decisive phase seconds later.

"Where are the British?" Staftoy turned the wheel of their jeep to avoid a farmer and his cow.

"Buddy boy, your guess is as good as mine. Last I heard, they were supposed to take over this area in six days, not ten."

They slowed to cross a river near Soviet-controlled territory and heard a broadcast in German blaring through loudspeakers: "German rocketmen, please to come over from the American side. There is a bonus of fifty thousand reichsmarks to anyone who knows the whereabouts of Professor Wernher von Braun or scientist Ernst Rees. German rocketmen! Please to come…"

They heard the Soviet bulletin played over and over until they drove out of range.

At the established perimeter of Dörnten, Cory showed their passes to a twenty-four-hour guard.

At the mine entrance on the mountainside, they were relieved to discover dozens of soldiers loading a convoy of trucks with the rocketmen's secret cache of documents. No booby traps had been triggered, and the recovery mission was on plan.

At 6:00 a.m., six days later, Majors Staftoy and Cory drove ahead of the loaded trucks into the American zone, only hours before the British set up roadblocks and searches. They stored their treasure at Nordhausen for another five days until two ten-ton semitrailers arrived. Cory arranged armed guards and two jeeps to accompany the trailers to Paris, where the documents and drawings would be shipped to the Foreign Documents Evaluation Center at Aberdeen, Maryland.

"I kinda feel sorry for the Brits," Cory said, watching them go. "After what they went through, morally speaking, they kinda deserve this junk more than us."

"Maybe. But they're in terrible shape." Staftoy sucked on his pipe. "Washington doesn't think they have the backbone, or the money, to develop these plans where they need to go."

Cory stuck out his lower lip, and Staftoy slapped him on the back. "Cheer up," he said. "Now we just need to convince a bunch of Nazi assholes to work for peanuts—and to show us how the damn things work."

Chapter 57

"Germans Were Getting V-2's Ready to Plaster U.S. by Next November; Himmler Bites a Poison Phial, Dies at British H.Q."

—*Daily Mirror,* London

Garmisch-Partenkirchen, Germany
Monday, May 28, 1945

An American major waved a loaded .45-caliber automatic in Dornberger's face. "C'mon, Mac, spill it or—"

"I suggest you try another method," said the German in German, "or I will not answer any more of your idiotic questions."

"Put that away!" Lieutenant-Colonel Carlson told the American major.

The three men occupied a small office with a view of the Austrian Alps through a barred window, Dornberger seated, the two Americans on their feet facing him.

The major holstered his gun.

Carlson had come into the picture when the U.S. Army had transferred von Braun, Dornberger, and as many of their engineers as they could find to Garmisch-Partenkirchen. The army had converted the mountain resort town's facility; Carlson's outfit had requisitioned two of its long three-story buildings for intelligence teams from the navy, air force, and Combined Objectives Subcommittee to conduct interrogations.

"I apologize for my friend," Carlson said in German. "Please tell us, did you ever try to kill Hitler?"

"No."

"How 'bout Roosevelt?"

In an adjacent room, an officer grilled von Braun: "Suppose you were working for us and we had another war with Germany?"

"Not likely in my lifetime," von Braun replied in English.

"Suppose it happened, though."

"Then I am still a German."

The officer shoved his hands into his pockets. "You'll never make it to America talking like that!"

* * *

During lunch, on the German side of the large, noisy canteen, Sunny Boy ate his overcooked peas and poked at a kind of meat stew. His huge cast made it awkward to eat among colleagues seated close on either side of him.

"To think all this used to be the snow units' headquarters," Dornberger lamented.

"Dith you hear thath Himmther goth kith?" asked engineer Julius Riedel. Unlike the other Germans, he'd been discovered hiding in a small village and two GIs had kicked out his front teeth before handing him over to intelligence.

"*Ja.* I did. Cyanide," Debus said, chewing. "Too bad."

"What about Kammler?" Magnus asked.

"Reported killed in a dozen places. Yet it is we who are prisoners."

"We are civilians with no criminal charges against us." Dieter shoveled stew into his mouth. "There is no legal way they can detain us, except for the *Generalmajor*—sorry, sir."

"Their methods and offers are embarrassing," Dornberger said, looking at each of them. "I heard from Gröttrup's wife and the kitchen staff, which, incidentally, is riddled with Soviet spies, that the Russians are offering houses and huge salaries. You can stay with your families in

Germany. The British have offered to billet us in first-class hotels. What have the Americans offered? Short-term employment, no possibility of citizenship, modest salaries. You will have to leave your families behind."

"They are simpletons, it's true," said von Braun. "But keep it down. We do not want to play hard to get. We want to continue our work. This is the most important."

"I showed one American captain my six trunks full of reichsmarks," said Dieter. "I told him what we need is *dollars*! I cannot feed my parents with reichsmarks. What will happen to them if I go to America? I have to be able to send American money that can buy apples or bread or milk *here*, in Germany."

"Gröttrup and his wife are fools if they believe the Reds," Debus said, eyeing his green Jell-O suspiciously.

"Of course they are." Von Braun swallowed the last of his peas. "The Russians will say anything to get what they want. You would have to be insane to trust them."

He took two blue pills from the table and downed them with some water.

"We must nevertheless hold out for better terms from the Americans," Dornberger said. "Three-year contracts. We have to act as a team—anyone who breaks rank and makes a deal without the consent of myself and Professor von Braun will be punished."

Dieter and the others finished their meals without looking up.

On the American side of the mess hall, Major Staftoy drank coffee to stay awake after breakneck trips back and forth across Western Europe to ensure that the Mittelwerk's contents were transported to the States. He'd made over fifty trans-Atlantic calls to drum up support for the importation of as many rocketmen as the U.S. Army could handle.

"So what do you think of them?" Staftoy asked Carlson, who gnawed on a stick of beef jerky.

From their position near the kitchen door, they could see von Braun and the others conversing.

"Questioning didn't go well," Carlson admitted. "I didn't know what to ask them. It's like they're talking Chinese to us, with all their technical jargon."

"Don't worry about that. I have it covered. What about them as people?"

"I've analyzed it, and I'd say there's three types," he said, chewing. "The ones who are nutty for space. Von Braun and Dieter fall into that category. The ones just doing their jobs would describe most of them. But the real Nazis…Debus is one of them. There's a couple of others. Overall, they're a frightening group."

"Why?"

"Because of what I'd call tunnel vision. To a man, not one of them has expressed any remorse or second thoughts about Germany's war. When I asked them about the V-2s exploding in London and Antwerp, and the civilian deaths, von Braun answered that his group had nothing to do with selecting targets. It just didn't concern him at all. Not a one of them seems to feel anything but satisfaction about their work." He took another strip of jerky out of his packet. "In fact, it's abundantly clear they think we're fools. They think we're wasting their time because a war with the Soviets is just around the corner."

"I happen to agree with that sentiment," Staftoy said.

But the thought made him tired, and he sat down.

"No kidding?" Carlson joined him at the end of a table crowded with GIs and CIC men. "Well, that bastard Dornberger and a few other Krauts may be willing to throw in their lot with the Asian hordes if we don't meet their demands."

"Their demands, huh? Looks like we're ready for round two."

While they ate frankfurters and beans, Staftoy explained his plan to Carlson.

* * *

On that unusually cold afternoon, Staftoy faced von Braun.

"Cigarette?" he asked.

"Yes, thank you." Von Braun took one from a pack of Chesterfields.

"Keep the pack."

"Thank you."

The American was sitting on the edge of an antique desk in an office.

"Professor von Braun, I'm going to be blunt. Your folks are pushing hard when you should be grateful. Don't you think we might decide to have you arrested and punished? Some of you might hang."

"Ve are not pushing." Wernher looked surprised. "Ve would not have treated your scientists as war criminals, and ve don't expect to be treated as bad men. No. I am not afraid. The rocket is something ve have and you do not have. Naturally, you want to know all about it."

With constant practice, his English had already improved.

"Well, we have the rocket now. In fact, we have plenty of 'em. We'll figure out how they work."

"Do not be so sure. It is a precision instrument. Without us, you vill spend perhaps a year, perhaps two, to understand the mechanisms. You vill not be able to make the new ones. The ones only in planning stages. The first intercontinental ballistic missile.

"So, yes, let us be blunt." Von Braun smoked his cigarette aggressively. "Our rocket, which was born of idealism, like ze airplane, was employed in the business of killing, which we never wanted. Ve designed it to blaze a trail to other planets. However, it was also too late for ze rocket to stem the tide. We needed another year. *Der Führer* did not seem to realize how immature our weapon still vas."

Listening to von Braun's contradictory words, Staftoy realized that he had the ethics of most of the Germans he'd met: blinkered and amoral.

But I need this particular Nazi.

"Okay, c'mon." Staftoy straightened up. "There's a couple of fellows I want you to meet."

Accompanied by three MPs—Staftoy had already foiled one plot to kidnap the engineer—he led von Braun to an enclosed courtyard within the long casern. One of the captured V-2s had been placed on several sawhorses, its inner workings exposed as if for an autopsy. Two men in winter clothing were closely examining those workings.

"Before the war, I believe you corresponded with these gentlemen," Staftoy said.

At the sound of his voice, the two others turned.

"Professor von Braun, may I introduce to you Professors Robert Goddard and Theodore von Kármán."

For the first time since his surrender, the German was speechless.

Von Kármán, his white hair curly around the temples, his eyebrows bushy, had a simulated rank of major general with a corresponding uniform. Goddard had wrapped a thick woolen muffler around his throat and appeared weak, but his eyes were clear and angry.

The three MPs took defensive positions. Goddard took a step toward von Braun and pointed back at the missile. "It looks like one of mine. The rocket I made in the spring of 1941 is practically identical." He stepped back and indicated several of its components with a wave of his hand. "Similar fuel; centrifugal pumps. Both pump drives, turbine. Stabilizing and blast vanes. Similar layouts. Too similar."

Wernher remained silent while the older man circled the missile.

"The apparatus for igniting liquid fuel is nearly identical to the one I patented," Goddard said. "So is your mechanism for directing flight, its gyroscopic steering, and your method for cooling the engine. In short, Mister von Braun," his voice rasped, "you have stolen my work—and used it to commit murder."

Staftoy and von Kármán smoked their pipes, waiting.

"Ve…ve were always perplexed at the lack of interest in America for your achievements. Ve—"

"That German, Oberth, probably helped you copy my work. Or perhaps spies—"

"Herr Oberth moved beyond your work to the mathematics of spatial trajectories," von Braun defended his mentor. "He vas our teacher." And then softened. "But you, Professor Goddard, you ver my boyhood hero."

Staftoy concealed his astonishment at the German's shamelessness, though his words sounded oddly sincere.

"Sir, you ver ahead of us all. But surely you must have known your patents ver translated and circulated. You blazed the trail, I freely admit.

You saved us years of work. I also admit zat we infringed on your patents, which enabled us to perfect ze A-4 years before it would have been possible. We had to move beyond your work. It was war."

Von Braun lit another Chesterfield.

Christ, he adapts quickly, thought Staftoy.

"Yes, we moved beyond. Ve established an enormous operation and spent millions and millions to do it."

"Stolen money," Goddard spat out.

Von Braun exhaled cigarette smoke.

"Professor Goddard, with all due respect, you failed to do what ve did. You must therefore realize zat the era of ze lone inventor is over. The scientist who works in his garage and amazes the world one day when he opens his door—vell, he no longer has a place in zis business."

Von Braun's lips formed his most seductive smile, and Goddard took a step backward.

"Unlike you, I cannot smile, Mr. von Braun," von Kármán said. "I'm surprised you can. I've been to Nordhausen. I've seen the walking corpses and the unburied dead." He switched to German and jabbed the stem of his pipe at von Braun. "Have you no remorse, no humility in the face of what you and Germany have done? Where is your conscience?"

"Someone else would have done the job if I had not," von Braun replied sharply, also in German. "Rockets were a new idea—and a new idea is stronger than one man's feelings, one man's conscience, or even a whole nation's." He reverted to English and addressed Staftoy. "Once civilization is committed to a technical advance, it is our duty to keep going. Ve cannot go back to a pastoral age. But you don't have somesing for notsing. Zer are strings attached. But do you actually think I should be blamed for ze V-2s hitting London? Military orders zat kill thousands are transmitted over telephone. Why not blame the inventor for zat?"

Goddard slumped against a sawhorse. "I'm sick," he said. "I despise you. My work is my message to the future. Your work…"

Von Kármán took Goddard's arm, and they slowly left the courtyard.

"Well?" Staftoy relit his pipe. "Those two are just the tip of the iceberg. You see, we do have some talented people at home. They hate you, but that doesn't matter to me because you and I agree about one thing: danger from the East."

"Well?" von Braun repeated the question to himself while making a thousand calculations. "Hm. I will convince the others to accept your terms. Our rocket must go to the West. In this, let us hope our historical contribution is not lost."

"Fine," Staftoy puffed. "Draw up a list of who you'll need." *You pretentious prick.* "We're not taking everyone."

Nuremberg, Germany
Tuesday, May 29, 1945

In the Palace of Justice, in a room off the main courtroom, two CIC officers questioned Albert Speer. Neither of them spoke German, so a translator had joined them again for their third day. A desk with a single chrome-shaded lamp illuminated the former minister's face.

"What about Schomberger?"

"I told you. I do not know the man," Speer answered. "Though I heard of him."

"Do you know where he is?"

"No."

"If you knew, would you tell us?"

"Yes."

"What do you know about 'vortex compression' and 'spin polarization,' weapons using antigravity propulsion?"

The senior officer went on to describe a saucer vehicle in great detail; Speer was impressed at the extent of their knowledge, which surpassed his own.

Perhaps Patton's Third Army had—

"If you know something, you'd better spill it!" barked the second officer.

Speer responded in English: "Why don't you ask Kammler?"

Chapter 58

"Moscou a Reussi à Imposer Son Gouvernement à La Pologne (Moscow Has Succeeded in Imposing Its Government on Poland)"

—*La Liberté et le Patriote,* Winnipeg, Canada

Nordhausen, Germany
Tuesday, July 3, 1945

Korolev headed south in his red Horch roadster at a terrific speed.

At the Mittelwerk, he hunted down a few charred engines on broken-down railway cars. He strolled through the tunnels and saw they'd been stripped of everything but scraps, at least at first glance. He and his team of engineers conducted a two-day investigation, however, and discovered hundreds of components and subassemblies for the construction of the rockets, along with thousands of machine tools.

A Soviet intelligence officer rooted out a former Czech prisoner willing to lead them to more war booty. Korolev took him in his shiny car, confiscated from a Nazi industrialist, and they tore through the countryside to the loud purr of its eight-cylinder in-line engine.

They uncovered a spherical object under a pile of rags in the dark corner of a basement. Korolev suppressed his stupefaction—it was a next-generation gyro-stabilized platform. At their next stop, toward the bottom of a dead-end drift in a potassium mine, they unearthed several guidance system components and range control, lateral correction radio sets. In a forester's cabin on a hunting reserve, they picked up two sets of relay boxes and firing control panels. In a sand quarry, more than fifty brand-new combustion chambers and crates, with enough fuel pumps, injectors, and engine parts to fill sixty railroad cars.

Among the contents of a safe in the back office of a restaurant were documents and blueprints. On one was carefully written "A-9"; on another, "A-10."

Korolev took advantage of the kitchen staff to order food for his starving informant. He poured vodka, which they drank together.

Back in his Horch, Korolev slammed his foot on the accelerator. He didn't want to be late for his call from Moscow.

* * *

"This is intolerable!" Stalin yelled.

In a derelict office at the Mittelwerk, empty drawers strewn on the floor, Korolev held the receiver away from his ear. They'd yet to meet, but he'd already had several emphatic telephone conversations with the general secretary.

"We have obliterated and slaughtered the Nazi armies," Stalin ranted. "We have occupied Berlin and Peenemünde, but the Americans have the rockets—and the leading rocket engineers? What could be more revolting and inexcusable? How was this allowed to happen?"

"Comrade Stalin, we have rounded up about three thousand of their rocketmen, at Bleicherode, Sondershausen, and at Kleinbodungen," Korolev replied. "They are not the leaders, but they have the expertise to operate existing physical facilities."

"In other words, we shall have to learn from the leftover dregs?" Stalin paused on the line. "This is good. Give the order to recruit as many of these people as possible. Promise them whatever you need to. Be kind to them. You must persuade one or more of the most capable to come to the motherland."

"Right away, Comrade Stalin."

"What we need to know are the details concerning the rocket's potential speed, distance, altitude of flight—and payload. Above all I would like to know about their accuracy of delivery."

"Comrade Stalin, I have already in hand plans for a rocket with a distance of five thousand kilometers. That is much more than the V-2." Korolev could see through the window his men putting rocket parts into large crates. "This is clearly an intercontinental missile. With a rocket such as this, our enemies would tremble. From this, we will also learn science."

"You are quite right, Comrade Korolev: a rocket is science and defense."

The line clicked off.

* * *

A complete V-2 rolled off the assembly line only weeks afterward, manufactured by Germans under Soviet supervision. They test-fired new motors nearby. Korolev had easily recruited local experts and craftsmen, who were afraid they and their families would starve.

His prize for the general secretary was Helmut Gröttrup. He and Korolev, with an interpreter, had walked together for hours discussing technical matters. The Russian recognized an intensity and brilliance in the thin-faced blond. "You will be in charge of an entire rocket project," Korolev promised Gröttrup, "equal in status to Wernher von Braun's at the height of the war."

A Soviet intelligence advisor had discovered a schism, competition between the two former German colleagues. Korolev aimed to exploit it.

"We will provide you with a house, car, food, servant privileges, and a good salary. You are fortunate. You and your Irmgard will be safe."

"Tell me one thing: My wife and I will never have to leave Germany?"

Korolev puffed his cigarette. "The Soviet authorities have agreed to that, yes."

As they strolled down the main tunnel beneath electric lights, Korolev marveled at Gröttrup's naiveté.

Chapter 59

"Churchill Is Defeated in Labor Landslide; Attlee Promises Prosecution of Pacific War"

—*The New York Times*

London, England
Friday, July 27, 1945

Two cars drove carefully through a dewy morning fog on Battersea Park Road. Both drivers had their wipers on.

The chauffeur of the black Rolls-Royce stopped before a row of ruined houses, while the other car parked a block ahead.

Dornberger, Debus, and von Braun, whose cast had been removed, exited from the Rolls to explore the wreckage. After a quarter of an hour they reconvened on the sidewalk to talk shop. Passersby, hearing German spoken, regarded them with suspicion.

The trio was on loan to the UK before their trans-Atlantic journey to America. When Debus's wife, Gay, had got wind of her husband's contract and was told that he'd be leaving her and their children behind in Germany, she'd attempted to swallow a cyanide capsule. Debus had knocked it out of her hand and slapped her face twice. He'd hoped to bring his wife to her senses, and was disappointed when she cried.

While Debus compared notes with his colleagues, their driver watched them. He was MI6, part of Operation Backfire. His report would indicate that his passengers betrayed no emotion akin to sadness or regret or sympathy for the damage caused by this particular V-2, which had hit last November. He would note that each morning since the German engineers had arrived from Cuxhaven, he'd taken them by a different route from their billet in Wimbledon to a different scene and not once had they exhibited empathy. Theirs was a clinical interest only. The military man, Dornberger, discouraged anything but a martial attitude toward their work.

Before the engineers could return to their car, a truck roared up and screeched to a halt. Three men in Soviet military uniforms leapt out from its rear and blocked their path. Another in civilian clothes climbed out and loitered nearby. Two large men stayed immobile in the cab.

"I am sorry," said one of the men in English, whose slightly Asiatic appearance was accentuated by his greased-back black hair. "Can we have word?"

The MI6 driver slipped out of his car quietly and, hands in pockets, took up a strategic spot. The second car circled slowly back.

"Who are you?" von Braun asked, also in English.

"I am being Colonel Glushko." The uniformed man extended his hand and von Braun clasped it instinctively. "He is being Captain Yuri Pobedonostsev. It is that you like for a few drinks?"

"No," said Dornberger, who had picked up some English. "It is… too early for drink."

The Soviets didn't budge.

Debus looked at "Captain" Pobedonostsev and the camera around his thick neck and calculated that this burly Russian had never taken a professional photograph in his life.

"No drink? I am to be direct. It is that we pay double what Americans offer."

"You to have personal car," Pobedonostsev added with a grin.

"We did not appreciate your attempt to kidnap Professor von Braun at Cuxhaven, and we do not appreciate it now," Dornberger said in German and pushed through the Russians, followed by von Braun and Debus.

Glushko hesitated, then waved to the MI6 man before he and his associates climbed back into their truck.

The British agent would add the surprise encounter to his report. He signaled the second car, and both vehicles drove away. A kilometer to the north, near Saint James Park, his passengers disembarked for their ninth day of interrogation.

Inside the cozy lobby of the Ministry of Supply, as they had been each morning, the trio was met by Sir Alwyn Douglas Crow, director of guided projectiles. Crow led them to their small conference room with shuttered windows and a long oak table. A woman secretary-stenographer already occupied her position at the opposite end. Upon their entering, a man in an ultramarine suit and matching tie stood up from his chair.

"Gentlemen, this is R. V. Jones, chief of Air Scientific Intelligence, MI6," Crow introduced him. "He has long been a student of your work."

"Yes, indeed," Jones said, shaking their hands. "If you don't mind, I'd like to become more familiar with the other end of the V-2's trajectory."

"Yes, certainly," said von Braun.

They settled round the table. The Germans wore gray or dark-gray suits and ties, with white handkerchiefs in their breast pockets.

"As you know we have only another day or two," Crow said. "We have already covered the preparation of your rocket and supplementary equipment, so this morning we would like to address the handling of fuels and flight control, if this is agreeable to you."

"Of course. I must admit that each day I expect your attitude to change," said von Braun. "I thought you might be unfriendly to us, but I am glad to say I have been wrong."

Jones and Crow swapped knowing looks. The Germans were oblivious to the Englishmen's real feelings. Those undercurrents remained hidden. Questions and answers flowed for the next hour and a half, to the delight of the Germans only too glad to expound on their technological achievements.

A rap on the door was followed by a very tall man in a long gray raincoat who entered without waiting for a response.

"Sorry to barge in, but I was told I'd find you here," he said. "No time to lose, what."

"Ah, Major Smith," Crow said. "Not a problem. What can I do for you?"

"Well, sir, we heard that you were entertaining a Major General Dornberger."

"I am *Generalmajor* Dornberger."

Smith paused and his narrow face seemed embarrassed. "Major General, I must apologize. You see, I've come to take you into custody in the name of the British War Crimes Investigation Unit."

Dornberger opened his mouth in shock, but von Braun placed a warning hand on his arm.

"You will accompany me to Bridgend in South Wales. There, you will be questioned by Sir Harley Shawcross, who is constructing a case against you. I can assure you, however, that though the trial will be lengthy, it will also be fair."

"This is absurd," said von Braun. "*Generalmajor* Dornberger had no command function over the rocket launches. War crimes? British and American air attacks on German cities caused thousands more civilian deaths than the V-2."

"That may be," replied Major Smith, "but the future of Major General Dornberger is at present a matter over which only Sir Harley and the British cabinet have jurisdiction. Though I may add for your edification that he is not to be tried for the use of rockets as weapons but for the use of slave labor and murder in production of those very same V-2s."

Dornberger blurted out, "I will protest to the Americans!"

Major Smith smiled. "Yes, take it up with Ike, why don't you."

Chapter 60

"Atomic Bomb Rocks Japan—Single Air Missile Equalling 20,000 Tons TNT Hits Hiroshima"

—*Free Philippines,* Extra Edition, Manila

Antwerp, Belgium
Wednesday, August 15, 1945

Before the USS *Augusta* docked at Antwerp, Brigadier General Eisenhower and a CIC officer climbed aboard, with helping hands, at a prearranged hour and place.

A captain escorted the brigadier general and the blond officer to the wardroom, where they shook hands with Secretary of State James Byrnes, Major Bruce Staftoy, and Secretary of the Navy James Forrestal, dressed in a pin-striped suit with two-tone shoes. Churchill, whom Eisenhower had not seen for a while, also greeted them, standing with his scientific advisors Lord Cherwell and R. V. Jones.

Onshore, crowds awaited to greet the new U.S. president, Harry S. Truman, whose protection, once on land, would become Eisenhower's responsibility. This more private meeting at sea had been agreed upon to avoid the public and press on the mainland.

Several folding chairs had been arranged in a circle beneath a low ceiling and exposed cables running overhead, freshly painted white. A carafe of water and glasses had been placed on a corner table, near the stenographer.

Ike lit a cigarette and said, "Well, let's get the difficult part over with."

"I've spoken with President Truman and I will be representing him in these critical matters," Byrnes said, using just the right amount of southern charm.

The ex-PM had accepted the secretary's role in advance. They'd met before at several events. Although defeated in the recent election, Churchill's presence was essential.

"Go ahead, Lord Cherwell, let's have the summation," he grunted.

A smile rippled quickly across the professor's face. He anticipated needling Jones with relish, one of his graphs in hand. "Our analysis of the V-1 and V-2 and their relative merits is as follows: When we consider the flying bombs, the results are in favor of the enemy. They did a great deal of damage. Over a million structures destroyed and over twenty thousand civilian casualties. We had to spend close to four to one to defend against it, while it cost the Germans relatively little."

He paused and consulted the reverse of his graph.

"The V-2 is another story. Approximately two hundred thousand German and enforced laborers worked ceaselessly from the beginning of the war to its end to little effect." The Prof eyed Jones. "By last summer, the V-2 was an extravagant irrelevance. Each rocket cost some £12,000 and proved inferior to any other form of bombardment. It was an extremely expensive and most inefficient form of attack, for only about fifty percent of the rockets fell within an eleven-mile radius of their target."

"So your conclusion is the V-2 had little to no military effect on the war?" Ike asked, cigarette in hand. "I doubt that."

Lord Cherwell looked at Eisenhower as if he were an ignorant schoolboy. "General—"

"Our records show a total of over five hundred rockets fell on London," Staftoy said. "Over twelve hundred on Antwerp, with about twenty-seven hundred civilians killed in London alone."

"Nevertheless," Churchill said, "I'd like to add for the record that my review of the Professor's minutes clearly show that his views on the possible scale of attack were, on the whole, very right. And the estimates of the alarmists…very wrong."

"In *my* mind it was a close call indeed," said Jones, and Eisenhower's eyes told him that the brigadier general agreed. "While carrying out their fascist romantic ideals, these men singularly advanced certain revolutionary techniques. What's more, from what we've now seen on their drawing boards, the missile will most likely become a deciding factor in any conflicts to come."

"That may be," Churchill conceded.

Staftoy leaned forward. "I don't want to change the subject, but I've seen with my own eyes the human toll the work had in Germany itself, and it's horrifying. I know some of you have seen it, too, either in person or on film. We estimate that in the concentration camps anywhere from forty to eighty thousand prisoners died to produce those rockets. Mostly, they were worked to death."

Eisenhower stubbed out his cigarette. "Germany must be occupied. For a long time."

"That's right," Byrnes said.

"More than this, the war-making power of the country should be totally eliminated."

"This brings us to the crux of the matter," said Churchill.

"What to do with the top Nazi engineers..." the Prof mused.

"Despite my personal feelings," Eisenhower said, "Order 1067 of the Joint Chiefs of Staff directs me to acquire as much German research as possible, which may include personnel. Major Staftoy here has in our custody over four hundred of their top research-development men. These men developed the V-2 and were planning more long-range rockets. Our scientific directors are of the opinion that this group is twenty-five years ahead of us."

"We believe that these selected engineers, if taken to the U.S., should go on with their research," said Staftoy. "Most are under thirty-five and know no other type of business. They're extremely anxious to carry on in whatever country will provide them the opportunity to do so. They'd prefer the States." He looked at Churchill. "No offense intended."

"None taken," said the PM without smiling.

"There is one, Major General Dornberger, whom we may wish to retain," Jones noted, "indefinitely."

"We would have preferred an SS officer named Kammler," said the professor, "but no one, it seems, can find him…"

"We have no qualms with your plans to import these diabolical scientists," Churchill continued. "We are sure the Soviets are doing the same. And, may I add, that my prediction for the years to come is not a rosy one. God help us if America is not the first to put an atomic explosive on the end of one of these missiles. You *must* be first. The Soviet armies were marching where they pleased until news of the atomic bomb put a stop to all that."

"Wouldn't it be a novel idea," the professor added, "if America forced a showdown with the Soviet Union *before* the latter acquires a bomb of their own?"

The PM, with the help of a cane, got to his feet.

"Gentlemen," he said, "goodbye. I believe we're done."

The British contingent was escorted out.

"He's right—it's done," Staftoy said to the remaining American quartet. "Operation Overcast will send Nazi rocketeers to America."

"Well, the Brits might be okay with army plans," said Byrnes, "but the Department of Justice sure as hell is not. No, they're not at all happy with the idea of FBI agents tied up watching over hundreds of German scientists. One or two of them might be those exact Nazis whom we should be putting on trial."

"That argument cuts both ways." Major Staftoy lit his pipe. "If we allow those Peenemünde boys to work in Germany or Russia, we would be perpetuating the activities of a group that could contribute to either country's ability to make war—with us. As it is, some of the more fanatical SS lovers, like engineer Wolfgang Sänger, we're not bringing. But that also means he and his kind will be able to work for whoever wants them."

"It doesn't matter. The State Department says they won't have a damn thing to do with it. But…as long as the War Department brings the German scientists back *in custody* and eventually returns them to Germany, they don't want to know what you're doing. They don't want to know any of it. If news of their presence in the States leaks to the press, it's going to be your necks."

"Mr. Secretary, many of those in the War Department are also against this. Our acknowledged purpose is temporary military exploitation for as long as it takes. It's not ideal, but we don't have a choice."

"Let's call a spade a spade," Ike said. "While Truman negotiates with Stalin, the Soviets will be carting off entire laboratories and their staffs. We can't stand by idly. And let's not forget the secret weapons."

"So where *is* Kammler?" Forrestal asked. He had a boxer's broken nose, a tight mouth, and small eyes. "I've recently seen some of his advanced weapons in Poland. You can believe the reports. The technology is…fantastic. We need to run him to ground quickly."

Forrestal and his protégé, war hero John F. Kennedy, had learned a great deal on their tour of Germany's secret manufacturing facilities. Forrestal would have liked Navy Intelligence to be in on the hunt for Kammler, but he'd been outmaneuvered.

"Donald," Eisenhower addressed the CIC officer. "Anything?"

"We have a bead on him," said the blond man with nearly white eyebrows.

"Good luck," Staftoy said. "And be careful. We may have some devils on our books, but you're on the trail of Satan himself."

ACT III

Chapter 61

"Opening Scenes at Nuremberg War Crimes Trial; Goering and Company in Good Spirits"

—*Evening Telegraph and Post,* Dundee, Scotland

Montevideo, Uruguay
Tuesday, March 19, 1946

Rachel quietly picked the lock of an apartment door on the fifth floor of a fashionable building.

She took a measured breath and withdrew her silenced automatic pistol from a holster inside her short jacket.

Noiselessly, she cracked open the door. A Uruguayan youth was packing a suitcase.

"Shh…" She held a finger to her lips.

He whirled about as shots erupted from the bedroom, narrowly missing Rachel, who moved sideways into the apartment.

She flattened herself against a wall, as the youth escaped down the exterior hallway.

When her attacker foolishly stepped into the living room, she grabbed his arm and broke it. The man cried out in pain and sunk to his knees. He was of average height and build.

"Where's Kammler?" Rachel asked.

He swore and tried to point his gun at her. "Blood and honor!"

She fired two bullets into his head, and he splayed backward onto the carpet.

Her search revealed only a worn valise with a flimsy lock. The Nazis in South America were loosely organized and making mistakes, shedding weight as their Third Reich disintegrated. Some former officers and high-level bureaucrats hid themselves well; others went by their real names.

Kammler, however, had disappeared. He hadn't even been tried in absentia at Nuremberg.

She picked the lock of the valise and went through its contents: antigravity formulae and a paper on the importance of gold's molecular structure.

Papers in a secret pocket of the dead man's suit confirmed his former command of an SS killing unit in Latvia.

She stuffed the ID papers into his mouth for the local police to find, then left the apartment to inform her superior, who would contact several intelligence teams.

Chapter 62

"Unite to Stop Russians, Churchill Warns of Iron Curtain"

—*The Stars and Stripes,* South Germany Edition

Fort Bliss, New Mexico/Texas
Tuesday, March 26, 1946

The Germans were playing Monopoly.

Wernher von Braun, Kurt Debus, Ernst Rees, and several others were taking it quite seriously. Arthur Dieter took a break from the board game and combed back his red hair.

He surveyed once again their new environment, so strange to him even after a few months. The "prisoners of peace," as they called themselves, were confined to four clapboard single-story barracks, a feeble mess hall, a functional center office, and several supply buildings. Most of the Germans were billeted in building "H," a drafty converted hangar made of wood.

The desert sun had brought out freckles on his puffy face. The heat and clear air had eventually washed away Rees's lingering cold.

Beyond the wire fence, Dieter saw engineers in the desert, mechanics and crew working on a launch complex and firing pit. On the farthest edge of the horizon rose up the purple Organ Mountains, so different from anything he'd seen before. The fences of Fort Bliss bound the

Germans' limits, but lizards, mice, snakes, scorpions, and large spiders crawled or slithered wherever they pleased.

He turned his head at the sound of low, indistinct voices and spotted Majors Staftoy and Cory on the other side of the lawn, shaded by a large cottonwood tree in the twilight. He waved to them.

"How long have they been playing?" Cory asked, waving back. He'd been away for a few weeks.

"Fifth day in a row." Staftoy puffed his pipe. "They've modified the rules to include provisions for holding companies and cartels." He puffed again. "The three remaining tycoons in the game, as I understand it, are involved in trilateral negotiations so convoluted that each of them has hired an assistant to administer their real-estate and mortgage deals for their imagined property."

"You've got to be kidding me." Cory squinted at the hotels on the board.

"I kid you not."

"Well…the last of the V-2 parts should be delivered soon, and they can get started."

"You know, it's become clear to me that a comprehensive evaluation of the V-2 was never undertaken by Nazi High Command," Staftoy said, knocking out his pipe on the gray bark. "Not even in the thick of it. The police state they lived in just couldn't stomach the idea of a single person knowing more than they had to. Maybe Kammler had the big picture, but…he's still missing." He lit his pipe again. "Or so I'm told."

"I heard something about a new identity and the Middle East." Cory lit a cigarette. "But are you saying these guys can't do the job?"

"Oh, they can do it. But only as a team. As such, by our office's estimates, the army will save over seven hundred and fifty million dollars in rocket research alone."

"No small change. By the way, I got a memo. Operation Overcast is now Operation Paperclip."

"That's right. Truman okayed it. We're the proud owners of 111 Germans of various and dubious character."

"Can we trust them?"

"It's a little late for that, but they're being watched. Watched and evaluated. Even when they go into El Paso, to a restaurant or shopping, we've got men there. They're going to the movies to learn English. Some of them spend all day there, which has given rise to some strange accents. Some of them are getting cozy with persons in town of German descent. They're using Schneider's Grocery as a gathering place. A few aren't afraid to cross the border into Juarez and frequent the ladies of the evening."

"World War II is dead. Long live the Russian war. Wasn't it Thucydides who said, 'War is the father of us all'?"

"Heraclitus of Ephesus—'War is the father of us all, King of all. Some it makes gods, some it makes men, some it makes slaves, some it makes free.' I learned it by heart at West Point… Here he comes."

Von Braun sauntered over the green, well-watered lawn.

"What can I do for you, Wernher?" Staftoy asked.

"I'm sorry, Major, but I must offer my resignation again. You have ignored my phone calls and my memos, so I cannot go on. Now I must answer to a pimply captain with only an undergraduate degree in engineering. It is humiliating." He lowered his voice. "I have pressure from others as well."

Cory looked him up and down. Von Braun's blond hair had become even fairer, his eyes bluer, his teeth somehow whiter. His face was a soft shade of red thanks to months under the sun. He spoke better English, too, with a marked Prussian accent, which made the softest words sound hard. Cory and Staftoy both thought they shouldn't like him, but they did like him. A little.

"Wernher, I appreciate we're in a difficult and somewhat trying situation," Staftoy drawled; he nodded to Cory, who took out a notepad. "I cannot accept your resignation, but I can listen. Spill it."

"We are disappointed. Some of our group is wondering if they were too hasty in accepting your offer to come to America. We are underpaid and we miss our families. You are counting pennies while we both know we must create long-range atomic missiles capable of reaching Russia, which will cost millions."

"That's the way it is for now, Wernher; I can't change that. I can say that we're working on the family difficulties."

Von Braun relaxed. He considered the major a fair man. "This is good of you," he said. "Last but not least, as you say, we ask you to remove the rattlesnake from the back of the Coca-Cola machine in the clubhouse. The snake rattles each time a nickel is dropped in, which frightens some of the men."

"I'll have it taken care of. I also have some news, good and bad. Professor Goddard is dead."

Von Braun sighed. "The world has lost a great and underappreciated man."

"The other news is that your friend Major General Dornberger will soon be released from prison. He won't be able to join you, but he's coming to the States. We'll find a place for him."

"Thank you for telling me, sir." Von Braun was content his former superior would be freed but employed elsewhere. He'd coolly resolved that the reputation of his group could not be tarnished by a German military officer accused of war crimes. "I will inform the others."

"Not so fast." Staftoy removed his pipe and planted himself close to von Braun. "You've had your say, now I'll have mine. You and your German colleagues were brought over for three reasons—and three reasons only: to serve as consultants to American industry and research institutions, to assist in the assembly and launching of the V-2s, and to propose new guided missile projects. If you want your families to come over, if you want to stop being treated like so-called prisoners—then your group better be patient, do its job, and shape up. Understand?"

Von Braun extended his hand. Staftoy glanced toward the clubhouse and saw the others, even the Monopoly players, observing them.

Staftoy took the proffered hand and shook it.

"Understood," von Braun said.

He walked away, hesitated, and turned back.

"One more thing: my staff addresses me as 'Professor.' Could you do the same?"

Staftoy puffed his pipe. "I'll think about it."

Chapter 63

"Stalin Sets a Huge Output Under New Five-Year Plan; Expects to Lead in Science"

—*The New York Times*

Bleicherode, Soviet Occupation Zone
Tuesday, April 2, 1946

Boris Evseyevich Chertok appreciated his luxurious abode. His office had its own telephone and a well-stocked shelf of fine vodka. He wished his father, Yevsey, could see him. He would have told him how everything, his entire career, had blossomed the day Yevsey had taken him as a boy to see *Aelita: Queen of Mars* at Moscow's Ars Cinema.

"Anta... Odeli... Uta...?" the beautiful Aelita had sensually asked of Man. *"Where are you, son of Earth?"*

A signal straight from Mars!

Chertok had become crazy for radio engineering. He'd studied it ceaselessly, even neglecting his mathematics, for which his father had thrashed him.

Chertok clapped his thighs with both hands.

He wore an officer's uniform, TT pistol, and two magazines in his belt. He'd been flown from the Soviet zone of Berlin in a B-25 because of his rare talents and his fluent German. As provisional leader of the Institute RABE, or Raketenbau und Entwicklung, Chertok had been assigned to organize an ad hoc base where German rocket and engineering specialists, scattered by the war, could be reunited. A temporary place where Chertok and his colleagues could learn more about the V-2s.

Today the Soviet team was assembling for the first time.

A loud knocking and he opened the door to Vasily Pavlovich Mishin and Mikhail Klavdievich Glushko, whose trousers and polished black boots were crusted over with dust and thick mud.

"What a journey. Give us tea—or something stronger!" Glushko plopped down on the couch. "We drove from Nordhausen the whole way with our car pulling badly and smoking. They say you have some good repair specialists; I suggest they get to it."

Leonid Alexandrovich Voskresenskiy arrived next, an engineering expert, like Mishin, and an efficient manager. Not tall, but with a markedly pointed nose.

Chertok poured out another glass of vodka and remarked, "Look at us gathered here, the best, but we are still missing one."

"He will be here," Glushko grumbled. "Unfortunately."

A commotion in the courtyard drew them to the window. Astride a magnificent brown stallion, a woman in a beige riding suit was berating the mechanics examining Glushko's car because they were blocking her way.

"Who the hell is she?" Voskresenskiy asked.

"That formidable monster is married to von Braun's former deputy," said Chertok. "Irmgard Gröttrup, the 'Amazon.' She supposedly hates fascism and was even arrested once. She and her husband are prepared to work for us if given complete freedom. But either way, she is taking it." He downed his glass. "Listen to me, you really do not want to get in her way."

"We will have to teach her how to behave," Glushko said from the couch.

Those at the window then saw a mud-splattered Horch roar into the courtyard and scatter the mechanics. The car careened off Glushko's smoking sedan like a pool ball, causing the stallion to rear up and bolt into the fields with Irmgard barely hanging on.

The spectators fell over each other laughing, and the Horch rolled to a gear-grinding halt. A powerful man leaped out of the vehicle and ran over to the cowering mechanics and swore at them.

An elegantly dressed woman and a young girl also emerged from the Horch.

"The family Korolev has arrived!" Chertok announced.

"Your car is not a fighter plane!" Lyalya shouted at Korolev.

"But I have a driver's license *and* a pilot's license!" Korolev retorted and swiveled back to the mechanics. "I demand that the owner of this other wreck, who parked so idiotically, be horsewhipped!"

In Chertok's office, Korolev introduced Lyalya and Natasha, "my eleven-year-old sprite," who snuck away to a comfortable chair in the corner to read a book.

Chertok liked the three of them immediately.

Korolev's uniform fit him well, but the absence of medals on his clean tunic gave him away as a civilian officer. His soft leather boots were the finest in the room. While they made small talk, Chertok remarked that Korolev's dark eyes had a merry sort of sparkle, an air of curiosity and attentiveness. He had a noticeably high forehead; his large head on his short neck gave him the compact look of a boxer.

"I have a feeling I will be working with you a lot," Korolev said to him.

"Good," Chertok replied, and Glushko glared.

"Do not be a spoilsport, Mikhail Klavdievich," Korolev chided him.

"What's the matter with them?" Voskresenskiy whispered his question to Mishin.

"Their positions have been reversed," Mishin whispered back. "Sergei Pavlovich has been named First Deputy and Chief Designer of long-range missiles by Stalin himself. Mikhail Klavdievich Glushko has been demoted to Chief Engineer."

"Why?"

"Ask Stalin."

"Another toast," Korolev exclaimed, "to our new team. We will learn everything we can about German rocketry. And to my wife, Kseniya

Maximilianovna, a brilliant surgeon. You have no idea what it means to live fifteen years with Korolev. No, you cannot imagine such a thing. But she has endured this heroically, so for her I drink this toast to the last drop!"

He emptied his glass, but Chertok noticed that Lyalya averted her eyes from her husbands'. Dressed in black and without makeup, she seemed forlorn, and Chertok felt sorry for her. Korolev's reputation and appetite for women, unshackled and promoted, had become prodigious.

"Now to business." Korolev poured another glass and his men gathered round. "We must begin by reproducing the German technology faithfully, before we can make our own. I know some of you will not like this, myself least of all. We are burning with desire to go our own way." Glushko cracked a smile at last. "But those are our orders. For the next few months we must prove to Stalin and Comrade Minister Ustinov that we can do as well as the Germans. And anyone who says we are stealing from them forgets that we have paid for it all with a great deal of blood."

Chapter 64

"Hirohito Tells Subjects He's Not Divine; People Asked to Abandon Master Race Illusions"

—*The Washington Post*

White Sands Proving Ground, New Mexico
Friday, June 28, 1946

Riding in the back of their jeep, Jack Parsons and Professor Theodore von Kármán were amused by a freshly painted orange-and-white sign on the main street of Alamogordo that proudly proclaimed it, HOME OF THE ATOMIC BOMB, CENTER OF ROCKET DEVELOPMENT!

Motorists clogged the highway out of town, so their driver had to zigzag among the sedans and station wagons overcrowded with sweaty passengers, picnic baskets, squirming children, and barking dogs. It looked to Parsons like the nearby towns of El Paso and Las Cruces were funneling themselves toward the noonday launch, attracted by the spectacular nature of the rocket—a glimpse of the future—and a chance to see the beast, the V-2, one of Hitler's mechanical devils.

Their jeep swerved from the road into the desert to pass a bus with the words INTERNATIONAL ROCKET SCHOOL in red on its side. Their driver gunned it, and his passengers bounced by more trucks and coaches loaded with Boy Scout troops, ROTC collegians, National Guardsmen, and boisterous civic clubs. Farther along, but still several miles from the launchpad, they skirted a chaotic public parking lot and pulled up in a cloud of dust by a corrugated steel hangar.

The professor, in a gray suit, clambered out, followed by Parsons, who had black hair and a rugged physique. An actor, if he'd wanted to be, he wore a crimson leisure jacket and green plaid pants. He'd never graduated from anything, but as a highly intuitive chemist he'd developed an important formula for rocket fuel during the war. On the basis of his discovery, he and the professor had formed a company together, the Jet Propulsion Laboratory.

They were just in time for the VIP tour. Fort Bliss and the Proving Ground were inundated with brass from the Pentagon, West Point, and Annapolis.

"I think every goddamn retired Mexican general is here!" Staftoy said when he greeted them.

He and Cory shook their hands.

"Where's von Braun?" von Kármán asked.

Cory pointed to a man in a civilian suit and tie talking with a number of site workers.

Inside the assembly building, Staftoy guided the VIPs to the assembly line. "Gentlemen, the V-2 rocket is being rebuilt by ordnance crews in order to carry out what we're calling 'cosmic research.'"

He escorted his thirty-plus visitors down the line, where they could see the rocket's glass-wool insulation, before a large fuel tank was lowered into the fuselage.

"To the rear of the alcohol tank is another tank for liquid oxygen," he pointed out. "Specially constructed frames that roll on tracks make the assembly easier."

Crew pushed the tail housing into position.

"For our purposes, as you can see, scientific instruments have replaced explosives in the nose head."

The VIPs watched the rocket being placed on a special wagon, which would tow it to the firing range. Staftoy then took Parsons, von Kármán, and a few others to von Braun, who was huddled with his department chiefs in the shade of a two-ton Jimmy truck.

As they neared, Staftoy heard Debus complain, *"Ich bin es leid, den Unterricht von Kindern—amerikanische Dummköpfe!"*

"Ahem!" Cory cleared his throat, and the Germans spun about.

"I told you guys to cut out that 'American stupid' stuff!" Staftoy roared.

Debus and the others flattened their backs against the truck, whipped off their hats, and shouted in unison, "Good morning, Major!"

"At ease," Staftoy grumbled. "Good morning, Wernher."

Parsons extended his hand to von Braun. "Glad to meet you, Professor," he beamed. "You may not remember me, but we corresponded before the war."

Von Kármán studied the Germans uneasily. In the intervening years he'd read the reports and attempted to overcome their bad taste. Behind them, trailers with equipment and ground crew rolled toward the launchpad.

"Of course I remember," von Braun said. "I never forget. Never. There were only a few of us to see the potential of rockets."

"Today, we are a few more," von Kármán said as he puffed his pipe.

"Thank you, Professor." Wernher bobbed his head. "We owe you a huge debt of gratitude for your support."

"Let's get this shoot going!" Staftoy signaled Cory. "We don't want to be late, or there'll be a riot on the highway."

Cory led the group of military and civilian VIPs westward along a path that paralleled hundreds of electrical control cables, through hot swirling winds and dust, to a white concrete blockhouse with thick walls and a thick roof.

Staftoy was left with von Braun and his inner group.

"You know, Major," Rees noted, "we have begun to call ourselves Operation Icebox instead of Paperclip, because we are being 'kept on ice.'"

The major did not return his smile. "Look, Rees, you should consider yourselves lucky to be eating three squares. Besides, I have good news. I'll make it official later, but I'm telling you now that you can apply to bring over your families."

"I do not understand, Major," von Braun said. "You seem to hate us, but you are happy to deliver this wonderful gift."

"Wernher, it's simple: I have faith in mankind." He knocked his pipe against the side of the Jimmy truck. "I believe you can change."

"But there is nothing wrong with us."

"Nothing that time, faith, and patience can't fix. There are those who disagree with me, but I'm counting on you."

* * *

In the pleasantly cool, crowded interior of the bunkhouse, many of the group unbuttoned their jackets. The mayor of Las Cruces, Sam Klein, loosened his tie. General "Hap" Arnold adjusted his cap. Behind Staftoy, personnel attended to tiny running lights and pulsating clicks on a bank of instrumentation.

"Gentlemen," Staftoy said, "the rocket we're about to launch is equipped with an ultraviolet spectrograph; skin temperature gauges on its nose, midsection, and tail; and three propagation transmitters for ion density studies. There's also a Geiger counter telescope to identify primary radiation."

"Major, can you tell us non-eggheads—what's the purpose of all this?" Klein asked.

"Yes, sir, I can explain," said von Braun, taking what he assumed was his rightful place by Staftoy's side. "At present we know as much about the sky upstairs as a fish knows about land. People can criticize the weatherman, but there are certain unaccountable winds for which he cannot be blamed. We want to launch a satellite one day so that America will have a constant check on cloud movements and pressure patterns. The weatherman will be able to predict hot summers ahead or cold winters beyond those summers."

"Gentlemen, this is, uh, *Professor* Wernher von Braun," Staftoy said, "who has been helping us to prepare the rocket."

"From Germany?" Klein didn't have to be a linguist to pick up on the name and accent.

"Uh, yes," Staftoy replied. "The Germans we have here are educating personnel in the mechanics and principles of guided missiles. We have officers here from Canada, Britain, France, India—in short, every allied country with an interest in the subject. But let's move on." He kept up a patter over Klein's visible distress. "We'll be gaining valuable knowledge about currents, temperatures, and pressure patterns of the stratosphere, even the ionosphere and the E layer."

General Arnold grunted. "As if atomic bombs are going to be any good without guided missiles."

A flare pistol outside signaled the three-minute mark before launch.

The countdown terminated at 12:03 p.m. and the V-2 erupted in a sudden and violent burst of flames.

Once free of the tower, it lifted up at a tremendous rate.

Out on Highway 70, families and spectators seated atop their cars or on blankets in the nearby fields watched the missile soar above the serrated peaks of the mountain range. They clapped as it sped higher.

The VIPs also applauded, crowded round the blockhouse's three windows, narrow slits of thick laminated glass.

"Beautiful!" Parsons proclaimed the loudest.

"Quite astonishing," von Kármán seconded.

At one mile up, the sound was still deafening.

"Telescopic cameras are charting the course of the missile," Staftoy shouted and gestured at a table. "Automatic recorders plot signals from the rocket on these large horizontal sheets."

"It's a keeper!" a technician called out.

* * *

After the launch, the crowds and VIPs went home or to grab a bite to eat. Von Braun, Parsons, Staftoy, and von Kármán circled the launchpad on foot. In the bright afternoon light, the German answered dozens of technical questions posed by his two visitors.

"It's not that we Germans are smarter, it's just that we old-timers have been working on these things for so long," he explained. "We've had twelve more years to make mistakes and learn from them." Buoyed by the day's success, he let his guard down. "Germanic culture has always been the leader of Western culture. Western culture is now being championed by the United States against Russia's Eastern ways. The United States has thus become the champion of Germanic culture, and therefore it is normal for us to work together. We are teaching you, showing to you our *Geheimnisse*, our top secrets."

"That's a neat syllogism," von Kármán remarked. "Worthy of Goebbels."

"Professor, did Hitler involve you in any of his occult workings?" asked Parsons, who was elated to be in the company of a kindred spirit.

"I heard some talk of this," von Braun replied, "but I was never a part of any, shall we say, black magic. Why do you ask?"

"Just curious. Have you noticed we're standing at Launch Complex 33, but there's only one launchpad? Where are the other thirty-two?"

"So?"

"You're unaware of the Thirty-Third Degree Mason? The army is full of them. Omar Bradley. James Doolittle. 'Hap' Arnold is one of them, and so is—"

"This is not so important," von Kármán interrupted. "I am descended from Rabbi Judah Loew ben Bezalel of Prague. My distinguished ancestors are reputed to have created a golem. It's all nonsense."

"I have heard of Freemasonry, of course," said von Braun. "I am unaware of what a golem is. But, gentlemen"—he planted one foot on the fender of an army hospital truck—"my interest is rocketry, missiles. We live in an atomic age. If you, Mr. Parsons, or you, Professor von Kármán, can help Major Staftoy to find for our team a proper base and funding, we can make missiles ten times more effective than what you saw today."

"I'll do what I can when I'm in Washington," said von Kármán.

"What about space travel? Have you abandoned that?" Parsons asked. "Surely you know the dangers to your soul if you make more weapons of mass destruction."

"Surely *you* are aware of the tension with the Soviets." Von Braun lit a cigarette. "Let's not be naïve. The only way to win a third world war is to prevent its outbreak. The most decisive step in doing so is to establish observing posts in satellite orbits. You see, rocketry is capable of solving many of the world's problems." He inhaled. "But to answer your question, no, I have not abandoned my youthful dreams. In my spare evenings, I am writing a book about a trip to Mars."

"Wernher wants to go to Mars, or the Moon," Staftoy said. "That's his real passion. Don't be fooled. War or peace on Earth comes after. He talks about missiles just to get his funding, like a huckster selling snake oil."

"If I start talking about trips to the Moon, I think you will not be believing anything I tell you," von Braun laughed. "Anyway, if you went to the Moon, the real problem is not getting there, but getting back. The return trip is the difficulty, though Earth's gravitational pull would be working for you."

"I'd like to read your story about Mars," Parsons said. "I'm working on the creation of a Cosmic Child, who will usher in a new golden age on Earth." He stamped his feet and recited, "Dear Thou Me, for I am the angel of Paphro Osoronophris. This is thy true name handed down to me by the prophets of Israel…"

* * *

When Staftoy accompanied the visitors back to their jeep, von Braun hitched a ride to Fort Bliss in one of the military's open trucks. Holding a flashlight in one hand and a few pages torn from a vocational dictionary in the other, he busied himself with learning a plumber's technical vocabulary.

"Faucet." "Valve." "Pressure washer." "Sealant." He recited the words aloud in the dark, to the amusement of exhausted GIs sprawled about him.

"Hey, professor," one GI called out. "Ya worried that one of your missiles is gonna go down the toilet?"

Chapter 65

"Goering, 12 Other Nazis Sentenced to Be Hanged at Nuremberg"

—*Jackson Daily News*

Bleicherode, Soviet Occupation Zone
Tuesday, October 22, 1946

In a two-story house assigned to the Gröttrup family by Korolev, Frau Irmgard Gröttrup picked up the ringing phone in a daze. Blonde hair hung over her face and through her tresses, she noticed the hour—3:00 a.m.

She was going to respond angrily, but a hysterical voice wailed, "Are they taking you, too?"

"What do you mean?"

"To Russia!"

"Are you out of your mind? What a time for practical jokes! Why should I go to Moscow? I am not a potential suicide."

She slammed the phone down and was half asleep minutes later when it trilled again.

"Are you being sent to Siberia?" a voice sobbed. "The soldiers are already here. Your husband must help us!"

"What nonsense! Are you all in league against me? Who do—"

The loud sound of vehicles outside cut her breath short.

Phone in one hand, she pulled back the drapes and saw a caravan of dark-green trucks emblazoned with large red stars, motors running; black sedans parked up and down the street. Soldiers with submachine guns swarmed in a cloud of gray exhaust smoke.

"They are here, too," Irmgard whispered and let the phone drop.

She put on her nightgown and ran downstairs to the back door to see if she and the children might escape—but was confronted by the barrel of a gun and a broad face staring blankly at her.

"*Nyet.*"

The front door quaked under pounding fists and her doorbell rang again and again.

They can't kill me—Helmut is too important!

She opened the front door and Soviet soldiers pushed by her, followed by an officer.

"Frau Gröttrup, please to pack your bags," he said politely. "You and your family are going to Russia."

Irmgard fled upstairs to her bedroom. She obtained a free line and got her husband on the phone.

"You must come home and stop this!"

"Stop what?"

He gradually understood despite his vodka haze.

Over Helmut Gröttrup's head swung Chinese lanterns of red and orange in a banquet room with loud music and air thick with cigar and cigarette fumes. Over a hundred guests milled around an open bar stocked with lager and liqueurs. The German engineers had been invited to a fete in their honor.

"We have been betrayed," he said. "There is nothing I can do. Nothing at all. I am in a room full of generals and officers. I may be home tonight, but I may not be able to see you again until we are on the train. Try to keep calm."

"Keep calm? How can I? They are packing up our things, even our furniture! What about the children?"

"Do what you can for them—take them with you whatever happens. I am sure it will be all right."

He hung up and Korolev appeared, drink in hand.

"Did you know about this?"

"Of course," Korolev replied. "General Serov and I made up the lists ourselves. Comrade Gröttrup, you are so innocent."

He emptied his glass and signaled a waiter for another.

"Do not patronize—"

"You should be proud. Your section will be Bureau Gröttrup!"

"Proud? You swore—"

"My word meant nothing. You should have known that. The Potsdam Agreement entitles the Soviet Union to deport five thousand Germans to help with the reconstruction of facilities—destroyed by your Nazi armies." Korolev took the glass offered by the waiter. "Besides, if you blame anyone you should blame the Americanese. They are demanding an investigation of the occupation zones to stop us from building missiles. We have no choice but to deport the lot of you."

Korolev drank. He didn't care to admit that he and Glushko, and many of their colleagues, had been against the forced evacuation.

"What if we refuse?"

"If you are that foolish, I imagine you will be sent to work in the mines of the Ural Mountains, where, believe me"—he put his hand on the German's shoulder—"you would not survive."

* * *

At dawn, hundreds of families on a railroad platform scrambled in search of loved ones and their belongings before finding assigned passenger cars.

Helmut heard a Russian officer counsel a bewildered technician, "If you do not want to take your wife, take a mistress."

"Can I do that?"

"Sure, why not?"

The Germans had been taken away indiscriminately. Anyone caught inside a designated house was shipped out, regardless of qualifications or relations.

Trucks parallel to the station were loaded up with what couldn't be carried by train.

Searching, Helmut saw men pushing a cow and throwing chickens into a railroad car.

Are they taking the whole farm? Madness…

He found Irmgard and his frightened children about to be trampled by horses.

They located their designated compartment and waited.

And waited…

* * *

On the fourth night, their train pulled into Podlipki, not far from Moscow. A heavy snow fell. The train's passengers, dazed and disoriented, disgorged from the cars. Soldiers on the platform showed them where to go: a foreboding camp surrounded by a high barbed-wire fence, with guard towers and searchlights strafing concrete buildings.

A few Russian children gathered at the fence shouted words they'd learned in German. "Nazi shit!"

"Welcome to Moscow!" Korolev said upon locating the Gröttrup family. "What have you brought for me? A cheerful mood, I hope."

He wore an opulent fur coat with red stars on his epaulettes, a gray Persian lamb cap on his head. The Germans had on lighter clothes.

"My dear Korolev," Irmgard said coldly and handed him a matchbox. "For you."

Korolev opened it and laughed. Inside were bedbugs. He offered cigarettes from his pockets, chocolate and candies for the children.

"Do not worry, Comrade Gröttrup." Korolev took Helmut's bare hand in his two gloved ones. "Scientific Research Institute 88 is only where you will work. I am also working there. You and your family will be lodged in a dacha, with six rooms. Your wife will even have a Hoover vacuum cleaner!"

Other Germans passed by. Coming upstream, two Russians, a man and woman, in thick fur coats sprinkled with snowflakes greeted them.

"Dobro pozhalovat!" said the larger man with an oily expression.

"Here is Minister of Armaments Comrade Dmitry Ustinov," said Korolev. "The beautiful woman who translates is Nina Ivanovna Kotenkova."

Kotenkova translated.

"Why am I here, I would like to know." Gröttrup crossed his arms to keep warm.

The snow fell harder.

"When will we be allowed to return to Germany?" asked Irmgard.

Ustinov chuckled. He and Kotenkova spoke rapidly. She had a round, pretty face and red lips, and risked a furtive, interested glance at Korolev.

The armaments minister smiled and Kotenkova said proudly: "Comrade Minister Ustinov declares that you can leave when your husband has made a missile that flies as far as America."

Chapter 66

"Nazi Scientists Aid Army on Research—Hundreds Are Revealed to Be in U.S. Showing How They Built Rockets, Other Things"

—*The New York Times*

Ross Sea, Antarctica
Friday, January 10, 1947

The USS *Mount Olympus* steamed into Ross Sea at the fore of Central Group. Two supply ships and two icebreakers trailed. A submarine, the USS *Sennet*, cruised well in advance of them under the ice shelf of Antarctica.

The *Mount Olympus* planned to rendezvous with East and West Group in a pincer maneuver that was being complicated by high waves and subzero temperatures. On the bridge of the 450-foot-long flagship was Rear Admiral Richard Cruzen, U.S. Navy, Commanding Officer, Task Force 68. On his shoulder was a patch with laurels and "Operation Highjump" spelled out. Rear Admiral Richard Byrd Jr., advisor and the only one experienced in that part of the world, was Officer in Charge. He adjusted an ornate ring on his finger; under his cap, he wore his hair comparatively long.

The other deck officers had on winter clothing, either navy issue or whatever they'd scrounged up. They'd shipped out in a hurry.

Rachel stood to the rear in a long wool coat. She'd been hastily added to the command crew as an unofficial observer, for she was one of the few people who could identify Kammler. She'd obeyed orders, but she thought they were on a wild goose chase.

"Sir, we've received a radio report from the *Sennet*," the communications officer said. "All scouts report Retreat 211 has been abandoned for some time."

"No sign of life?" Cruzen, a small-boned man, wanted to be sure.

"They scoured the area beneath Queen Maud Land and found several entrances to a warm-water lake. But the only remains were scrap metal. Nothing alive on the surrounding shore, though scouts report finding three tunnels to parts unknown."

Cruzen looked at Byrd, who nodded. "Have them check those tunnels and tell the *Sennet* we're coming in for a closer look," Cruzen ordered. "Tell the landing crew to prepare for an expedition tomorrow at dawn."

"Yes, sir!"

Rachel assumed they'd find nothing of importance. The Nazis had never seriously tried to establish a base in Antarctica.

She noticed a sudden commotion on deck. From the bridge, she and the others saw sailors bent over the rail looking at the ocean below. More men ran over despite the crashing surf.

"What's that light?" Cruzen asked, pointing to the south.

"Sir!" a radioman shouted from his post, "the *Yancey* reports they're under attack. The captain is requesting destroyers *Brownson* and *Henderson* emergency rendezvous from East and West Groups."

Cruzen gave the order, while a glow beneath the waves grew larger—blue and yellow lights.

"Either many objects or a solitary big one," shouted the deck officer. "They're breaching!"

Thirteen saucer-shaped discs shot out of the sea at a terrific speed, water streaming off them as if from a duck's back. Three broke off from their V-shaped formation and buzzed the *Olympus*. They ran its length, then reversed over its antenna array without a sound.

Shooting up quickly to rejoin the others, they gained cloud cover in seconds.

Those on the bridge kept their eyes riveted on the clouds until the colors vanished.

"Nazis?" asked the radioman.

"I didn't see any markings," Cruzen said.

No one had.

"Not Russian either."

"What do you think?" Cruzen asked Byrd.

"A show of force." Byrd rotated his ring. "A warning."

But Rachel knew it was more.

Chapter 67

"Violentes Manifestation Anti-Américaines en Chine (Violent Anti-American Protests in China)"

—*Le Petit Marocain,* Morocco

Fort Bliss, New Mexico/Texas
Wednesday, April 9, 1947

During his relatively idle days and weeks at Fort Bliss, von Braun told his friends that he was being purified by the desert sun. He explained to Staftoy that he was reverting to his younger self, perhaps his true self, unsullied by war.

"I wonder if that's possible for any man," Staftoy said one day outside their clubhouse.

Of late the American judged the German more charismatically imposing. Von Braun never worried unduly. Staftoy believed it was one of the reasons he had remained the leader of his often disgruntled, mutinous colleagues.

"I thought your group was mostly bored here. I thought they were angry about Washington's neglect."

"This is also true."

At night von Braun wrote his book for hours. In elegant cursive, he dreamed up adventures for his seventy crewmembers in huge spaceships on their long voyage to Mars. He described how the astronauts glided down in a detachable craft with long skis to land on the planet's icy north pole.

One predawn morning that smelled of early spring, he laid down his pen and closed his eyes.

He slept for two hours.

Upon waking, he showered and shaved, dressed, and easily slipped into his more extroverted persona.

"Good morning, Rees!" he said.

They stood on the threshold of their clubhouse, a converted garage of crooked boards and tar paper

"Herr Professor, you should have taken the Greyhound bus ride with us yesterday," said Rees with wide eyes. He'd developed a habit of making exaggerated faces while talking about mundane subjects. "We went to a resort area near the Rio Grande and saw a tennis match, Bill Tilden against Fred Perry. So much fun."

"Maybe next time," Wernher demurred. "Maria wanted to go to the movies."

"Ah, yes, you must keep your lady happy!" said Dieter, trotting up to them. "It's so hot here, no domestics, and—"

"The young newlywed!" Debus exclaimed. "Herr Professor, you won't be able to go out with the boys anymore."

They joined their colleagues, about twenty of them, for their daily operational meeting around the long pinewood clubhouse table. They'd furnished the clubhouse "living room" with sofas, easy chairs, rugs, and a bar stocked with rum, gin, tequila, beer, and lots of soda. They'd even installed chrome slot machines and, on the porch, two Ping-Pong tables under fluorescent lights so they could play at night while battling mosquitoes. Long Monopoly games were still popular.

"I tell you it wasn't easy to get married!" von Braun declared. "A sea of red tape was traversed, and so was the Atlantic."

"Herr Professor, we have bought something for you." Dieter pointed to an object on a shelf beneath stag heads, covered by a blanket.

Rees approached and, with a flourish, pulled off the blanket to reveal a large cuckoo clock. "Sent all the way from the Black Forest!"

The group applauded and von Braun said, "*Wunderbar!* When Maria and I have a home of our own, we will hang it in a place of honor."

Von Braun noticed the absence of his brother Magnus.

Dieter was chewing on something and Debus asked, "What is that in your mouth?"

"Gum." He blew a bubble.

"It is quite unseemly. Why are you doing that?"

"Because I saw Americans doing it. Why do you drink whiskey and listen to jazz?"

Three others sang out, "Because I saw Americans doing it."

"Gentlemen," von Braun said, "there is nothing here but room to grow."

"Of course," Debus sneered. "No one else wants to live in this radioactive desert. What difference are a few more rockets."

A loud debate ensued on atomic energy and nuclear fallout, and whether the Americans would put warheads on their missiles.

Von Braun tried to put the meeting back on track. "Gentlemen, we are in the middle of what you might call a public relations war. We must do more to be accepted here by the local community. Myself, I am going to speak at a Rotarian club, but I am welcoming ideas from you now."

"We could have our children sing 'The Eyes of Texas' at the next school assembly," proposed radio guidance expert Willy Mrazek.

Hans Hueter, keeper of the minutes, jotted down the idea.

"We must learn to recite the Pledge of Allegiance from memory," offered Rees.

"We could have a contest to speak English better, to help our children be more American," said Dieter.

"Our classical music group could play in public…"

At the meeting's close, von Braun encouraged his colleagues, as he often did, with an inspirational maxim. He'd chosen a cavalry call from World War I that urged soldiers to overcome every obstacle: *"Man muss sein Herz über den Graben werfen!"* he shouted.

"We will!" the others shouted back.

Outside the clubhouse, off-limits to women, von Braun took the hand of his eighteen-year-old bride, Maria Luise von Quistorp, now Maria von Braun. They walked together in the hot sun.

Fellow engineers doffed their hats or inclined their heads in deference.

She wore a simple Kerrybrooke blue dress, which she'd ordered from a Sears catalog, with a belt of the same color and black leather shoes. They took an elevated walkway through a large flower garden, and passed a plot of green grass next to a little creek whose banks had been planted with forget-me-nots and marsh marigolds.

"How is your book progressing?" Maria asked.

She had a pleasant voice and spoke in German.

"My dear, Major Staftoy has invited me to become a member of an exclusive club. It is extremely important. I already accepted, because I am sure you would want me to."

"I will see you even less."

"You will have more time to practice your English." He took both of her hands. "I will ask Arthur to take you to the movies. My dear, I am sure you want me to be happy as you are."

"Then you must do something for me."

"What is that?"

"I've discovered a little Lutheran church in Alamogordo. You will come with me on Sunday mornings."

"Of course I will."

They ducked through a hole in the fence to walk among the dunes. Maria noted the bunny ear cacti in bloom. "Aren't they enchanting."

"It is not much of a place, is it?" He gazed at the violet mountains. "But it is beautiful. Quite unlike anything at home."

"*Ja*, it is beautiful. And peaceful. Do you think it has changed you, my dear?"

"Maria, do you think I need to change?" He looked at his young spouse. "You are not the first to suggest that I should."

"*Nein*," she smiled. "But it is so different here…"

When they returned to the confines of Fort Bliss, Major Staftoy approached at a brisk pace.

"Good afternoon, Mrs. Von Braun," he said. "Ma'am, I'm sorry, but I need to have a word with your husband."

Maria excused herself, and the two men moved toward one of the supply huts.

"It's about your brother."

"What has he done?"

"Now let's not blow this out of proportion." Staftoy sucked on his pipe. "It seems your Magnus sold a bar of platinum for a hundred dollars to a jeweler in El Paso. The MPs caught him in the act. They brought him back and confined him to his room. He's admitted he brought the bar to the United States in violation of customs laws. I already called the Justice Department. They're not too happy about it."

Staftoy had never seen von Braun's face so red.

He hastened to add, "I can understand why any of you…Magnus might need the money, but regulations are regulations."

"Major, may I be permitted to deal with this in my own way? After all, he is my family." Staftoy gave him an inquiring look. "I guarantee no German in this camp will ever break a rule again."

"Okay, Wernher. Let's go."

They quickly covered the short distance to a little barrack beneath the hot sun. Magnus had been given his own lean-to because of von Braun's importance and had decorated his door with wine-cup flowers picked from the desert.

Staftoy dismissed the MP standing guard, and von Braun entered without knocking.

The major hesitated, then walked away.

Magnus lay on his cot in a tank top and gray slacks but jumped up immediately upon seeing his brother. He quickly read Wernher's expression and realized at once what he intended. Magnus was astonished by his acceptance of it.

Wernher slapped his brother's face hard, knocking him to the floor, then straddled him.

"What were you thinking?" he shouted with raised hand.

"I am sorry. You must forgive me."

"Der Zug ist schon abgefahren!"

Wernher clenched his fists and struck him once, twice, and bloodied his nose.

Another blow nearly broke his jaw. Wernher had tears running down his face, yet he didn't hear Magnus's cry of pain with each blow.

"Must I teach you a lesson you should already know?" he panted.

Magnus cradled his battered face with red hands.

"Do you want to ruin everything—everything we have worked so hard for?"

"I am sorry, I am truly—"

"Why do you do this to me—to us?"

Wernher collapsed on the cot and pulled violently at his hair.

"Why?"

The two brothers were silent.

The elder von Braun washed his hands in the tiny sink and left to find Maria.

He would say nothing of the affair to her.

* * *

The next morning before dawn, Magnus hurried across camp in a topcoat with a small tan suitcase in hand.

At the gate, the guards were perplexed by the German's irrational request to leave without permission; they threatened to report him.

Magnus returned to his room with bowed head.

Chapter 68

"Truman Acts to Save Nations from Red Rule; Asks 400 Million to Aid Greece and Turkey"

—The New York Times

The White House, Washington, DC
Friday, April 11, 1947

"I can assure you, these saucers are real," Admiral Byrd said to President Truman. "They are not constructed by Russians or Germans."

"Well, they sure as hell weren't built here," Truman said from behind his desk in the Oval Office. "If they do exist, the question is, are they constructed by any power on this Earth?"

"That remains to be seen," said Forrestal. "The theory—"

"Show me!" Truman said, pointing to a plaque next to his ink blotter. On one side was the motto, "The buck stops here," and on the other, facing Byrd, "I'm from Missouri."

"I'm from Missouri, the Show-Me State. You've got to *show me* the evidence. Where are your photographs? Didn't anyone have a camera to take a picture of the flying whatchamacallits?"

"Mr. President, I've seen them, too," said General Eisenhower, who'd come home to be chief of staff of the United States Army. "I read many reports during the war, and I can say we're definitely dealing with something solid."

"The Nazis knew about them before we did," Forrestal got in. "A man named Kammler and his SS organizations were back-engineering their own saucers. They had some success, but the end of the war put a stop to it. I've seen what was left behind."

Forrestal, Eisenhower, and Admiral Byrd had been invited to President Truman's "daily digest" meeting, during which he was briefed on the latest intelligence. Also present were Dr. Vannevar Bush, Major Bruce Staftoy, and General Twining, the last framed on the opposite side of the room by gray drapes and gray-green walls.

"Do we have any idea where the ships are from and who's flying them?" Truman asked.

"No, sir," Twining replied.

"Do we know what these SOBs are after?"

"We don't know that either." Twining looked to his boss for support, but Ike wasn't making eye contact, so he went on. "Sir, I'm a military man. This isn't the first time they've penetrated our airspace, so we have to treat them as hostiles."

"We won't want the newspapers or radio getting their hands on any of this," said Vannevar Bush, who chaired the Joint Research and Development Board of the Army and Navy. "We were in a similar position on the Manhattan Project, Mr. President. It was war; we couldn't tell anyone. This is war, too. Same thing. It can't get out. Not now and probably not for many generations."

"There's no need for dramatics, Van," Truman said. "The government doesn't need to cover itself up. It's so inefficient it will do that all by itself. But what do we say if they land in front of the White House? We have no control over this at all…"

He rose from his desk and scratched his head.

"We'll create less panic in the streets if we disclose what we already know," Forrestal argued. He didn't agree with Bush on the subject of secrecy. "Besides, we can't stop the papers from—"

"But we don't know anything real," Bush interrupted with a condescending, professorial air. "Not a thing until we can acquire one and analyze it, or somehow question one of the pilots. And that's assuming we can even find a way of talking to one."

"They've snooped around a dozen bases," Twining said. "They mean us harm, and we know it. The problem is, we can't do anything about it."

"Where is this Kammler?" Truman asked.

"None of my Germans know," Major Staftoy answered. "We've been watching them closely. We monitor their mail and telephone calls."

"I thought Donald Donaldson was tracking Kammler down," Forrestal said.

"That's right." Eisenhower smoked his cigarette. "But Kammler could be in several places. He may have gone to ground behind the Iron Curtain or in the Middle East or South America. His death has been reported too many times to be true—wishful thinking, I say—but Donaldson has leads."

"I'm organizing a VIP group," Truman announced. "With Van in charge and Forrestal as balance. They'll collect and evaluate any saucer information. We need solid evidence one way or the other."

"I have to agree with Twining." Byrd pulled at his ring. "General MacArthur has confided to me his fears that we'll be attacked. I for one urgently advise that our current security be strengthened."

"Major Staftoy," Truman said, "that's where the army might come in. What about 'your Germans,' as you call them?"

"Von Braun and his team have been cooperative in the extreme," Staftoy said. "We're now proficient in launching V-2s, and they're itching to make a better rocket. They have a number of useful ideas about potential weapons in space."

"We could be in a real pickle here." Truman sat on the arm of a chair. "Word is out they're here on American soil, and people don't like it. I may have trouble getting funding." He scanned the room. "I want you all here while I talk to Dingell. We're in a bind. You'll hear it for yourself."

Truman threw a switch on his intercom. "Tell him to c'mon in."

Twining and Eisenhower took a seat on the office's red couch. Through the window behind them in the White House gardens bloomed red roses, yellow daffodils, and grape hyacinth.

John Dingell, Democrat from Michigan, entered with a file in his hand. He had a crew cut and glasses. “Thank you for seeing me, Mr. President.”

“What can I do for you, Congressman?” Truman took up a position behind his mahogany desk.

“Mr. President, many of us in Congress have heard disturbing stories from our constituents about a pack of Germans the army has brought over. They are currently residing at Fort Bliss.” He opened his folder. “May I read just a couple of headlines?”

“Go ahead.”

“‘German Scientists Plan Refueling Station in Sky en route to Moon’ is one. ‘Jobs for German Scientists Opposed’ is another. I have many more. What we want to know is, what exactly are these former Nazis doing here and why were they smuggled in?”

“Well, I’ll tell you why. To utilize their expertise and shorten the last war. At first. As it turns out, we’ve also prevented them from falling into the hands of the communists. The communists have their own pack of Germans, but we have the cream of the crop.”

“May I say for the record,” Dingell said, looking defiant, “I’ve never thought we Americans were so poor mentally that we had to import scientists for the defense of our country. I’d also like to read from a letter sent to your office last December, for I also received a copy.” He withdrew several typed pages from his folder. “Strangely you haven’t seen fit to release this letter to the press. As you know, it was written by a group of prominent individuals, including Albert Einstein, Rabbi Stephen Wise, and Norman Vincent Peale. It reads, ‘We hold these individuals (the Germans) to be potentially dangerous carriers of racial and religious hatred. Their former eminence as Nazi Party members and supporters raises the issue of their fitness to become American citizens and hold key positions in American industrial, scientific, and educational institutions.’”

“Look, I don’t like it all that much either,” Twining said from the couch. “But we sure as hell can’t let the commies get ahead because we’re too particular about our country’s guests. It’s distasteful to some degree,

I admit, but if our country of 130 million Americans can't absorb 350 German engineers, no matter what their former politics, our so-called democratic values aren't worth a damn."

"Right." Truman addressed Dingell: "But I assure you—not a single one of these men will get citizenship on my watch. Does that satisfy Congress?"

"It does," Dingell replied. "For now. Major Staftoy, can you guarantee these Germans under your charge at Fort Bliss and elsewhere pose no immediate danger?"

"We're keeping them on a tight leash."

At a sign from Truman, an aide opened the door. The meeting was over.

Chapter 69

"Flying Disk Fever Spreads to Tehran, Iran"

—Denton Record-Chronicle

Moscow, Union of Soviet Socialist Republics
Monday, April 14, 1947

Chief Designer Korolev had been summoned by Stalin. At the Kremlin's Senate Building, Sergei Pavlovich had to pass through numerous checkpoints and was searched twice before being allowed to walk down a long corridor made silent by an equally long green carpet.

He ascended a marble staircase, at the top of which a staff member showed him into a plain waiting room already occupied by three men with vacant eyes. Thick purple drapes on two windows blocked out most of the sunlight. Korolev, in his dark-brown suit and light-green tie, sat on an uncomfortable bench built into the wall. With his briefcase on his knees, he pondered the unpredictability of the regime. He usually shut out memories of his arrest and years of hardship, but in the circumstances he couldn't prevent his mind from reaching back.

Corpses dumped in frozen ditches.

He liked to think his reprieve and rehabilitation permanent, but he had no illusions. Glushko often said that too much success could be equally dangerous, and Korolev trusted him, despite his recent petulance.

Korolev's thoughts about Stalin had not changed, however; he preferred to believe his leader bore no responsibility for his imprisonment, that he knew little about the extent of the purges carried out in his name.

He waited with the other three in silence. Each judged it better not to speak. When a bald secretary addressed one of them, an older bureaucrat in a poorly tailored suit, Korolev saw the older man stiffen and wipe his sweaty hands on a dark-yellow handkerchief. He picked up his crumpled valise and vanished into the adjoining suite.

Korolev leaned back against an uncomfortable wooden headrest. He resented the presence of Nazi engineers in Russia but wasn't sure what to say to Stalin.

He closed his eyes.

I will let the moment decide.

An hour later he proceeded through a pair of massive oak doors into a cubbyhole-like anteroom where two bodyguards frisked him yet again and confiscated his briefcase.

On the threshold, Stalin's personal secretary warned him, "Do not become excited. Do not even think about disagreeing with him. Comrade Stalin knows everything."

A door opened to a short corridor that led to a study. At a large desk on four sets of paired wooden legs, Stalin smoked his famous pipe with its black shaft and golden band. A detailed map of the Soviet Union hung on a wall of paneled oak; in the left corner, by a conference table covered in thick green felt, was an ornate red stove with gold trim.

"Good morning, Comrade Stalin," Korolev said.

The general secretary looked up but did not extend his hand.

"Welcome, Comrade Sergei Pavlovich Korolev," he said slowly, in a low voice. "Sit."

Korolev positioned himself squarely on a solid wooden chair opposite the general secretary, whose face, ravaged by smallpox, was half lit by a bulbous lamp. A stationery set, a silver ink blotter, and a plain black phone at the front of the desk acted as a wall between them.

Stalin gazed at a family photo, and for a moment his mind visibly wandered. "What a curse they are," he muttered before shifting his eyes back to Korolev. "Give me a report on the Germans and your progress."

Sergei Pavlovich, without his briefcase, recited his prepared notes from memory; Stalin listened in silence, puffing on his pipe with half-closed eyes.

When Korolev went into more technical details, Stalin remained interested and even posed questions. Korolev sensed that Stalin, unlike many of the generals he'd briefed, had a grasp of what rockets were about.

"In Germany," Korolev concluded, "we formed the most valuable basis for a solid team of forward-thinking Russians with similar ideas and enthusiasm."

The general secretary removed his pipe and said quietly, "I am concerned about accuracy of delivery. This is something we must improve."

"Of course—Comrade Stalin, I have to admit we no longer need these Germans. They are receiving two or three times the salary and much better food than our Soviet counterparts. Without these Germans, we will carry on and we will improve on their work with a more accurate rocket and a longer range. We can go beyond the V-2."

"Your OKB is eager to start on the Paketa-3, this I know. Stalin will authorize its production." The general secretary's reference to himself in the third person was a well-known habit. "Stalin would like the P-3 to be operational within the year. How difficult would it be?"

"We will have to obtain some hard-to-find materials, but it can be done."

"Good. We must be patient. When we have milked them dry, Stalin will send the Germans home." He knocked ashes from his pipe into a tin ashtray. "Let's face it: technology decides everything. Technology will make it easier for us to talk to shopkeeper Truman. Then Stalin will confound him with rockets."

He circled his desk, which allowed Korolev to see the whole man. Stalin was dressed in a green military uniform and black military boots. The two men measured the same, about 1.6 meters tall. He moved deliberately as he spoke—"Come with me"—and stepped toward a portrait of Lenin. He put his hand behind the molding into a hidden recess and pressed a button.

The wall and painting swung inward to reveal a paneled corridor.

"You will tell no one of this."

Korolev followed the general secretary into a windowless room with a row of tall filing cabinets along two gray walls. Stalin flipped a switch and a single bulb lit up five orderly piles of photographs and documents on a narrow table.

"I want you to go through all this," he said, tapping each of the piles. "You will tell me what you think of it." He looked at his watch. "You have two hours."

He returned to his office, and Korolev began sifting through the papers. He'd learned enough German and English to understand many of them. He studied photos of a damaged saucer at Christchurch, New Zealand. He read articles and examined more photographs, these from Missouri, dated 1941, of a large silver disc split in half and three small bodies, about a meter long, weird humanoids with oblong heads and large black eyes. Close-ups showed symbols on the saucers that looked to Korolev like Egyptian hieroglyphics.

Some of the documentation from other countries had been translated, and he skimmed them quickly. His colleagues often talked in private of the saucers, but he was taken unawares by the general secretary's interest in the phenomenon.

Precisely two hours later, Stalin lumbered back. His slitted amber eyes impressed Korolev with their cunning. He reexamined several photos before asking, "Well, what is your expert opinion, Chief Designer Korolev?"

"My opinion is that none of these craft are manufactured in the United States or any other country. Nor are they aggressive. Not yet anyway. Their technology is of a different order from ours. If I could study one up close, I—"

"Good." Stalin seemed satisfied. "I can tell you that your opinion is shared by a number of other specialists."

Korolev hesitated. "There is a man the Germans speak of when they are alone. Kammler," he said. "And another, named Schomberger. We should find them."

"The Zionists have taken Schomberger. Fortunately, our intelligence team confiscated his research papers from a flat in Vienna; I will have copies made and sent to your office. As for Kammler, we are trailing the American spy who is trailing the Nazi pig."

In his study, Stalin added, "I will read your reports with interest, Comrade Chief Designer."

Minutes after Korolev had shut the door behind him, Stalin picked up the black phone on his desk and told his personal secretary, "I like this man. He rings true. Stalin must have another talk with him soon. In the meantime, increase surveillance."

He hung up and walked to the corner window and gazed across Red Square. The stately view always calmed his anxieties.

Kapustin Yar, Union of Soviet Socialist Republics
Tuesday, June 17, 1947

Korolev and Gröttrup surveyed workers rolling out the first A-4 to be assembled in Russia. Its vehicle number 010T was stenciled on one side. To ease its approach to the firing stand, snowplows had leveled the yellow sandy soil.

Gröttrup wore a long wool coat that hung loosely over his suit; he knew he'd been sent for only because Ustinov was in a panic. The rocket's automatic control had malfunctioned. Measurements had been carried out again and again, but the tricky testing instruments would not register a correct deflection. The Russians couldn't launch if they didn't find a solution soon, which put several careers in jeopardy.

A dry wind swept swirling dust and tumbleweed across the rocket's path.

"I pray the test stand holds," Gröttrup said.

It had been brought piece by piece from Germany and, to his astonishment, reassembled within a few days by a welding brigade recruited from nearby Stalingrad.

"It will hold," said Korolev, who sported a Lenin cap and a short jacket over a long tan peasant's shirt, with pants tucked into knee-high boots caked with gray dust. "You should be thinking about answers. Be more concerned with your rocket. Even if it launches, it will be watched closely and we will be judged. All of us."

"What will you do if we cannot find a remedy—will you shoot us?" Gröttrup sneered. "It is not our idea to be here."

Their spoken language switched from German to Russian when Ustinov, Glushko, and Chertok joined the two engineers. While the A-4 completed its slow journey to the firing stand, they discussed the problem in raised, nervous voices. While the A-4 was straightened into position, the group moved closer and chanced to see a workman fall off the scaffolding with a surprised scream. He plunged sixty feet onto a concrete slab, where his skull cracked open with a high-pitched pop. Gröttrup blanched, but the others barely took notice.

"These peasants monkey about cheerfully enough," Ustinov remarked.

* * *

Late at night, differences in rank and class ceased to exist. Russians and Germans became a united and wildly excited family. Past wrongs were forgotten during two hours of open, heated conversation. They pinpointed the source of their suffering: a gyro relay, two thin wires to signal the oscillation of the rocket to the control point, which was reacting unduly to shocks and vibrations.

That early morning, they made adjustments, and the gyro behaved as planned in a controlled test. A single cloud wafted pink in a clearing sky, and they rejoiced. Workers and technicians ate their breakfast standing up, too edgy to do otherwise, chewing on mutton, rice, and melon, thinking only of the launch. Constant winds churned up tall pillars of sand that spun across the steppe.

Fueling took another two hours. Korolev studied reports from weather stations. Instruments were synchronized.

At zero minus five, the launching platform sagged sideways. One leg of the test stand had given way.

A crew dashed from a wooden barrack to the stand. They winched up the platform and the fully loaded, highly combustible rocket, using girders as props, while a second crew replaced a pyrotechnic device.

"All clear!" Korolev announced. "Zero minus four, minus three… fire!"

At 10:47 a.m., a sonic blast ripped the sand off the testing field.

The heat of the flames warmed Korolev and Gröttrup even in the bunker. Stereo telescopes followed its course. Time recorders in the control room printed their strokes on paper.

The A-4 traveled 206 kilometers in seconds and nearly hit its target in the deserted steppes.

Ustinov embraced Korolev, who embraced Gröttrup. Korolev's black eyes shone. Stalin would be pleased. The German foreman of the launching squad laughed with his subordinates, who shook hands with a beaming Chertok and Glushko. Gröttrup had never seen such ebullient turmoil, which even infected his colleagues for a minute or two until they recovered their decorum. The Russians went on celebrating, whooping and shouting, showing the steel crowns in their teeth. Chertok pulled a soldier's flask of pure alcohol out of his pocket and passed it around.

"Does not our first launch call for rejoicing?" Ustinov asked Gröttrup, grabbing him forcefully by his shoulders. "Are you not eager for your reward?"

"We cannot play around here like naked savages," Gröttrup said. "There is more to come tomorrow. The next missile has got to be readied."

Chapter 70

"George Marshall Plan for Europe: Pledge, Warning—Grab in Hungary by Reds Blasted"

—The Times-Picayune

Fort Bliss, New Mexico/Texas
Tuesday, July 8, 1947

With a Brandenburg concerto playing quietly on his phonograph and a martini from the clubhouse at hand, von Braun labored over his trip to the Red Planet. A light tap on the window broke his concentration. It was Staftoy. Von Braun cracked open the window, careful not to wake Maria in the adjacent bedroom.

"Let's go," Staftoy whispered. "Grab your coat. We're taking a plane."

"May I—"

"No, you can't tell Maria anything."

Within minutes they'd boarded a Piper Cub and were flying through cold midnight air. Their pilot followed the highway below in a northerly direction until they banked east at Alamogordo.

"Can I be allowed to know our destination?" von Braun shouted to Staftoy.

"Sorry, no can do!"

They landed on a small private airfield with a bump. The two men jumped into the backseat of a waiting jeep, whose driver floored it.

"Keep your eyes on the road ahead of us," ordered the MP riding shotgun. "Don't look to either side—that's an order!"

A few miles later they stopped at a cordon of trucks and smaller vehicles with their headlights on. Armed troops patrolled the area. Several floods lit up the sky.

Staftoy and von Braun signed a security statement supplied by another MP and were issued white gloves.

"Follow me," a tall man in a black suit ordered.

With long steps, he led Staftoy and von Braun through a series of checkpoints, where their identification and credentials were repeatedly checked against a master list. "Major General," the man said without turning, "I'm Quincy Adams. With all due deference, I've been instructed to inform you both that when we arrive at the designated locale, you should not talk to anybody unless you are given permission. You will not be on a Hollywood movie set. It will be real, and it is highly classified. You cannot talk to your family about this. You may talk to no one about this. Do I make myself clear? You do not want to be erased. Disappeared. The air force has given us absolute control."

They emerged from a long green tent into what appeared to be a crash site. Dozens of military men and civilians were picking their way among debris that littered the ground and desert shrubs, illuminated by powerful lights on stands. In eerie silence, von Braun and Staftoy followed an indicated path until, some distance away, they spotted a damaged delta-shaped silver vehicle. It had apparently skidded along until it burrowed itself into a hillock. It had plowed up the earth for at least a hundred yards. Its topside tailfins pointed outward at forty-five-degree angles.

Amazing, von Braun thought.

About twenty men in uniform formed a human wall, shoulder to shoulder, and went on hands and knees inching forward across the ship's path. They stored any speck of found material in burlap pouches. Other workers loaded a large wrapped object onto a lowboy flatbed truck.

"I'm going to ask a few questions." Staftoy moved off to where air force technicians and signalmen had gathered.

With gloved hands, von Braun picked up a shiny fragment of what resembled at first glance to be flimsy aluminum foil. Its texture reminded him of a rattlesnake skin he'd come across at White Sands. Though it weighed next to nothing, the fragment was extremely strong.

"What do you think, Herr Professor? Is it Soviet technology?" Von Kármán approached, nearly shouting. "This is something new, is it not?"

"You there!" an MP ordered from nearby. "No talking!"

Von Kármán shouted back, "What are you going to do? Shoot us?" He said to von Braun, "Follow me."

Together, they proceeded to the vehicle wreckage and stepped inside a kind of open shell. Von Braun estimated it had been about ten meters across. A dim light emanated from its ceiling, where glass-like wires as thin as arteries twisted through a gray harness.

A junction. But where is the energy source?

He examined the back of two "chairs" built into the craft's infrastructure that had not been thrown clear. Looking out through a "window," he was surprised to see that the exterior landscape was visible in the darkness, lit up not by sun or lamp but through some artificial means.

"Two ranchers were sitting on their porch," von Kármán said, "and saw a large glowing object fall out of the sky from the southeast, going maybe five hundred to one thousand miles an hour. There may have been two or three. I believe they're trying to see what our nuclear bomb squadron is up to. The air force's best guess is that our radar doesn't agree with their machinery, whatever it is. Because when two powerful radars focused on it, the saucers came down."

He gestured to what may have been a single panel of instrumentation; a soft yellow glow radiated from its glyphs. "You and I are supposed to advise on what all this is. Who made it, where it comes from. I'm heading up an ad hoc council. We need you to tell us if this is a 'V' weapon."

"I can say it is definitely not the work of any German scientists I know," von Braun said, examining the panel. "I doubt very much it is Russian. The material is something I have never seen before. Never."

"Nor I." Von Kármán ran his gloved hand along the ceiling. "It doesn't appear to be made of metal as we know metal on Earth. Maybe something biological, such as synthetic skin. What about your Kammler? Was he involved with something similar?"

"Kammler? Let's be frank." He verified they were alone. "The German, Soviet, and American military have been aware of saucer-like flying vehicles for at least a decade. Probably longer. Aerial intelligence on all sides have monitored and photographed them."

"That's correct. But what about Kammler?"

"Your guess is as good as mine. Where are the pilots? The crew?"

"I'll take you to them."

Von Braun followed the professor out of the saucer and over a ridge, past Adams, who glared at them, to a tent marked with a large red cross. Two MPs parted a flap. Inside the makeshift hospital, Staftoy was discussing the situation with several military officers. Doctors and nurses in white scrubs hovered around two cots at the far end.

"May we approach?" von Kármán asked a nurse.

"Certainly," she replied. "One of them is gone. We've stabilized the other…"

She handed them surgical masks, and they walked over to the cots. Lying there were two creatures not more than three feet in height. Wernher thought they looked quite frail.

"You will note that their skin texture is similar to the 'skin' of their craft, but smoother," von Kármán said. "My theory is the creatures and their vehicle operate as a single unit."

Their heads seemed disproportionately large compared to their grayish reptilian bodies. In place of a nose and mouth, von Braun noted tiny slits, with ears not more than indentations. Above the cots, in a thick glass container hung from a rafter, something organic had been preserved, suspended in blue liquid.

You are right; interstellar space travel is possible.

Von Braun looked around, but no one appeared to have said or heard anything. He looked again at the live alien. It had rotated its head in his direction.

Noticing his puzzled look, one of the doctors asked, “Has it spoken to you? We’ve all been receiving telepathic messages. That’s how we’re keeping him alive.”

“Yes, uh, yes…I think so. I am not sure.”

The alien raised its large head. Its impenetrable black eyes took in the visitors and focused on von Braun, who felt his thoughts being pulled from his mind, even those from before birth.

It hurts…

He clutched his head, went down on his knees. Hands tried to help him, but he keeled over. In the few seconds it took, the German suffered no judgment, only acceptance.

Chapter 71

"RAAF Captures Flying Saucer on Ranch in Roswell Region—No Details of Flying Disk Are Revealed"

—*Roswell Daily Record*

Bern, Switzerland
Friday, August 20, 1948

Looking at James Jesus Angleton, the "cadaver," in the ground-floor apartment, Allen Dulles thought his emaciated friend's face matched his slight build. Angleton had driven all day from Rome to Bern and had been smoking ceaselessly since his arrival. Dulles had insisted that Angleton, as advisor on espionage to the newly created Central Intelligence Agency, formerly head of counterintelligence for the OSS, be present for their latest recruit's debriefing.

"We've always agreed that Germany should be a bulwark against communism, but you may balk at my choice," Dulles said.

"I doubt it." Angleton inhaled. "These are perilous times…"

Dulles, despite his mild appearance and scholarly glasses, appeared to Angleton as he was: a ruthless and brutal intelligence officer. He had succeeded in burying an OSS outpost in State Department bureaucracy and financing it with Nazi gold. He and Angleton, in cahoots with the CIA, could count on running their own foreign policy for the next decade.

"Where'd you find him?" Angleton coughed and drank from his glass of scotch on ice.

"South America. Just before the Zionists."

"What are we offering?"

"In exchange for blueprints and documents, which he claims number in the thousands, he'll work for us. He'll be *useful*." Dulles emphasized his favorite word and glanced at the cuckoo clock. "He stood at the pinnacle, knew everybody. We can reconstitute his intelligence network. He and Himmler dangled their technological *Wunderwaffen* in front of our noses for a good year before the end. We want—that is, the Group wants one of those saucers."

"SS. Of course."

"I'll propose a large sum of discretionary cash and the promise of protection. Maybe even citizenship. Trained killers are always *useful*."

"Our friends in Israel might object."

"That's your job. You'll convince them. The Nazi genocide is over. The Soviet menace is on the move."

They heard footsteps on wooden stairs climbing from the bank of the river to the rear entrance of their apartment. A coded knock. Angleton swung open the door.

Former CIC man Donald Donaldson entered in a rumpled gray raincoat. When he saw Dulles, he signaled to the figure behind him to come forward into the light.

The second man wore a black raincoat: Kammler.

ACT IV

Chapter 72

"Flying Saucers Now Top Secret—Armed Services Won't Talk About Them Any More"

—*Detroit Free Press*

Bethesda, Maryland
Sunday, May 22, 1949

James Forrestal, until recently Secretary of Defense, was being held against his will in a naval hospital. He'd been removed from government office, stripped of title. He'd physically collapsed a few days later. He hadn't functioned well in the Group. These were facts he'd readily admit to, but he hadn't given his consent to be drugged and driven to the hospital by Vannevar Bush's chauffeur. He didn't want a naval corpsman standing sentry in the adjoining suite. He suspected more guards loitered in the hallway, to screen visitors and deflect newspapermen.

Forrestal wrung his hands and glanced at a bank of fog pressed against the window glass. The effects of the medication they'd been forcing him to take—and inexplicably stopped—had worn off. He'd avoided taking his prescribed sedative. They'd been using sub-shock insulin therapy on him, so he'd gained weight. He'd eaten a thick steak for lunch and had meticulously shaven. They wanted him to behave, though he knew, and they knew, he wouldn't.

A light tap on the door and his former protégé, John F. Kennedy, entered. He'd recently been elected congressman for Massachusetts's Eleventh District.

Forrestal had on a bathrobe over blue pajamas.

"Truman asked me to resign and I refused," he said. "What's the official story?"

"Nervous breakdown. Your diagnosis in the press is, er, involutional melancholia. A serious depressive condition."

"Oh no." Forrestal sat on the edge of the bed. "It never ends. They're trying to get me…I'm glad you're here. They've been monitoring who goes in and out. I want to brief you."

"I heard you were giving unauthorized briefings, even to the opposition." Kennedy crossed his arms. He thought it odd that hospital authorities had put a potentially suicidal man on the sixteenth floor and strange that he hadn't been able to talk with Forrestal's psychiatrist, who'd left abruptly for Canada.

"Yes, I've decided to come clean. I thought the president would support me. He didn't. Instead they put me here. He sent LBJ and Dulles to see me. I used to like Allen—until this morning. Jack, I didn't take you to see those secret facilities in Germany for nothing. You've seen the craft with your own eyes. Von Braun and those Paperclip bastards—they've known for years."

"And yet it's still hard to believe."

Forrestal's thin mouth became so tight, he seemed to swallow his lips. "That's why news of the alien existence has to come from on top. Me. My brother Henry's coming tomorrow to get me out of here, and I'm coming clean. About everything. The cover-up is terribly wrong, Jack, and what I'm going to tell you will make you vulnerable. It's more than you think. They're watching you, too. They're watching Byrd and anyone in the know."

Forrestal has always been drawn pretty fine, thought Kennedy, who detected an inner wobble in his friend. Forrestal had been twisted out of shape by what they'd seen.

"You feeling okay, James?"

"The doctors have been giving me stuff, shooting me with needles. They won't tell me with what. Jack, we're both Catholics, born and raised, but this phenomenon means a whole new cosmology. I admit to you that I'm afraid of being punished, of being labeled a bad Catholic—even though the Vatican has known for centuries! They're terrible liars. That's how I'm getting out. My brother's been pulling strings. Jack, the word 'secrecy' should be banned in an open society." His mind wandered. "But we're not secure either; America's always at risk, always…"

Kennedy made his mentor drink a glass of water; he brewed some stale coffee he found in a kitchen drawer and made him drink that, too.

The two men talked until early morning. Kennedy told Forrestal that his priest had tried to visit him six times but had been blocked.

Not long after the congressman left, Forrestal was packing his things.

He hadn't noticed that the naval corpsman had vacated his post.

Nor did he sense the others in his room.

"You're not leaving here," said a flat voice.

Forrestal spun about to see two large men.

A third was standing quietly behind them, his face in the shadows.

Forrestal's mind seized up. It couldn't be, but it was. He knew him from photos and a long hunt. The perfect Dulles recruit. Kammler.

"An example must be made of you," Kammler said. "Punishment for treason is dishonorable death."

Forrestal tried to wedge himself through the two thugs, but the larger one grabbed him by the scruff of his neck. The other, with clenched yellow teeth, shoved a towel into his mouth. Forrestal surged forward again and was yanked back harder. Two strong hands squeezed his throat shut. He gasped for air, tried to gouge out their eyes.

The larger man shattered a glass vase against his head, and his body sagged.

The other stripped the belt from Forrestal's robe and cinched it round his neck. He smiled and peered closely into the ex-Secretary of Defense's face.

"The syringe," Kammler snapped.

His men ripped off Forrestal's pajama top and gave him a shot.

They dragged him into the kitchen and opened a window. Cold air smacked their faces. They heaved Forrestal feetfirst into the wet night, but he came to and pushed against them. His taut fingers scratched at the windowsill.

They let him pull himself up, before punching his face and ripping his hands from the sill.

Forrestal fell through the air to a splashing, crashing thud on an elevated passageway between two wings of the hospital.

"Quickly!"

They tied one end of Forrestal's dressing-gown sash to the radiator and tossed the other end out the window to make it look like he'd tried to hang himself.

In the elevator down Kammler thought, *Dulles will be grateful.*

The high-level assassination had gone off without a hitch. A test. His organizational skills were as sharp as ever.

Having slipped into America without detection, Kammler boarded a TWA morning flight for Paris.

Chapter 73

"Red Korean Forces Invade South"

—San Antonio Sunday Light

San Antonio, Texas
Tuesday, November 6, 1951

Von Braun ducked out of a conference on upper-atmosphere medicine and stepped up to the hotel bar. He was looking for someone and ordered a drink.

Now the Soviets have the atom bomb, he thought. *Korea. War has once again...*

Staftoy wanted his group to concentrate on surface-to-surface guided missiles. With atomic warheads.

Finally. Improved laboratories for guidance. Better computers. More technicians...

Von Braun intended to "drum up business," as he liked to say, at the conference. His evangelical fervor needed another outlet, for the hyperenergetic German had been unable to find a willing publisher for his book.

He spotted the man from *Collier's* magazine gazing at a crystal highball between his two hands.

He moved to a stool next to him.

"Too much math?" von Braun asked. "I could not understand physics when I was younger. But to go into space and travel to Mars, I had to learn it, so I did."

The man from *Collier's* looked at him. "Professor von Braun? We've met before."

"Are you the fellow who—"

"Cornelius Ryan. Former war correspondent; today, editor at *Collier's*." Ryan had an accent borne from his youth in Ireland and had a long, handsome face with red arched eyebrows that matched the color of his receding hairline. "They sent me down here to find out what you 'serious' scientists think about the possibilities of exploring outer space." He scowled, threw his head back, and gulped down his highball. "But I don't know what half you people are talking about. Most of what I've seen is a lot of eggheads covering blackboards with mysterious signs. Our readers will never understand that. They'll think they're being hoodwinked."

"Let me see if I can summarize Professor Strughold's theory."

"If you can explain what that old Nazi said, dinner is on me."

Ryan wanted to see how von Braun would react to his choice of words, but the German let it wash over him. Experience had taught von Braun that although many of those he encountered initially despised him, they also secretly admired him for having survived as a former servant of Lucifer, Beelzebub. *Der Führer.*

A jazz quartet played an Irving Berlin tune. The bartender delivered a martini, and von Braun popped a blue pill into his mouth.

"Strughold's theory is, to put it simply, that though many scientists have set the boundary between the atmosphere and space at about six hundred miles from Earth, the *biological* conditions of space begin much lower. At about fifty thousand feet. Therefore, manned orbital flight at an altitude of nine miles, or fifteen kilometers, would be, for all practical purposes, *space* flight. That is where we can begin. We already have rockets that can go higher quite easily."

"You win."

Ryan invited an illustrator from *Collier's* named Chesley Bonestell, who happened to be at the other end of the bar, to join them for dinner as they walked over to the hotel restaurant.

"Dr. von Braun, have you ever thought of going to the Moon?" Bonestell asked enthusiastically.

Wernher laughed. "Every day of my life. But, to be honest, I am more interested in going to Mars."

"Care to convince us of that possibility?" Ryan asked.

"I will need some allies," Wernher said upon spotting two colleagues. "The stake is an article in your magazine."

"Another bet? I already lost the first one."

"This is a bet you want to lose."

The German led the magazine men to a table, where he introduced Fred Whipple, chairman of Harvard University's Department of Astronomy, and physicist Joseph Kaplan from the University of Berkeley, California.

"My friends will help me to convert you," von Braun smiled.

A brunette waitress in an orange cocktail dress set their drinks and appetizers on a fine white tablecloth.

"Look, Mr. Ryan, the best way to convince your readers is to show them. That is where your friend Chesley comes in."

With a ballpoint pen, Bonestell was drawing rockets on a paper napkin.

Ryan inclined his head toward a nearby table. "Rival magazine editors from *Look* and the *Post*," he said. "Let's keep it down, fellas."

"But you see the potential interest," von Braun said confidently. "If we can establish an effective collaboration, I think you will get a good response from your readers."

"I just don't see how you're going to pay for it," the magazine editor said.

The jazz quartet launched into a rendition of Duke Ellington's "Cotton Tail."

"Ah, you're letting loose your inner taxman," Kaplan said.

Von Braun roared with a laughter designed to make him the center of attention. "Funding is important, of course," he said. "Yet, dear colleagues, we must be honest and look at history."

"Uh-oh," said Whipple.

"Every great nation has controlled either the land or the sea. In the last war America controlled the skies, and the German armies were annihilated from above. What I am proposing is that America control space itself, via a network of satellites armed with nuclear weapons. No country in its right mind would ever dare to pick a fight with us."

"I don't know..." Kaplan objected.

Ryan considered the idea. "That would get Uncle Sam to foot the bill. Maybe."

"Hold on," Whipple said. "If you were to publish Dr. von Braun's plans, your magazine would be accused of scientifically and economically bankrupting the United States. Are you prepared for that?"

"So the spoonful of sugar is weaponized space," Bonestell mused while sketching.

"Gentlemen, you are not paying attention." Von Braun took a sip from his third martini. "A rocket is also science. The Soviet Union is already planning to launch an artificial Earth satellite. But if we are first, the most deadly weapons would be in the hands of a democracy. Perhaps we could kick off a Pax Americana such as the world has never seen."

"Or an arms race that ends in global apocalypse," Kaplan said.

But von Braun had calculated well. He could see it in Ryan's eyes. The latter's realm was magazine sales, and they had all seen enthusiasm for space travel grow, thanks in part to the UFO craze; Bonestell had already filled up a dozen napkins with wild musings.

Von Braun could probably sell anybody anything he damn pleases, Ryan thought. *He's come a long way since surrendering. A long way.*

"Looks like I lost the second bet," Ryan said.

Chapter 74

"Перестало Биться Сердце Мудрого Лидера И Учителя Коммунистической Партии И Советского Народа—Иосифа Виссарионовича Сталина (The Heart of Wise Leader and Teacher of the Communist Party and the Soviet People, Joseph Vissarionovich Stalin, Has Stopped Beating)"

—*Pravda,* Moscow

Gorodomlya Island, Soviet Union of Socialist Republics
Sunday, March 15, 1953

"'All German specialists are to return to their country.'" Irmgard Gröttrup reread the directive aloud to their friends. "'They must leave within two days of Sunday. We take this opportunity to express our thanks and for the lessons taught to a new generation of Soviets.'"

The long-awaited ordinance.

She laughed.

"Stalin, our 'Little Father,' dead—and we are being sent home just when we were starting to enjoy ourselves."

Helmut Gröttrup kissed his wife on her forehead. "Our work has not been wasted, as we so often believed. The R-5 has made the conquest of space a definite possibility."

Though not a single one of them had been allowed to see the R-5's launch, the Gröttrups and their friends were confident in their contribution to its success. Hans Zeise and Franz Fibach, aerodynamicists, drank black tea in thoughtful silence. Others downed vodka from large glasses.

"Your brains have also made the destruction of our own country a distinct possibility." Irmgard sniggered and drained a glass. She was overdressed in a black skirt and silk blouse that would have been more appropriate in Berlin. "A full-blooded atomic bomb carrier born from seven years of infidelity and drunkenness. My best friend killed herself, a strong rope around her neck, and your friends, Helmut—they preferred to shoot themselves. God only knows how many mental breakdowns I've seen."

"Maybe you're right." Zeise staggered to his feet, his once thick head of hair thinned to scraps. "So many long years of work for really nothing."

"It is the politicians who ruin everything," Helmut admitted, "from that Hitler lunatic to the Americans."

"As usual you refuse to take responsibility." Irmgard leaned back in her chair. "But I am as guilty as you are. I like to live well."

* * *

Irmgard climbed into a sleigh next to her husband and their children.

"Stalin kaput! Good for you," an old peasant woman said to her.

The Gröttrups had bad hangovers.

They had said their farewell to pupils, servants, workers, mistresses, and lovers, and not without regret. They had no idea what awaited them in East Germany.

At a command from their drivers, strong horses pulled, and the single file of sleighs slid forward. Large snowflakes wafted down, but not enough to stop their winter caravan from crossing the frozen lake to the train station. A group of student engineers and locals in thick coats and fur hats peered through the falling snow until the conveyances disappeared into a white mist.

Not a single Soviet official had come to say goodbye.

Kapustin Yar, Soviet Union of Socialist Republics

A powerful ZiS 110 black limousine sped through the gates of the facility. The workers and technicians who jumped out of its way glimpsed a figure in a brown leather jacket hunched over the wheel.

At 8:30 a.m., Korolev went from his vehicle to an office building. Under his leather jacket he wore a beige linen shirt on the outside of gray trousers. He shook hands with everyone in the reception room, swiveling his compact body from one to the other. Black eyes scrutinized those who wanted money, work, or favors; he was wary of officials who wanted to steal his rubles.

In a second outer room, he removed his hat and jacket and greeted typists and assistants.

In a third room, his aged personal assistant, Antonina Otrieshka, introduced to him a younger woman: "This is Natalia Rundrov, your new secretary, Comrade Korolev."

Rundrov curtsied in a navy-blue dress bought in Moscow, where she'd also had her hair done. "Good morning, *Gospodin* Korolev," Rundrov said.

"Good morning," he said and examined her. He approved of her prettiness and divined her age at about twenty-two. Korolev had requested a young woman. He could do that now. He didn't drink to excess like his colleagues, and he was faithful to neither wife nor mistress. His colleagues and subordinates admired him for his sexual conquests.

He thanked Antonina and showed Natalia into his private office.

"Take a look," he said.

She noted tasseled red curtains and dried mimosa in a cut-glass vase on an antique stand, family photographs on the mantelpiece, and a thick hand-woven carpet.

Her boss pointed at the desk. "I picked it out myself. I must have a bouquet of lilacs on it every morning, when they're in season—and this, this is of utmost importance: no one, not even you, is allowed to touch or disturb anything."

"Yes, Comrade Korolev."

"I write in black India ink. Please make sure I never run out of that. Or paper. I have established a tradition: anybody who wishes to venture into Korolev's office must first clear it with you, Natalia Rundrov. If I am in a good mood, you will smile at them and give a slight nod, and they will enter. If I am angry or in a bad mood, you will shake your head ever so slightly, which means they are risking their neck. If I have summoned them by phone and cursed them out, you will gaze at them sympathetically and say, 'May God help you.' We will talk more later."

He dismissed her with a pat on the rear. "Now I believe my daughter—"

Natasha skipped in without knocking. "Hello, dear father. I came for the launch!"

She was the only one the Chief Designer permitted to address him using the informal *ti*. She kissed him on the cheek, as Natalia Rundrov closed the door behind her.

"Good." He reclined in one of the room's two armchairs. She plopped down in the other. "I will need someone on my side."

Natasha was eighteen and had selected, after much deliberation, a light-green party dress for her special visit. She had braided her long brown hair in two tresses, and her black eyes matched his. Although she planned to be a doctor like her mother, not an engineer, she doted on her father. Because Natasha didn't see him often, she'd been delighted when he'd sent a car to fetch her.

Korolev picked up a copy of *Collier's* with von Braun's name on the cover. "This German and I, we should be friends," he said without looking at her. Natasha thought her father sounded strange. "Look." He showed her an illustration of a space station. "These Americanese are going to beat us into orbit."

He paused.

Natasha bit her lip.

"You have grown up, my dear—you can understand many things yourself." She sensed disaster. "Your mother and I… Authorities finalized our divorce some time ago. Perhaps she told you? Well, I am telling you.

More importantly, two months ago, Nina Ivanovna Kotenkova and I were married."

Natasha cringed at the sound of her name, which she had sworn never to pronounce herself.

The translator whore has seduced him.

Her father went to the safe.

"I just remembered—you will need money."

He twirled the tumbler back and forth, swung open the reenforced steel door, reached in, and pulled out a wad of rubbles. He handed it to Natasha, who accepted the money dutifully.

She followed him without a word to the draftsmen's building, where she knew he controlled everything, down to the thickness of the lines on the technical drawings.

But I will no longer obey him. Like my mother I will love and hate him.

"You have made an error," her father said to a draftsman. "The Moon's surface is solid."

"At Bauman Institute, they say no serious scientist can support such a statement," the young man replied. "There is no proof, only speculation."

Natasha hoped the young man would make a fool of her father.

She saw her father write in his notebook, "The surface of the Moon is solid."

He tore out the page and gave it to the draftsman. "There is your scientific proof," he declared.

At another desk, for reasons incomprehensible to Natasha, he exploded. "Get over to the typing pool and dictate an order firing yourself—*without* severance pay—and bring it to me for my signature!" Despite the presence of his daughter, he swore at the mortified middle-aged man. "I will send you and this whole gang to Siberia on rails! I can make it happen!"

When he and his daughter entered the facility's canteen, over a hundred men and women fell silent. He strode to the counter and picked up his lunch, all the while shooting questions to subordinates, who shouted out answers.

Can't they see what a monster he is? Natasha glared at her father. *He is fat and his new, disgusting wife will leave him.*

At one of the long tables, a man she recognized as Comrade Chertok told her father about an argument between two men. Her father ate meat dumplings in a vinegar and mustard sauce and grunted, "I don't have the patience to sort it out. Give them another twenty-four hours to reach an agreement or I will sack them both."

The middle-aged draftsman arrived and handed his typed termination order to Korolev, who yanked it away and yelled loud enough for everyone to hear, "What? You want to go home and sit on your ass drinking tea with jam? Get back to work immediately!"

He ripped the order to shreds.

Korolev noticed his daughter hadn't touched her food, but he had other things on his mind.

* * *

As the sun set, the R-5 shot up into the sky, but Natasha had left her father's side in the blockhouse to cry in the shadows of the assembly building. She could nevertheless hear the earsplitting roar of the rocket and feel its stomach-jarring rumble.

Chapter 75

"Truce Is Signed, Ends Fighting in Korea; Eisenhower Bids Free World Stay Vigilant"

—*The New York Times*

Burbank, California
Wednesday, January 13, 1954

Ward Kimball grimaced at the mirror screwed to his animation desk at the Walt Disney Studio.

He scrutinized his own expression, then sketched a grotesque sort of cowboy with a big hat. Bill Tytla stopped by and looked at the result. Kimball had on blue suspenders over a yellow shirt; Tytla, a black vest over a cream shirt with rolled-up sleeves. Both wore dark-gray slacks and black loafers, and both were in between projects, trying to come up with gags.

Two telltale coughs from down the hall of the Animation Building told them Walt Disney wasn't far off.

Another cough and he walked in, wearing one of his blue suits and a matching tie.

"Fellas, it's driving me crazy—I've got nothing for Tomorrowland and the damn TV show!" Disney rarely beat around the bush anymore. "You guys are modern thinkers. Heck, Ward, you're practically a beatnik. Can't you think of something?"

Disney pulled out a cigarette, lit it, and slowly took a puff. He'd aged fast, his face heavy and shoulders wide, his gait slowed.

"How about something based on Edison's ideas?" Tytla suggested.

"Bill, Tomorrowland is about the future, not the past."

"How about a planet where everything is Lilliputian in size?"

Kimball sorted through a pile of magazines on a small table. "Well, there are these pretty reputable scientists who think we can go to Mars." He opened an issue of *Collier's* to a large illustration of a space station. "This guy Bonestell's terrific! I could give them a call..."

Tytla looked over Disney's shoulder as he flipped through pages of words, more illustrations, and photos, including one of von Braun.

"They make a good case that exploration of the solar system is possible," Kimball added. "There's been a series of articles, so they must be selling."

"That sounds good." Disney took another long drag. "Work something up. You're the director."

Surprised by his sudden promotion, Kimball's mind raced. "I'll phone that guy von Braun first."

Disney was halfway out the door when he turned back, tore off a blank sheet of paper from a pad on the animation desk, and handed it to his director. "Here," he said. "Write your own ticket."

Tytla's eyes practically popped out of his head. He ran his two hands through his hair and waited for their boss's footsteps to fade.

"Wow. I've never seen that before."

"Me neither."

"Either Walt's getting soft, or you've discovered his hidden Shangri-La."

* * *

Six months later two former members of the Berlin Rocket Club, Wernher von Braun and Willy Ley, were reunited at the Walt Disney Studio, brought together again by space travel. Wernher teased Willy about the weight he'd put on in America as they strolled down a hallway into the storyboard room.

Dieter was already lecturing about a theoretical Mars expedition to Kimball, Tytla, and several artists; one, sitting on a piano bench, was sketching out an idea.

"It would require a ten-ship expedition and a crew of approximately two hundred," Dieter said. "Crew quarters would be arranged in a donut-shaped parasol, whose motion would provide artificial gravity. It is all quite possible."

"That is, if pesky Martians don't bother you too much," Kimball said.

"We will have to go bearing gifts," von Braun remarked.

Tytla sighed. "I wonder what Martian women are like?"

"Gentlemen, we will certainly meet creatures from other planets," said Ley, his stomach heaving. "I suggest you prepare yourselves!"

Walt Disney walked in and asked, "Well, where are we?"

"Bill and I have come up with a few rough ideas." Kimball gestured toward layouts and drawings pinned to cork panels on the walls.

Disney examined their work.

"Not bad." He fixed on Tytla. "But we're trying to show man's dreams of the future. We should show that man has been constantly seeking a way to get up into the air. Now he wants to get out to the Moon, he wants to land on Mars, see what it looks like. People are curious; they want to know what they might find."

"The kids really get this space stuff," Kimball said.

"*You'd* better believe it, too"—Disney jabbed a finger at Kimball's chest and coughed—"if you want this story to work."

"Well, Walt, I'm skeptical," said Tytla.

"Skeptics don't accomplish a helluva lot. We'll get there; *I* believe it."

"To the Moon?"

"To Mars."

"Mr. Disney, by going into space," said von Braun, "we discover other Earths. The Moon and Mars are baby steps. Those other Earths, this is what we want to discover."

"And it is mathematically certain," Ley heaved, "that these Earths are inhabited by intelligent creatures, like ourselves. Perhaps not made like us, but doubtless with a brain or something like a brain."

"Exactly." Disney coughed and turned back to the drawings, and coughed again. "We have to set it up right. The show should combine fantasy and you experts dealing with facts." He said to Ley, "You know, too many people grow up, they forget. They don't remember what it's like to be six or nine or twelve years old. They patronize and treat children as inferiors. Well, we won't do that."

"We could add humorous notes," von Braun suggested. "One of the crew could say, 'Get your feet out of my face.' A giant loudspeaker on the ground could say things that are all wrong."

"Yes, that's good."

"I think we have enough to go on, Walt," said Kimball. "We'll keep working with the professor, Arthur, and Willy here, and have more to show you soon."

"I'm counting on it. Can't you scientist fellows dream up something even more modern, something new but technically feasible?"

"How about a spaceship powered by a nuclear-electric generator," Dieter proposed. "Or solar-electric propulsion. A nuclear reactor or solar collector could drive a turbine to provide electricity."

"Great. That's what we need."

Disney coughed so hard, the effort bent his body in two. "Uch, uch, uch!"

"For crying out loud, Walt!" said Kimball. "Why the heck won't you give up smoking?"

Disney looked at him, his eyes watering. "C'mon, Ward. A guy's gotta have a few vices."

At the door, he added, "You know, if you have enough of that new material, we'll do two shows, maybe three or four."

Chapter 76

"Eisenhower Signs Anti-Communist Law— Bill Is Aimed at Party, Red-Infiltrated Unions"

—Honolulu Star-Bulletin

Pullach, Federal Republic of Germany
Wednesday, November 17, 1954

Kammler strode through the pouring rain under an orange full moon low in the sky. He laughed to himself. The people he worked for—Dulles, Angleton, Donaldson, their CIA—they appreciated his cleverness, as well as his connections and character. His ruthless efficiency. Years ago he'd directed them to his cache of design documents and the valuable prototype, twelve thousand tons of it, smuggled out on Ju 290s. Papers on advanced weapons and technology had prompted joint operations between the CIA and the Group and allowed him to be a secret actor in both.

In the town of Pullach, through the agency of the Gehlen Organization, Kammler had reconstituted his old intelligence structure within the American national security system. His was the de facto spy agency for West Germany and, by extension, for Europe and the White House.

When Adenauer was maneuvering to become head of the new Federal Republic of Germany, American officials had not regarded him as suitable. Kammler's shadow contacts in the U.S. State Department had gone to work. Kammler despised Adenauer for his weak-kneed politics, but he was malleable and they both wanted Germany to regain its rightful place in the world.

Kammler walked down a clean street of his compound; only those with the proper clearances knew what went on inside. CIA agents and deputies lived next door to ex-Gestapo and ex-SS officers, sealed off from the outside world within a four-kilometer ring of walls and steel fences topped with barbed wire. Families socialized together; their children attended the same one-room schoolhouse. They went on joint skiing trips.

Kammler never tired of doing his part. Communists were already feasting in France and Italy.

He entered a two-story white stucco house.

In a meeting room, he surveyed the men sitting at a long table: Dr. Franz Six, a balding former *Brigadeführer*, whose sentence at Nuremberg had been reduced thanks to Dulles; two seats away was one of Kammler's former employees, Konrad Fiebig, who had overseen the extermination of Jews at Belarus; to his left, former *Obersturmfürhrer* Hans Sommer, who set Paris synagogues on fire. Sommer was making small talk with agent Quincy Adams and two members of Algeria's Eleventh Choc killing unit.

A few of East Germany's Ministerium für Staatssicherheit had also been invited. Though their superior resided in the Kremlin, Kammler had learned that certain divisions preferred the old way—his way.

He glanced behind him at the silent observers of this crucial summit, CIA director Allen Dulles, Angleton, and their darling: Reinhard Gehlen, former general of the Wehrmacht, former head of intelligence for Foreign Armies East. With his large ears and eyes, he gave the impression of an eager but starving rodent.

Dulles looked over Kammler. Electroshock therapy had polished off some of the German's rough edges, though he was as full of hate as before, in particular for von Braun. The latter's growing public persona was a painful thorn in Kammler's side. Mention of the rocketeer elicited tirades from his former boss. Von Braun, whom Kammler considered a heinous chameleon, strutted across the front pages of newspapers and magazines as a celebrated "scientist," while Kammler and their covert actions against communism had to be carried out in secret.

"Our friends in Moscow call it *dezinformatsiya*," Kammler began. "Our friends in America, as well as our enemies, call it *active measures*. Both definitions mean we must drive deep wedges into existing political structures, including NATO. We must sow discord among communist countries to weaken them in the eyes of Europe and America. Above all we must guard against the dangerous and foolhardy incompetence of leaders everywhere, for only we have all the facts. Only we see clearly.

"You may open your folders."

In unison the counterintelligence agents and assassins, wearing three-piece suits and ties or long coats, reached for the manila envelopes in front of them and spilled their contents onto the table: passports, foreign currencies, photographs, mission parameters.

"Some of you will be given scientific papers to peddle. Others will be assigned to teams developing satellites and rockets in the East or the West. Egypt is a priority. Quite frankly, some targets will have to be liquidated. In most cases, you won't have to do the dirty work. You will create witch hunts in government infrastructures through planted evidence. They will assume double agents are everywhere and will do the job for you."

Behind him, Dulles smiled.

"As part of Operation Splinter Factor, some of you will have accounts reserved for funding antiwar movements."

"The American Army is full of idiots," Adams said in a loud voice. "They can't be trusted. Castle Bravo, what a fiasco. That bomb blast wasn't just ten times more powerful than what those morons expected—it was a hundred times. The locals…hell, I'll be surprised if any of those radioactive bastards live past thirty."

"You are correct," Kammler said. "Idiots, all of them. Consequently, there is an international call for a ban on nuclear testing. They have played right into our hands."

"What about the saucers?" Adams asked.

He wanted to see Kammler squirm.

The ex-SS man's face did flush, but it was Dulles who replied, "President Truman's original Group was nothing less than a government within a government. They ruthlessly guarded their secrets. But a power struggle has developed within the Group itself. We will exploit this rift to bring it into an even closer relationship with us."

"You all have your assignments—study them," Kammler ordered. "Individual briefings will follow tomorrow morning."

Afterward, Dulles, Angleton, Kammler, and Gehlen walked along whitewashed corridors past red fire extinguishers.

"We'll have to be subtle about it." Angleton held a burning cigarette. "Washington officials are worried. And the British are saying we've sold our souls to you Germans due to our, quote, frantic and hysterical desire to thwart the Soviets. Unquote."

"There are few saintly archbishops in espionage," Dulles said. "Let us not fret. We'll win the war in the press, too. I'll give Luce a call over at *Life*."

"You had better do something to get the army do-gooders and Red journalists out of our hair," Kammler snapped. "I cannot abide their interference."

"Of course, Hans."

Dulles almost never lost his calm. He prided himself on being above crass emotions. Yet the CIA director remained an admirer of Kammler's tireless zeal. He'd been *useful* so far. He saw him as "Captain Germany" fighting for liberty. Kammler hadn't winced at the unfortunate but necessary bloodshed, like that of the rogue Forrestal. Dulles had made sure Kammler had access to highly classified information and reported, through him, to the Office of National Estimates, Washington's senior intelligence evaluation center, which in turn reported to the president. Kammler was their expert on the USSR's clandestine networks—most importantly, Kammler gave Dulles a leg up on the alien science so coveted by the Group. That knowledge would enable the merger.

They exited the building into a park.

"It's a complex world," Dulles said, and Angleton nodded. "Our job is to make it secure. Right now that means assuring the superiority of our space programs, both public and…not so public."

"I know of someone who can help," Kammler said as they walked through the park toward their homes. "Viktor Schomberger. You should have grabbed him years ago."

"Schomberger? The Zionists have him. They won't give him up."

"That's right," Angleton said. "If he perfects his antigravity work, they may even go public."

"That's a terrible idea. It would alter the balance of power."

"I can procure Schomberger," Kammler said.

Dulles thought for a moment.

"Okay. Go get him."

Chapter 77

"Reds 'Awful Close' to War, Dulles Says; Russia Close to H-Bomb, Churchill Says"

—*The Albuquerque Tribune*

Podlipki, Union of Soviet Socialist Republics
Friday, January 21, 1955

Korolev led the tour. First Secretary Nikita Sergeyevich Khrushchev was accompanied by three Presidium members wearing thick brown or black fur coats: Molotov, the aging diplomat, whom Khrushchev judged calculating and shrewd; Kaganovich, overweight and unfriendly; Kirichenko, tall and arrogant.

Khrushchev and his trio looked up through a gaping hole in the roof at a cold yellow sky. The First Secretary had been told about Korolev and the secret ballistic missile program only after taking Stalin's place at the head of the Communist Party. Upon meeting the Chief Designer, Khrushchev had been surprised when Korolev had referred to Stalin's passing as a "tragedy" and had stated in absolute terms that he admired him greatly.

The group exited the building, and Korolev suddenly thought of his daughter, Natasha. She hadn't written him in nearly a year. He banished her from his thoughts and said, "We will work in earnest to fix up this place, mostly in the areas I have designated—housing, a culture center, a stadium. We will have our own city. But our food supply is inadequate.

People who have a cow or more than three goats are not allowed to have bread. Most of the workers depend on their kitchen gardens."

They walked by grimy brick buildings and rusty hangars. Khrushchev glanced at his rectangular pocket watch, set in a steel case, and asked, "Is it true nearly two thousand laborers have left or been sent away for medical reasons?"

"Yes," Korolev replied as they entered the administration building. "The truth is I have to spend as many hours managing the welfare of my workers as I do managing research. At this rate, we will most certainly fall behind the Americanese. Fortunately, I have a plan."

They followed Korolev through his office into an adjoining room, where Ustinov, Glushko, and Chertok waited. In a corner on a polished wooden table, a red silk covering hid an object. A map of Europe on the wall had in its upper right-hand corner an inscription: "Highly Classified. Of special importance. Copy number three." Lines radiated from Russia to Europe. Korolev took up a position by the map.

"Which countries are in range?" Molotov asked.

"The R-5 can strike every nation in Europe, except Spain and Portugal."

"How many warheads would be needed to destroy England?" Khrushchev asked.

"Five. A few more for France, seven or nine, depending on the choice of targets."

"Terrible."

"Wonderful," Molotov said. "Until recently we could not even dream of such a thing. But the appetite grows by what it feeds on. Comrade Korolev, is it not possible to extend the rocket's range to America?"

"No. A new missile would be required. The R-5 is already history—so!"

Korolev pulled away the red silk to reveal a detailed scale model.

"The R-7."

Khrushchev gawked at the bulky cigar-shaped tube, about a meter in length, with a belt of smaller rockets around its base; it was a combination he couldn't imagine flying. He kept his mouth shut, however; he considered himself out of his depth.

"Comrade Glushko will make its engines," Korolev stated, and Glushko nodded. "Its five boosters will consume nearly two hundred and fifty tons of fuel in only four minutes. One million pounds of thrust will hurl it over eight thousand kilometers at a speed of over seven thousand meters per second. The Semyorka, our own R-7, will be the world's *best* ballistic missile. Its real secret is its new electronic guidance system."

Chertok nodded.

"How long will it take to fly to the United States?" Molotov asked.

"Less than thirty minutes. But it won't come cheaply; each site for the R-7 will cost half a billion rubles."

"What will we do?" the First Secretary balked. "We will be without our pants!"

"The alternative is that the Americanese, led by Professor von Braun and his German friends, will beat us into orbit. Poor Tsiolkovsky is already turning in his grave because not a single Russian satellite is yet in space. Under the czar, we would have had several up there long before now."

Korolev dared to mention the previous hated regime because he knew of the lingering insecurity and guilt in the hearts of his country's leadership.

Khrushchev removed his fur cap and rubbed his white scalp with a stubby hand. "The budget for military research is already several times greater than in America," he said. "Six times greater as a percentage of the Soviet gross national product."

"Intelligence reports say the Americanese are making only little progress," Korolev pressed. "This is an opportunity to be bold. We will beat them militarily and scientifically. Of this I have no doubt—*if* I am given the necessary financing."

"Tell me absolutely, is it possible to make this rocket work?"

"It is theoretically possible," Glushko replied. "According to my calculations, I—"

"Do not drag us into the technical details. That is your business." Khrushchev turned over in his mind the situation's many components. "Comrade Korolev, now that you are a party member, it will make things easier. Go ahead. Work on it, and we will see…"

Chapter 78

"Vietnam Becomes Red Police State"

—*The Stars and Stripes,* European Edition

Mount Carmel, Israel
Saturday, March 12, 1955

Night.

Rachel was well hidden. Angleton had warned her that morning, and she'd raced over from Tel Aviv before sunset. She knew from which direction the three bounty hunters would come—and when they appeared in the woods, she had a good view of their approach route through a glade toward the wooden cabin.

Inside the cabin was their prize: Schomberger.

Rachel killed the first man with a shot from her silenced Luger.

The soft thud of the weapon on the quiet forest ridge alerted the other two, so, to cover her movements, she crawled between two trees and paralleled a babbling creek. She'd cut her brown hair short.

The second bounty hunter was within a hundred yards of the cabin. She increased her pace and took a length of tensile wire from her jacket pocket.

The second bounty hunter was dead minutes later.

She fingered a pendant in the same pocket. She felt no malice toward the fallen agents—that was part of the change within her—but was disappointed Kammler didn't number among them.

These thoughts distracted her, however, and she lost the third man.

He'd double-backed behind her, and, taking aim with his weapon, inhaled. She heard it and would have been killed—had she not clenched her fist and twisted it. The bounty hunter twisted too, like a marionette, and missed. She threw her arm to the right, and he sprawled to the right on the ground.

"Was ist los?" he gasped, searching for his weapon.

Rachel ran over to him, gun in hand, and kicked his weapon away.

"Tell Herr Kammler this target is off-limits," she hissed. "Go back to your Stasi rat den and tell him that we will never back down—tell him the number of his days are known to me."

She allowed the bounty hunter to scramble to his feet and retreat toward the access road.

Rachel walked back up the ridge. One light shone in the cabin, where Schomberger was intent on his antigravity experiments. She'd procured for him limited funds and necessary materials.

Alone in the forest, she took a moment to consider her standing with Mossad. It provided cover. She understood the world's geopolitical situation and acted on long-term objectives even if that meant having to deal with those she abhorred: Angleton, Dulles, their CIA. Others. She wasn't sure why Angleton had double-crossed Kammler and told her about his designs on Schomberger; perhaps he'd had second thoughts about working with ex-Nazis and fascists. By the same token, she couldn't touch Kammler and his cronies if Israel wanted to maintain American goodwill.

She checked her weapon and reloaded, then headed for a shed to the rear of the cabin.

She thought of the Soviets' guided missile work behind the Iron Curtain, and that of the Americans, in public. She'd heard rumors about Egypt's clandestine rocket plans.

It should all *be out in the open.*

An antidote to the secret organizations. She fought parallel to those who schemed and killed in the dark—that was her job—but she wished to help the rocketeers who struggled in the light of day for the future of their species.

She grabbed a shovel from the shed to dig a shallow grave for the two corpses.

Chapter 79

"Satellites Which Circle Earth Are Due in '57"

—*The Russell Daily News*

Huntsville, Alabama
Thursday, March 17, 1955

Von Braun boarded a plane to Washington, DC, for a meeting arranged by Frederick Durant III, president of the International Astronautical Federation, with Commander George Hoover. Von Braun had met Durant, a test pilot and rocket engineer born into a rich family with connections, at a conference years before. Hoover was headman in the Office of Naval Research, and he wanted to get rolling on a spaceship.

Von Braun had been appointed head of the Guided Missile Development Division of the Ordnance Missile Laboratories at ABMA (Army Ballistic Missile Agency) in Huntsville, Alabama.

He opened his briefcase, took out a report to read, and considered the positive effect of the *Collier's* articles. The response had been larger and more enthusiastic than he or Ryan had ever anticipated. He received three large bags of mail every week, results of his new fame and his sudden emergence as "the greatest expert in the world on space travel." He wrote replies to everyone, children and professionals.

We are finally going somewhere, he thought.

Texas Instruments would be selling portable transistor radios in a few months, using some of the technology from the saucers. He considered the various applications for space travel to be of paramount importance.

The stewardess handed him a martini, and he swallowed two green pills with his first sip.

* * *

He met Staftoy at the airport and they shared a taxi. Staftoy had been promoted to brigadier general. The two of them oversaw nearly four thousand ABMA employees at Huntsville.

It took them a while to locate the correct room within the vast Naval Research Laboratory.

When they joined the others in an office with a view of the Potomac River, Commander Hoover was saying, "Everybody is talking about a space satellite, but nobody is doing anything about it."

Around the table were Hoover; Durant, who had the refined good looks of the patrician class; a few academics and aeronautics experts; von Kármán; Senators Lyndon Johnson and Allen Ellender from Texas and Louisiana, respectively; and Philip Corso, an ex-military man on Eisenhower's staff, who would advise and report back to the president.

"I'd like to get started with a small satellite," Hoover went on, "carried into orbit by a combination of existing rockets."

"Do we have the means for orbiting a set of lightweight scientific instruments?" asked Johnson.

"Yes," Staftoy replied. "And so do the Russians."

"Our team in Huntsville can launch a vehicle made from a Redstone missile with upper stages," said von Braun. "Topped by a small satellite of five to seven pounds."

"How much will it cost?" Hoover asked.

"We could do it for a hundred grand," Staftoy said.

"That's not much."

Ellender spoke in a southern drawl. "But the chosen vehicle for launching these satellites is the navy's Vanguard rocket, is that correct, General?"

"To be frank, the navy's Vanguard rocket is mired in technical difficulties. It's behind schedule. The army's Jupiter C test rocket is much further along."

"The Jupiter C is a military rocket. Isn't it true that the Vanguard is more suited for civilian entry into the competition? The Vanguard is an elegant composite, I'm told."

"This is not a design contest," von Braun pointed out.

His somewhat high-pitched German accent jolted Corso. It reminded him of von Braun's origins.

Bad idea to have the first American satellite launched by a prominent ex-Nazi, he thought. *Ike will never go for that. Von Braun just doesn't get how much he's disliked by this administration. Oh, they'll be polite, but…*

"This is a race to put a satellite into orbit," von Braun continued. "To claim the Vanguard possesses more dignity than ours is a weak argument. A rocket is a Cold War tool. How dignified would your position be if a man-made star of unknown origin suddenly appeared in our skies?"

"Are you talking about a Soviet satellite or a UFO?" Ellender quipped.

"Well, I'll be damned if I'll sleep by the light of a Red moon," said Johnson. "Soon they'll be dropping bombs on us from space like kids dropping rocks on cars from highway overpasses. Simply put—whoever rules space, rules the world."

"I could not agree more," said von Braun, who made a mental note to remember the senator.

"Perhaps the establishment of an independent civilian space agency could accomplish all of our mutual goals?" suggested von Kármán. "I have heard this idea thrown around before—"

"Senator Ellender," said Staftoy, "I would like to say for the record that the Soviets are much closer than the government thinks to launching their own satellite."

"The launch of a man-made satellite," von Braun emphasized, "no matter how humble, will be a scientific achievement of tremendous impact. The Soviet Union may even be ahead of us. It will be a terrible blow if we don't do it first."

"It may not be as simple to get approval as you think, Professor," Corso said. "Interdepartmental rivalries may sink you from the get-go."

The first meeting adjourned with the Vanguard still the government's rocket of choice.

The second meeting consisted of only the six members of the Robertson Panel, formed on the recommendation of the Intelligence Advisory Committee to look into possible threats posed by the saucers.

Corso had been told that Staftoy and von Braun had clearance because they needed to know certain things for their work and because of their aid in the government's reverse-engineering and antigravity programs. Yet he was uneasy passing along information to them.

Durant, on the other hand, trusted von Braun. He knew they were going to need him and Huntsville in the years to come and prayed the White House hotshots would back him despite their misgivings.

Hoover briefed them on recent encounters. "It's our belief that the entities are not so much interplanetary visitors as time travelers. I know it's hard to believe, but they may even be *us* from a future Earth."

Durant, von Kármán, and Corso had already heard this theory and didn't buy it.

It came as news to von Braun and Staftoy.

"In certain circumstances, they can manipulate reality around them. They've demonstrated this. They've also led us to believe that human beings have far more potential than we've ever dreamed of. But, and this is a big 'but,' we are early in our evolution.

"Of more concern today is the antigravity work," concluded Hoover. "Gentlemen, we need to achieve parity with the saucers."

When von Braun and Staftoy flew back to Huntsville, a car was waiting for them.

They didn't want to be late to the next official function, and the driver tore off.

Von Braun's new hometown had accepted his team of Germans, though neither the mayor nor the town elders had greeted them with open arms. Nobody would sell or even lease a house to their former enemies, so the Germans had organized. They raised more than $7,000 and purchased thirty-five acres on the crest of Monte Sano Mountain to build their homes.

Over the years, the Germans had proven themselves, and prominent locals had changed their attitude. Increased employment and a much healthier economy, spurred on greatly by the rise of ABMA, hadn't hurt.

Their car took a turnoff to the valley.

Wernher had chosen to live closer to ABMA than his compatriots. With its refurbished metallurgical and chemical laboratories, test stands, and supersonic wind tunnels, the facility reminded von Braun of Peenemünde. He wanted their new base to surpass their old one. Huntsville had road and rail hubs, a small harbor on the big Tennessee waterway, even a landing strip—everything they needed.

In the driveway of their home, Maria and their two young daughters squeezed into the car, and they sped off again.

Maria was pleased that von Braun, Debus, and their associates had helped establish St. Mark's Evangelical Lutheran Church. Only Magnus had strayed from their extended family; he'd gone to work for Chrysler, the automobile manufacturer, in Detroit.

Minutes later, the von Brauns and Staftoy jumbled out of the car and rushed into a high school auditorium packed with friends, coworkers, and town officials, who hooted and hollered and clapped their hands.

"I am so happy that the United States Army chose our modest town for their rocket base," the mayor of Huntsville proudly told the audience of over a thousand. "I can recall of no other group that in choosing America has given us so much pleasure. They have brought strength and economic vitality to Huntsville, and, I might add, made one great TV show."

Forty Germans with white carnations in their buttonholes fanned out behind the mayor. President Truman had been followed by President Eisenhower, whose office, despite misgivings, had not blocked their applications for citizenship.

Two federal district judges administered the oath to von Braun, Debus, Dieter, Rees, and their compatriots.

Many of those in the audience waved American flags. The town band played a traditional German song.

"I had my doubts," said Staftoy at the microphone. "But I'm happy to say the army has never known a better and more talented group."

Von Braun walked up to the podium, larger than life, a television star, and the crowd cheered. Some of the women and girls in the audience nearly swooned at his blue eyes and broad shoulders.

"This is the most beautiful day of my life," he said and threw up his arms. "It is like getting married for the second time!"

He kissed Maria.

* * *

A few days later von Braun was chatting with Eisenhower; to the president's right, Walt Disney and Ward Kimball occupied two plush chairs in the front row of the screening room in the White House's East Wing. Behind them, the Pentagon's top brass, various advisors, and cabinet members filed in and took their seats. Kimball tried not to gawk at the VIPs or the long, stately room, its floor-length yellow curtains, and light-blue walls with gold trim.

As the first reel of the Disney episode flickered on-screen, he was still amazed he hadn't been fired. He'd taken Walt at his word and filled in that blank check for about $250,000, a fantastic sum for a single TV show with little chance to recoup its costs.

He was relieved that their history of rocketry, told via live action and animation, seemed to grab and hold the select audience's attention.

On-screen, von Braun described his proposals using a model and charts for a four-stage orbital rocket.

A trip to the Moon was simulated in a live-action segment. As their ship circumnavigated the dark side of the Moon, one of the astronauts announced "a high radiation reading at thirty-three degrees."

The radar operator announced an unusual formation coming up below.

A third astronaut launched a flare.

Kimball peered down the row at Walt, Ike, and Wernher. None of them exhibited any emotion as the flare revealed the unmistakable geometric shapes of an immense alien moon base that should not have been there. Its bright lights sparkled in orderly lines on the surface below.

Did the president lower his eyes?

Kimball had asked Disney about that shot introduced late in the edit.

"Don't worry about it," Disney had replied.

Kimball hadn't been able to find out exactly where it came from, but he figured Walt had asked Ub Iwerks to create the special effects image. If it had been described in a memo, he hadn't seen it. If it was the professor's idea of a joke, he wasn't owning up to it.

But here it is, broadcast to all of America.

When the lights came on, the audience praised the two shows.

Eisenhower stood and said, "Over one hundred million people have seen these, but I wanted to make sure everyone in this room saw it, too. I'm going to have it shown here for a couple more weeks, so everyone can have their staffs see it."

In a drugstore booth downtown, Disney, Kimball, and von Braun ate hamburgers and fries.

Rain sprinkled outside. The minute hand on the wall clock approached midnight.

On their second cup of coffee, Disney said, "Wernher, did I tell you George Hoover wants us to do a fourth picture—a UFO picture?"

"George told me himself. I think they're ready to go public."

Kimball couldn't believe his ears. "I knew it! All these guys, and you, you know UFOs are for real. They *are* real, aren't they?"

The drugstore was empty except for a busboy wiping down the counter.

"Sure they are, Ward," said von Braun.

"I knew it. I've been collecting material—I have a cupboard full of it, every report. All the books. If we're going to do a fourth show, we've got to end it with some real stuff. We've got to!"

"You'll have it," Disney said. "A Colonel Miranda over at Wright-Patterson has the footage we need. Everything taken by fighter pilots. We'll go over there soon and have a look."

"I just knew it!"

"Ward, calm down!" von Braun laughed. "Take a pill..." He rummaged in his pockets.

"Film of flying saucers? I don't suppose they have anything good."

"Oh, hundreds of feet of it." Disney coughed and sipped his coffee. "They told me, confidentially, they have great shots, beautiful footage. Oh, the ships come in all shapes and sizes."

Through the drugstore's large windows, von Braun caught a pedestrian looking at him, smoking, from the street outside.

Something in the pedestrian's posture marked him as military.

The stranger touched his hat before vanishing into the darkness of a summer downpour.

Chapter 80

"Nasser in Egypt Says Palestine to Be Regained"

—Middletown Sunday News Journal

Tyuratam, Union of Soviet Socialist Republics
Tuesday, June 11, 1957

Korolev had moved his entire operation to a secret facility in Kazakhstan. He and his chief technicians, along with thousands of workers, were transforming an arid desert steppe at Tyuratam into a full-blown launch town.

He began his day by inspecting their vast assembly hangar, which a railway connected to a fire pit the size of a large rock quarry. A construction crew was at work on underground propellant storage tanks, not far from a cement bunker and their five-thousand-square-meter launch platform made from sixteen massive bridge trusses.

These activities distracted his mind from the rupture with his daughter.

Later that sweltering night, he and his department heads toiled in the blockhouse for nearly twelve hours enduring one aborted countdown after another.

"Take it away. I never want to see that rocket again," Korolev told Mishin. "We are criminals. We just burned away the annual budget for a small city."

Seven attempts and seven failures to launch one of their R-7 rockets. The harrowing three-day affair had decimated the launch crew's morale.

Lights blinked red on a control panel.

Lower-echelon technicians made themselves scarce, running for cigarettes and a cold supper.

Glushko stared at the flickering board.

"What can they do to us?" Chertok asked.

"They are not going to jail us or send us to a gulag," replied engineer Voskresenskiy. "That period has passed."

"Do not be so sure," Korolev grumbled. "*Khlopnut bez nekrologa*—they will throw us in a ditch, and there will be no obituary."

"The reaction may not be so severe," said Glushko, "but your rocket will be put into the hands of others."

"Never. Our ministers will understand. We are gaining tremendous experience." Korolev headed for the door. "We will try again. Soon—in a month."

Friday, July 12, 1957

At 15:53, the R-7 rocket, series number M1-7, lifted from a tulip-shaped gantry the same height as the Eiffel Tower.

Thirty-three seconds later it disintegrated.

Korolev, Glushko, and the others rushed out of the blockhouse to see debris raining from the sky several kilometers away.

It had been another month of sleepless nights and terrible food. Filthy accommodations, inadequate facilities.

For nothing.

"I told you to leave my engines well enough alone!" Glushko's mind snapped, his eyes slits of rage.

"It is not right!" Voskresenskiy slammed a fist into his palm.

"The rocket will fly," Korolev said quietly.

Glushko raised trembling hands. "Maybe one day—but not in time to save us."

"There is no reason to keep up these tests!" Mishin lamented.

"You must understand—the Americanese..." Korolev kept his eyes on the falling debris. "The Americanese are so close, so—"

"Fifteen of my engines destroyed!" Glushko ranted. "My production line cannot sustain it. You and your rocket... You have put Khrushchev under a spell, but, Sergei Pavlovich, have you not become arrogant? It's one goddamn problem, one goddamn failure after another!"

They surrounded their chief, towering over the shorter man in sweaty 130-degree heat.

Korolev felt their anger and desperation but protested: "You should understand there are no *Korolev* rockets. These are *our* rockets with *your* engines, Mikhail Klavdievich. And they are magnificent." He looked at Chertok and Voskresenskiy. "These are rockets with *your* radio guidance, Boris Evseyevich." He pointed to Vladimir Barmin. "And *his* launchpad." To Viktor Kuznetsov. "And *his* gyroscopes. A rocket can fail, but each time it is a failure of *our* rocket."

Chertok smirked. "You are a cunning person, Sergei Pavlovich. You spread so much stink on us, while perfuming your own shit."

"I would not mind so much if my engines served their purpose," Glushko still fumed. "Why should I suffer from somebody else's mistakes?"

"Because it is *our* fault! Remember, the perfect is the enemy of God."

"We are in no danger of perfection," Chertok laughed. "We need to take a break and improve things. Particularly, the nose cone."

Korolev nodded. The worst of their fury had passed.

"In place of the cone, I will try again to convince the First Secretary to let us launch a satellite. It will take his mind off warheads, at least for a while. I must; I have to beat the Americanese."

None of them missed Korolev's reversion to the pronoun "I."

Friday, October 4, 1957

"Get him out of here this instant or I am aborting!" Korolev thrust an accusing finger at a military observer. "He's the one sending false reports to Ustinov."

Mishin escorted the observer out of the bunker.

Glushko eyed Korolev. They had argued frequently and heatedly, nearly coming to blows, until their first R-7 had successfully flown two months before.

All Korolev really cares about is the satellite. That's why he doesn't want the military about.

Glushko accompanied him to the assembly hangar. Though the launch clock ticked, he wasn't surprised that Korolev wanted to inspect the *prostreishiy sputnik* once more.

Inside, Korolev blew up at a technician: "You stupid fool! The surface of our little PS-1 must be absolutely perfect—you are polishing it like a pair of old boots!"

"But—"

"The lifespan of this baby satellite depends on its smooth travel through spacc!"

"But—"

"Any roughness, even the smallest bump, will cause it to heat up or burn to a cinder!"

"But Comrade Chief Designer Korolev," the technician managed, "this is only a replica." He pointed to another worker across the room. "Dmitri is working on the real one—over there!"

"Idiot! Two times—three times idiot!" Korolev cursed him. "Of course you are working on the replica! Did you ever stop to think that *yours* is the one that will be seen in the museum many centuries from now?"

He winked at Glushko, who wore a pale-yellow silk shirt under his thick overcoat; his brown leather shoes had been ordered from Paris.

The technician stammered, "Of course, Comrade Chief Designer!"

Like everyone on the base, he was caught up in the excitement that radiated even off the cooks preparing their ham sandwiches and tepid soup. Korolev and Glushko could feel it in the dirty back streets of the nearby village and throughout the sprawling prefab town they'd transformed from dilapidated mud huts. Every man and woman wanted success.

They went over to Dmitri for their final check on what they called the "simplest satellite." They examined again the connections between its sphere and two pairs of whiplike three-meter-long antennas. The team had fretted over its small radio transmitter, batteries, and temperature instruments. Its skin measured only two millimeters thick, yet Sputnik would sit atop the giant rocket and, if all went well, would be ejected into an Earth orbit.

Korolev caressed its burnished surface with a gloved hand.

"We made it in only one month and with only one reason," he said to no one in particular. "To be first in space."

They toured the launch area where rail tankers pumped tons of kerosene and super-cold liquid oxygen through the intake valves. They proceeded under a spider's web of high voltage lines to the rocket, which lounged in its horizontal position on a concrete islet amidst overlapping sand waves blown by ceaseless gusts of cold air.

The Sun did nothing to heat up the men who had no proper clothing because they had never dreamed the launch would be delayed for so long. They labored in short sleeves, their arms and faces stung by the freezing breezes.

"How much more?" Korolev asked a crew member with an oily shirt.

"About five hours, Comrade Chief Designer, but there is a problem. A small liquid leak of oxygen between two sections of the pad."

He showed it to Korolev, who opened his coat, unzipped his pants, and peed on the joint.

The liquid froze instantly and he announced, "That will hold it until ignition."

* * *

After sunset, powerful spotlights illuminated the now upright frost-covered olive-green rocket and its "belt" of smaller rockets. It hissed white and gray plumes from its bleed valves.

Korolev and Glushko approached as close to the missile as they dared.

"Shall we see off our firstborn?" Korolev asked.

"Yes, my friend."

"T minus ten minutes," blared the loudspeaker.

The two men reunited with Chertok, Voskresenskiy, Mishin, and others in the bunker.

Ustinov, State Commission members, and several high officials squished between operators manipulating switches and dials on dimly lit control station panels.

"T minus one minute."

"Key to launch!" barked Korolev.

Glushko took a key attached by a chain to the main panel, inserted it, and turned it to the right.

"Key on!"

"Roll tape," Chertok ordered, and telemetry readouts rolled off a printer.

"Purge the system!"

"Key to drainage!"

"*PUSK!*"

Korolev pressed the launch button to initiate an automated sequence. Through one of the bunker's periscopes he saw the umbilical mast retract. The rocket switched to onboard battery power.

A blinding shaft of light shot through the periscopes' viewfinders and lit up the room. It was so bright that Korolev and the others covered their eyes or turned away.

An ear-splitting roar passed through the concrete walls.

When they looked again, the quivering rocket was belching out flames that engulfed it. Its five engines built up a stream of air that pushed the whirling red flames downward into the enormous unseen escarpment.

Brilliant glare from the missile's fireworks illuminated adjacent work towers in the black night and cast long shadows.

"Lift off! The missile has lifted off!"

Despite the terrific noise, Chertok heard the clear tones of a bugler.

"She is off!" Korolev shouted. "Our baby is off!"

Workers in the assembly hangar hugged and kissed. They danced.

The bunker crowd pushed toward the exit. Chertok squirmed in a knot of coats, pushing his way up the stairs.

Outside, their boots kicked up sand as they dispersed to celebrate or telephone superiors. Chertok scurried across the sand, hurried through another door, and sandwiched himself between Korolev, Glushko, Mishin, and telemetry engineers adjusting their instrumentation in an adjacent console room.

"We must hold off on the big celebration," Korolev cautioned. "If the upper stage does not fire or if the nose cone does not properly eject the sputnik—it could still be a disaster."

Chertok nodded. "We should wait to hear the signal after a complete orbit."

Time dragged.

Most of them had been awake for thirty-six hours.

Talk ceased after forty-five minutes. Korolev was conscious of his own breathing. He went over the calculations again in his mind…

At thirty thousand kilometers per hour and eight hundred kilometers above Earth, our sputnik should take around ninety minutes to complete one orbit.

He looked at the clock on the wall. Thirty minutes to go.

Pneumatic locks will activate, the nose cone fairing will separate, the antenna spike will be released from its stowed position, the pushrod will…

Only seconds to go.

We should hear it soon—

"We have the signal! We have it!" shouted a radio controller.

"*Bleep…bleep…*" a young telemetry technician imitated the sound, bent close to the receiver. "I think it's working…it's in operation—the sphere is flying!"

The assembled group craned forward so they, too, could hear the plaintiff *bleep bleep*.

Which were followed by stronger bleeps.

Korolev whispered, "This is music no one has ever heard before."

To Chertok's ears the faint bleeps vibrated at G-sharp, but he knew the sound depended on how the receiver was tuned.

They came in groups of four at ten-second intervals.

Bleep, bleep, bleep, bleep…

"Hurrah, hurrah, hurrah—hurrah!" they shouted.

Several men ran out to join those in the assembly hangar already drunk.

Korolev turned to Glushko, tears on his face. "I have been waiting for this day all of my life."

"I know you have, my friend. I know you have. It was my dream, too, long before I met you."

Around them, bodies jostled in more hugs and kisses, and they embraced.

Bottles of vodka were passed around, and the two men poured the cold liquid directly down their throats.

They subsequently learned their sputnik had barely made it. The satellite was orbiting at an apogee eighty to ninety kilometers lower than planned. But it was enough.

Bleep, bleep, bleep, bleep…

* * *

Toward midnight, Khrushchev returned from his dacha in the Crimea to his family's house on the Moscow River. His son, also named Sergei, carried their suitcases up the outside steps and a servant informed the First Secretary of a call on the White Line. He disappeared inside his study.

Sergei finished unloading the car with the valet while security men patrolled the perimeter that skirted a pine forest.

When he closed the front door to the cool night air, he saw his father going upstairs to bed.

"What was it?" he asked.

His father shrugged. "Just another Korolev rocket launch."

Chapter 81

"Ike Tells Why Army Sent to Little Rock; Negroes May Return to School Today"

—San Francisco Chronicle

Huntsville, Alabama
Friday, October 4, 1957

In the Redstone Arsenal Officer's Club, a phonograph blared big-band music into a roomful of Defense Department and army brass talking shop. They were enjoying their favorite liquors or beer while dining on thick sirloin steaks and crispy fried chicken.

Major General Staftoy played host at his table to Neil McElroy, whom President Eisenhower had recently named Secretary of Defense. After an afternoon tour and briefing, Staftoy had invited von Braun over so they could convince McElroy to give them a backup position behind the navy's Vanguard. With them was Secretary of the Army Wilber Brucker, bald with drooping eyes, who knocked his cigarette ash into their already overflowing ashtray.

"Congratulations, sir." Von Braun raised his glass to McElroy, who had a long, handsome face between graying temples. "I hope you will help us to get things done."

"Thanks, Professor." McElroy drank his scotch. "I assume by 'things,' you mean beating the Russians."

"Of course. Because infighting and politics are hamstringing our efforts here."

"Perhaps you'd prefer it like the good ol' days?" McElroy lit another cigarette.

"You would be surprised to know how much politics we had even back then, sir." Von Braun deflected what he and Staftoy considered a cheap shot.

A waiter approached with a yellow phone trailing a long cord. "Excuse me, Mr. McElroy. An urgent call."

"Sorry." He took the receiver and snubbed out his smoke. "Uh-huh… Got it. When will they release a statement? Okay. Good. Uh-huh."

He hung up. "This is difficult, so I'll just say it: Radio Moscow is reporting the Soviets have placed a satellite in orbit nine hundred kilometers above the Earth."

Amidst the room's laughing and loud talking, their table fell silent.

McElroy took another bite of his rare steak.

Brucker's drooping eyes saw Staftoy's face go from pale to crimson.

Wernher's left hand crumpled his paper napkin into a tight ball.

"I guess you're not surprised," McElroy said, chewing.

"If somebody tells me that he has the rockets to shoot"—von Braun was angry—"and tells me *what* he will shoot, *how* he will shoot it, and talks about nearly everything except the precise date…well, should I be surprised when this man shoots up his damn satellite?"

"Bastards." Staftoy tried to moderate his voice but banged his pipe on his ashtray.

Brucker wasn't sure if he was referring to the Reds or the politicians.

McElroy chewed another pink cube.

"We knew they would do it," von Braun said. "We could have done it with our Redstone *two years ago.*"

"Missile number 27," Staftoy explained sharply. "It could've gone into orbit—without question." He slammed his fist on the table, making his plate jump and causing those nearby to look over. "Jesus, McElroy! The hardware is *in hand!* The money we need to make the effort is small—*miniscule!"* He slammed the table again with his open palm. *"Damn it!*

We have a ninety-nine percent probability of success. Give us twelve million dollars and the *goddamn go-ahead!*"

"For God's sake," von Braun pleaded, "cut us loose and let us do something!"

McElroy listened while he chewed, and Staftoy saw the news wasn't affecting his appetite or his humor. Since the secretary had recently been briefed by Eisenhower, Staftoy suddenly realized the White House must have a trump card.

As the news made the rounds, others in the room reacted with disbelief and disappointment. Someone switched off the music.

"Bruce is right," von Braun said. "We have the hardware on the shelf. Vanguard will never make it. Never."

"Isn't that a little presumptuous?" Brucker asked.

"I don't think so. They will fail. We can put up a satellite in sixty days, Mr. McElroy. Give us the green light and sixty days."

"*Ninety* days," Staftoy corrected.

"Sixty."

"No, Wernher," the major general pulled rank. "Ninety days."

"Okay." Von Braun's mind raced. Hardware would have to be cleaned and retested, final assembly performed; experts from JPL would have to recheck the payload. Crews would have to muster strength at Cape Canaveral...

"Gentlemen." McElroy chewed a last morsel. "I'm flying back to Washington tonight."

"Sir, when you get back and find all hell has broken loose"—von Braun leaned in close—"tell them we can fire a satellite into orbit in *ninety* days."

But Staftoy could see behind McElroy's eyes—*politics...*

Chapter 82

"Russia Wins the Race Into Outer Space"

—*Daily Herald,* Delaware

The White House, Washington, DC
Monday, October 7, 1957

Outside the Oval Office, McElroy noticed the secretary's switchboard lit up with anxious telephone calls…

Sputnik, Sputnik, Sputnik…

He would've liked to have told von Braun, however, that he didn't encounter anything like panic inside the Oval Office. No hell had broken loose. Instead, he found President Eisenhower and his closest advisors in a more confident mood than anyone in the country would've imagined.

The president had other concerns.

"I want those U-2 flights stopped," he told John Foster Dulles, his Secretary of State. Ike had aged: bigger ears, a few more pounds, less hair. He had on a diagonally striped tie and a pale-yellow shirt, charcoal jacket and pants.

"Why?" asked Dulles. "Allen over at the CIA is happy. We're happy. We're getting great information, and their high-altitude flights probably helped push Khrushchev to launch his little Sputnik. The Russians have done us a good turn—I admit, unintentionally—by throwing up their little ball. A *really* good turn. They've established the concept of freedom in international spaceways. By God, if we'd done the same, the Reds would've screamed bloody murder."

"You captured the wrong Germans!" said General Pierre Gallois, a French dignitary with brushed-back hair who barged in after a brief knock.

He'd been expected—Europe's emissary.

"Not at all," Dulles retorted, shaking hands. "We could've launched a year ago. We didn't let our guys do it for the reason I just mentioned before you came in—the Russians would've caused a worldwide fracas."

Lieutenant Colonel Philip Corso sat with his back against the wall. He served on the president's National Security Council and had been called into the daylong meeting. He'd just returned from a mission in Rome and had exactly one thing to report. He saw on a tea table next to him an edition of the *New York Times*, whose headline roared: "SOVIET FIRES EARTH SATELLITE INTO SPACE; IT IS CIRCLING THE GLOBE AT 18,000 M.P.H.; SPHERE TRACKED IN 4 CROSSINGS OVER U.S."

"Isn't that right, McElroy?" Dulles asked. "We could've launched a year ago."

"*Two* years ago, if you believe our head German," McElroy replied dryly.

"Mr. President, aren't you the least bit worried about Russian military superiority?" General Gallois insisted. "People all over the world are pointing in the sky to the satellite and saying the U.S. has been beaten."

"They *can't* point to it," Vannevar Bush remarked from his red leather chair. "You can't *see* it. What they're pointing to is the last stage of the Russian rocket."

"That is a petty detail."

"No, I'm not worried, General," President Eisenhower answered. "Because they certainly don't have superiority. Intelligence reports that their R-7 is useless as a missile. Too big to be moved on anything but railcars, too slow to fuel, too easily blown up before launch."

"Then why is the panic button being pushed?" asked the general.

"It's not being pushed." Eisenhower walked round his desk. "Frankly, I can't understand why the American people have got so worked up. It's certainly not going to drop on their heads."

"It's a media riot," Dulles said. "Polls show the general public isn't much concerned. But the press and the Democrats, as soon as they heard Sputnik's first little beep, they ran to the bar like heavy drinkers hearing a cork pop."

"In France and the rest of Europe, *we* are concerned." The general remained standing; he knew it would be a short visit. "This spectacular Russian…thunderbolt has thrown NATO officials into a state. More Soviet missions could radically alter the balance of power and put us in a delicate position. Mr. President, what can you tell me, confidentially, to calm the waters?"

"You can tell Europe," Eisenhower replied, "that Sputnik does not rouse my apprehensions. Not one iota. They have put one small ball into the air. We are well aware of the situation, but we are, in fact, two steps ahead of them. Effective intercontinental ballistic missiles are still a long way off. Years off. So you can tell them we are going to weather this storm in a teacup and carry on with our plan—"

"Which in fact the Soviets have made possible," Dulles interjected.

"—and launch our own satellites in the near future. And ours will be significantly more useful. You can tell them that we have a plan, a good plan, and we are going to stick to it. Here and abroad, I want only cheerful faces."

He knows how to play the weak-kneed Europeans and the press, Corso thought, listening to the Old Man. *He doesn't miss a trick and he never shows his hand.*

"When you've worked out a good plan, a sound plan, the best policy is to stick to it. We can't go changing our program in reaction to everything the Russians do or do not do. We know they're going to launch a second satellite in two days. The cost of running these programs, even if we do nothing, will bankrupt them. So we'll just let them have their moment in the sun."

An only somewhat relieved General Gallois was shown out.

Eisenhower turned to Dulles and Bush. "How soon can we launch our own reconnaissance satellite?" he asked.

"It won't be ready soon enough to beat ABMA," McElroy answered. "But von Kármán at JPL has been working with a Professor van Allen on a research satellite that can be launched by Huntsville in ninety days."

"How long until Corona?" Eisenhower asked again.

Corso knew about Corona: a spy satellite. Like the U-2 flights, masterminded by the CIA. Corso also knew Ike couldn't be happy with the prospect, if Vanguard failed, of "a bunch of ex-Nazis" and that "publicity seeking" von Braun launching the first U.S. satellite. Ike's consolation prize was the much more strategic, much more secret Corona reconnaissance satellite, which was still in development.

"It's going to take a little more planning and preparation," Dulles said, removing and cleaning his glasses. "They're developing a special seventy-millimeter film, which we'll retrieve from orbit. The satellite will jettison a capsule and parachutes will be deployed. It all makes for a complex operation. But"—he put his glasses back on—"Corona will be completely invisible to the Soviets."

"How *long?*"

"Optimistically, eighteen months."

Eisenhower frowned. "I want you to shut down the U-2 program as soon as possible. But I'll approve one more flight."

Bush saw an opening to advance his agenda. "Ike, the Group is in favor of establishing a string of informal listening posts over the entire planet, in space and on the ground. They'd be able to report on the Soviets, China, and any saucer activity. We're fairly certain they have bases at the poles, but it behooves us to find out if they have other bases and to keep tabs on them."

"How many factions are we talking about, Philip?" Eisenhower asked the one question Corso had come to answer.

"According to the Vatican, at least five, maybe six separate alien groups. Each with their own agendas."

Corso saw the Old Man was shocked. Even Bush raised his eyebrows.

"That LBJ lunatic is right, even if he doesn't know why," Dulles said. "The Russians have left the Earth—and a race for control of the universe has begun."

Chapter 83

"Sputnik No. 2 Carries Dog on Space Flight—Soviet Rocket to Moon Hinted Already on Way"

—Cincinnati Times-Star

Huntsville, Alabama
Wednesday, December 4, 1957

Von Braun liked to sit in the living room and read his evening papers and scholarly journals. A telescope on a tripod stood near glass doors that opened onto a small garden.

Between articles, his mind went back to his late-night talk with Disney and Kimball—to the stranger outside the drugstore diner.

Ex-SS, von Braun surmised, *controlled by Kammler, or someone like him. Somewhere.*

He'd never believed the rumors of Kammler's death.

In business again with America's blessing. Probably CIA. Not army.

He would've heard something.

Psychological warfare.

Von Braun wanted to know who ran the Soviet space program, which group. He'd inquired, but nobody knew for certain. He'd noted a Soviet professor named K. Sergeev who tirelessly promoted space travel. Sergeev cultivated friendships with journalists and may have produced at least one film on the subject, but the foreign press never showed his face.

Could be him.

He looked at his Rolex.

"Iris, Margrit, *es ist Zeit!*" he called his two girls.

They skipped in, happy to take a break from homework. Iris rotated the TV dial to the right channel. She and her sister flopped on the beige carpet and propped up their chins on their palms. The cuckoo clock, their parents' wedding present, chimed the half hour.

Maria took a seat next to her husband, and they prepared to watch the broadcast he'd helped produce, "Mars and Beyond."

In black and white, Walt Disney introduced the show to millions of viewers: "In this exciting age when everyone seems to be talking about the future possibilities of space travel, there is much speculation on what we will discover when we visit other worlds. Will we find planets with only a low form of vegetable life? Or will there be mechanical robots controlled by super-intelligent beings? One of the most fascinating fields of modern science deals with the possibility of life on other planets. This is our story..."

"Daddy, who lives on the Moon?" Margrit asked.

"Russians," her father answered with a grin.

* * *

Two days later he reclined in the same blue easy chair to read his papers, this time with a good dose of *Schadenfreude*. Printed across the front pages were large photographs of the navy's Vanguard rocket blowing itself to bits on the launchpad. Articles described the embarrassing fiasco as, "FLOPNIK," "DUDNIK," even "KAPUTNIK."

He said to Maria, who stitched a purl, "*Jetzt sind wir an der Reihe.* Now it's our turn—and we won't fail."

* * *

Eighty-four days later, on January 31, von Braun joined Staftoy, von Kármán, and a host of military and Washington officials inside the Pentagon's Army Communications Center, the "War Room."

Von Braun recognized at least two top men from JPL: Bill Pickering and James van Allen making small talk with Brucker and McElroy.

Pickering had been named director of JPL. Even Hermann Oberth, his hair and broom mustache white with age, had been invited and mingled. At 9:00 p.m. they discussed politics and the economy while waiting for the promised countdown.

Unexpected high-altitude winds were causing delays.

President Eisenhower would receive the first real news via a dedicated telephone line.

Staftoy had insisted on scant publicity. There had been too many reporters to witness the Vanguard's debacle.

"Our rocket will be launched from Pad 26A, at Cape Canaveral." Von Braun had been asked to brief the assembled, a stalling tactic. "The Jupiter-C—'C' standing for 'composite'—a converted Redstone ICBM, old number 29. Atop this main stage are fifteen individual, much smaller solid-propellant rockets that use a formula based on the invention of JPL's late Jack Parsons"—he nodded at Pickering and von Kármán—"which are arranged in three additional stages. The thirty-one-pound satellite itself, which we have named Explorer 1, sits atop the rocket, about seventy feet above the ground.

"If all goes well, the satellite's orbital inclination will be thirty-three degrees. We expect it to have a perigee of about two hundred and twenty miles and an apogee of one thousand miles."

As von Braun moved aside for van Allen to speak, he added, "Our little Explorer is competing with the Sputniks in spirit only—in terms of rocket hardware, ours is much more sophisticated."

His boast did nothing to alleviate the many worried faces. For those present, America's short-term reputation and long-term hopes hung in the balance. While van Allen went over the satellite's research capabilities, three Teletype machines stuttered to life with an update from the Cape.

Trouble. A pool of liquid had formed on the pad beneath the launcher.

Staftoy pulled von Braun aside. "Could it be a propellant leak?"

"Debus will handle it."

Moments later, the Teletype machines spelled out the all-clear on several large-screen monitors, set up so everyone could follow.

At "X-45" the countdown commenced. 10:03 p.m. on the wall clock.

Conversations quieted, and von Braun could see in his mind's eye the action hundreds of miles to the south...

At "X-30," the rocket would turn on its lights, beautiful and awe inspiring—an austere but elegant black-and-white monolith, fins, and tapered nose.

At "X-10," current would be fed to the electric motors and the upper stages would start spinning.

Teletype machines chattered again, and the screens read, "X-1 minute, final weight measurements being taken. Spinner still running smoothly..."

Von Kármán and Staftoy flanked von Braun, as if their physical proximity might help elevate the rocket.

"X-20 seconds, 10..."

Von Braun imagined Debus casually nodding to his blockhouse crew, as he had done so many times at Peenemünde, before pressing the switch to ignite the engine. They would view the fireworks through heavy safety glass...

On the screen: "Firing command. Main stage. Liftoff... Slow rise, faster. Straight up through a hole in the clouds. Out of sight..."

10:48 p.m.

The first stage would cut off and the nose section, with the spinning tub, would separate.

Ernst, it's up to you! von Braun thought and glanced at Staftoy smoking his pipe.

Ernst Rees would have to collate the data from three tracking sources in a flash and calculate exactly when to press the button that would fire the upper stages. Even a slight error would ruin the mission.

Teletypes clattered again. "Second stage ignition okay."

"He's the man with the golden finger!" von Braun exclaimed, though only a few knew what he meant.

He looked at the clock and had the Teletype operator send a question: "Did third and fourth stages fire?"

"Do not know yet," came the reply from Cape Canaveral.

The JPL scientists fretted with the crowd. So far, so good.

"Professor, I'm sure it's in orbit," von Kármán said. His wild gray hair had recently been trimmed, and he looked dapper in a brown suit and dark-blue tie.

"We cannot know for sure."

Von Braun grabbed a glazed donut from the buffet table and took a bite. He poured water from a pitcher into a paper cup and discreetly swallowed two pink pills.

Staftoy returned to his side.

"The satellite has appeared over Antigua, but I've told the public relations officer we won't release a statement until it's circled back round. That should put it over the West Coast at...a bit past 12:30 a.m."

Cigarette smoke filled the War Room.

God willing, the fourth stage has ignited and the satellite has separated, thought von Braun.

He imagined it shooting through space at about eighteen thousand miles per hour.

He searched out Secretary Brucker and said, "If Explorer has achieved a successful orbit, it will pass over California in precisely 106 minutes."

Staftoy alerted the moonwatch station in San Diego to listen for the adenoidal beep at exactly 12:41 a.m. eastern time.

For the next hour, following receipt of downrange station reports, they endured an exasperating, if predictable, absence of information. McElroy and his flunkies sipped more coffee and smoked more cigarettes.

"This is just like waiting for election precincts to come in, boys!" Brucker drawled. "I'm out of joe and running low on stogies."

When the appointed moment approached, an even more unpleasant tension went round.

Staftoy juggled four telephones, one for each JPL tracking station on the West Coast. A few minutes before the exact orbital deadline he got an open line to San Diego.

"Do you hear her?"

He listened, then shook his head no to the uneasy throng.

The minute hand on the large wall clock ticked to 12:42.

"Do you hear her?"

Von Braun scanned faces with their own particular reasons for despair or anger.

From behind him a voice said, "If this dog don't hunt, your ass ain't gonna be worth a plumb nickel to the top brass—ain't that so, *Professor*?"

A southern two-star general smiled vacuously and stepped away.

Another minute.

And another.

And one more, without a sound from the satellite.

McElroy told Staftoy, "Obviously you and the professor were mistaken. Explorer never went into orbit—"

"Wernher, what happened?" Brucker grabbed von Braun by the arm.

"Why the hell don't you hear anything?" Staftoy yelled into one of the phones.

Another sixty seconds evaporated.

Seven minutes late! von Braun wanted to shout, but he drew upon his fount of optimism and told Brucker, "*Wait.* Let us wait a little longer, please."

At eight minutes, a colonel complained in a loud voice, "Boy, the Russkies are going to have a field day with—"

One of the smaller Teletype machines went *clack-clack.*

It wasn't connected to any screen, so an operator ripped off the message and handed it to Staftoy.

Von Braun held his breath.

"Goldstone has the bird!" Staftoy shouted to the whole room, pipe clenched in his teeth. "They hear her. They *hear* her!"

The four phones rang at once. Staftoy grabbed one; Pickering and van Allen seized the other three. Their words tumbled over each other:

"Clear, strong signal…!"

"Satellite transmitting…!"

"Orbit achieved!"

Joy lined Brucker's face where there had been recrimination, and he hugged von Braun. "Thank God," he murmured.

McElroy shook Staftoy's hand. Von Kármán and van Allen clasped arms.

Explorer 1 was orbiting Earth.

Victory whoops. The two-star southern general backslapped von Braun, enmity forgotten.

"Well done, Wernher," Oberth congratulated his former student.

"She was eight minutes late."

"Mysterious, yes," Oberth agreed. "We'll talk about it later."

McElroy retreated to a corner of the room with Brucker to put in a call to Augusta, Georgia.

"He's playing bridge," McElroy said.

Brucker picked up a second receiver and heard President Eisenhower say, "…that's wonderful. I surely feel a lot better now. But let's not make too great a hullabaloo over this."

We calculated it to the second, to the last variable, mused von Braun. *More than eight minutes late. The laws of physics cannot be changed…*

ACT V

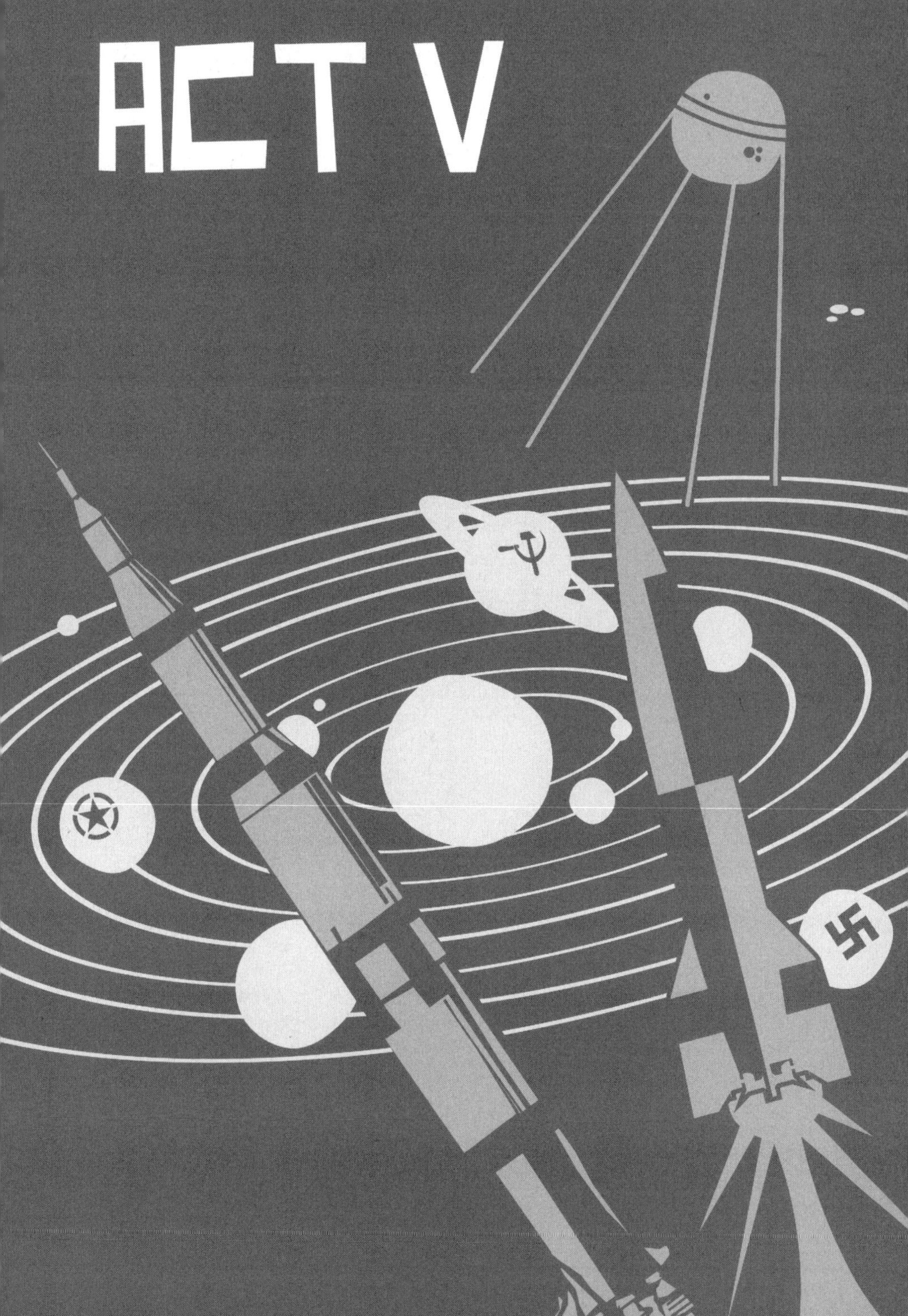

Chapter 84

"U.S. Satellite Up—Army's Jupiter-C Fires 30-Pound Moon Into Space"

—The Boston Daily Globe

Warrenton, Virginia
Sunday, February 16, 1958

"The cat is out of the bag," Angleton said.

"What does it matter?" asked Dulles. "So it flew a little higher and took a little longer."

"They'll add it up."

"We're way ahead of them," said Vannevar Bush. "It won't make a difference."

Their words reverberated in an underground relocation bunker designed to ensure government survival in case of a nuclear attack. Its bare rooms and chairs were functional, but comfortable. The hum of hidden generators and pumps was low, but permanent.

Dulles, Angleton, Bush, Kammler, Gehlen, Donaldson, Quincy Adams, and several organizational executives had come together to discuss next steps.

To Gehlen's left a special guest brooded. Nobody knew much about him, but Bush had assured Dulles that his special guest wielded great power.

The Group and the CIA had, unofficially, joined forces.

"Way ahead is not very far," Gehlen remarked.

"Look," Angleton coughed. "After Kammler's botched attempt to take Schomberger, we're getting him for free, so to speak. It pays to deal with the Mossad."

Bush leaned forward. "I agree. We're ahead. Increased funding, black budgets, our own advanced arsenal, soon enough. But unless we're first to beat gravity, unless we have our own saucers—"

"You will." The guest stroked his stiletto beard. "Herr Kammler and I will see to that—if you acquire what we need."

"Right." Dulles took some papers from a folder. "In exchange for Schomberger, we're letting them take a stab at these. Research based on the saucers. Material from Kammler. We win both ways."

"When you say *them*, you mean the Israelis?" Donaldson asked. "I hope so, because they have the best of that world."

"Right." Dulles handed the papers to Angleton. "Part of the deal."

Angleton put the papers in his briefcase and locked it. "If they find a way, they'll have to share. Kammler is sending Wolfgang Sänger, one of the ex-Peenemünde gang, to work for Nasser in Egypt. With a team of German specialists Sänger will make rockets—pointing right at the Jews. They'll understand."

Kammler smiled at the symmetry of it: allow the Zionists to do their bidding before blowing them off the map.

"We're also looking into the question of other dimensions," Bush said. "And the implications."

"So we feign cooperation," Adams said. "Like good spies."

"Yes, Quincy," said Dulles. "Schomberger will answer our eggheads' questions in case we need them. We'll keep everyone on a short rope. If necessary, we tighten the noose."

Gehlen smiled to himself, for he and Kammler knew that Dulles, the "gentleman" CIA director, was a plaything of the Group.

But who controls Rachel? He'd learned the name of the agent who had foiled their plans more than once. *Mossad? No. Then who?*

Chapter 85

"Cuba: Batista Wants Rule Extension—Castro, 2,000 Men"

—*The Stars and Stripes,* Pacific Edition

Huntsville, Alabama
Sunday, August 10, 1958

After Maria put their two daughters to bed, her husband mentioned that the evening would be a long one.

At the appointed hour, Rachel and two army intelligence officers led Viktor Schomberger from a black coupe to the house. She spoke calmly to the old Austrian.

Von Braun thought Rachel looked oddly familiar. But since he couldn't place her, he put it out of his mind. He made the necessary introductions in a jovial mood: "Herr Schomberger, I want to thank you for coming to my home. Germany is three countries. The Rhineland is the wine country. Bavaria is beer country. And I am from Silesia, so tonight we will toast our union with schnapps."

While he prepared their drinks, Rachel whispered, "You won't have much time. He is weak. You must ask your questions and tell others. His papers have been deposited with Staftoy."

"I understand," he said, but his manner was reserved.

Von Braun had read in the press how certain aircraft companies—Lear, Martin, Bell—had been on the verge of antigravity technology but had been aggressively shut down. Funding cut off. The message to ABMA and others had been clear: *keep your mouths shut.*

Rachel and the intelligence men took up defensive positions outside while von Braun and his guest adjourned to the study. Von Kármán and Oberth had flown in earlier and were seated on a small divan. Schomberger, breathing with difficulty, chose a plain wooden chair below a framed map of the world.

No one took notes. Nothing would be recorded.

"Are you all right?" Von Kármán asked.

"Yes, thank you."

They conversed in German. The Austrian felt easier with native speakers, after weeks of talks in English that had bordered on interrogations.

"The landing was bumpy," Schomberger said. "My chauffeur is a spy. I am tired. I am not used to the food here."

"Perhaps Maria can fix you something?" von Braun suggested.

"If you have strong coffee."

He left to get Maria.

"Herr Schomberger," Oberth said, awkwardly, "I am a great admirer of your work on the flying discs."

"What a disaster this has been…"

Von Braun returned and sat on the edge of his desk. "Please, let me get to the point," he said. "What we are going to discuss is something that must be kept secret."

He saw Schomberger's astonishment. "But Rachel has—"

"Since launching several Explorer satellites," von Braun spoke over him, "I have sent discreet inquiries to experts in physics and quantum mechanics with a puzzle as follows: the rockets are providing a larger than expected thrust, which results in higher and longer orbits than we planned. For example, 114 minutes rather than 105 minutes.

"We have checked and rechecked our calculations. We made no errors. Unfortunately, I have received no satisfying explanation for these consistent anomalies. I have consulted with my friends and colleagues here. I have exchanged letters with the theorist Burkhard Heim and with others who are not so rigidly attached to the theories of the past. I have asked them if there wasn't an alternate gravitational solution, something beyond trivial slide-ruler explanations…"

He sipped his schnapps.

"But because we made no error, based on the laws of physics as we now understand them, our problem, and it is a big problem…well, perhaps we are not understanding physics as we should."

The idea made von Braun uncomfortable, though his friends had come to the same conclusion.

"If this is true," von Kármán said, "if we are working in ignorance, we cannot launch spacecraft on precise, predictable trajectories."

"Military flyovers of intended targets also become impossible. Of more importance to me, to the people in this room, we cannot send missions to the Moon or Mars. Herr Schomberger, I have been told that you might be able to help us."

Schomberger grumbled, "I won't be here much longer. I've had my work ripped from me—I have been foolish—I thought the world could benefit from my studies…"

"Herr Schomberger, we are, as they say, all ears. Can you not help us?"

"Perhaps you are searching for an antigravity effect." His eyes were milky. "Or perhaps, like that fellow Hitler, you are looking for a field-propulsion technology?"

Von Kármán winced at the comparison.

"Perhaps you are telling the truth and wish to find an easier way of sending rockets to other planets. A predictable way. Let us pray that is so." His voice became clearer. "I have studied your blueprints. The rocket's upper stages have a spinning midsection, yes?"

"Yes," von Braun replied. "The 'tub' is set spinning before launch to provide gyroscopic stability against the uneven burn of the solid rockets."

Von Kármán leaned back, cerebrating.

Maria entered from the kitchen with a coffeepot, small sandwiches, bourbon and soda, and cakes. She placed her crowded tray on the desk and the coffeepot on a small table next to Schomberger's chair.

"*Vielen Dank*," he said.

She poured coffee into a china cup and he drank.

"It is good," he said. "And strong."

Maria smiled and left the room, closing the door behind her.

"Are you implying that rotating objects, spinning objects, go higher because they somehow acquire free energy?" von Kármán asked.

Schomberger sipped more of his coffee. "It really is good." He paused. "Herr von Kármán, I had to abandon the Euclidean model of straight line and circle long ago. All the functional surfaces of my machines employ beautiful spirals, the curves which we find in nature, in the streams and the plants. Their holistic shapes produce life-affirming energies which stabilize and enhance. They are abundant, free, and they rehabilitate. How old do you think I am?"

"I wouldn't venture."

"In nature everything pours out electromagnetic energy without any observable energy input, except sun and rain. Nature is served by rhythmical, reciprocal unfoldings. Without increasing reserves of energy, there could be no evolution or development, yet this occurs in nature without end. This abundance results first and foremost in the collapse of the so-called conservation law of energy. In consequence, the law of gravity and other rigidly backward, dogmatic premises also become unstable. We ignore this at our peril—for how do the large celestial bodies revolve on their own axes?"

"I would have to answer, God," said von Braun. "But there are other theories."

Schomberger nodded. "Yes," he said energetically. "But even God has laws, and you must predict with absolute precision your rocket's trajectory. So you must give up Newton's law. You must accept the fact that these enormous spinning entities absorb energy from the ether. The same is true for the smallest spinning creature or object. So it is true for the atom and smaller particles yet to be discovered. You know," he chuckled, "the whirling dervish, the dancers, make reference to spinning planets that harness the energy of the universe. The number of your Thirty-Third Degree Masons, it is a reference, a sign, of that physics, too."

He stood up on bowed legs to make his next point.

"*Tremendous energy* is embedded in nature everywhere, all around us. It flows in from other dimensions, the power to create stars, the power of solar systems, to seed planets with the wonders of infinite nature. It *is* God-like, Professor von Braun, if not God himself."

"Then we better make rockets that don't spin." Von Kármán smoked his pipe. "At least until we figure out how to calculate for the increased energy in the equation. I'll have JPL get to work on new designs immediately, if you agree?"

"Of course," said von Braun. "It's too late to make changes for the next launches. But as soon as we can, we will adapt."

Schomberger collapsed into his chair. "You must also tell the world."

"I'm sorry, Herr Schomberger," von Kármán said, re-lighting his pipe. "Even your presence here is a kind of gift. Our work is closely monitored. Moreover, you are considered by many to be, shall we say, unorthodox. Maybe later."

"It is not their decision," Oberth explained.

"Carry out tests," Schomberger pleaded, "and you will see that I am right. You have the means."

"What about the flying discs, which seem to spin as well?" Oberth asked. "My theory is that saucers are time travelers, jumping from one time-space dimension to another."

Von Braun lit a cigarette. Maria wouldn't be happy, but the nicotine helped him think. "They're using some sort of antigravity electromagnetic propulsion," he said. "That's for sure."

Schomberger took a long draft of coffee and poured another cup. His face had, if possible, become more haggard. "There are at least twelve races that have been visiting Earth for hundreds of thousands, maybe millions of years," he said, as if in confession. "Some resemble humanoids. Some of their ships come from bases here, others from near Orion's Belt or farther afield. Their saucers use a variety of nature's laws to function, including those I mentioned, at levels far beyond yours. Most are not too concerned by us. I believe them to be peaceful, but one or two of them might have their own plans."

"How do you know this?" Oberth asked.

"They told me, the ones with the large black eyes. I have met them in the forests, not always in physical form—"

"This is why we have to go our own way," von Kármán said to von Braun and ran a hand through his gray hair. "I'm sure you realize, Professor, assuming for a moment that this is true, that *we* are playing a regional game, while *they* confront a potential extraterrestrial threat. Our problem is that the functioning of the Group is now managed by individuals within the intelligence community. And they are not talking to us."

Von Braun stubbed out his cigarette in a glass ashtray. "It's another good reason why we must say nothing," he agreed. "For the present, we need only to launch our rockets in a predictable manner. We must encourage space travel anyway we can, without complicating matters."

"Yet it strikes me as surreal," Oberth said, "that here we are, learning about saucers and zero gravity, while we insist upon using such old-fashioned methods of propulsion."

"Teacher, there are aborigines in New Guinea who are still using sticks and knives made from stone and wood."

"Different tribes," von Kármán concluded. "Subgroups of a primitive species with emotional handicaps. That's all."

"I have told you everything I can, I have fulfilled my duty," Schomberger mumbled in his corner. "You must choose your path. This secrecy, this hiding, is nothing more than a mask upon your own shame. You serve your masters and will do only what is expedient."

He was finished with them.

Von Braun signaled Rachel. She would take him back to Israel.

Less than a month later, those who had spoken with him that night learned Schomberger was dead.

Chapter 86

"Batista Flees; Castro in Control"

—*New York Daily News*

Hampton, Virginia
Tuesday, June 30, 1959

The seven astronauts were ill at ease in their tuxes, but made the best of it, smoking cigarettes and chatting with stylish women in white gloves and elegant hats. A bar had been set up in the back of the Space Task Group's Mission Control room. Pretty waitresses in yellow cocktail dresses handed out a steady stream of strong vodka sodas, gin and tonics, and straight liquor.

Staftoy and von Braun mixed with the other guests, cocktail and martini in their respective hands. Over the PA system a Lawrence Welk record crooned and drowned out the air conditioner.

The bulk of the room's population formed successive waves toward von Braun, drawn by his magazine-cover appearances, TV stardom, and perceived power, but the Mercury Seven were coming up fast.

"It's strange to be working with the same people we hated during the war," Chris Kraft commented to his boss, Bob Gilruth. "Before I meet him, tell me what I'm in for. What's von Braun like?"

The flight director had worked long enough with the director of the Space Task Group to know his question was unwelcome. It was a subject they'd been avoiding.

"Von Braun has an ego," Gilruth replied reluctantly. "He can and will be stubborn and opinionated. Like me. You'll find that out soon enough. What's more, he's gunning for our astronauts. He wants to control the whole show."

"But...we need him?"

Gilruth pushed out his lips. Of medium height, he was bald on top and had inky black eyebrows. "Yes. Our astronauts are going to ride von Braun's rockets. Training those astronauts is our job."

They watched von Braun and Staftoy fraternize with the Mercury Seven astronauts: Carpenter, Cooper, Glenn, Grissom, Schirra, Shepard, and Slayton, or "CCGGSSS." The brotherhood. Two of the astronauts laughed. Gilruth had already observed that whenever von Braun joined a discussion, without a word of excuse before butting in, he tended to monopolize it.

"You are welcome in Huntsville anytime to see the Redstone," von Braun invited Alan Shepard. "I will fly you there myself."

"At last, a stick-and-rudder man I can talk to," Shepard said.

Von Braun had heard Shepard described as goofy looking—high forehead and thick lips—but his demeanor conveyed a personality competitive as hell, an astronaut determined to be the first man in space.

Staftoy caught Kraft looking at them and whispered "diplomacy and charm" to von Braun. The two men excused themselves and headed over.

"Doctor, I'd like to introduce you to flight director Chris Kraft," Staftoy said. "You already know Bob."

Von Braun extended his hand and Kraft took it. "You have done a wonderful job. Your astronauts are the most wonderful people. They are no daredevils by a long shot; they are serious and dedicated."

"You know that already?" Gilruth asked.

Staftoy changed the subject. "If NASA gets von Braun and ABMA, promise me you'll treat them well. I feel like I'm losing a son."

"I feel like a bride with two suitors." Von Braun smiled. "The air force and Space Task Group want our rockets. I admit I'm a little bit afraid. All I really want is a rich uncle."

Von Braun thought his words amusing and the Americans smiled politely, so he forged ahead. "The other day I met with some finance people and they asked, 'How much funding do you need?' I said, 'How much have you got?'"

He laughed at his own story.

"Doctor, let me show you the control room," Kraft suggested, and the two moved off.

"Von Braun doesn't care what flag he fights for," Gilruth said.

"Now, Bob, I've worked with him for over a decade. He's the real deal. He's just…" Staftoy smoked his pipe. "Well, he's just a natural showman. He can't help it."

Kraft and von Braun walked slowly between the first two rows of Mission Control consoles, the second of which was elevated by a step, so each aisle would have an unobstructed view of the large Earth map on the facing wall.

"I suspect we will have to pass Russian customs when we finally reach the Moon, no?" Von Braun kept trying to make the American laugh.

"We can give them a run for their money," Kraft said. "This room is a significant step in that direction. We've put together a huge team, which we hope Huntsville will be a part of. We've designed a space-going system, a worldwide tracking network, and this center." He pointed to a control station. "There's one console for environmental systems, another for the flight surgeon, and so on."

Von Braun listened; he'd read the reports and considered their system excessively restrictive.

"Only one person, probably another astronaut, will talk to the capsule. Any messages, commands, or questions will go through CapCom. The Control Center will also monitor launch guidance, coordination with a range safety officer, trajectory calculations, and retrofire."

Between the second and third row, von Braun said, "You know, we at ABMA have estimated that NASA is going to cost taxpayers a billion dollars a year. Our job is to catch up with the Russians—but God help us and Congress if we ever do."

This time, Kraft chuckled. "The engineer at his console will be a decision maker. But each console position will be backed up by a team of experts." He gestured to two rows of comfortable-looking armchairs, with an ashtray stand between each. "You'll be in one of these seats, behind the partition up there."

"I wish I could be in the capsule. You know, those seven men are thrilled by the challenge, but they deeply resent the suggestion that they are human guinea pigs rather than test pilots. Chuck said they are 'spam in a can.'"

"Of course they're not guinea pigs. But ultimate control of the mission has to be *here*, in this room."

"Mr. Kraft, I thank you for the tour. Yet I must inform you that your concept for mission control is all wrong. The astronauts agree with me. Completely."

Kraft couldn't believe his ears.

"I have extensive experience as a pilot, like those men over there." Von Braun gestured toward the brotherhood. "So I must insist that the flight of a Mercury capsule will not be any different from piloting any other flying machine. The pilot must have autonomy. He must."

The two men faced each other, drinks still in hand. A few of the guests looked their way, sensing something amiss.

Although his face projected kindness, Kraft was a perfectionist, a hard ass, not someone to let von Braun get away with what he considered an asinine point of view.

"No, that's not right," Kraft countered. "We've thought about this for a long time—much longer than you—and it's different. The astronauts can't possibly keep track of all the parameters. Frankly, I'm surprised, given your unfamiliarity with our setup, that you'd say anything about it."

"So you will treat them like robots or a monkey," von Braun shot back. Of late he couldn't abide anyone disagreeing with him. "That will not work. They *must* have the power to act independently of ground control. They must."

"You don't know what you're talking about. Listen—"

"You will never have your way." Von Braun jutted his big head at Kraft. "Let me tell you, I met the other day a man who will perhaps be the next president, Mr. Kennedy—and *he* understands the importance of the astronaut in the space program."

"The astronaut is damn important, we all know that, but you're in over your head." Kraft was pissed. "And let me tell you something about Kennedy. Jack once had an older brother named Joe. He flew a Liberator during the war. It blew up on a secret mission. He and his crew were killed because their explosives went off too soon. You know what they were going to bomb? *Your goddamn secret vengeance weapons!*"

Kraft's empty right hand balled into a fist.

If this Kraut says one more word…

From the corner of his eye, he saw a poised, well-dressed woman with coiffed blonde hair detach herself from the spectators and glide over. She smiled at Kraft as she whispered in von Braun's ear. His face relaxed.

"Thank you again for the tour, Mr. Kraft," he said in a high-pitched, conciliatory tone.

Von Braun and the woman retreated.

Gilruth came over and Kraft asked him, "Who was that?"

"Maria von Braun, his wife." Gilruth put a hand on Kraft's shoulder. "Take a deep breath. It's hard to believe I asked him to be a part of NASA." He pronounced each letter of the acronym, N-A-S-A. "So you better get used to the man."

* * *

Wernher and Maria strolled through the humid night air to their rented car. He considered himself blameless, though it bothered him that others still judged him guilty of anything.

"My so-called celebrity status only goes so far," he said to his wife. "*Sie hassen uns noch.*"

Maria looked forward to their return to Huntsville. She wished to persuade her husband to take their family on a vacation to Disneyland. His cherished mother had died and he worried about his father, alone in West Germany. A break would do them all some good.

Chapter 87

"Vice-President Nixon, Khrushchev in Bitter Public Quarrel"

—Los Angeles Evening Mirror News

The White House, Washington, DC
Friday, August 21, 1959

Vannevar Bush stuck his legs out from a red velvet antique sofa beneath a life-size oil painting of George Washington and crossed his ankles.

"Our reconstituted Group must have complete autonomy within the CIA," he again urged President Eisenhower. Eisenhower was sitting next to him smoking a cigarette.

Philip Corso bided his time by the grand piano and saw that Ike didn't like the idea. Not at all. He was sure George Washington would have hated the idea, too.

John and Allen Dulles stood on the parquet floor, facing Bush and Ike on the sofa. The Dulles brothers and Bush looked like triplets: same fixed stares, same sanded faces.

Dull, Duller, Dulles, Corso thought.

He didn't think much of the sixth man in the East Room either: Nelson Rockefeller, Ike's advisor on government reorganization. In the light of three brass chandeliers Rockefeller was only a silhouette, a two-dimensional shadow of himself. Corso hated the Old Man's deference to the Rockefellers and Big Business. Big Business serviced the country's covert machinery of violence, which Allen controlled.

A shiver went down Corso's spine.

"I couldn't agree with Van more," said Rockefeller. He'd pressed hard for this meeting. "The Group must be autonomous. They must be able to function without direct oversight of the president's office. Ike, be reasonable. *You* understand. What if the next man doesn't?"

"It's inconceivable," Allen said, "that a secret intelligence arm of the government should have to comply with the overt orders of the government. Of course the CIA will help out where it can. Corona is working at long last."

Eisenhower smoked, and Corso thought back to the recent hullabaloo: when the Group had refused to hand over their antigravity research, the president was going to send in the First Army and rip them apart. The Group had relented, but now they were maneuvering to outflank the executive branch.

Silk curtains billowed in a strong breeze that blew through open windows.

"It's the only way to safeguard the advanced technology, the assets," Allen insisted, "from the whims of the unprofessionals. There have been leaks and close calls. You wouldn't want it all to become public now, would you?"

Eisenhower took a long breath. He'd seen how the press had whipped the public into a frenzy over Sputnik, a tiny, insignificant ball in space…

There's the rub, Corso thought. *The Old Man doesn't trust Allen, the CIA, or the Group, any more than I do. But it'd be worldwide chaos if the CIA or the Group went public with the alien phenomenon. People wouldn't be able to handle it. Period.*

"Very well, Nelson," the president said. "I accept your recommendation."

Rockefeller stepped out of his shadow to reveal a tanned, orange face and slits for eyes. "You won't regret it, Mr. President."

"I already regret it."

"This will speed up your underground construction fund."

His words failed to cheer the president, who dismissed everyone but Corso. When they'd gone, Ike asked, "Is the Vatican talking?"

"They are." Corso spoke softly. "And the legate *a latere* sends this message: 'The poles are still off limits to any and all satellites.' I should know more in a week or so."

Eisenhower rose with effort.

"Philip, I'm going to sign this afternoon a document to make Hawaii the fiftieth state. We've finally overcome the resistance and prejudice of southern congressmen to the islands' nonwhite population. Can you imagine what they'd say if they heard us here…"

Chapter 88

"Khrushchev Says U.S. U-2 Plane Shot Down, Dangles Rocket Threat If Flights Continue"

—Bennington Evening Banner

Heliopolis, Egypt
Wednesday, May 11, 1960

As part of a covert team, Rachel had broken into two Egyptian embassies and a consulate in Europe to photograph top-secret documents. An employee from the Zurich office of United Arab Airlines had allowed her to go through mailbags twice a week for a month in a safe house. Through these and other clandestine sources, she and Mossad had gained a thorough understanding of the Egyptian missile project and its captain, Wolfgang Sänger.

Rachel was the only one of the team assigned to penetrate Sänger's base, Factory 333, outside Heliopolis.

Getting in was easy. Dressed for the part in a short skirt, she posed as a representative of a Turkish company sympathetic to Egypt's goals that specialized in guidance components. She was given a tour of the facilities, test fields, and laboratories, which she knew had been built with laundered money provided by the CIA.

She was left alone in the luxurious living quarters of the German expats, a stately room with Louis XVI furnishings, buffet, large gilded vitrine, cabinets, and overstuffed pillows. She chose a door and found the library. With his back to her was an overweight man. She'd heard Sänger had been bored working for the French and had jumped at Egypt's lucrative offer, which had the bonus of targeting Zionists. He was flipping through a Mercedes-Benz catalog.

"What can you tell me about strontium-60 and radioactive cobalt?" she asked.

He turned his bulk and looked her up and down. He approved of her legs in nylons. "I just nabbed a silver 220 SE. What do I care about cobalt?"

"Radioactive waste and gas-filled warheads on your nine hundred rockets, this doesn't interest you? I thought you were in charge."

Rachel positioned herself in a lemon-yellow desk chair between him and the door.

"Exaggerations made for more money. Are you a reporter? They told me you had something to sell."

"Should we wait to see if you and your buddies can pull it off?"

The ruse was over. "You are another Israeli pig?" he asked.

"For someone who hates them, you've done so much to help Israel."

"What do you mean?"

She concentrated on Sänger and improvised. She pulled away the veils between his hidden self and his conscious mind and sped up his heartbeat to a dangerous level. "All this couldn't have happened without your Nazi friends."

Sänger clutched his arm, then his chest. With both hands, he ripped open his silk shirt. His eyes rolled into his head.

He made a silent, contorted scream and died on his antique sofa.

* * *

In Tel Aviv, Rachel knew she was being tailed. She could sense that the two CIA men several cars behind her motorcycle would have liked to kill her—she'd just destroyed a rocket program and upset the organization's delicate power play—but they needed her destination's coordinates.

She swerved off the two-lane road and sped across a rugged field, where they couldn't follow. She came out on a narrow street that bisected a small desert village and sped down a lane adjacent to crops being watered. She accelerated on a gravel path beneath a row of date trees and closed her eyes.

They're lost.

Twenty minutes later, she cycled into an underground parking lot in a nondescript neighborhood. She walked past the vehicles with a sense of disappointment. Despite the promise of Schomberger's work and his revelations in America, nothing had been made public. Nothing had changed. She was critical of her own naiveté. On the other hand, the trajectories of American rockets would soon be predictable.

A key-activated freight elevator took her down to the research department of Mossad, where she knocked on an unmarked door.

"Come in," said a voice.

A windowless office, long and narrow, overwhelmed with books, old and modern, stuffed into shelves, stacked on the floor at odd angles like stalagmites.

"Ms. Rachel, the papers you gave me are interesting," said Goshen, a professor of Biblical philology and physics. In a white cotton shirt and old gray flannel pants, he maneuvered between the detritus to remove a battered teapot from a heating coil. "I can recognize only a few of the glyphs and maybe one or two characters of the symbols."

"Nor can I read more than a fragment," she admitted. "But it *is* related to the saucers' ability to travel beyond light speed."

"May I ask why they are allowing us to study these papers?"

Enlarged photos of the glyphs were thumbtacked to the walls.

"Because both sides have tried and failed. It's in their interest for you to have a go at it."

"Something that prosaic?"

"Both sides fear the saucers will prevent them from making weapons and exploring space. They want control of the heavens, same as us." She sipped her tea. "Perhaps, Professor, if you invite others from the fields of Egyptology and biology, combine disciplines, you can discover their means of propulsion. Antigravity."

"That could take years."

"I wouldn't take that long. They'll withdraw funding."

"I'm surprised, frankly, that Mossad is getting involved."

"This building is Mossad, but I am not Mossad."

"And if we don't succeed?" he asked, stirring honey into his cup.

"Then we'll have to find a more primitive way to fight back. They're too dangerous to let be."

"And if we *do* succeed?"

"Then they will come for you."

Chapter 89

"Winner Kennedy Asks Aid in Choosing Running Mate"

—Kenosha Evening News

Huntsville, Alabama
Thursday, September 8, 1960

Von Braun, in his most immaculate suit, watched the *Columbine* touch down on the tarmac. Its chrome and silver exterior shimmered in the sun. The door of Air Force One opened and President Eisenhower stepped out, wearing dark gray, and waved to a crowd of congressmen, military brass, and rich Huntsville families.

He was greeted by von Braun, Governor Patterson of Alabama, and Major General Staftoy, in full regalia. ABMA had become a part of N-A-S-A—a civilian outfit—Gilruth, Kraft, and the rest of them. JPL and von Kármán had been absorbed, too. One of the first steps had been to rechristen the "Army Ballistic Missile Agency" the "George C. Marshall Space Flight Center." A more peaceful moniker.

Shaking hands with Eisenhower, von Braun pushed aside the fact that he was looking into the eyes of the former supreme commander of Allied Forces. Instead he anticipated their conversation about budgets.

The president, for his part, had to suppress once again something akin to hostility.

They rode in an open white convertible adorned with NASA decals on its sides. Their motor cavalcade passed by a sign on the road that read, HUNTSVILLE, ALABAMA—SPACE CAPITAL OF THE UNIVERSE.

Arriving at the assembly building, Eisenhower admired the rudiments of the enormous Saturn launch vehicle, even though it was only partially constructed and lying on its side. He put on his glasses for a better look as von Braun related the rocket's history, as well as its symbolic and practical value.

He's eloquent, Ike admitted to himself. *Passionate.*

"It will achieve 1,500,000 pounds of thrust."

"As much as the Soviet rocket?"

"We think so."

Dozens of reporters snapped hundreds of photos while shouting questions at them and the others. Society men in polished shoes and women in high heels, jewelry, and chic dresses ogled the immense machinery.

Ike laughed as they walked past another sign: LATE TO BED, EARLY TO RISE, WORK LIKE HELL AND ADVERTISE.

"That's our motto, sir," von Braun also laughed.

At the test area a Saturn engine had been installed on a stand. Von Braun asked Eisenhower to put on a proffered hard hat.

"What kind of payload can it put into orbit?"

"Maybe as much as 4,500 kilograms," answered von Braun. "But its upper stages won't be available until '61 or '62 at the earliest. They will not meet the DOD's requirements for heavy loads, so we would like to build an even bigger and better rocket in the future."

He knew that wasn't the answer the president wanted, because it meant more money. Eisenhower said something to an aide, who asked the reporters to back off, while he, von Braun, and Staftoy slipped into a private office.

"You see, Mr. President, with more powerful rockets we will have the means to lift tremendous cargos into space." Von Braun was still selling without realizing Eisenhower wasn't buying. "From telecommunications satellites to—"

"Nuclear warheads?"

"Scientific survey instrumentation," Staftoy intervened.

"You believe the United States should weaponize space, don't you, Professor?" the president said.

"Sir, I am afraid if we do not, the Soviets will." Von Braun enunciated each syllable carefully. "We cannot close our eyes to the military aspects of outer space simply because the idea may be frightening to the public. The question of space superiority is as important today as the concept of air superiority was forty years ago."

"I don't like that kind of thinking." Ike crossed his arms. "After all, you and I and the general here know there are other forces at work. It's no longer that simple. We don't exist in a vacuum, and neither do the Soviets."

Eisenhower saw from Staftoy's face that he made up the minority, not that he cared one way or the other.

"Whenever I open a magazine," Eisenhower went on, "I see every product being sold with a picture of a Redstone or an Atlas missile. It's an insidious penetration of our minds that tells us the only thing this country should be engaged in is weapons. But I'm telling you both we can't afford that. Every rocket fired is stealing money that could be used to improve the everyday lives of citizens. How much would all this cost? Tell me straight."

"Sir," Staftoy said, "the Apollo program will run between thirty-four and forty-six billion dollars."

"I just don't see how much safer we'll be or how much scientific knowledge you can fish out of space to justify that investment. I'm not going to do it. I'm not going to play the outer-space game and try to one-up the Soviets. It's just not worth it."

"Sir, aren't you concerned about their penetration of our airspace?"

Ike knew what he was referring to.

"There are cheaper, more effective, and quieter ways of dealing with all that," he said. "I'm not about to hock our country's jewels for one gargantuan program. Gentlemen, I'm sorry, but my administration won't back Apollo."

Von Braun lit a cigarette and his optimism kicked in. *Maybe the next president will*, he thought. The election loomed only months away, Nixon vs. Kennedy.

A half hour later President Eisenhower reboarded Air Force One.

"I know we are on the critically correct path," von Braun said to Staftoy as they watched the plane take off. "Of that I'm sure."

"I agree." Staftoy puffed his pipe. "Our problem is all that money going into black projects."

"Yes." Von Braun smoked. "Our civilian agency, a public one, well, it's going to be even harder to acquire the budget. And no bucks, no Buck Rogers..."

Chapter 90

"Nixon and Kennedy Debate Cuba, 'Regrets' Over U-2, Civil Rights and Schools in Second TV Clash"

—*The New York Times*

Tyuratam, Union of Soviet Socialist Republics
Monday, October 24, 1960

Korolev cursed himself for feeling self-pity.

6:44 p.m. Final prelaunch operations.

A few hundred meters from the pad, instead of observing its activity, he brooded over his daughter's steadfast refusal to return to him. Though Natasha had written twice, she would not see him. It had been years since he'd kissed her face…

What does she look like now?

Korolev's KGB protector, Colonel Grigoriy Yakovenko, pretended to mind his own business. Since Sputnik, Korolev had been assigned a security detail. To keep his mind off his depression and the recent failures of the Mars probes, he had come to witness the launch of the prototype R-16 missile. He hoped it would be a success, but since his arrival he'd noted a casual inattention to safety procedures, a crew tired and desperate to hurry things along.

Korolev had soothed Khrushchev by assuring him they could soon achieve another historical first: man in space. The two saw eye to eye on that subject, and Khrushchev had named Korolev Principal Designer.

With the countdown at thirty minutes, Korolev ducked into the designated smoking area, which was crowded with agitated engineers and supervisors going over last-minute procedures. When he clicked on his metal lighter, its little flame seemed to illuminate the whole room in a blinding flash.

Korolev bolted outside with Colonel Yakovenko and the others.

Something had exploded in the launch area. Flames shot off to the east. Propellant splashed out of the missile's tanks and soaked the scrambling test crew. A fire devoured them and flared to the west and north. Several men, trapped and frantic on the service platform, jumped straight into the flames. Other men fell, killed by poisonous vapors.

Korolev's mouth clenched his unlit cigarette.

A wave of heat hit the onlookers and singed their clothing.

Those workers too close to the conflagration bogged down in molten asphalt. Screeching and screaming, each exploded like the red top of a struck match.

Technicians in brown coats streamed from the blockhouse to escape the furnace, but the top part of the rocket fell onto the second. The detonation ignited monstrous fireballs that engulfed the technicians in mid-stride.

Korolev saw the burn zone widen, killing everyone in its path; he felt the violent, earthshaking blows simultaneous with solid-fuel engines and high-pressure tanks bursting skyward.

He spit out his cigarette.

Even as he dodged the fires, running to help those who had made it to a safety ditch, he thought, *Perhaps Natashka will forgive me if she thinks I'm dead.*

Chapter 91

"Americans Concerned About the Missile Gap"

—Biloxi Daily Herald

The White House, Washington, DC
Tuesday, January 17, 1961

President Eisenhower faced the television camera. Democrat John F. Kennedy had won the election. Although a disappointing break in political continuity for the seventy-year-old, Nixon's loss had not been the most distressing thought on his mind the last few weeks.

Sitting at a wooden desk with a tabletop lectern in the East Room, he adjusted his clear-rim glasses and began his farewell address at 8:30 p.m.

"Good evening, my fellow Americans," Eisenhower read from notes into two microphones.

Behind him, a curtain backdrop would appear to television viewers on their black-and-white screens to be the same shade of gray as his suit. Among the small group allowed to witness his speech, standing behind the TV camera and photographers, were Nixon, CIA director Allen Dulles, and Philip Corso.

"Three days from now, after a half century of service, I shall lay down the responsibilities of office as, in a traditional and solemn ceremony, the authority of the presidency is vested in my successor."

He spoke haltingly. Parts of his speech had been rewritten only hours before. Ike had a more assured air when he read from the later unchanged sections on the Teleprompter.

"Today, we face a hostile ideology, global in scope, atheistic in character, ruthless in purpose, and insidious in method. Unhappily, the danger it poses promises to be of indefinite duration."

Nixon and Corso had agreed on this point.

"Until the latest of our world conflicts, the United States had no armaments industry. American makers of plowshares could, with time and as required, make swords as well. But now we can no longer risk emergency improvisation of national defense. We have been compelled to create a permanent armaments industry of vast proportions."

Nixon shifted his weight from one foot to the other. He'd read the speech beforehand and reported its contents to Dulles.

"This conjunction of an immense military establishment and a large arms industry is new in the American experience. The total influence—economic, political, even spiritual—is felt in every city, every statehouse, every office of the federal government. In the councils of government, we must guard against the acquisition of unwarranted influence, whether sought or unsought, by the military-industrial complex. The potential for the disastrous rise of misplaced power exists, and will persist.

"We should take nothing for granted. Only an alert and knowledgeable citizenry can compel the proper meshing of the huge industrial and military machinery of defense with our peaceful methods and goals so that security and liberty may prosper together."

Eisenhower removed his glasses.

"We must also be alert to the equal and opposite danger that public policy could itself become the captive of a scientific-technological elite."

* * *

"Just who did you mean when you mentioned the 'military-industrial' cabal?" Dulles asked afterward.

He, Nixon, and Corso had accompanied Ike to the Oval Office. The latter reclined, smoking, in a big green chair upholstered in a floral pattern.

"Well, I suppose you should know what I meant, Allen," Ike said. "I meant people like the cabal, but primarily Teller—and that Wernher von Braun."

"Is that all?"

"They need to be watched."

"The FBI and our folks keep pretty close tabs on them. Are you sure that's all you meant?"

Eisenhower exhaled. "I'm sure."

Nixon sweated, while Corso, sitting as far from Dulles as he could, kept his eyes on the floor.

"Okay," Dulles said and left the office.

"Dulles'll stick you in the back if you're not vigilant, Dick."

"He's Kennedy's problem now," Nixon said. "You did what you could."

"No. I failed. I wasn't careful enough with that damn Group, or Allen and his CIA." Eisenhower inhaled and exhaled smoke. "I trusted them, and at present it's all being run by schemers and corporations and God knows who. Their actions are going to wind up being detrimental to the country or worse. Much worse."

"It's not too late to force them to deemphasize their weapons nonsense"—Corso looked up—"in favor of intelligence gathering and analysis."

"I've tried. I cannot change Allen Dulles."

Corso saw that his president's confidence had been badly damaged.

"Then it's up to Kennedy and his guys."

Ike frowned. "I don't think he's up to it, frankly. None of this is going to be in the best hands. None of it. Jack's inheriting a legacy of ashes."

Nixon wiped beads of perspiration from his brow. A look from Ike told him to leave, so he did.

Alone, Eisenhower said to Corso, "I want you to go see General Trudeau. I want the two of you to handle advanced technology dissemination. Maybe you can salvage something. Help that Kennedy bastard if you can."

"Yes, sir."

"Did you send my message to Rome?"

"Yes, sir."

"And?"

"And…nothing. The Vatican's legate sent no reply. Their silence is… ominous."

Corso had his hand on the doorknob when Ike asked, "What about Forrestal?"

He half turned.

James Forrestal? Why is the Old Man asking about him?

"Before I brief the new guy in the Oval Office, I need to know the truth." Eisenhower had read his thoughts. "I've been remiss here, too. I never believed he jumped. If Dulles was behind it, and he most surely was, Kennedy has to know. He needs to know everything."

"Yes, sir."

Chapter 92

"35th President Sworn In:
Kennedy Calls Mankind to 'Quest for Peace'—
Says U.S. Will Pay Any Price to Stay Free"

—*The Arizona Daily Star*

Tyuratam, Union of Soviet Socialist Republics
Saturday, April 8, 1961

Korolev lived in a prefab three-room wooden house apart from the main cluster of buildings, about fifteen minutes by car from the launching pad. As he'd requested, young poplars had been planted to shield him from two identical structures nearby, and a carpet of red flowers led to his door. The closest house was crowded with cosmonauts, the "Vanguard Six."

Sergei Pavlovich would visit them later, after finishing his daily correspondence. In his study, he leaned over his desk and took paper and ink. The sun had yet to rise, so he switched on a green-shaded lamp.

On a table behind him, Western magazines were fanned out, those with articles on the "Red" satellite, those with photographs and comments from prominent scientists. None of them knew about Korolev. His identity remained a secret to all but his team and the highest officials, but he appreciated the praise, even if the forced anonymity rankled him.

After scribbling a note to Mishin, he put his hand in a side pocket of his jacket and removed a delicate glass vial. He took a yellow pill from it, which he placed under his tongue. His heart had been acting up lately.

On his desk lay a letter from his daughter. He'd sent a car for her the day before. Natasha had written her letter to explain why she hadn't come: "Grandfather Maximilian Nikolaevich told me that mother would be upset and I would break my word by coming. So I took off my party dress and I cried. Grandpa reminded me that I had no right to cry or to visit my father without my mother's approval. I screamed and sobbed, and gave up finally. I will regret it all my life."

* * *

The sun rose in a clear blue sky above the beige steppes. It was four days before the first manned launch of the Vostok.

Inside the MIK assembly hall, Korolev, Chertok, Glushko, General Kamanin, and a film crew of five visited the Vanguard Six, shorter men, because they had to fit inside the small capsule. Gagarin, Titov, Nelyubov, Popovich, and the two others were practicing getting into and out of their cosmonaut suits.

Afterward they changed back into their blue training outfits.

"We are able to put the suit on in twenty minutes," Titov reported. "To take it off, we need only fifteen."

"Good," Korolev said. "The ejection seat is not designed to float, and the spherical reentry capsule is no better. I am therefore telling you the only option is landing on Soviet Union soil."

He dismissed the camera crew. The six candidates suspected the Principal Designer was going to make his choice.

He asked each of them a few technical questions, and each answered correctly. It seemed to Nelyubov that Korolev favored Gagarin.

"As of today, six Vostoks have been launched, of which four reached orbit, and two landed successfully. Not great, but not bad for you. You've had a chance to read the manual. What do you suggest?"

"We think only a shortened version of this manual should be put aboard the spacecraft," Gagarin joked, and the other cosmonauts laughed.

Korolev noted that, similar to his friend Chertok, Gagarin's boyish face always seemed to be smiling.

"Comrades," said General Kamanin, "the nation's honor will be in your hands. We dare not lose the space race to the Americans. They are pushing to match us in launch vehicles and they have already surpassed us in electronics, communications, and, I must admit, telemetry."

Chertok lost his smile. Communication with Venera 1 had failed at a distance of less than two million kilometers from Earth. The Americans had maintained radio contact with a satellite at more than thirty million kilometers.

"With their new civilian agency they are concentrating all their efforts in one space organization. It is to be admired. But we can show them once again who is the more daring and the more inventive."

"I also want to make sure each of you understands the risks," Korolev said, looking squarely at Yuri Alekseyevich Gagarin. "Let us be frank. You have not chosen an easy path. You have chosen a dangerous one, but it is impossible any other way."

He approached a scale model of the Vostok that stood three meters high. Reaching up, he ran his palm over the capsule surface. "You will not have much room in there or much control," he spoke gently. "The centrifuge, altitude chamber, and the rest are absolutely essential and are therefore automated. Otherwise, you would not survive out there in space."

"We are pilots," said Gagarin, who had blue eyes and pale skin. "Danger is the lot of the profession."

Yes, he is young, Korolev thought. *Yet he already seems to understand life.*

"In our days, you cannot smolder," Nelyubov said. "You've got to really burn."

"Go ahead, talk all you want," Popovich blurted out. "But I will fly first."

"Truly spoken—flying is a profession for the bold," Korolev said. "There is no greater happiness on Earth. I envy you. One of you will be the first to storm outer space. One of you will step on the surface of the Moon. And, eventually, on Mars."

“That is the mission for me,” Titov declared.

Korolev turned back to the model. “This is a *kosmicheskiy korabl.* And why not? There is a sea ship, a river ship, an airship, now we have a genuine spaceship.” He scanned their faces. “All of this has to function faultlessly. Only talented people could have created such technology. Only artistic people, wise and gentle as a mother, could have created its forms.

“I have here six cosmonauts, each ready to complete a flight. But I have chosen Gagarin to fly first. Others will fly after.”

Korolev shook Gagarin’s hand and said, “We wish you success, Yuri Alekseyevich!”

* * *

Four days later, at T minus two hours, a bus drove Gagarin to the launchpad. A larger number of well-wishers than anticipated hugged him in his orange spacesuit.

The last to bid him goodbye and kiss him that predawn was Korolev.

“Take this, Yuri Alekseyevich.” Korolev handed him a sealed envelope. “It contains the numbered sequence to override the computer. Use it if you have to. Unlike Glushko and the physicians, I sincerely doubt you will be going insane up there.”

“Thank you.”

Gagarin would now have a fighting chance if any of the automated systems broke down. He would be more than an animal locked to a chair.

The cosmonaut took the elevator up, and the Principal Designer headed toward the bunker.

The Vostok itself hummed. Over two hundred electric valves, over six thousand transistors, over fifteen kilometers of wiring.

In the bunker Glushko thought only of his engines. He was confident they’d perform adequately as long as the man inside the capsule could do nothing to disturb their functionality. But when Korolev entered, he perceived his friend’s betrayal.

“Ignition, preliminary, main…and lift off!” a technician shouted.

The nearly forty-meter-long Vostok rocket shot clear of the launchpad with a thrust of about six hundred tons.

"Po-ye-kha-li!" Gagarin shouted over the radio, his words nearly drowned out by thundering engines. "Visibility is excellent! Out the window, I see Earth, clouds, the launch site; I see rivers… It is beautiful. What beauty!"

Soon Gagarin in his capsule was orbiting the planet, a hundred nautical miles up.

"Let the capitalist countries catch up with us!" Khrushchev cried over the phone when he'd been connected to the first man in space.

Chapter 93

“Человек В Пространстве—Капитан Первого Звездолета—Наш Советский Человек! Великая Победа Разума И Труда—Мир Аплодирует Юрию Гагарину (Man in Space—First Starship Captain Is Our Soviet Man! Great Victory of Mind and Labor—World Is Applauding Yuri Gagarin)”

—*Pravda,* Moscow

Huntsville, Alabama
Thursday, April 13, 1961

Von Braun’s twelve-year-old daughter, Iris, roller-skated ahead of him on the waxed hallway floor. Her father walked behind her, in steel-blue suit and beige tie, while skimming the latest reports from his thirty-five chief engineers.

He nodded to an employee without looking, who nodded back.

A letter informed him that the fourth Disney show had been cancelled.

At the outer door of his office he said, “Now skate back to your mother. You cannot miss your afternoon class.”

“But, Dad, it’s going to be a substitute.” Iris circled him in her light-blue blouse and darker blue skirt.

"You cannot miss even one period of science, ever." He patted her cheek as she passed. "Can you imagine what they would say about me?"

His daughter made a face but rolled backward obediently.

He'd opted to eat lunch at home, to take a break, to look in on his new infant boy, Peter, and to escape for an hour the grim mood at work.

"James Webb called," his secretary Carol Holmes informed him. "And I quote, 'NASA is not showing the film to Congress.' Unquote. Mr. Webb said the top brass decided that a traumatized chimp after Gagarin would be…uh, quote: 'embarrassing.'"

"Thank you, Carol."

Von Braun closed the door to his inner office. He knew nearly everyone in the building disagreed with him.

He was thumbing through a pile of paperwork on his desk when the door was flung open and Alan Shepard barged in. "Kraft told me *you're* the one responsible for our monumental fuckup! Goddamn it, Wernher. We had 'em by the shorthairs—and you let 'em go!"

"Alan, please close the door."

Von Braun could see Carol standing behind Shepard, helpless.

Shepard didn't close the door. His blue eyes bulged and even the stubble on his face seemed angry. "You goddamn *bastard!* You and your goddamn German testing! Test, test, and more testing!" He took a step into the office, and Carol was able to shut the door and prevent two curious employees from seeing more. "'We're *asleep* down here.' What kind of message is that to the world, for chrissake? You need to wake the hell up!"

"Alan, please calm down." Von Braun thought the astronaut might hit him. "Have a seat. I can see you're upset."

"Don't patronize me. You robbed me of my place in history. The others in the brotherhood feel the same goddamn way."

"We could not risk it, Alan." He stayed seated, his face pale. "I am sorry, but we could not risk your life, or anyone's. We would have lost everything—all financial support—if something had gone wrong."

"Bullshit! Don't underestimate us. You're not American and you never will be. I heard one of their cosmonauts *did* die! That didn't stop the Reds—and it wouldn't stop us. You had one banged-up monkey and you put everything on hold, for chrissake! Kraft and Gilruth—they were ready to go!"

"Alan, look on the positive side." He put his hands forward on the desk. "Gagarin's flight clears away the medical blocks. You will fly in the next few weeks. Kennedy has to give permission now."

"Soon is too late! Fuck Washington! And fuck procedure. You blew it."

Shepard slammed a knobby fist into his open palm. Von Braun couldn't help noticing that the astronaut looked about ten years older than the cosmonaut in the newspaper photos. The Russians were choosing younger men.

Are they emphasizing health over experience? Interesting.

"The test flight should have been a *real* flight." Shepard slammed his fist again. "With me in it—and we would've beat those goddamn commie tractor drivers!"

"Alan, it is a long, important race, and we cannot make a mistake by rushing."

"You're kidding yourself, Doc. It's just another commercial enterprise, where being *first* is everything." His face softened a little. "Look, Doc, you're scared. You've never launched a human. For the first time your objective is to keep someone alive instead of killing a whole bunch of 'em. So listen carefully: I'm not scared, even if you are."

He ripped the door open and rapped it closed behind him.

Carol jerked it open again. "He just stormed right by me, Doctor—I couldn't stop him! I'm so sorry—"

"Don't worry about it, Ms. Holmes. Alan had only to blow off some steam. This is a dramatic business."

Chapter 94

"Castro Claims Victory; Moscow Blames U.S. for Attack"

—*The Arizona Republic*

The White House, Washington, DC
Thursday, April 20, 1961

Vice President Lyndon B. Johnson had told his staff that the Bay of Pigs invasion had been a huge "fucking fiasco," so he wasn't surprised to be called into an urgent meeting with Kennedy two days later. A single word had been typed in the subject line—"NASA"—and Johnson chaired the National Aeronautics and Space Council.

Jack's been stalling, he thought. *But everything's changed with the one-two punch of Gagarin and Castro.*

Upon entering the Oval Office, Johnson saw three men he knew fairly well already standing with Kennedy: budget director David Bell, science advisor Jerome Wiesner, chief administrator of NASA James Webb.

The president's brother Robert, United States' attorney general, occupied a window seat.

"All right, gentlemen, let's get started," Kennedy said when he saw Johnson. "Lyndon, can you tell us about the status of the space program and what, er, we can do to catch up? I want to know what *needs* to be done, uh, what *should* be done, and what *can* be done."

"Mr. President, the short story is we are not making maximum effort or achieving the results necessary if we want this country to reach a position of leadership in space."

Johnson had decided to be aggressive from the get-go. He knew Wiesner was plotting to thwart him. Bell, a bean counter, would push against him, too. Johnson's proposals weren't going to come cheap. Webb would back him.

"Is that all?" Kennedy asked.

"No. The Russians just did something spectacular—again. At NASA they are frustrated and angry. Stories critical of their efforts are in the papers, and they know it's not their fault. They can and should get going. They want to. But the morale of the entire team is pretty damn low." He said to Wiesner, "I should say Jerome's report is getting a lot of heat. You're not popular down south."

Wiesner's expression showed he didn't care. "If the newspapers printed a dispatch announcing the Soviets were sending the first man to Hell," he said, "the press would shout, 'We can't let them beat us!'"

Johnson turned red and moved closer to Wiesner, whose sagging face suddenly betrayed a touch of fear.

Shit, Wiesner thought. *I'm going to get the* treatment.

Johnson's eyes narrowed. "When Khrushchev stopped by the UN, Soviet delegates joked that the United States of America needed third-world aid; you know—handouts." He thrust his face an inch from Wiesner's. "But I'm sure *you* know we're on track to take the lead—so *don't get in our way*."

The Kennedy brothers watched, amused at Johnson's bullying tactics.

"Lyndon, what about, your, er, your von Braun—can we trust him?" Jack asked.

Johnson pivoted to him and Wiesner sidestepped away.

"Ike didn't," Johnson replied. "He hated him. But my feeling is that von Braun is a realist. He's the key guy, with a couple of others, down in Huntsville. I've seen this with my own eyes. There's a certain amount of hero worship."

"Well, I don't care if he's the janitor over there, as long as he knows how to get us going."

"As long as the janitor is named von Braun." Johnson took a drag on a Lucky Strike. "He wrote me a letter describing how we could catch up and surpass the Soviets. I'll forward it to your office."

"Do those southerners know about his membership in the SS?" Wiesner asked pointedly.

"They know he was arrested by the Gestapo." Johnson stayed focused on Kennedy. "He makes a point of broadcasting *that* story. My feeling is von Braun has been more than willing to play ball. He's an American citizen and he goes to church."

Wiesner wasn't impressed, but he saw Jack easily swayed. The science advisor knew he'd have a tough rearguard fight to curtail what he considered fiscal madness.

"Jim, the Gemini program has slipped how much?" Wiesner asked.

"*Slip* is the wrong word, sir," replied Webb, who had a square head with no discernible lips and small eyes.

Johnson wanted to throttle Webb on the spot for his bookish semantics.

"Jim," the president asked, "can you tell me when the, er, two-man mission round the world will be?"

"An *unmanned* suborbital flight is scheduled for August of '63. The first orbital with two men is planned for February '64."

"Two men, one week?"

"Two men, one week."

Johnson now wanted to throttle both of them for getting off track. Instead, he forcefully stubbed out one cigarette and lit another.

"I see." Jack paced. His steel-rod-and-canvas back brace, tightened and cinched around his torso, kept him ramrod straight for each painful step. "Gentlemen, do we have a chance of beating the Soviets by putting a laboratory in space, or a trip round the Moon, or with a manned rocket to the Moon? Jim, is there any other space race we could win?"

They knew Kennedy liked to win. A look from Johnson told Webb to keep his mouth shut.

"Sir," Johnson said, "we have a good chance of beating them to the Moon with a manned crew."

"Before we go to Congress, we'll have to decide. Once we decide—Lyndon, you can do this—you'll have to get key members of Congress to back us. We make up our mind first, then pull 'em in."

"Yes, sir. We'd face reasonable odds. With an all-out crash program, we could achieve it by '67 or '68."

Webb coughed. Johnson's dates were designed to please the president. That's all. Jack would want to be in office when they landed.

"Bob Gilruth told me 1970. Can we really do it before?"

Kennedy had asked the room, but again, it was Johnson who replied: "Yes, sir. We know the Russians can't reach the Moon. Not yet. They don't have the ability, and the Saturn rocket is further along than their equivalent. A Moon landing would give real drive to our space program. We'd be able to say—and it would be true—that the program can develop skills and capacities on a broad technological front. That's leadership."

"That's what you think?"

"That's what I know." He knocked the ash of his cigarette into an onyx tray. "NASA will launch Shepard on May 5. That'll help sway opinion. We've also already solved a problem the Soviets haven't—Corona has taught us how to recover astronauts in their capsule. Since we can land in water, we can have bigger and safer payloads."

"It's going to cost billions," sighed Bell.

Johnson kept his gaze fixed hypnotically on the president.

"Jack, if you want to *win*, you've got to back Gemini all the way. Much more importantly, you've got to back Apollo. You've got to back them loud and clear."

"We'll beat them at every turn, you can bet on it."

His brother Robert tapped his wristwatch. It was time for Jack's evening medication.

"I'm going to do more than back them," Kennedy said. "You'll see."

Chapter 95

"First U.S. Spaceman Rockets 302 Miles on 5,100 M.P.H. Journey in 15-Minute Flight"

—*Fitchburg Sentinel*

Juniper Hills, California
Sunday, January 28, 1962

The sun rose on a small cabin surrounded by forest. Inside the cabin a little girl nicknamed "Muffie" was dying of pneumonia, after six months of agony, the terrible consequence of an inoperable brain tumor. She lay still beneath the covers. Her parents stood by her bed.

After Muffie had breathed her last, Neil Armstrong showed little emotion. No one there, not the doctor or the two family friends, doubted his strong feelings, yet they didn't dare reach out a hand to console him. They felt it wouldn't be right, Neil wouldn't have wanted it. Nor did he reach out toward his wife, Janet, whose heart, like his, broke that day, their sixth wedding anniversary.

He'd been away the previous week on air force business, and Janet had suffered with Muffie in isolation.

Did she wait to see me once more before dying? Neil asked himself. *Why did I stay away?*

* * *

The day of his daughter's funeral, Neil's friends at the Flight Research Center grounded their planes. She'd almost made it to the age of three.

One cousin whispered to another at the reception afterward that the Armstrongs had lived on a base in Nevada where the government had conducted atomic testing.

"That fallout, lying around in those hills," he said, "it got into the water systems…"

The second cousin nodded knowingly.

* * *

On Monday, Armstrong flew fast in his F5D.

Shortly after his test flight, he walked down a tree-lined street to his neighborhood mailbox. He slipped into the chute an application for the next round of astronaut selection.

His thoughts lingered on Shepard's flight and Kennedy's recent speech committing America to a manned Moon landing.

"Before the decade is out," the president had challenged Congress.

The Mercury and Gemini programs had open slots. Armstrong wanted one of them.

He would make it up to Muffie.

Chapter 96

"Ranger 4 Crashes on Moon—Spacecraft Feat Hailed by Leaders"

—*The Phoenix Gazette*

McAlester, Oklahoma
Wednesday, June 6, 1962

"Let me remind you that Americans have always been explorers and pioneers. If Americans want to continue as world leaders, America must establish a leadership role in space!" Von Braun, the celebrated director of the Marshall Space Flight Center, was sweating in the hot air of a high school gymnasium and delivered the last words of his stump speech to a packed crowd of students and their families.

They applauded. Their enthusiasm and confidence in the space program had never been higher. Astronaut John Glenn had circled the globe three times only months before, and they gave a lot of credit for his success to the man on stage.

Von Braun thanked them and shook the hand of Carl Albert, Speaker of the House, who had introduced him. He then took questions.

"Are we going to beat the Russians to the Moon?" asked a shoe salesman.

"I cannot be certain, but we will do our best."

"Couldn't this money be better spent on something here in Oklahoma?" asked a schoolteacher.

“NASA is a stimulant and catalyst for the development of new technologies and for research in the basic sciences.”

“What do you think about UFOs?” asked a student.

“It is as impossible to confirm UFOs in the present as it will be to deny them in the future.”

A few folks in the audience pondered his surprising certainty, while a chief of the Choctaw tribe presented von Braun with a shield and a colorful full-length headdress of eagle feathers. The elder Native American announced to the crowd that he’d given the German American a new name: “*Oskinaki Ninakhushi Eya*! Grand-Chief-Who-Sends-Arrows-of-Fire-to-the-Moon!”

People leapt to their feet as if von Braun were a pop star to give him a standing ovation. Ever the showman, he donned the floor-length headdress and posed for pictures. Waving goodbye, sans headdress, he climbed into a waiting government sedan, which peeled out in the direction of the airport accompanied by a high-speed police escort.

“Is there anything about America you don’t like, Doctor?” Carl Albert asked in the sedan.

“I don’t like being treated like a foreign spy,” replied von Braun. “I am a citizen, but everywhere I go the FBI has me followed. I cannot even go to the bathroom without an FBI man tailing me. Look behind us.”

The congressman turned.

“That blue car has been following us since we flew in. They’re always around. My telephone is bugged, and they read more of my mail than I do.”

“Doctor, my brother-in-law is law enforcement and I have some experience in the intelligence world,” Albert said. “That’s not FBI. No, sir. You have somebody else on your tail.”

* * *

The next morning von Braun took a chair in a meeting room of the Manned Spacecraft Center, formerly the Space Task Group. Another name change. This one due to its move from Langley to Houston. Gilruth had begged Webb to keep his team in Virginia, but it had been a political decision, a "pork" decision. LBJ wanted the MSC in Texas, so that's where they went.

In a suit and tie, von Braun made awkward chitchat with what he considered a contentious group, all of whom, Gilruth included, had on the same gray pants and white short-sleeved shirts: deputy for systems engineering Joe Shea, flight director Chris Kraft, and aeronautical engineer John Houbolt. Two astronauts had also been invited, Alan Shepard and John Glenn. They'd assembled to decide at last how to fly a man to the Moon.

Von Braun eyed Shepard warily. He saw that Kraft was on edge. Von Braun had accepted that Kraft and Gilruth would run the astronaut program from Houston, but he still had the rockets and the press in his pocket. The public had the impression von Braun orchestrated the whole shebang, even if he didn't. Whatever Kraft and Gilruth thought of him, he knew they had to woo him to their way of thinking.

The group from Houston had already made up their minds and had been lobbying the rocketman for months. The astronauts would cast the deciding vote in case of a tie, their star power against his.

"I used to be a voice in the wilderness," said Houbolt, who had silver hair and noticeable bags under his eyes. "I could never understand why Nova, with its ponderous size, was being accepted without the right questions asked."

Glenn glanced at Shepard, who suppressed a grin, for von Braun had long championed Nova and its direct ascent to the Moon. A giant craft, Nova would have landed on the Moon and taken off again for a return trip. But its allure had faded due to impracticalities and calendar constraints, to its detractors' delight.

"If we really want to send a manned mission to the Moon," Houbolt concluded, "lunar orbit rendezvous is the only way to go."

"We've been over the specifics," Gilruth took over, "the weight advantages of LOR, and its advantages in time and money. Even over Earth orbit rendezvous."

"Yes, but if they fail in Earth orbit, they can splash down," von Braun said. "If your orbit rendezvous fails above the Moon, the astronauts are dead."

"That's a risk we're willing to take," Glenn said.

"Look, we've already lost too much time debating," Kraft said. "Two years of this decade are gone. We have to do what's possible in the years left. That means LOR and its shorter flight testing program."

"We will need mighty good computers," said von Braun. "The Apollo program is going to be the most technological endeavor in the history of civilization. In terms of finance, manpower, and other resources, Apollo will have no parallel. It is unique."

Who is he talking to? Kraft wondered. Even though he'd been in dozens of meetings with von Braun, the latter's grandstanding still baffled him.

"We'll have to become more proficient in rendezvous techniques, that's for sure," Shepard said. "Mercury's a capsule, not a spacecraft. We can point it this way or that, but we have no ability to maneuver in orbit. Max, you'll need to build something with a lot more flexibility, and"—he looked at them all—"Doctor von Braun can have as many practice shots as he needs."

Shepard saw his barb sting the MSFC director, but von Braun shook it off.

"Can we get the 'bug' into the Saturn?" he asked.

"The lunar module? Yes, I'm sure of it," Houbolt answered.

"This is of paramount importance. If you can get the bug into the area which joins the command module to the guidance slice, we will save on vehicle weight and length."

Von Braun's mind raced. LOR meant he'd be in charge only of building the rocket, whose mission would be over minutes after launch. The rest would be up to Gilruth, Kraft, and their Mission Control team. Either he signed on or…

I have no choice.

They outnumbered him, and their reasoning was sound.

"Marshall will back LOR," he said, and Gilruth smiled. "I think it has the highest confidence factor of success. I will weather the storm of criticism I will no doubt face back home for accepting your proposal." He looked at Shepard before borrowing the astronaut's coinage. "I am A-OK with lunar orbit rendezvous. Let's go."

Jesus, he's not even going to consult his own team first, thought Kraft.

He and Gilruth had hoped to sway von Braun but hadn't expected a complete capitulation.

"What made you change your mind?" Gilruth asked, standing up as the others filed out of the room. "Confidentially."

"Ranger 4," von Braun replied without hesitation, also standing. "The probe hit the Moon when and where we predicted."

Gilruth understood.

"Webb and Wiesner will need convincing," von Braun added in the doorway.

"I'll convince Webb. No one cares what Wiesner thinks."

* * *

Von Braun arrived home to find family members out shopping or at a friend's house. After taking off his jacket and tie and throwing them on the living room couch, he stepped into his study to relax and read the papers—but found Hans Kammler already at ease in his recliner.

On either side of Kammler loomed large men in gray suits.

"Surprised to see me, Professor?" Kammler asked, crossing his legs.

Von Braun stared—Kammler hadn't aged much. He'd never seen the ex-SS commander in a suit and button-down shirt.

"*Ja*, I am surprised," he said and reached for the phone.

"There is no need for the police," Kammler said and raised his hand. "If you say I broke in, I will say you invited me. We are both Germans, they will see. I have proper papers like you, Professor. Funny, isn't it? When one has secrets"—he tapped his temple—"one can obtain many things."

"Why are you here?" Von Braun changed tack and opened a cabinet, from which he withdrew four shot glasses and a bottle of whiskey.

"These men won't be joining us," Kammler said. "When did we last have the pleasure of speaking? The Haus Ingeburg? Yes."

"We heard you were killed, but I never believed it." He handed Kammler his whiskey. "Soda?"

"No," he said, and added almost as an afterthought, "NASA cannot go to the Moon. You would do well to cause delays in the program until they must give up."

"Preposterous—"

"You cannot go. If you go, and they land, it will be worse for you."

"Are you threatening me, Herr Kammler?"

They both drank.

The two muscular men didn't move.

"Relax, Professor! I am here to tell you how things are, so you will obey. Just like the good old days. You cannot go. That's it. And you cannot mention to anyone the energy source your spinning rockets unlocked."

Surprise washed over Wernher's face before he could check it.

"Of course I know all about your meeting with Schomberger. You can just forget about your plans for the Moon *and* Mars."

Von Braun cleared his throat and took Kammler's empty shot glass.

"On what authority do you speak?"

He filled up the glass.

"I worked for a gentleman you know of, Allen Dulles. Today I work for his successor and his superiors. Influential people, and I don't mean the president. If you don't know them personally, you have more reason to do as I say. You have more reason to fear. For your own sake and your family's." He drank. "Two young girls, I believe, and a little boy."

Von Braun switched on a light. He had to fight to control his fear and anger.

"More threats."

"Professor, it is your own fault because you are so stubborn. You flounder and you beg for pennies, but neither NASA nor the White House makes policy. You believe you are aware of what is happening, but you are not."

"I know what's happening." Von Braun lit a cigarette. "Americans have their Corona spy satellites; the Russians have their Kosmo spy satellites. Both countries develop laser particle beam and kamikaze weapons. Each side researches orbital nuclear explosives. We spy on each other, and we keep an eye on the flying discs. Within this confusion, we are trying to do something worthwhile. Do you think we are all stupid here?"

"You are extremely stupid, yes. That is your main problem, though you have many others." He drained his glass. "*Your* security clearance does not give you access to what *I* know. In the absence of good management, you bump into each another like idiots in the dark. You make a hash of everything. You let communism in through a hundred open doors."

He poured another glass himself. Von Braun saw blue varicose veins in his hands.

"That's not true. At NASA we have agreed to open a back channel to military planners and intelligence. We will know of hostile activities conducted by any country or extraterrestrial. We know about their Moon base, but we need to have a presence there, too."

"Impossible, I'm afraid." Kammler nodded to the large man on the left, who moved quickly and grabbed von Braun from behind.

The technical director fought back too late, held in place by powerful hands that threatened to break his arms.

Kammler stepped close to his former employee and struck him across the face.

"That is for abandoning the fatherland," he said and slapped him again. And again. And again. "That is for working with communists and Jew scum." He grabbed von Braun's face with his left hand and squeezed hard. "This is only a taste of what I can do, believe me. I care nothing for your family, your plans. Nothing."

He took a step back and nodded to the other man, who grinned yellow teeth and socked von Braun in the stomach. His partner released the technical director, who fell to the ground. Kammler kicked him in the side. He took out a gun with a silencer and pointed it at his head.

"I've always wanted to do this," Kammler said. "I should have had you all shot when I had the chance."

"Will you kill me?" Von Braun turned his bloody face to Kammler. "Even if you do, the program will go on."

"True…I…I need you to slow down that program. But I also wish to see you suffer." He lowered his weapon and raised his eyes to the ceiling. "What am I to do with imbeciles such as yourself?"

He suddenly exited through the sliding glass doors into the garden. His two associates followed him.

Wernher put his hand on a table and pushed himself up.

He took a step after them, then thought better of it.

"Remember who I work for," Kammler shouted without turning around. "And, if I may, you are far too nonchalant about your wife's whereabouts."

He and his associates descended the hill.

Wernher kept his eyes on them until they disappeared behind some trees.

Furious, he rubbed his cheek and considered his options.

None of them were satisfactory.

Chapter 97

"Kennedy Urges All-Out Race to the Moon— A $20 Billion Plan"

—San Francisco Chronicle

Moscow, Soviet Union of Socialist Republics
Monday, June 11, 1962

Korolev and Glushko walked through Staraya Square and into a six-story neoclassical building. They didn't speak to each other in the elevator going up. They lived their anonymity, forced on them despite their successes, like an interminable prison sentence. In their solitary confinement from the rest of the world, they grew wary of each other. Korolev suspected Glushko of plotting against him; Glushko felt that Korolev's ambition had shoved him into the camps of others.

When the doors opened on the dreaded fifth floor, Sergei Pavlovich shivered slightly, despite the suffocating warm air. The atmosphere still reeked of Stalin's secret police.

A tired-looking bureaucrat showed them into a large room with light-blue patterned wallpaper and a mahogany coffered ceiling. Khrushchev sprawled on a sofa in a tight-fit suit.

Dapper in pressed shirt and pants, Ustinov surveyed the city lights from the balcony. He'd become heavier and, turning, spoke in a loud voice. "We'd better take the Americans seriously. Whoever gets to the Moon first is the real winner."

"There are only two ways for the Americans to get to the Moon," said Glushko. "Earth orbit rendezvous, many missions and delicate maneuvers, extravehicular labor, life support. Things that do not exist. Or… they can attempt a direct flight, which would require a first-stage booster with as much as sixteen million pounds of thrust. Nor does this exist."

"It would be nice to fly across the ocean," Korolev said, "and have a look at what they're planning."

Ustinov stepped inside. The two visitors remained standing on a thick red carpet; Korolev seemed to be studying its pattern. A phone rang repeatedly, but no one answered it. After an awkward pause, Khrushchev clapped his hands. "Kennedy is a small man. I've met him and his boasting is pure propaganda. Comrade Korolev, we will follow your blueprint."

"Comrade Khrushchev," Glushko sputtered, "what about the plans of Vladimir Chelomei—?"

"We will have *two* programs," Ustinov said.

The family connections of Chelomei have paid off, thought Korolev.

"Comrade Chelomei will lead a project for a two-man lunar flyby," Ustinov explained. "But we will also approve Korolev's draft plan for a Moon landing in 1966." He glanced at Khrushchev and back to Korolev. "Perhaps a space walk can take place sooner?"

"Yes, I think so," said Korolev, who snapped his head back up. "I am as committed as ever, but I must be frank: at NASA, they have three men doing my job."

"And many more doing mine," Glushko said.

"Don't let the Americans have the Moon." Khrushchev kicked at a stack of papers moodily. "What resources you need, we will find them."

"And let us not worry unduly." Ustinov settled into an armchair. "The American Congress will never approve their president's budget. It is too outrageous."

"If they get cheap, it will be good," Khrushchev agreed. "And we will remain bolder."

In the elevator down, Korolev kept his black eyes straight ahead. He would have to create a new kind of rocket to fly to the Moon, while fending off Glushko, Chelomei, and their cohorts.

He and Glushko took separate paths through the square, where a sculpture of a muscular water god battled a serpentine dragon in a fountain.

Korolev imagined the waters surging up to drown the beleaguered deity.

Chapter 98

"Berlin Wall Set on Fire; Reds Shoot at West Hecklers"

—*The Stars and Stripes*, European Edition

Huntsville, Alabama
Monday, September 10, 1962

Von Braun looked at his Rolex.

Five minutes.

He smiled at the thought of Mariner 2, which had blasted off weeks before. It would perform the first interplanetary flyby of Venus and succeed where the Soviets had repeatedly failed. The second launch of the Saturn rocket had also defied skeptics.

That late afternoon in his office at Marshall, he admitted to himself that he hadn't seen his wife or his children much lately.

Fortunately, Maria is an excellent mother.

He'd hired a security guard to watch his house at night but had said nothing to her about the threats.

He had another drink of bourbon and swallowed three green pills.

He hadn't phoned Staftoy either, for his friend and mentor had been eased out of NASA. Their civilian chiefs had been uncomfortable with a military man around. Staftoy hadn't been surprised. He understood politics, and had welcomed an early retirement. Von Braun had seen that the alien phenomenon weighed more heavily on him. The revelations had upset his worldview.

Voices in the hallway.

Carol Holmes waved in Dieter, Debus, and Rees, each in casual slacks and white short-sleeved shirts. They'd adopted the NASA look. Oberth followed, in his usual tweed jacket and bow tie. Retired, he lived nearby.

"Greetings, gentlemen. Greetings, teacher."

Oberth took one of the armchairs. Rees took another. Debus preferred to stand; he rubbed his dueling scar. Dieter leaned against the closed door, his red hair aglow in the setting sun's light.

Von Braun poured drinks.

"I will start," Oberth said. "Who do you think Kammler is working for?"

The conversation switched from English to German.

"CIA. Dulles." Von Braun lit a cigarette. "Or he used to. He mentioned someone higher up; must be a part of old Gehlen's network. It's not surprising when you think about it."

"He could be KGB." Debus also lit a cigarette.

"The way he talked about the communists, I sincerely doubt it."

"It does not matter *who* he is working for," said Oberth. "He is a natural troublemaker and a psychopath."

"He told me we could not go to the Moon." Von Braun exhaled smoke.

"Did he imply somebody would stop us?" Debus asked.

"*Ja.* Or something worse."

"Sabotage?"

"Much worse."

"What if he's working for one of the alien groups?" Oberth suggested.

"That seems farfetched."

"At least the military here is ready to fight," Dieter said. "We have over two hundred missiles, compared to Russia's meager reserve. Who knows what the Group has; I've heard they're making their own ships."

"Is it enough to shoot down the flying discs?" Debus looked at him. "No one can be sure."

"It is not anything like that," Oberth retorted. "I must insist these flying saucers have been investigating Earth for centuries. This is why they already have a base on the Moon. It's probably been there for millennia."

"They won't want us anywhere near that base," Rees said.

"Has Kennedy been briefed?" Debus emptied his glass.

"I would say no," von Braun replied. "Nobody in Washington trusts him. I have reliable information that he's been trying to wrench control of S-4 away from the CIA. It's a power struggle. It could be as simple as this: Someone high up sent Kammler to piss on the president's pet project."

"True," Rees said. "Kennedy fired Dulles, yet the man is still pulling strings. That's real power."

"Kennedy had to fire Dulles," Debus snorted. "That *idiot!*"

"Maybe the president will mention it tomorrow during his visit," Dieter said.

"With all the reporters around? Unlikely."

"What should we do?" Von Braun leaned back in his chair. "Can we act without proof? We are already costing so much, and Dulles has many connections in Washington. Nearly any excuse will be a good one to shut us down."

"There are too many factions to act," Oberth said. "Herr Professor, we must forge ahead. We have to believe that those who are supporting us are also protecting us."

The others nodded.

"So," von Braun said as he poured more drinks, "I will increase security, but everyone should be on guard."

* * *

The following day von Braun's voice boomed over the PA system: "We have the president of the United States with us!"

He did his best to impress Kennedy, eager to please and not immune to the American president's charisma. He and Webb gave Kennedy, LBJ, and their entourage the complete tour, from checkout and structural fabrication hangars, surface treatment shop, fuel test facilities, and engineering buildings to the computation division, one of the labs, wind tunnel and test stand, even the technical materials warehouse.

"We are practically the only self-contained organization in the nation," he boasted. "We are capable of developing a space vehicle from conception through production."

Several hundred Marshall employees applauded on cue when they stepped inside the assembly building.

They walked the length of a 152-foot Saturn C-1 in its horizontal position. A few of the trailing newspapermen, the more informed and curious ones, noted that the same man leading Jack Kennedy into a rocket hangar had led Eisenhower two years before, and had led Adolf Hitler through his missile facility some years before that. They asked themselves how a group of ex–German Army, ex-SS, pro-America, anti-communist, politically conservative, fish-out-of-water space-happy dreamers had managed to occupy key positions at MSFC.

"Thanks to your initiative," von Braun said to the president, "several arms of the military and thousands of civilian companies are now engaged with NASA in the business of making rockets."

"And thanks largely to your team's good work." Kennedy wiped his brow in the ninety-two-degree humidity.

Webb patted his own forehead with a handkerchief.

"The next Saturn's five-engine cluster will generate the equivalent hydroelectric power of eighty-five Hoover dams. This is the vehicle that will fulfill your promise to put a man on the Moon."

"You don't say," Kennedy purred. "Did you hear that, Lyndon?"

"I did," LBJ beamed.

"Doctor von Braun says he'll get us to the Moon, Lyndon," Jack repeated, and LBJ kept on smiling. "How will you track the rocket to the Moon?"

"Our people in Houston have built tracking sites from the Canary Islands to Australia, Hawaii, and Mexico. Two ships in the ocean will also be monitoring the rockets. The whole world is wired for communication."

Flashbulbs were popping when Kennedy added, "I understand Dr. Wiesner doesn't agree with your plans for lunar orbit rendezvous." He looked around. "Where is he?"

A presidential aide ran off to find him.

At a nod from Johnson, they moved behind a row of metallic barrels to distance themselves from the press and the crowd. Von Braun and Webb were concerned by Kennedy's sudden wavering; Wiesner, whom they saw being ushered over, was not on the agenda.

"LOR is no good," Wiesner said. "Earth orbit is better. Something without *any* astronauts would be the best."

"I could not disagree with you more," von Braun said.

Kennedy folded his arms across his chest. Johnson hung his head and listened.

"We'll launch incrementally, Jerry, as we always have," Webb mediated. "We'll solve each problem as it comes up."

"But there may be too many problems at once—or one big problem you can't solve." Wiesner stood his ground, his face covered by a thin layer of sweat. "Let's be practical. American launch vehicle technology isn't far enough along, and the Soviets are way ahead of us. Human spaceflight is a high-risk enterprise with a high chance of failure. We should keep playing to our strength: space science. We're already beating the pants off them there. And what about the four hundred million dollars?"

"Good point," Kennedy said. "Jim, what is, er, our schedule?"

"Mr. President, it's hard to say." The underarms of Webb's shirt were visibly wet with perspiration. "We used the best information we had and settled on late '67 or early '68 as the landing date. But we want to have some leeway within the decade."

Leeway, my ass! Johnson thought. *He'd better have the landing before Jack's second term is out—or* he's *out.*

"But, practically speaking, every program at this point has grown by a factor of two to three in cost." Wiesner addressed Kennedy: "Sir, you're going to have to face increasing costs year after year after year. Mercury is up to five hundred million dollars already…"

"Only two dollars and a quarter for each person in the United States," Webb said.

"...and when the Mercury program ends, we'll *still* be behind the Russians."

"With the Gemini program, we'll move ahead," Webb countered. "Long-duration flights, rendezvous and docking, reentry and landing, the effects of weightlessness—all four important for getting to the Moon."

"Exactly, Jim," Kennedy said. "Getting to the Moon is the top priority. Whether we like it or not, we're in a race. If we get to the Moon second, it's like being second in anything—nobody cares."

"Why can't it be tied instead to preeminence in space?" Wiesner insisted. "Which are your own—"

"Because, by God, we've been telling everybody we're preeminent in space for five years and nobody believes it. Because *they* had the first satellite. It doesn't matter to anyone that we've put up more satellites and better ones."

"But we don't know a damn thing about the surface of the Moon. We're making wild guesses about how we're going to land there. We—"

"That's their problem and they'll deal with it. Jim will decide if we're going with LOR. But..."

Johnson knew what was coming and was mighty unhappy about it.

"...there is an alternative. Jim, would NASA consider a joint mission to the Moon with the Russians?"

Webb had heard rumors about the president's thinking. Von Braun had not.

"Many folks in Congress are, er, and rightfully so, it's true, concerned about spending. They're asking why we and the Russians are working on the same things, each in our corner. A joint operation would save billions and end our cycle of mistrust."

"NASA would, hmm..." Webb stammered.

"Mr. President," Johnson said. "I think the vast majority of the people and Congress want to see an *American* flag planted on the Moon. If you invite the Soviets, you'll be crucified."

"But we're already over budget."

"Of course we are." His tone told everyone else to butt out. "We all said in the beginning what they *wanted* to hear. It's the oldest game in the book, and we knew it. They knew it. And they went along with it. Everyone knew it would cost more, much more. Now, Jack, now we've got to see it through."

"You're damn right we're going to see it through. But if we throw out there the idea of a joint mission and the Russians don't accept, they'll look awfully bad."

"It's not worth the risk."

Von Braun assumed KGB operatives, manipulated by Dulles and Kammler, were feeding disinformation to the White House to trick them into thinking the Soviets would cooperate.

The Reds will take all they need and sabotage the rest. Has the president forgotten their past aggressions? Or—

He checked his thoughts when he noticed that Kennedy's features had contracted, as if some invisible fist had knocked the wind out of him.

"Lyndon, let's discuss it later. Enough," Kennedy said. "At this rate, I might not live to see the Moon landing. But if that happens, I'll be up there in my rocking chair enjoying the show. I'll have the best view of all."

Chapter 99

"Soviet Blonde Orbiting as First Woman in Space"

—*New York Herald Tribune*

Podlipki, Soviet Union of Socialist Republics
Friday, June 21, 1963

The door opened and, preceded by her KGB minder, the Seagull entered a small suite in the Experimental Design Bureau of OKB-1. Chertok, Glushko, Mishin, and their three chosen men jumped up from their seats. The Seagull had a noticeable dark-blue bruise on the bridge of her nose.

A souvenir from her rough landing, thought Chertok.

They intended to interview Valentina Vladimirovna Tereshkova, the first woman in space. Khrushchev himself had selected her. Chertok thought it a clever publicity stunt to demonstrate the superior qualities of the "New Soviet Woman."

Another Russian first.

They would have two hours and were forbidden to ask for autographs.

"Comrade Tereshkova, we would like to thank you for taking time out of your busy schedule," he said. "We would like to hear the true story of your three days up there. Obviously, we need to know details in order to plan for future flights."

Beneath a bouffant of blonde hair Tereshkova smiled weakly with crooked teeth. Glushko could see she suspected a trap.

"Perhaps you could begin by telling us about your difficulties with the Vostok's manual control," Chertok suggested. "Or anything which hampered control and activation of communication modes. We welcome your free criticism of everything. Here, we must be honest."

The door flew open and Korolev walked in. He appeared more haggard than usual. Chertok had remarked a pattern of increasingly authoritative behavior in Korolev coupled with a physical decline. The race with the Americanese was closer than they would've liked, and it hurt Korolev in every way.

"Excuse me, comrades," Korolev said. "I need to talk to the Seagull in private. I will give her back to you in ten minutes."

He nodded at the KGB man and ushered her through a side door to an adjacent lounge.

"What is all that about?" Mishin asked.

"Too many mistakes." Glushko took out a cigarette.

On the other side of the wall, Korolev, fifty-six years old, glared at Tereshkova, twenty-six. She sat upright in her chair facing him.

"You stayed up there way too long. Why?" he asked. "Tell me."

"The automatic orientation system of the capsule was incorrectly established."

Her tone was more confident than he'd expected.

"I noticed immediately on orbit insertion that it was oriented ninety degrees from the intended direction. If retrofire had been initiated, I would have been sent to my death in a higher orbit."

"And you advised ground control of this and they didn't believe you?"

"Correct. They finally verified and sent signals to the spacecraft on the second day to offset it."

Korolev rubbed his chin. "So clearing up this problem delayed your return. This is the story you're sticking to. Do you think they would have believed you sooner if you had been a man?"

"I could not say for sure."

"Let's face it, you are a well-meaning woman, but a woman who had no business being up there. You were forced on me by politics, and when you became the first cosmonaut to vomit in space, I should have brought you down. Luckily, we will not be telling that story."

"That was due to the poor quality of the food."

"I cannot believe my ears."

"I was ordered to remain strapped to my seat, so I developed a cramp in my shin—by the third day the pain was intolerable."

Though Korolev saw she hadn't been given time to recover from her ordeal, he persisted. He felt that the mission's events and faulty communication required his hard questioning. Persistent difficulties with his ex-wife and daughter made it satisfying.

"You had more problems than a bitch in heat," he grumbled. "A sore on your head because of your helmet, an itch that could not be scratched, a rash. It is frankly beyond belief. I intend to write in my report that you were on the edge of psychological instability. Would you agree?"

"No. I only had tasks assigned for the first day. When ground control extended my flight for two days, I had nothing to do. In fact—"

"In fact they wanted you to fail. Is this what you are saying?"

Tereshkova avoided his eyes and focused on the wall. "I never complained," she said. "I completed the flight program to the last letter."

"Good. That is what I wanted to hear. I believe you did what you could. But I will not allow any other hysterical women in space."

When Korolev exited the lounge, alone, it had been more than ten minutes. The others questioned him with their eyes, but he left without a word.

"He gave it to her," Chertok said. "Even though our woman logged more hours up there than all the Americans combined, it wasn't enough."

"Comrade Tereshkova was easier to offend than a thick-skinned fellow would have been," Glushko sneered. "A woman, even a cosmonaut, is still a woman."

Tereshkova emerged. She'd applied makeup to her nose and around her eyes.

"I am sorry," she muttered.

The KGB man followed her out.

Chapter 100

"Cuba Blockade!—Sensational Move by Kennedy—Ultimatum to Kruschev 'Move Those Missiles'"

—*Daily Sketch,* London

Langley Research Center, Virginia
Wednesday, October 30, 1963

Rachel and Professor Goshen showed their passes, clipped to lanyards around their necks, to two MPs, who directed them to a large hangar guarded by soldiers. Rachel noted a sniper on a nearby roof and knew others had to be hidden elsewhere.

Once their eyes had adjusted to the somber interior, they went over to one of the long tables. NASA technicians in civilian clothes were assembling 35mm photos into large mosaics of black-and-white moonscapes.

Goshen whispered, "Potential landing sites for the Apollo mission."

Rachel went off to find their contact.

Left on his own, the professor discovered geometric shapes in one of the panoramas, towers, spherical structures, and what resembled radar dishes. He bent down and removed his glasses to examine them. He estimated that some of the towers had to be enormous, taller than any skyscraper.

"Don't worry. We'll airbrush out anything sensational."

He looked up to see Rachel by the side of a handsome military man, whom she introduced as Lieutenant General Trudeau.

"And this is Philip Corso, head of the Pentagon's Research and Development section," she said, indicating a shorter man who joined them. "I've already briefed Professor Goshen on your efforts to capitalize on alien technology. But we can't talk here."

"This way," Trudeau beckoned.

They emerged through a side door onto a large field near a tunnel facility. A Chinook helicopter awaited; its two whirring blades blew their clothes back.

The fuselage door opened and a man waved them in.

"Uh-uh. Not him." Rachel refused to move. "Tell him to get lost."

Corso ran over and shouted in the man's ear. Unhappy about it, he jumped to the ground and strode away.

Within the copter they took crew seats on facing benches, and the Chinook lifted off with a lurch. No one spoke as they flew out to sea.

Trudeau had to shout to be heard above the turboshaft engines. "You've made progress?"

For several minutes Goshen explained his team's methodology, tapping his briefcase to indicate its valuable cargo.

Rachel's eyes were on the cockpit door.

"We have turned a corner, but it will take some effort and perhaps many years before you will be able to construct a full-fledge antigravity vehicle. A means must be discovered to—"

A large, muscular man in a black suit emerged from the cockpit and spotted the professor.

Rachel lunged across the space between them and wrapped one arm around his thick neck. She pressed her strong fingers into rubbery flesh and his angry eyes.

The large man squirmed violently.

She pinioned his firing arm.

He punched her twice in the stomach.

She absorbed the blows, maneuvered him into a headlock, and applied more pressure.

He weakened.

She released her grip and he slumped over, his gun with silencer clattering to the floor.

Rachel picked it up, adjusted the silencer, stepped into the cockpit, and pulled the trigger. The pilot's brains splashed over the windshield.

She grabbed hold of the control stick and took the copilot's seat.

Turning back, she shouted to Corso, "We're in an unofficial war zone!"

"Uh…"

"Your organization is riddled with traitors. Military officers assigned to CIA missions are sent back to their military posts as disciples. Your people are sick with men such as Gehlen and Kammler."

Corso collected himself—he'd seen plenty of bloodshed in his day. "We should've vetted the crew," he admitted. "The grasp of Dulles is long…and long-lasting. It's a mistake we won't make again."

Trudeau slid Goshen's briefcase to his side of the cabin. "We'll get this into the right hands."

Corso grabbed the first corpse by the scruff of his suit jacket and dragged him past the shocked professor to the fuselage door. He shoved out the body, which dropped into the sea hundreds of feet below.

In the cockpit, he unbuckled the bloody pilot.

"The longer it all stays underground and black, the greater the danger to everyone," Rachel shouted. "More hidden deaths, more fascist states." She turned again to Trudeau. "Those in the Pentagon, those still uncontaminated, they must be persuaded to go public. With everything—antigravity, lasers, alien contact. Everything!"

"There's still a Cold War on."

"Make them see the bigger picture."

The second corpse made a silent splash.

Chapter 101

"Shock...Disbelief...Grief—Sniper's Bullet Cuts Down President; Jacqueline Cradles Dying Husband; Johnson Sworn In—John Fitzgerald Kennedy, Born in Brookline, Massachusetts—Shot and Killed in Dallas, Texas, at Age of 46"

—*The Boston Globe*

Huntsville, Alabama
Friday, November 22, 1963

The paperwork didn't matter anymore, but he kept at it automatically in his office. Two assistants filed his reports. But it didn't matter and they didn't matter. Nothing mattered to von Braun, because President Kennedy had been assassinated earlier that day in Texas.

A vision kept replaying in his mind, even though he hadn't seen it himself. Not of the assassination, but of a scene on a recent Air Force One flight to Berlin. Frederick Durant had been a passenger and had described it to von Braun: "The whole matter is out of my hands," the president had said while doubled over in pain. "Dulles, the Group. They killed Forrestal, and others. Terrible. Just terrible... Now we *all* have to deal with it. I was going to splinter those murdering bastards into a thousand pieces and scatter them to the winds. Now...it's out of my hands."

A small black-and-white TV in the background broadcast the latest news. In shock, Carol Holmes loitered in the doorway and watched her boss reach over to switch it off.

"Has everyone gone home, Ms. Holmes?" he asked. "Tell them to say a prayer for his family."

"Of course, Doctor."

She nodded to the two assistants. They left and Carol closed the door.

Wernher bowed his head into his hands. He would stay in his office for a while to avoid having his children see him cry.

* * *

A month later, he had a window seat on a flight to Austin, Texas. His hand held the response to a condolence letter he'd sent to the president's widow. Jacqueline had replied: "Please do me one favor—sometimes when you are making an announcement about some spectacular new success—say something about President Kennedy and how he helped to turn the tide, so people won't forget."

An hour after landing a chauffeured black Cadillac drove him through the twilight to President Johnson's big two-story ranch house. Yellow and white Christmas lights bathed its white paneled wooden exterior in a warm glow.

Johnson; his wife, Lady Bird; and a local congressman with a bow tie, Albert Thomas, nursed their predinner cocktails in the president's home office. A domestic handed von Braun a martini, and everyone shook hands. The First Lady, her face framed by a perfect semicircle of jet-black hair, wished Maria well.

"Yes, thank you." Von Braun sipped his martini.

"Incredible!" Johnson grinned. "One of your satellites beaming Jack's funeral all over the world. Things like that are changing everything."

"Mr. President, I must be honest and say that particular satellite flew on a modified Thor booster. Air force, not one of ours."

"You don't say…I guess we have rockets coming up all over!"

Waves of baggy yellow flesh under Johnson's eyes contrasted with his festive mood.

Von Braun had expected to find a mournful president.

"Wernher, I invited you out here because I'll be shit-canned if we let the Reds win the race to the Moon." Johnson moved closer. "I wanted to tell you this in person. I'll get the NASA budget through Congress, if that asshole Byrd will deal, and you can tell that to everyone back in Huntsville."

"Thank you, sir. This is the best news."

Johnson put his arm around the Marshall director and guided him behind a claw-foot desk flanked by American and Texan flags. A painted portrait of one of LBJ's beloved beagles hung on a wall of knotted pine. The president took a white Texas Stetson from a bookshelf.

"Doctor," he said, "I want to see this cowboy hat on the Moon. You'll get it there for me, won't you?"

He handed the stiff Stetson to von Braun, who put it on his large head. "Mr. President, we will do it or be damned shit-canned."

Johnson laughed. "Wernher, you may be both!"

Huntsville, Alabama
Wednesday, January 8, 1964

The Moonwalkers had arrived.

Several manned-flight veterans, Gus Grissom and others, strolled in, followed by a trio from the New Nine, Neil Armstrong, Frank Borman, and Jim Lovell. Another hailed from the third group of astronauts, Buzz Aldrin. Three of these pilots would fly on the most coveted mission of all. Today, they joined von Braun, Debus, Rees, Dieter, and a host of department chiefs in the long conference room at MSFC for another matter. Deke Slayton and Al Shepard were the last to find chairs.

A number of supervisors had to stand, backs to the wall. Heat from bodies in close quarters and blown in through vents warmed the cold air.

Sitting next to the MSFC director at one end of the table, in a brown suit, was a stranger to most. "Gentlemen," von Braun said, "I'm pleased to introduce our new deputy associate administrator to the Office of Manned Space Flight—George *Mueller*." He clapped his hands and the room clapped with him.

"It's pronounced *Miller*," Mueller corrected him.

"*Miller*. Of course," von Braun apologized. "You must excuse us first-generation Americans. As head of the Apollo program, perhaps you have something *else* to tell us?"

Mueller laced his fingers together on the bare table before him. About forty-six years old, he wore green-rimmed glasses and had a high forehead and a narrow chin that jutted out. "Gentlemen," he said, "the way we are doing things now, NASA will never make it to the Moon by the end of the decade. We will never make it—unless we adopt a more forceful approach to our rocket development program."

Silence.

"My plan is to take advantage of what I learned over at the air force's ballistic missile program by implementing an *All Up* approach. It worked there and I'm confident we can make it work here."

Mueller glanced at von Braun's poker face.

Waiting to see how it goes, Mueller thought. *Hanging me out to dry.*

More silence.

"Rather than testing components separately," he went on, "I'm asking Doctor von Braun and you, everyone here, to test the full Saturn V rocket all in one go."

Silence—until Dieter blurted out, "It cannot be done!"

Mueller ignored the outburst. "Instead of testing a ballasted first-stage flight followed by a live second stage only after the first has been proven flightworthy, I propose that the first Saturn V test-fly with all three stages—live. *All Up*. I also want that first flight to carry a live command-and-service module, so its systems can also be tested in orbit."

He paused to clear his throat.

"The command module will reenter the atmosphere as though it were returning from the Moon. That'll add a heat shield test to the program. *All Up*. Everything tested at one go."

Silence—until a section chief protested, "But this is ludicrous—haywire!"

Mueller held up his hand.

"Gentlemen, I welcome your thoughts, but keep in mind I've already talked with NASA's field center directors. Everyone has agreed—this is how we can put Apollo back on schedule and back on budget."

Dieter, Debus, and the rest of the Germans down both sides of the table looked to von Braun, who met their eyes. He knew exactly what they thought.

Heresy, pure and simple.

Von Braun pronounced his words slowly in his best high-toned, lilted speech. "Director *Miller*, change will not come easy here. I think you know that. There are also some compelling arguments against you. What if the first stage fails? Our expensive upper stages will be lost and no performance data will be obtained."

German and American heads nodded in agreement.

"True," Mueller said. "But stage-by-stage testing spreads the risk of failure across *multiple* tests, rather than my approach, which minimizes them in one. And don't forget that time doesn't favor the more tedious sequential approach."

"Perhaps. But we have learned, the hard way I might add, that testing piece by piece is the best way to make sure each of those pieces works." More nods. "It never pays to introduce more than one major change between tests. Never."

"But you've said yourself, Doctor von Braun, that when water is used in the upper dummy stages, it gives your rocket different dynamics from real propellant, so why not put liquid hydrogen in the tanks?"

"Okay, sure," von Braun said.

The room wasn't sure what he'd agreed to.

"Why not go ahead and light their engines, too?" Mueller pressed.

"George, your logic is flawless, I must admit." Von Braun scanned his section chiefs, as if to say, *You are missing something.* He turned back to Mueller. "So the whole stack sits there and when somebody pushes the button, we shall have our reputations riding on it. Yes, I have to admit, I no longer have a strong argument against it."

His about-face was too much for the others.

Veiled panic and fear became outrage.

"Insane!"

"Stupid!"

One department head after another leapt up in anger.

"Irresponsible!"

They entreated and scolded, and several arguments broke out.

"Gentlemen, gentlemen, please!" von Braun shouted. "Let us be calm!"

"Development programs cannot be run this way," Debus insisted.

"You are simply tossing into the refuse heap all of our existing plans," said Rees, his face contorted in disgust.

"I believe management has lost their mind!" barked Willi Mrazek, structure and propulsion chief.

"You must give me a *technical reason* why we cannot do it," von Braun barked back, "not your same old conservative opinions!"

"It may be a good approach for unmanned tests," Neil Armstrong spoke up, "but it does seem like a dangerous approach to manned flight. I've been brought up in step-by-step testing—"

Others more impatient to voice their objections drowned him out.

The debate went hard and long. Von Braun watched them go at it. He appraised Mueller—gaunt but strong; arrogant yet smart. Mueller was also Bob Gilruth's boss, and von Braun assumed Gilruth had already agreed to the idea of All Up.

Politics. Politics and expediency.

He'd been a master of the two demons since the rocket club. His methods hadn't changed. He'd calculated that if he agreed, Debus, who headed up Cape Canaveral, would also accept the radical proposal. If von Braun disagreed, he'd be going up against the board of directors. Although he sat on that board, Gilruth and the others would fall in line with Mueller and undermine him.

Mueller will take the blame if we fail. If we succeed, the praise will be spread around...

About forty-five minutes into it, Mueller still spoke louder than the others. "Look!" he shouted. "If we announce that the purpose of an early launch is a plain old first-stage test, even if we do well, we'll get a nice pat on the back from Washington. On the other hand, if we launch All Up, and if we don't fail, it will be a quantum jump ahead of the game. In that case, Washington will give us everything we need. Everything. And when we need it."

A tired silence.

"Look, fellows," he went on. "You are the most experienced group of rocketeers in the world. You know how to do things. You have twenty-five years of learning from your mistakes. You won't make more mistakes. I know you can do it."

Time to tell them.

"We must think about All Up in solid engineering terms," von Braun said. "With our static test firings, I think we will be in pretty good shape. Let us not forget that in Washington, we are already under attack for spending too much. The faster we can show our competence in rendezvous technique, in control and guidance systems, in better propulsion, all of which have military significance, the faster we can contribute to military activities in space. And that means dollars."

"In other words," Debus said, divining at last von Braun's strategy, "if we do as good a job as we claim to have already done, we will have nothing to worry about."

Everyone laughed. Most of the Moonwalkers even seemed excited by the idea of an accelerated timetable.

"Gentlemen," von Braun concluded, "America has been described as the land of the free—and home of the committee…" More laughter. "So I am making a kind of unilateral decision. No more hand-wringing. We have got to move!"

To Mueller he said, "Mr. *Miller*, you can count on us. We are all in for *All Up*."

Chapter 102

"Vietnam Crisis Grows; Red China Would Send Troops"

—Los Angeles Times

Syracuse, New York
Thursday, December 9, 1965

Two F-102 Interceptors were scrambled from Syracuse Air Force Station as soon as the Semi-Automatic Ground Environment Data and Combat Center picked up the blips.

Traveling at Mach 1, their pilots had the strange orbs in view.

"Wildflower 564, off to our three o'clock," radioed Captain Butterman. "I've got some definite strobes and discs out here."

"That's a restricted area," HQ replied.

"They don't seem to care. The saucers're goin' up and down an'—holy shit!—they just left in a hurry."

The Interceptors kicked in their afterburners and attempted to pursue the lights at over eight hundred miles per hour, but they soon fell far behind.

HQ came back on. "Can you verify lights out?"

"That's A-firmative," replied Butterman, looking out his cockpit window. "We have no house with lights on below us or anything. Not a one."

5:20 p.m.

Kecksburg, Pennsylvania
Thursday, December 9, 1965

5:25 p.m.

A young mother in a yellow apron and her youngest son, in a knitted blue sweater and dungarees, were gathering wood in their backyard when a roaring sound and a bright light made them look up. They saw a burning red ball with an orange plume making its way across the horizon toward a dark forest.

"What's that, Mama?"

"I don't know…a meteor or who knows what." She pulled her boy by his sweater to her.

She knew it wasn't a meteor when the object slowed and rose back up before making a controlled descent. The acorn-shaped object glowed as it disappeared behind treetops several miles away.

Mother and son retreated into the house. She telephoned as many authorities as she could think of, including the police.

A friendly operator told her she wasn't the only one seeing something strange.

Her son spotted through their living room window two military flatbed trucks speeding down the main road.

"They're driving too fast, Mama!"

A pale-blue cloud wafted over the forest like smoke from an unseen chimney.

Then the power went out.

Stonewall, Texas
Thursday, December 9, 1965

5:45 p.m.

An aide found President Johnson stretched out napping on a green couch and awakened him with the news. LBJ jumped on the horn and rampaged through his ranch home. His staff converted several of his offices into combat suites, where men and women spoke urgently on several phones in loud, competing voices.

LBJ had prepared for this scenario by erecting three microwave towers outside his compound, and they now made use of the secure coded transmission facilities.

High on adrenaline, he stampeded from room to room, from staffer to staffer, followed by three assistants collating the latest developments while he gave orders.

Lady Bird advised White House personnel who always traveled with them to prepare bedrooms for officials who would be staying the night.

Chief NASA administrator Webb arrived by private jet.

An hour later the motorcade of Vannevar Bush; General Earle Wheeler, chairman of the Joint Chiefs of Staff; and their support staffs roared to a stop outside the front door.

They caught up with Johnson in a small anteroom by the cryptographic section.

"Eight or nine northeastern states and parts of southeast Canada have lost all power," said the thin-lipped general. "Completely blacked out."

"Which states exactly?" asked Johnson.

"Connecticut, Massachusetts, Maine, New Hampshire, New Jersey, New York, Pennsylvania, and Vermont, we know those for sure. Maybe Virginia, too. Major Keyhoe reports an important relay in a Syracuse station was tripped by a huge power surge, probably care of our saucer friends."

"There are UFO sightings being reported throughout New England," Bush confirmed. "But we believe all that's a cover for what's going on in Kecksburg, Pennsylvania."

"And what the hell *is* going on, Van?" Johnson growled.

"We're trying to ascertain that, Mr. President," Webb said. "A NASA team is already on the spot working with an army and air force team to recover whatever came down. It isn't Russian. We know that already. Some kind of hieroglyphic symbology is etched around its lower perimeter. We're trying to decipher it. But it's only one of probably a hundred probes that penetrated our airspace tonight."

"A hundred?"

"Yes, sir. At least. And some kind of aluminum material is raining down over parts of the Eastern Seaboard. We're having a spectral analysis done on that."

"Sir, we may have a bigger problem," General Wheeler said, black telephone in hand. "Colonel Bourassa is picking up nuclear alerts from System 210-A, Bomb Alarm. We've got yellow lights and sites that have gone down. Salt Lake City and Charlotte are showing red—red for detonations. The colonel has placed Mount Weather on full alert."

"Oh, for crying out loud—make sure that idiot doesn't start World War III!" Johnson roared. "Don't do anything—and tell *him* not to do anything—until we get eyewitness confirmations of nuclear detonations!"

"Yes, sir." Wheeler put the phone to his ear and exited the room talking loudly and trailing a long extension cord.

"Mr. President." An aide poked his head in. "I have the governor of Pennsylvania on the line. He wants to know what's going on."

"Tell him to get his ass up here—and tell him I don't want local law enforcement involved. Tell them, politely, to fuck off!" Johnson stomped out of the room, only to lean back in. "Jim, get the word out to people we trust. I don't want the media to cover this. Van, have the Pentagon crack down on any papers who print any of this UFO bullshit."

"I second that," Bush said coolly.

"A while back," Webb said, "I had to squash a report that there might be life on the Moon."

"Life on the Moon? Are you kidding me?" Johnson's face cavorted between rage and disbelief. "Jim, we've got aliens coming out of our assholes right *here!*"

The Pentagon, Washington, DC
Thursday, December 9, 1965

11:15 p.m.

Philip Corso entered General Trudeau's office, third floor, outer ring.

"NASA is getting all of it," said Trudeau. Behind him was a row of dark-olive military cabinets, their drawers crammed with advanced technology paperwork. "Whatever's going on, the probes, the fallout, they'll lock us out."

"Probably just one of their objectives. The president's office says it's worse. There may be satellites up there being switched on, or something that looks like 'on.' They're getting heat readings. Those things are active, for chrissake."

"If that's the case, we're even more vulnerable than before."

Kecksburg, Pennsylvania
Friday, December 10, 1965

10:02 a.m.

Mother and son were shopping at a local grocery store where others were excitedly discussing the night before.

But the papers they bought contained nothing on what they'd seen. Nothing was on the radio either. No one had heard anything from an official agency or news desk. Those who had ventured into the woods hadn't been able to approach the area because of posted military guards.

Eyewitnesses told fantastic stories, but the electricity came back on and life quickly returned to normal.

Chapter 103

"Two Geminis Fly 6 to 10 Feet Apart in Man's First Space Rendezvous; Crews, Face to Face, Talk by Radio"

—*The New York Times*

Athens, Greece
Saturday, December 18, 1965

Delegates strolled past signage for the sixteenth International Astronautical Congress in the King George Hotel.

Von Braun and Mueller had flown in to deliver lectures in the hotel's large conference room. Afterward, they separated to mingle and sip cocktails in the banquet hall, where congregated scientists and engineers, journalists and officials. The walls and tables of the room had been staged with so many bouquets of red roses and blue forget-me-nots that the hall seemed to be in full bloom.

"Traveling to the Moon is a reconnaissance mission," von Braun explained to Leonid Sedov, chairman of the USSR's Space Exploration Program. "I compare it to what an army does before it penetrates an unknown territory. After the Apollo program, the real conquest of space begins."

Cosmonaut Leonov, the third man of their group, thought the German arrogant. "If America is so technologically superior," he spat out, “why did you not have before us your own Sputnik, your own Gagarin, your *own* Voskhod 2?”

“Because your own chief designer is a far more determined man than I.”

“Would you like to meet him right now?” Sedov asked.

Leonov’s jaw dropped.

“That’s what I’m here for,” von Braun replied quietly.

Minutes later he faced Sergei Pavlovich Korolev in an empty ballroom. Its mirrored walls provided multiple views of the two rocketeers and their translator, who wore a floor-length dark-green evening gown; in her hand, a notepad and gold pen; a silver bumblebee clasp held her red hair. Lily, a Greek national employed by the state department, had been jointly agreed upon by the executive offices of the United States and the Soviet Union. Arrangements had been made in the utmost secrecy; not even Leonov had been told, nor their nations’ respective intelligence services.

“I am sorry to have kept you waiting,” von Braun said. “I am never late. Never.”

Korolev removed a small book from his suit pocket. “I believe this once belonged to you,” he said in Russian and Lily translated. “I…borrowed it from your house at Peenemünde. A most interesting visit.”

Von Braun took the notebook and flipped through its bloodstained pages, which had become gossamer with age. He recognized it and had to force back a wave of nostalgia.

“Thank you.”

“It contains Kondratyuk’s theory of lunar orbit rendezvous. Is this what inspired your idea?”

“No. In fact it was not my idea; I fought it…” Von Braun looked troubled. “I brought nothing to give to you.”

“Don’t worry. You may consider the notebook my apology for our attempts to kidnap you and your friends.”

They both smiled.

"It wasn't much of an attempt." Von Braun slid the notebook into the pocket of his blue suit. "I cannot say how much respect I have for your stupendous work. I have always said that if I had the opportunity to meet and talk with any one of the true space pioneers, I would pick you."

Lily translated, and Korolev felt better than he had in months.

"I could not be allowed into the conference because my identity must remain a secret," he said. "But I listened to your speech. While I still think we shall be first, let me also congratulate you on your progress. I also wish to say, without being arrogant, that if Gagarin's flight had ended in failure, you would not have a space program."

"You may be right," von Braun readily conceded. "Shall we sit down?"

He held a chair for Lily. The three sat at the ballroom's only table, in its center beneath concentric chandeliers. Agents detailed from the prime minister's office guarded the doors.

"Please tell me, are you the famous 'Professor K. Sergeev'?"

Korolev grinned. "*Da*."

"Like me, you have been tireless in promoting space travel. I sincerely hope one day you may stand up and be appreciated. You and I both know that we drive our programs. But to feed our energy, we need recognition."

"It is hard living in shadows." Sergei Pavlovich switched to English. His regular reading of Western periodicals had increased his vocabulary. "So it is strange; no, *hard* to meet you, someone who can be in the… spotlight." He sighed. "In public and at official gatherings, we Russians have to criticize you Americanese; in private, some of us express our admiration. Premier Khrushchev used to say, 'We have lots to learn from capitalists. They may be rotten to core, yet they keep coming up with things.' You see, he and I, we both wanted to overwhelm the Americanese with our achievements. But you are German."

"Naturalized. I'm an American citizen, but certainly a capitalist from the West," Wernher said in English.

The translator, out of work, continued to take notes.

"We also…'borrowed' some Germans," Korolev said. "It didn't work out. Of course, there was some bad blood."

"Of course."

"Even today there are spies everywhere. On both sides."

"Yes."

"We both have our satellites for 'national' and…technical means of verification."

"Yes." Wernher lit a cigarette. "At one time, President Kennedy wanted our two countries to work together."

"Germany and Russia?" Korolev chuckled.

"I am referring to his national security memorandum of November 12, 1963."

"I know."

"He needed you. Our budget frightened him."

"Now I need you."

"Let us continue to say what we mean." Von Braun inhaled. "We will go to the Moon. Then we will go to Mars. I hope this second mission will be a joint mission. A Russian and American mission. That's why I'm here, apart from my considerable curiosity. I represent those who feel our work should be supranational, for obvious reasons."

"Our…communal problem…" Korolev searched for the word. "Extraterrestrials."

"Yes." After a moment's hesitation, von Braun added, "After a lifetime of secrecy, I am also so bold to say that our work, as much as possible, should be made public. It's better to be in the sun."

"My friend, you and I understand." Korolev put his hands on the table. "But there are still many who do not. Who will not. Never. For the moment, we Soviets are too weak to share. I say that because I know your spy satellites have revealed this much to you. If we show America the guts of what rockets we have, those at the top fear you shall steal what few advantages we have."

"I'm sure that's true." Von Braun shouted to one of the guards, "Can we have a bottle of your best vodka, please? And three glasses."

Lily said it in Greek, and a sly grin swept over the guard's face before he disappeared.

"Some of your politicians have said that whoever masters space shall be master of world," Korolev said. "So Americanese missiles, of which there are enough to blow us to pieces over and over, are really for flying discs, correct?"

"I'm not sure even they know."

The guard delivered a bottle of Stolichnaya and three crystal glasses on a silver tray; he returned to his post as Korolev poured. The Russian had almost given up alcoholic beverages—doctor's orders—but they toasted each other's successes, past and future.

"You are reverse-engineering their technology," Korolev said. "I have heard we are trying, too, without success."

"I have heard it, too." Von Braun drank. "Regardless, we have to come together eventually. Isn't this so? I'm here to assure you that NASA wishes its exchanges with your academy—of *all* information—to go on indefinitely. If the exchange stalls, it is no good for anyone."

"That should not be problem. But..." Korolev gulped down his vodka. "An international mission is not happening today."

"Well, let us not waste this opportunity." Wernher leaned back and lit a second cigarette. "Tell me about Sputnik..."

Korolev lit his own and the two men talked, while Lily took notes but did not drink.

* * *

A month later Korolev collapsed in his Moscow home at 3 Ostankinskaya. Nina Ivanovna wanted to call an ambulance—for weeks she'd been urging her husband to see a doctor—but he refused and called a taxi.

He stumbled past a waist-high bronze statue of a youth launching a small rocket, past framed photos of the Vanguard Six and a black-eyed girl whom he hadn't seen in years. He made it to the living room and took several files off a pink marble mantelpiece. He knocked over some books and seized his collection of science-fiction stories by Stanislav Lem. He stuffed it and the papers into a satchel.

The taxi drove them to Kremlin Hospital, and they took an elevator to the third floor where the Minister of Health, Anatoly Vasiliyevich

Petrovskiy, greeted them. After giving the nurse instructions, the minister led Korolev to a hospital room with a beige floor and two white walls facing two pale-blue walls.

"This is no big deal, only polyps," Petrovskiy said. "A lot of people have this kind of surgery. It's less complicated than an appendectomy. Comrade Korolev, you should be back at work within a week."

"Doctor Anatoly Vasiliyevich, you are our friend." Korolev took the minister's hand and placed it on his heart. "Tell me, how long can I live with this?"

"Worry about that later. Today the polyps, tomorrow we will take care of your heart. Do not fret. You will live many years."

Not long after surgery had begun, a nurse reported to Nina that the polyps were not worrisome and the tumor benign. Nina relaxed, though she'd disagreed with her husband when he'd insisted that a high medical official perform his operation instead of a practicing surgeon.

An hour later, two nurses in white scrubs hurried out of the operating room and whispered to two orderlies. Another nurse explained to Nina that they'd found a sarcoma; she saw them wheel a machine of some kind through the surgery's double doors.

More equipment followed.

A second surgeon, Aleksandr Vishnevskiy, was called in.

Nina walked unsteadily to the nurse's desk and dialed Natasha's number on a beige telephone.

The operation went into its fourth hour, and she knew before they announced it that her husband was dead.

"We did all we could, but his heart couldn't take it," Petrovskiy said to her, pulling off his gloves. "We were unable to insert the respirator tube into your husband's trachea, due to the peculiar way his large head is positioned on his short neck. His jaw must have been broken years ago and it never healed right."

She hardly noticed the bluntness of the minister's language and only half understood that the gulag had killed Korolev at last.

Nina was left on the bench alone, until Aleksandr Vishnevskiy asked if he could speak with her.

"In the end, your husband made a mistake having a minister perform the operation," he said. "In my opinion they have too much in their heads to concentrate. Even if they were great before, they are not in shape for this kind of thing. Petrovskiy did not conduct a thorough pre-op examination, and the cardiopulmonary bypass machine hadn't been prepared in advance. It is partially my fault, too." He took her hand in his. "I should have been there from the beginning. They could not stop the hemorrhaging after they removed the polyps."

Three floors below Natasha leapt out of a taxi and ran up the stairs…

Chapter 104

"U.S. Bombs North Vietnam Again"

—*The Age,* Melbourne, Australia

Merritt Island, Florida
Friday, January 27, 1967

At the end of a long, tiring week at the Kennedy Space Center, astronauts Grissom, White, and Chaffee trudged along a skeletal corridor lined with snaking cables. From the gantry they headed to the command capsule to complete a job none of them wanted to do: a preflight plugs-out communications test.

The facility's director, Kurt Debus, had observed the three-man crew of Apollo 204 boarding the elevator of Pad 34 and had remarked to himself that the program's earlier enthusiasm was gone. However, he considered the exercise necessary; things would improve with its success.

At Debus's side, Carol Holmes took notes for von Braun. She thought the three men had looked exhausted and pale.

As she and Debus got in a car for the short ride back to the center, she thought, *It's the mood of the country.*

She'd read a newspaper on the flight down to Cape Canaveral, or "Malfunction Junction," as they were calling it. Things were going badly there and everywhere. She sympathized with the young people demonstrating for peace and civil rights, but she opposed their anti-Vietnam rhetoric.

At the capsule door thirty floors above, the three astronauts missed Guenter Wendt, their good-luck charm, their "midwife to the stars." Wendt had seen off each and every Mercury and Gemini mission, but due to a change in capsule manufacturers from McDonnell to North American Aviation, he'd been dismissed.

Grissom, unhappy enough about the whole venture, hung a lemon over the hatch.

He became increasingly unhappy in the cramped quarters when systems faltered for two hours.

"How the heck are we going to get to the Moon if we can't even talk between three buildings?" he radioed Mission Control.

Problem after problem, five more hours, and the simulated clock remained on hold at T minus ten minutes.

The trio couldn't leave the capsule until they'd completed the countdown.

Disaster struck at 18:31.

* * *

At the White House, President Johnson was enjoying a great triumph. To celebrate the passage of his treaty prohibiting weapons of war in outer space, he'd invited heads of NASA and Congress to the East Room. Webb chatted with von Braun, Gilruth, and Kraft. High-ranking officials welcomed ambassadors from Great Britain and the Soviet Union.

Nearly everyone had a cocktail or a martini in hand. An aide tapped a crystal glass with a spoon. Simultaneously, a White House butler whispered to Webb, "Telephone, sir. It's urgent."

The two left the room discreetly just as Johnson began in a loud voice: "The signing of this treaty—hold on." He looked at a notecard. "I'm going to read the whole darn title…" He cleared his throat. "The signing of the Treaty on Principles Governing the Activities of States in the Exploration and Use of Outer Space, including the Moon and Other Celestial Bodies…well, its signing is an inspirational moment in the history of the human race."

His guests applauded.

"This is a great and important step for several reasons, first—"

He spotted an aide making her way toward him through the crowd. She handed the president a folded piece of paper. Irritated, he unfolded and read it. When he raised his head, he looked ill. "Ladies and gentlemen, I have a sad announcement to make. Earlier today a fire broke out in the capsule of the first Apollo crew under test at Cape Kennedy. All three men were killed."

There were gasps, and two women had to be helped to chairs.

"We don't know for sure if it was the primary or backup crew, but we believe it was the primary crew of Grissom, White, and Chaffee."

He lowered his hand holding the note. Someone cried softly.

Guests stayed to finish one last drink or wandered off.

Johnson huddled with Gilruth, von Braun, and Kraft; Webb returned, having received the same news over the phone. Kraft knew that he and Gilruth would remember this awful day the rest of their lives. He saw that von Braun didn't look too good either.

"Mr. President," Webb said, "we can only do what's right, and we know what we're doing is right."

The furrows on Johnson's face contracted, deep and sickly. "Um…"

"We can't be discouraged and depressed to the point where we throw up our hands. We're going to find out what went wrong and we're going to correct it. We're going to continue."

"My feeling is the same, Mr. President," von Braun said. He remembered Shepard's blunt words about risk and death. "The country will be willing to accept failure and press on, if we do."

Johnson breathed heavily.

"You cold bastards may be right. The American people are slow to start, but hard to stop."

Chapter 105

"Tiny Spark Ended Lives of Three Apollo Astronauts in Ball of Fire"

—*Santa Maria Times*

West Berlin, Federal Republic of Germany
Monday, April 24, 1967

At Devil's Mountain, where the U.S. National Security Agency had built a state-of-the-art, five-hundred-foot-high listening post, three communications technicians could hear transmissions to and from the Soyuz space capsule. The trio formed part of ECHELON, a global intelligence-gathering network. Around them, hundreds of tape machines secretly recorded thousands of conversations. The one between cosmonaut Komarov and the Soviet blockhouse at Tyuratam had attracted their attention.

The capsule had suffered several system failures as it passed through the atmosphere. Antennas hadn't opened properly; power was compromised, navigation difficult. Nobody could help on the ground.

Colonel Vladmir Komarov was going to die.

"I think he's cursing the people who put him in a shitty spaceship," said a young captain from Wisconsin who spoke Russian.

Komarov had been scheduled to rendezvous with another Soyuz, but its launch had been canceled due to thunderstorms. The first crewed Soviet launch in two years, it would have been a triumph for Brezhnev.

Instead, the three Americans gathered round their high-tech equipment could hear somebody sobbing.

"It's coming from the blockhouse—Jesus," said a private from Mississippi.

The captain from Wisconsin translated, the Soviet capsule's parachutes weren't opening. "The poor bastard's telling 'em the heat is rising in his capsule… He's cursing them again, all of 'em, engineers and officials. For killing him."

The captain didn't need to translate the Russian's loud cries of rage and pain.

They heard a last, brief crackling before the capsule slammed into earth.

Chapter 106

"Russ Spaceship's Plunge Kills Pilot— Chute Fails; Craft Crashes"

—Santa Monica Evening Outlook

Huntsville, Alabama
Wednesday, April 26, 1967

Late at night, in pajamas and robe, von Braun fidgeted in his recliner, under the same roof but distant from Maria and the children. A light shone on his desk. Nothing moved. Although von Braun maintained a confident air at work, he feared that the several NASA teams were in danger of falling apart.

So many deaths. By bomb, machine gun, pistol, gas, rocket. Assassination. Incompetence. Grissom, Chaffee, White. Now Komarov. The other two cosmonauts, one in a fire and another...yes, a faulty ejection seat. Korolev.

Korolev, the man he'd competed with for so many years, had passed on. Sluggish mail service between communist and capitalist countries meant that he'd only read that evening the translation of an article published a year before in a Soviet scientific journal by one "Professor K. Sergeev." His fingers traced its title, "Strides Into the Future" and its last words, "The human mind knows no limits."

Wernher silently agreed.

But Kennedy murdered. Disney dead. Oddball Jack Parsons blown to smithereens. Dora... Not my fault.

Deaths of revered colleagues. Terrible risks. Those at the top…

Do they even know what they're doing?

Kammler calling at midnight or before dawn, waking us all hours. Warnings and more threats…

Von Braun still had nothing to act on.

The madman has powerful protectors. No one is talking. No one can help. And I…I cannot… Please, God.

He put his hands together and prayed.

His thoughts strayed to the news…

I used to be bolder…

At Marshall…

Deadlines unraveling…

Marriages destroyed. He knew of scandalous affairs.

Weeping children. Careers ruined. Spirits broken.

More problems with the Saturn V. The fire, a spark and flammable oxygen, had pushed out the date. They were slipping. Even with Korolev gone, the communists remained active.

He smiled slowly and said to himself out loud, *"Aus seinem Herzen keine Mördergrube machen."*

We will persevere.

He would rally the troops. Everything depended on the first launch—All Up.

Everything.

He put down the journal and from a pile of periodicals on his reading table picked up a *TV Guide*. A cover article about a television series had caught his eye. "*Star Trek* takes us on a journey into the unexplored regions of space aboard the USS *Enterprise*, a huge starship…"

The creator was one Gene Roddenberry.

Von Braun remembered his name. An early script by Roddenberry had crossed his desk at Marshall. The FBI had sent it over for review because of its subject matter: the story of a pair of aliens debating if a primitive blue planet called Earth had the technology to retaliate against infiltration and invasion.

What of the extraterrestrials?

He'd examined the acorn-shaped craft, but it had since "disappeared."

More strings pulled. No doubt commandeered by the Unholy Alliance. I'll never see it again.

He rubbed his eyes and went to his desk.

Leaning on one hand, he opened a drawer and withdrew a bottle of pills. He thought of Dieter, who criticized his increased dosage. From a carafe he poured water into a glass and swallowed five red ones.

White Sulphur Springs, West Virginia
Friday, April 28, 1967

"Where the hell are the astronauts going to land?" Gilruth asked. "I thought we'd already settled that."

At their emergency meeting Gilruth, von Braun, Webb, key NASA supervisors, and space scientist Dr. Farouk El-Baz, nicknamed the "Pharaoh," consulted large, detailed photographic mosaics placed on long tables in a conference room of the underground installation known as "Greenbrier."

More bad news had come. An unmanned lunar lander had stopped sending transmissions only minutes before landing. The Pharaoh believed the lander had smacked into something artificial on the Moon. A tower.

A secretary called von Braun. An urgent phone call.

"Hello?"

"You will never make it."

Kammler.

"How did you get this—?"

"Shut up. Professor, perhaps you've heard of a certain Thomas Baron. A safety expert assigned to investigate the fire which burned up your astronauts. Well, Baron is dead now. Killed instantly. Killed with his wife and stepdaughter. A train struck their car at full speed. Professor, do both of us a big favor and please think about that."

The line went dead.

Webster, Texas
Friday, May 5, 1967

The men from Huntsville parked their rental car in a gravel lot, and von Braun, Debus, and Dieter sauntered toward what looked to them like a saloon from the Old West.

"Hey, Doctor von Kraut!" A stranger in a black suit jumped out from between two cars. "Hey! How's it going? How're the Martians doing?"

Von Braun didn't stop walking, but asked, "Mr. Adams, is it not?"

Dieter saw that his boss was embarrassed but recognized the interlocutor.

"I'm trying to yell in your ear to see if you'll levitate!" Adams strutted alongside. "Don't you understand physics? Didn't that Schomberger guy tell you anything before we killed him?"

Dieter and Debus would've restrained their strange assailant if von Braun hadn't motioned them away.

Adams waved his arms up and down. "You dummies are using outdated gizmos! Haven't your operation chums told you about anti-grav propulsion yet?"

Von Braun kept ahead of Adams, his colleagues a step behind.

"Man, you Germans are uptight! Ulcer city! That's your problem. The other Kraut, Kammler, he's loosened up. But you guys—you guys still think you're *Übermensch*!"

Adams sprinted round to cut them off, and von Braun said, "Mr. Adams, can you tell me the meaning of this outburst? If not—"

"Look at this!" Adams pulled up his shirt to reveal a raised scar, long and yellow, across his lower abdomen. "See that! That's just a taste of what your phooey astronauts will get if you send 'em to the Moon." He cackled loudly. "Oh, yeah! I battled two alien bastards with a radiation laser—but who knows what they'll have up there! Huge towers, wasted cities—you know it! You *know* it!" He looked at Dieter. "How about you, Herr Dieter-Eater, have you been told about the right stuff?"

"For God's sake, tuck in your shirt!" von Braun snapped.

They entered the saloon, with Adams shouting after them, "I warned you, Wernher baby! Don't say I didn't warn you!"

Inside, von Braun said to Dieter and Debus, "Obviously we will speak to no one of this unfortunate incident."

They nodded.

Once their eyes had adjusted to the dim light, they found themselves among cheap tables and chairs, thin wooden paneling, a gaudy décor. It was the preferred hangout of the astronaut group, already crowded, reeking of beer and cigarettes.

The Huntspatch trio had come to get drunk with them.

Some of those already dancing to a Rolling Stones record on the jukebox had left work early and driven over from the Manned Space Center down the road. Von Braun spotted Gilruth, Kraft, Glenn… everyone who was in town. Most of the astronauts wore Ban-Lon polos. Supervisors had taken off their suit jackets and unbuttoned the tops of their shirts, but kept their ties.

Armstrong drank at the bar with Deke Slayton; a few feet away, alone and simmering, astronaut Frank Borman signaled the barman with his glass for another round.

"There's Al," von Braun said to Debus and went over to shake Shepard's hand.

He ordered a whiskey for the American and a martini for himself. He welcomed the alcohol.

He drank next with Gilruth. It had taken years, but von Braun's unceasing civility was wearing him down. On occasion, Gilruth referred to the German as his friend.

Von Braun was sipping his third martini when Gilruth asked for everyone's attention. Someone switched off the music and the dancing stopped.

"Gus, Ed, and Roger burned to death in their test capsule. On the ground. Not even during a mission. An undeserved, horrible disaster. I know people are angry. I'm angry. I've shed tears with their families. We all deserve some of the guilt; some of us more than others…" Gilruth swallowed his feelings. "In Washington there's talk of stopping this or that, and we'll deal with it soon enough. But I wanted everyone here to know, God willing, we'll get through it. The public wants the missions to keep going. So do the policy makers and the moneymen. Truth be told, we always have the Soviets breathing down our necks. Anyway…here's to those three good men."

Everyone raised their glasses and drank.

Von Braun was chomping at the bit, and Gilruth gave him the go-ahead.

"We have lost three valiant pioneers; I lost three good friends." Von Braun's voice raised. "But I think we all understand we are not in the business of making shoes. This is a dangerous endeavor. Their sad loss reminds me of what a German glider pilot once said before making a fatal flight: 'Sacrifices must be made.'"

Many in the smoke-filled bar had mixed feelings or worse about the MSFC director. No man of space had done more and received less credit than *their* boss, Bob Gilruth, yet von Braun still received the lion's share of public attention.

"We have built the Saturn V not just to go to the Moon and pick up a handful of dirt. We have built it to explore space, to reach for the stars. The Saturn V will be the most powerful damn rocket in the world. The first Apollo manned flight is no more than eighteen months away. We are working hard to make it. We will move beyond this tragedy—and when the first ship with the three lucky astronauts blasts off, I will be on the sidelines rooting you on, shouting with all my lungs, bursting my heart."

He raised his glass and the others, some grudgingly, raised their own and drank again.

But the mood was still somber and grim; suddenly Borman shouted from his place at the bar, "All right, folks, let's cut out the *bitching!*"

Von Braun, Gilruth—everyone turned to the pissed-off astronaut.

Bored and frustrated, he slammed down his shot glass. "*Get on with it!* Enough! Let's do the job. It is time…to…*fly!*"

"Are you a turtle?" Shepard shouted out.

Borman cracked a smile. "You bet your sweet ass I am."

Cheers and loud hoots. Laughing.

Someone switched on the jukebox and the Kinks' "You Really Got Me" blared and rocked. Couples danced again.

Von Braun spotted Dieter chatting with a younger man.

He ignored them, found Debus, and elbowed him hard in the ribs, which caused him to choke on his drink. "Now we only have to beat off Congress, eh, Kurt?"

"What is this"—he coughed—"about a turtle?"

"Nothing." Von Braun drained his martini. "Astronaut mumbo-jumbo. They do it to embarrass each other. But, Kurt, tomorrow we fly back to our mistress, you and I."

"She is almost ready. Just a few more—"

"She *is* ready. I can hear our sexy Saturn calling us…"

Chapter 107

"29 Million in U.S. Say Vietnam War Morally Wrong"

—*Vietnam Summer News,* Massachusetts

Merritt Island, Florida
Thursday, November 9, 1967

A worn-out pad crew labored intently on their tasks up and down the gantry. Beneath them von Braun chatted with a few of his team at the base of the monolithic Saturn V.

He then walked off to be by himself, a rare pause in the early morning darkness to reflect.

He thanked his teachers, one by one, naming them in his mind: *Oberth, Dornberger, Becker, Goddard, Staftoy...*

He thanked God, for he believed his consciousness launched with each rocket.

A van drove up and several astronauts jumped out. They, too, wished to savor a moment before the first launch of the 500 series, the *501st,* the "Stack," the Saturn V. Borman, Lovell, Anders, Armstrong, Aldrin, Schirra, Collins—combinations of them would be riding the behemoth soon—and they stared up at their ride.

Not yet, but soon.

In the months since the fire, the astronauts and the engineers, the bureaucrats and the technicians, had reorganized. They'd solved problems, and now they wanted to admire their monster together. They could feel its tremendous heart beating.

The greatest rocket ever made, thought von Braun.

It would fly All Up to save months and money. *All Up*, the enormous gamble.

Mueller had insisted, and von Braun had agreed, on the Saturn V being equipped with an empty command and service module, as well as ballast to stand in for the lunar module. Each and every stage would be checked out in one go. The only thing missing from the Apollo 4 would be its crew.

If something goes wrong, there will be hell to pay—we'll be finished. Twenty thousand industrial units out of business. Over 2,000 contractors, 18,000 subcontractors. The work of more than 377,000 people…

I'm beginning to sound like Dieter.

There it stood, majestic, tangible evidence of the planet's collective desire.

"Let us build a tower, whose top may reach unto heaven."

Wernher circled the rocket's wide perimeter, strolling quietly among technicians. From his mobile vantage point, he had a good view of its five elegant, massive F-1 engines. They would lift the first-stage booster forty-two miles in seconds. Their most magnificent object reposed on top of the most powerful single-nozzle liquid-fueled engines ever made.

"Let us make for ourselves a name, lest we be scattered upon the face of the Earth."

Each stroke in their metallic chambers, housed in six concentric bands, would mix and burn thousands of pounds of fuel and oxidizer quickly to create…

The adrenaline. Great kings built it.

…1,500,000 pounds of thrust…

…6,000 miles per hour. Fast enough to reach the abode of the gods…

…200,000 gallons of propellants incinerated per minute to generate 160,000,000 horsepower.

Von Braun saw the sun on the horizon.

An end to gravity's bondage.

He thought of the other engineers and scientists working on saucer-like propulsion…the Apollo Guidance Computer calculated using integrated circuits similar to the ones discovered in the alien disc. He had confused feelings about the innovations…

Kammler.

He put his torturer and the hypothetical theories and craft out of his mind.

We were born to fight alone, to snap our chains amidst fire and lightning.

The Saturn V.

The astronauts climbed back into their van and it drove away.

Liftoff was scheduled for 7:00 a.m.

* * *

"It's trial by death!" Dieter cried in desperation.

With his two hands he nearly pulled out chunks of his red hair by their sweaty roots. He'd turned sixty-one that morning, but instead of a celebration, the Saturn V was pulverizing his nerves. Its countdown should have taken four days, but that Thursday the countdown turned seventeen.

One engineer moaned, "Goddamn it to hell, we've tried—"

"Shut up, *shut up—shut up!"* Dieter cursed him.

Inside a small office near the main room at Mission Control, they'd encountered problems with the readings, fuel tanks not loading properly.

"What is the rate of consumption of liftoff plus twenty seconds?" Dieter demanded of another engineer.

The engineer slammed open a thick binder full of notes.

"You do better or I send you to Dr. Mueller!" Dieter shrieked. "You will have blood on your face!"

Moments later a cooler engineer pinpointed a faulty gauge. Dieter told them to fix it and left in a hurry for the big firing room at launch control.

He entered with von Braun and they took their places in the row reserved for mission managers. Debus, his hair a silver-gray, Mueller, and others were already in place. Wernher's wardrobe now fit in with the unofficial code of Mission Control: dark slacks, a white short-sleeved shirt, thin sober tie.

Terse greetings or none at all.

Engineers at their computers in the lower rows ran through prelaunch checks, double checks, and procedures. Launch Director, Flow Director, and Payload and Orbiter Directors spoke to each other in short bursts over their communication system headsets.

Gene Kranz was "Flight" at the Manned Space Center back with Gilruth in Houston. From that Mission Control room Kranz interfaced with Florida.

"Booster, Retro, Fido…"

With two minutes to go, von Braun and his stony-faced colleagues swiveled in their chairs and trained their binoculars through hazy morning light on the distant pad.

"Ninety seconds and counting…" came a voice over the PA system. "Houston now confirms they are 'go' for the flight… Pressurization… hydraulics commit."

Wernher's fingers clenched his armrests.

All Up—all or nothing.

"T minus sixty seconds and counting… We have transferred to internal power… T minus thirty seconds and counting… Stages reporting ready to launch."

Dieter conferred quickly on a black phone and hung up.

"Eleven, ten, nine, ignition sequence starts!"

The five F-1 engines became pure fire. A hot mass of flame erupted in silence, for the sound wave hadn't yet reached them.

Several engineers couldn't contain themselves and leapt out of their chairs—"Yeaaaaaahhh!"

"Five, four—we have ignition," the PA system said. "All engines are running. We have liftoff—we have liftoff."

When the first sound wave hit, the Saturn V was already speeding upward.

Von Braun bounced up, too, and howled, "*Go, baby—go!*"

The public and the hardened press, unprepared for the massive physical effect of the blastoff—which shook the wooden grandstand of onlookers and buffeted crews in the vehicle assembly building—felt powerful shock waves beating hard on their faces and chests.

The rocket's thunder violently rattled the corrugated iron roof of a mobile studio, where TV anchorman Walter Cronkite, broadcasting live, was pelted by tiles and debris from the ceiling. "Our building's shaking here—the big blast window is shaking!" Cronkite emoted into his microphone, "Oh, it's *terrific!* Look at that rocket *go!*—into the clouds at three thousand feet! You can see it. You can see it! Our roof is coming down, but, oh, the roar is *terrific!*"

The rocket climbed higher, and mission managers grabbed ringing phones. Congratulatory calls poured in, clogging up intercoms and telephone lines, some from Washington, some from Houston and Huntsville.

Wernher picked up a phone to call Arthur, even though he sat just seven chairs away—a practical joke. With a flick of a switch, he made sure the whole room could hear them over the PA system.

"Arthur, congratulations!" he exclaimed.

"Who is this?"

"This is Wernher."

"Wernher who? I know quite a few *Wernhers!*"

"You son of a bitch!" von Braun exploded. "I'm the one that goes to Washington and gets all the money for you to play your funny games!"

Arthur looked down the aisle with a comical expression. "Oh... Wernher *von Braun!*"

Others fell over laughing. Von Braun came over and slapped Dieter on the back. "I would never have believed it could happen," he said.

"The *501st* is up and gone." Arthur clasped the hand of his friend in his two hands. "But never—never—to be forgotten."

They hoped the Saturn would perform as planned.

* * *

They celebrated all night at the Cocoa Beach Holiday Inn with the astronauts and anyone else who joined them at the hotel's restaurant-bar.

People ran in, had a drink, and ran out to the next party, electrified by their success. Music played and couples gyrated; people jumped into the pool with their clothes on; others had ecstatic sex in the bathrooms.

Von Braun approached Dieter, who was speaking too loudly and standing too close to a good-looking engineer with longer hair.

"Watch it, Arthur," he warned and moved off.

At the bar, he sipped a martini.

Mueller's gamble had paid off. Each stage of Apollo 4 had performed to expectations. The launch's air pressure wave had been detected more than one thousand miles away. Reporters were comparing its blastoff to the explosion of Krakatoa. At about nine hours after launch, the command module had splashed down in the Pacific not far from the recovery ship.

Yes. Von Braun took another sip. *Mueller has saved hundreds of millions of dollars and shaved months, if not years, off our time.*

They had a real shot at a manned mission to the Moon within the decade.

All Up had changed everything.

Chapter 108

"Korolev Gets Pravda Credit; Korolev the Nameless 'Chief Designer'"

—Washington C. H. Record-Herald

Tyuratam, Union of Soviet Socialist Republics
Sunday, December 10, 1967

Mishin had been named Chief Designer in Korolev's place. He, Chertok, and Glushko circled launch site 1/5. They walked quickly to stay warm and avoid frostbite during a fall night's glacial chill.

"If Korolev were around," Glushko said to Mishin, "it would be different, but you are acting up and you do not listen to good advice. A year and a half without a successful launch. Longer. I don't see how we will deliver a circumlunar flight, much less a Moon landing."

Chertok silently agreed but noted that Glushko had quickly forgotten his differences with the deceased.

They passed beneath electric lights strung on wires high above them. The tulip-shaped launching towers cast long shadows on the officers and technicians milling about. Glushko glanced up at the Luna E-6LS, which crowned a Molniya carrier rocket. The snow on its nose made it look festive.

"The ministers are not stupid," Mishin grumbled. His hair had become coarse, black at the roots and gray at the ends. "Each of them understands the difficulties we face, but when they get together, they decide to order us to do the impossible. They say, 'Do not give away the Moon to the Americans,' but it is not ours to give or take."

"The Kremlin no longer believes our promises," Chertok spoke softly. "We've missed every deadline for every decree."

"You know, Boris Evseyevich, there is a certain beauty to our Luna program." Glushko grasped at a last straw. "We could fly it to the Moon. We could pick up some rocks on its surface and bring them back—*first*—before the Americanese. We will be glorified and they will be humiliated. They will look foolish to the world."

The trio continued in silence for several minutes.

A fierce wind made the lights sway above them. They looked again at the rocket in the crisscrossing glare of searchlights and a thicker snowfall.

"Your idea, Mikhail Klavdievich..." Mishin said. "Your idea has merit."

Chapter 109

"Robert F. Kennedy on Brink of Candidacy"

—*The Rhinelander Daily News*

Houston, Texas
Saturday, January 6, 1968

Astronauts Buzz Aldrin, Neil Armstrong, and Michael Collins proceeded down a light-green hallway of the Manned Spacecraft Center and, in single file, through the open door of Deke Slayton's office.

Behind the air force eyes of their boss, Slayton, simmered excitement and a little jealousy.

"You're *it*," Slayton said.

Adrenaline exploded through the three men's nervous systems, but they didn't show it.

They exited and went their separate ways.

Each would tell their wife in a different manner.

Chapter 110

"Bobby Expected to Lead Dems"

—Hillsdale Daily News

Los Angeles, California
Wednesday, June 5, 1968

Kammler and his team had slipped over the Mexican border to kill the American politician. The man was a threat, in their eyes, like his brother. A hypocrite, weak. He wanted to make public what should be secret; he intended to destroy their network, undermine their objectives.

At a few minutes after midnight, they entered the Ambassador Hotel and melted into a crowd that trailed Senator Robert F. Kennedy, who was taking a shortcut through a dimly lit kitchen pantry. He'd just won the California presidential primary, was on his way to a press conference, and would most likely be the Democratic candidate in the upcoming national election. Well-wishers flowed toward him from the opposite direction.

The politician had an entourage, but no security. Kammler, on the other hand, had several CIA associates in strategic positions: David Morales, Chief of Operations at JMWAVE, not far from Kennedy; Gordon Campbell, Chief of Maritime Operations, in the lobby; and George Joannides, Chief of Psychological Warfare, among the throng that also included their assassins.

In a room upstairs, old Dulles and Gehlen waited for word.

"We got that son of a bitch in Dallas," Gehlen had told Kammler, "and now we have to get his little bastard brother."

Kammler helped patrol the periphery while two more assassins edged in. He spotted their patsy, Sirhan Sirhan, approaching Kennedy as if in a dream, drugged to the eyeballs, but functional enough. A young Palestinian-Jordanian immigrant. Hypnotized. A Manchurian drone, a graduate of Dulles's mind control program, MKULTRA, on a heavy dose of BZ, or 3-Quinuclidinyl benzilate.

The real killer was almost behind Kennedy, almost…

The senator shook hands with two of the kitchen staff. Sirhan stepped out of the crowd, shot and missed.

The assassin, face hidden by his hat's low brim, shoved a stylish woman in heels out of his way, pulled out his gun, placed its muzzle behind his target's right ear, and fired.

Blood exploded from the candidate's face. The other assassins had their guns out— shooting. Sirhan got off one more round before he was tackled.

More bullets struck Kennedy in the back, smacking him against a table. Another bullet passed through his suit jacket. His eyes bulged in pain, his muscles gave out. He crumpled. A bystander took a bullet through the head. People ran toward and away from the victims.

A red pool gushed out on the floor.

"Senator Kennedy has been shot!" a reporter on the outskirts broadcast on the radio. "Senator Kennedy has been shot! Senator Kennedy—oh my God!—Senator Kennedy has been shot. His campaign manager, possibly shot in the head. *Oh my God!*"

Outside the hotel, old Dulles and Gehlen silently greeted Kammler. They and their agents, except for their patsy, unhurriedly took preplanned routes to safety.

Shouf, Lebanon
Sunday, June 23, 1968

Kammler's Group contact spread thick red jam on his toast. They both felt at home in their wicker chairs on the enclosed sunporch of the Mir Amin Palace Hotel. The ancient Middle East.

"That was good work in California. Now I want you to plan for an operation behind the Iron Curtain," the contact said. "Assign it to Quincy. He speaks a few languages. Take whatever experts you need. Spend whatever's necessary."

The only other guest dozed at the opposite end of the long, hot porch.

Kammler sipped his Koshary tea and looked out the large windows at the valley below, then back at the agent, whose real name he didn't know. He saw him soaked in blood. The contact stroked his stiletto beard and saw Kammler in the same light.

"The Soviet probe they intend to land on the Moon," he continued, "well, it should be a big problem for the American astronauts."

"The one in the Luna series?" Kammler asked.

"Yes. When that probe crosses paths with the Apollo team, it should kill them. For your troubles"—the bearded man took another piece of toast from the tray—"you'll have a novel kind of explosive. They finally have a handle on chlorine trifluoride gas. You'll remember it as N-Stoff. From the war."

Kammler did recall the incendiary weapon and its unrealized potential and imagined the devastation it would cause.

"This special brew kills anything within ten miles. Washington will assume the Soviets have committed an act of war. A natural conclusion to the information you've been feeding them."

Kammler crossed his legs and took another sip, satisfied. The Group, the CIA, and sundry clandestine organizations in their umbrella network had ultimately become what he'd always imagined himself to be—an agent for change. They would wipe away useless outdated systems to install a superior *reich*. They would pull the strings of puppet leaders in their more perfect world.

No one will interfere with our plans, he thought. *They are too perfect.*

Chapter 111

"Nixon Wins—Pledges Unity"

—Toronto Daily Star

Waco, Texas
Wednesday, April 2, 1969

Buzz Aldrin strolled from his car to the entrance of the Grand Masonic Lodge of Texas. Apollo 8 had successfully splashed down a few months ago, and the hot afternoon breeze smelled right. He knew it wouldn't be too hot inside, though the lodge lacked air-conditioning. He stopped to admire the edifice's stately proportions. Its concrete wings balanced nicely its two rectangular towers, which flanked the center building to form a giant "H" that dwarfed pedestrians and motorists.

Before passing through the tall door of the main building, he wiped his brow with a white handkerchief embroidered with a gold astronaut emblem. He'd come straight from an official function for which he'd worn his regalia and was overdressed. On the lapel of his immaculate suit a Phi Beta Kappa key dangled on a slim chain from air force pilot wings; on the opposite lapel, a gold membership pin from the Society of Experimental Test Pilots. A souvenir Gemini spacecraft was pinned to one white cuff. More germane to his visit, he wore a ring with a Masonic emblem in precious stone.

Inside the cool hall a long stained-glass window featured an all-seeing eye; candles, symbolic of enlightenment, burned before it. A United

States flag hung on a pole. He walked past painted portraits of grand masters, one per year since 1837, some of them Texas governors.

He thought of earlier days when he'd strived for the approval of a Scottish Rite Mason, his father. When Buzz had first applied to be an astronaut, Eugene Senior had predicted he wouldn't make it. Buzz hadn't; he'd been devastated, but applied again. Not long afterward, his father telephoned him. A friend in Washington had informed him that Buzz had been rejected a second time. His father sounded content. Turned out they were wrong.

"I am a gardener. I am a Mason," Aldrin said, shaking the Grand Master's large hand in his office.

"Brother Aldrin, nice to see you," the Grand Master said. "Ready for your trip?"

"We're ready, but they still have us going through endless tests and whatnot, like trained monkeys."

"Do you think you'll meet with opposition?"

"No one's objected so far," Buzz said. "My fellow astronauts, Neil and Michael, seem to be okay with it. NASA won't mention it, though they know I'm taking it to the Moon."

"Do they understand its significance?"

"Oh yes," Aldrin nodded. "There are plenty of brothers around."

The Grand Master had white hair and wore a plain business suit with a dark tie. He went to a drawer behind his desk, opened it, and withdrew a bundle of soft fabric. "Here it is."

He unfolded the protective crepe to reveal a rectangular flag of silk cloth embroidered with the words, "The Supreme Council, 33°, Southern Jurisdiction, USA." It also had a motto, next to a double-headed eagle, which Buzz read aloud: "*Deus Meumque Jus*. God and My Right. Beautiful."

The Grand Master wrapped it up again and handed the package to the astronaut. "The presence of this banner on your historic flight will signify Masonry's universal goals and importance," he said solemnly. "When man reaches new worlds, Masonry will be there. Godspeed."

"The truth has to be revealed."

Aldrin shook the Grand Master's hand farewell.

"Yes, it does. Yes, it does. Everything is changing, mass consciousness, too, since that photo taken by your colleague up there."

"Earthrise?"

"Earthrise."

Houston, Texas
Monday, May 26, 1969

The Apollo 10 crew had descended in their lunar module to within about ten miles of the lunar surface; a few days afterward they splashed down safely in the Pacific Ocean.

In Mission Control, Chris Kraft beheld the room, its celebrations, the backslaps and handshakes. He even exuded warmth for Mr. Teutonic Man, von Braun, who grasped his hand, then left for a plane back to Huntsville.

Kraft lit up a big cigar he'd reserved for the day and put his feet on a console. He took a deep breath.

"Practice is over," he said to no one in particular. "Next time—we land."

Chapter 112

"Czechoslovakia Invaded by Russians; They Open Fire on Crowds in Prague"

—*The New York Times*

Baikonur, Union of Soviet Socialist Republics
Thursday, July 3, 1969

Since Lebanon, Kammler had been a busy saboteur, using every asset available to him through the Gehlen Organization—kidnapping, spying, a forest dead drop. Months of aerial photography, mapping, and long nights. Interrogation, bribes, and recruitment within the Soviet bunker that would be monitoring the Luna probes. Even language lessons.

It had been worth it. Although Gehlen had retired and Dulles had died, the Group and its affiliates exerted more power than ever, and they appreciated his efforts. The Group maintained at the State Department a telephone contact service—"extension 11"—on his behalf.

Those fools have no idea what we are planning.

Kammler had pinpointed weak spots in the emergency procedures protocol at the Soviet launch facility. Adams had been useful, too. The CIA man had so successfully manipulated his moles within the KGB that its own *Diversionno-razvedyvatelnaya gruppa*, the sabotage and reconnaissance unit, had promised an arms package would be waiting.

Kammler lit a cigarette while in the sitting room of their safe house. Three agents with AK-47s monitored the radio, windows, and door. The flat had been secured for their mission by the Twelfth Department. It occupied the back end of the building's top-floor third story on a cul-de-sac with two escape routes through the fields behind it.

"Well?" Kammler demanded.

"They're in," replied the radioman.

Kilometers away, dressed in military garb with a colonel's rank, Adams and a local technician with gambling debts blended in with those assigned to the Cosmodrome's assembly building.

Nightfall.

They opened a gray locker in an empty dressing room. Inside were a Cherepakha mine, three explosive charges, four Ugolok devices, and three detonator fuses. Much more than required.

"Eenie, meenie, yep-yep," Adams whispered to the Russian, who had already concluded that his partner was deranged.

The duo retraced their steps to the main area of the busy assembly hall. Technicians in the unbearable heat concentrated only on their own discomfort. The immensity of the hangar and its facilities made it easy to be unremarkable.

Adams looked at his wristwatch. A department supervisor, who wished to defect with his family, arrived on time for the handoff, took the satchel containing the locker's contents, and headed for his clandestine job in the launch complex.

"Calm yourself," the technician warned Adams in Russian.

The Soviets' Cosmodrome, roused from its summer stupor, churned in preparation for the unmanned test launch of the Moon rocket, the N-1, their answer to the Saturn V. Adams had calculated that a hitch in Soviet plans would provide cover for their mission.

By 9:00 p.m., hundreds of cars and trucks clogged the roads in sickly green-yellow dust clouds.

At 11:18 p.m., the mammoth rocket lifted off with hidden charges set by the saboteurs.

Seconds later, its turbopump—which supplied liquid oxygen to engine number eight—exploded.

Stunned personnel caught sight of bright shards falling gracefully from the N-1 booster's tail section. The rocket collapsed back onto the launchpad and its loaded fuel tanks erupted—massively.

Adams saw furious red-black clouds race through the hangar's open doors, followed by a shock wave that blew out its windows. He ducked as workers threw themselves to the ground.

Power was shut off to the entire center. In the dark, people ran outside to help.

The two agents snuck into an adjoining shop. They found the gray Luna spacecraft untended in a corner, an ascent stage mounted on top of a larger cylindrical descent stage with four protruding crab-like legs.

They opened a compartment containing the descent component's extendable arm and, with gloved hands, Adams coated the interior with a nonreactive substance. He placed a balloon-shaped receptacle of explosive gas into the chamber; its skin would deteriorate in a day to release the gas. Extravagant bribes ensured their handiwork would not be detected. Microscopic receptors in the lining of the compartment would enable the gas to be detonated on command or impact, whichever proved more convenient.

Five minutes later, when the lights came back on, the Soviet technician had returned to his post and Adams was speeding from the facility in an unmarked car. Other vehicles raced by him toward the flames. The launchpad had been completely destroyed, and the road was strewn with dead birds.

Adams shed a tear for the innocent creatures, sure he was going to Hell.

He entered the safe house and winked.

Kammler smiled and downed a glass of vodka. Nine days to launch of the Luna 15 Moon probe, thirteen to Apollo 11.

His radioman called Pullach and delivered the code word for success.

Chapter 113

"Luna 15 Races Out Into Space on a Secret Mission"

—Findlay Republican Courier

The Pentagon, Washington, DC
Sunday, July 13, 1969

Standing in the National Military Command Center, President Nixon had his hand on one of the hotline teleprinters. On the other side of the machine, security advisor Henry Kissinger said in a thick German accent, "They've been prepared and are standing by."

"Will Keldysh be there?" Borman asked.

"Yes."

NASA needed to know more about Luna 15—confirmation that it wasn't on a collision course with Apollo 11, during flight or landing—and Borman had made friends with several Russians at the USSR Academy of Sciences.

"Go ahead," Nixon said.

Mueller, also present, listened as Borman dictated their questions concerning the probe's orbital parameters and radio frequencies to a young communications officer, a member of MOLINK, the Moscow-Link team that monitored the diplomacy machines twenty-four hours a day.

The young officer conferred with a noncommissioned officer before inputting Borman's questions into a teleprinter. It would "talk" to the teleprinter in Moscow, one of four the United States had sent over equipped with the Latin alphabet.

While they waited for Moscow's reply, Nixon grumbled to Mueller, "Too bad their launch went well yesterday."

"Mr. President, it may fall apart, like the Zond 6 or the N-1. Fortunately, they're not blaming us for that disaster."

When one of the four Soviet teleprinters chattered, a third officer fluent in Russian decoded the message written in Cyrillic script. A MOLINK clerk quickly typed it up and handed the "Eyes Only" document to the president.

"Luna won't intersect any published trajectories," Nixon read and gave the sheet to Mueller. "No collision. Well, that's a relief."

"They're going to follow up with more details, but we shouldn't have any radio interference." Mueller frowned. "However, Luna 15 is already in an intermediate Earth orbit. It will beat Apollo to the Moon by a day or so. Its ascent stage can carry at least a hundred grams of lunar soil."

"So *their* rocks will beat *our* rocks back to Earth. Is that correct?" Kissinger asked.

Borman crossed his arms. "They're literally trying to scoop us!"

Chapter 114

"Astronauts Relax, Await Big Send-Off; Countdown Running"

—*Panama City Herald*

Titusville, Florida
Tuesday, July 15, 1969

An air force helicopter touched down on a manicured golf course, not far from the eighteenth hole of the Royal Oaks Country Club.

Von Braun, the keynote speaker, jumped out nimbly, head bowed, ogled by a crowd on the green, men in tuxedoes and women in tight dresses and minks.

The speaker was followed by Cornelius Ryan, and they shook hands with representatives of Time-Life, the publishing giant and sponsor of the night's gala event. The crowd couldn't hear their polite words over the whooshing blades, but it didn't matter. The evening's prelaunch extravaganza promised to overflow with celebrities flocking to an open bar. Energy surged through the thick, humid air.

The soiree was the last stop for von Braun on a long list of scheduled executive meetings, tedious management huddles, VIP photo ops, and back-to-back news conferences, domestic and international. Maria had chosen to skip the eve's festivities; she preferred to rest at their hotel and keep her strength for the next day.

"How are things at *Reader's Digest?"* von Braun asked Ryan as they bypassed the throng, escorted by a flunky into the club's banquet hall.

"Just fine. They want to know about your plans for Mars." Ryan climbed up the five steps to a raised platform. "Are you up for another article?"

"You know, usually I am ready to talk about Mars," von Braun laughed. "But tonight…one thing at a time."

Governors, mayors, congressmen and their wives, an assortment of film stars, corporate big shots, and high-level reporters had gathered in Titusville, "Space City, USA," to hear his talk, but he delivered it without his usual gusto.

From a table about halfway back, Norman Mailer studied him and figured the German's lackluster performance resulted from so many potentially hostile critics in one place. He spotted Italian journalist Oriana Fallaci near the podium.

When another journalist asked the inevitable question about the significance of the mission, von Braun replied, "I think it is equal in importance to that moment in evolution when aquatic life crawled up on land."

The room applauded. Some of the press got to their feet and clapped.

Mailer clenched his teeth.

Now that bastard is going to pour it on and make us all crazier.

Mailer, promised a hefty sum, had agreed to write a story for *Life* magazine. Author and heavy drinker, on speed, he mingled at the cocktail party afterward, making his way among the tables and potted mauve lilacs. He spotted Ray Bradbury and Arthur C. Clarke and said hello but focused on other guests, on the sexier ones, through bloodshot eyes. He blinked in the haze of a hundred cigarettes and cigars. He wasn't the only one hung over and fighting a headache.

Tonight I'm the scientist and von Braun is my rat. He has rat eyes. Darting rat eyes. Fascist darting rat eyes.

Mailer finished his scotch and left his glass upside down in a planter. He grabbed another drink from a passing tray and recognized Hermann Oberth from his file photo.

The eccentric nutjob of the group. Believes in UFOs. Jesus.

He had no interest in talking to him but recognized it wasn't going to be easy to penetrate the multilayered coterie surrounding von Braun.

Fawning peasants. Ol' Ryan actually seems to be concerned for the welfare of my prized rat. How touching.

Mailer knew Ryan from way back and saw an opening.

"Can you get me a minute?" he shouted.

"Of course, Norman," Ryan replied. "Hold on."

Ryan disappeared into the flesh.

He emerged, towing von Braun, who held out his hand to the American. "You must help us give a shove to the program. Yes, we are in trouble. You must help us. If we do not have public—"

"Who are you kidding?" Mailer cut him off. "You'll get your money. You're going to get everything you want."

The rat has revealed a confusing aura of strength and vulnerability—I mustn't forget to record this in my lab report.

Oberth joined them and another foreigner whom Mailer didn't recognize.

Von Braun gave Dornberger, his old boss, a wary look.

A visit long overdue, but at the wrong time, he thought.

Mailer swayed slightly. "I noticed during the biographical part of your introduction, they left out the word '*Nazi*.'"

Von Braun's face whitened.

"Norman, that's not fair," said Ryan.

Dornberger and Oberth moved away as quickly as they'd arrived.

"They might have also added '*cold-hearted murderer of civilians*,'" Mailer dug in, but von Braun had vanished, Ryan close behind.

Thus marks the end of my experiment. Another victory over Nazism and NASA-ism.

On the other side of the banquet hall, Ryan headed off to find a martini for von Braun, who had already dismissed Mailer in his mind.

Dornberger appeared again and said, "I think we both need a drink, Sunny Boy. That American, eh?" His words sounded cold. "What if we had perfected the trans-Atlantic rocket before the war's end? He would be singing a different tune."

"Keep your voice down," von Braun said. "You cannot know what you are saying."

He is drunk.

"Of course I know." Dornberger tottered. "*Professor* von Braun, you are doing what we both dreamed of doing… This much is true."

"I have some urgent business—goodbye, Walter. Thank you for coming."

Von Braun shoved off, and Dornberger gulped another shot of brandy.

"Goodbye, Herr Professor."

Outside on the crowded terrace, amidst flower boxes of red, purple, and yellow, von Kármán smoked his pipe and saw von Braun almost run by. He grabbed his arm and the German took a few seconds before recognizing the Caltech professor. When he did, the back of his neck tingled. He suspected that the Jewish gentleman had never liked him.

"Congratulations, Doctor," von Kármán said warmly.

"Thank you."

"I want to introduce you to someone."

He led von Braun to a group that included Rachel, Staftoy, and a few others. Von Braun's old friend had become an Episcopal priest, Father Bruce, with a close-cropped gray beard. What Staftoy had learned about extraterrestrials and the cosmos had cracked the foundations of his belief. Over the years that fissure had widened into a more evolved spirituality.

"How do you feel?" Staftoy asked. "How's everything back at the Cape—ready to go?"

"I feel like a tug captain with my boat in dry dock. All we can do is wait for its release." Von Braun sipped his martini. "As Kurt is fond of saying, 'When the weight of the paperwork is equal to the weight of the Stack, we must launch.'"

He recognized author and friend Arthur Clarke at Staftoy's side, but not the shorter jolly man, whose face betrayed a good deal of alcohol behind its evident good nature.

"This is Ray Bradbury," Clarke said. "He has some interesting views on your mission that I'm sure you want to hear."

"Doctor," Bradbury began, "I believe this is the most beautiful age humanity has had the good fortune to live in; the most audacious, the most privileged, the most stupendously blasphemous. When they say, 'Look, isn't that rocket marvelous?' I answer, '*Man*, who built it, *he* is marvelous!' We used to think of beauty and sculpt statues, paint pictures, and build palaces. Now when we think of beauty, when we think of God, we create something that burns and flies upward—engines, machines! We, you, all of us are making rockets. We are leaping beyond the Earth—we're leaving our prison behind us."

"I am humbled by your thoughts, Mr. Bradbury, but I cannot take all the credit since—"

"Nor am I giving you the credit, sir. We know it's a huge operation. Thousands of people. But tonight I am saying to *you* how important your work is to *all* of us—because we're afraid of death and darkness. Don't let us forget—the Earth can die—it can explode! The Sun can go out, it *will* go out. And when the Sun dies, when the Earth dies, when our race dies, Homer will die. Michelangelo will die. Galileo, Leonardo, and Shakespeare. Einstein will die. All of those who are not dead because we're alive, because we're thinking of them—they will die if we die. Your rocket carries more than three astronauts. It carries all of us."

"At least liquor has made one guest more eloquent instead of more idiotic," Clarke said.

"Mr. Bradbury, perhaps you can support us on our next mission?" von Braun asked.

"Doctor, I would gladly give you a part of my earnings for a seat on your ship to Mars."

Staftoy laughed and Clarke added, "Hear, hear! When we escape from this ocean of air, we'll move into a whole universe of new sensations. But I'm keeping *my* money, Wernher. You'll have to hit up some of the captains of industry at the next table…"

"Sirs—and ladies." Bradbury bowed slightly toward Rachel. "Let me conclude by saying that if we fear the darkness, if we fight against it—for the good of all, let us take our rockets and let us become Martians. Let us become Venusians. And when Mars and Venus die, let us go to the other solar systems, to Alpha Centauri—to the gates of Orion's Belt! People, let us drink—to Apollo!"

The small group drained their glasses.

The musicians hit a groove, and people danced inside and on the terrace.

While von Braun chatted with Ryan, who had returned with another martini, Rachel scanned the room.

"Let's dance." She pulled the German from his guests.

Wernher, surprised, put down his drink and let himself be taken onto the dance floor for a slow number; they slipped in among other couples holding each other close.

"Something is wrong," Rachel said. "You must tell me. Perhaps our troubles are the same."

He was suddenly overwhelmed—*a message*—he really did know her from long ago.

"Yes, it's true," she said. "We danced at Peenemünde. I wanted to kill you."

"You—?"

"Things have changed. Now I'm here to help. Tell me."

He hesitated, then went with his gut, because things *had* changed.

"There is a man, former SS—Kammler. You may have heard of him. He has threatened me, my family—more importantly, he is threatening the Apollo 11 mission. I feel his threat is real, but I cannot find out anything. He works for—"

"Formerly Dulles, now others. They've been protecting him for decades."

She pushed von Braun away.

"We're all compromised," she said. "I've waited too long, but my hands have been tied. I'll be in touch."

Von Braun watched her disappear into the crowd.

The night would be long.

Tomorrow would be longer.

Chapter 115

"Astronauts 'Unafraid' as Apollo Launch Nears"

—Fort Pierce News Tribune

Cape Kennedy, Florida
Wednesday, July 16, 1969

Armstrong, Aldrin, and Collins awoke for the countdown at 4:15 a.m. eastern daylight time. In their individual crew quarters within the Manned Spacecraft Operations Building of the Kennedy Space Center, they each took care of personal business. Buzz took off his rings before washing his face; Armstrong combed his hair; Collins carefully shaved.

In a larger room, the flight surgeon and three doctors gave the trio physicals and declared them flight ready.

In the morning's third locale they pulled up cushioned metal chairs to a Formica table with plates on a white tablecloth to eat a breakfast of orange juice, steak, scrambled eggs, toast, and coffee. In short-sleeved collared shirts and beige pants, they wolfed down the food with Slayton observing them.

"Just another mission," Collins said.

"Shut up and eat," Slayton suggested. "You know what generic slop you'll be getting for the next few days."

They kept up as casual a conversation as possible. They'd flown many dangerous missions. A stranger in the room, an officially appointed NASA artist, sketched them and their scene for posterity.

"Oh, I've got a question they want answered," Slayton remembered.

"It better be the last one," Buzz said.

"The question is, 'Do you feel the weight of the world on your shoulders?'"

Collins and Aldrin looked to Armstrong. After chewing some eggs and swallowing, he replied, "Seems like I've had that one before. You can tell them the weight is evenly distributed among thousands of people working on the program and hundreds of people backing us up in Houston, at the Cape, and at other NASA centers. Everyone. It's their mission as much as ours."

Their old friend Joe Schmitt was helping them suit up when Buzz noticed with alarm that his grandfather's Thirty-Second Degree Masonic ring was missing from his finger.

"You want me to check your room?" Joe asked.

"Yes—check the bathroom."

One of Schmitt's technicians ran off and in less than five minutes returned with the ring.

"Thanks," Buzz said. "I would've felt naked without it."

The three astronauts put their legs into their spacesuits, with assistance, then pulled the tops over their shoulders and pushed their heads through neck rings. Before they put on their "Snoopy" helmets, Slayton sent them off with an old test-pilot adieu: "Go and blow up."

The three astronauts no longer breathed outside air. Small portable tanks pumped oxygen into the sealed suits, which were inspected for leaks. During the next three hours they would purge their bloodstreams of nitrogen to prevent the bends later on. Aldrin, Armstrong, and Collins, after being checked out again, departed from crew quarters at 6:27 a.m.

Each astronaut carried his own oxygen supply in a valise for the short walk to the Astrovan. Over a hundred people had lined the road to the launch tower to cheer them on their way. Camera flashbulbs popped, and several onlookers shouted kind words and sentiments, but the trio heard only the sound of their own breathing inside their helmets. They waved goodbye and climbed into the van, which drove off, slowly, to cover the eight miles between those offering prayers for the trio and the giant rocket waiting on Pad 39A.

* * *

Von Braun had risen even earlier than the astronauts, due to an erroneous wake-up call from a confused hotel clerk. Unable to go back to sleep, he'd gone over in his mind each step of the mission and written a few postcards to family members.

He leaned down and kissed Maria at around 6:00 a.m.

"Pray for us," he asked.

"I will," she said, half asleep. "Bye and good luck."

He thought about Kammler on his short drive over. He'd asked the authorities to beef up security weeks ago, but they assured him that a fly couldn't buzz in undetected.

Crowds of onlookers along the highway buoyed his spirits. In every direction, cars, trailers, boats, caravans, tents, and campers jammed vantage points along the roads, waterways, and beaches. He saw a young man and woman in T-shirts and shorts setting up folding chairs and a picnic basket.

He was waved through the entrance gate and started his official day outside the four-story vehicle assembly building with retired GI, former private first class, Fred Schneikert of the Forty-Fourth Infantry Division.

"Hello there, Doctor von Braun," Fred said. "Thanks for the invite."

Schneikert had aged, of course: gray hair and lined face. They stood together in the warm early sunlight.

"Did you bring your family, Mr. Schneikert?" von Braun asked.

"Why yes. They're already seated on the bleachers with a fine view of the launchpad. Since we live nearby, it wasn't a long trip."

Reporters, sniffing a story, gravitated toward them.

"This is the man who captured me in 1945!" von Braun called out to them.

Cameras clicked and pencils scribbled on pads.

Schneikert wasn't used to being in the limelight and searched for words. "More like you…surrendered, sir. Who would've thought—"

"I would have thought!"

They posed for the press and chatted a little more. The MSFC director bragged again of winning their bet, having beaten the private back to the USA.

They said goodbye, and von Braun proceeded alone into the reinforced concrete building. On the southeastern side of its third floor, he entered launch control, the "fire room." He crossed paths at its double doors with several controllers who were rushing to restrooms with only moments to spare.

Von Braun had received no news from Rachel. Staftoy could no longer be of any help, and he didn't trust unknown military officials. Kammler had always been hard to predict.

* * *

At T minus two hours, forty minutes, the prime crew boarded an elevator from inside the "A" level of the mobile launcher. They didn't speak much going up to the 320-foot level. Collins and Armstrong walked across Swing Arm 9. They would enter the capsule first. Aldrin waited near the elevator. He knew he had about fifteen minutes and relaxed into a pleasant limbo. As far as he could see along the calm ocean surf stretched a swarm of people and vehicles of all kinds on the beaches and highways. He noted NASA ground personnel in their flame-protection gear and armored carriers. Looking up, he admired the superbly engineered capsule atop the taller-than-a-football-field Saturn V rocket. A work of art; what they'd trained and jockeyed for.

Gotta remember this moment.

One floor above Aldrin, Armstrong was preparing to climb into the capsule when pad leader Guenter Wendt, once more part of their team, handed him a small, shining crescent, carved out of Styrofoam, covered with a metal skin.

"For you," he said. "Your key to the Moon."

Armstrong folded Guenter's hand over it.

"You hold on to it until we get back." He pulled out a small printed ticket from beneath the wristband of his Omega watch and handed it to Wendt. "This is good for a ride in a space taxi between any two planets."

One of the crew called Aldrin and soon each man had taken his place. Armstrong in the left-hand couch. Collins in the right-hand couch. Aldrin in the center.

Collins, looking across while doing their checks, said, "Neil, I think that extra pocket they sewed to your pants is in danger of ruining our mission." He pointed at the abort handle not far from the commander's knee. "I'm pretty sure our goal isn't to be the laughingstock of the world."

Armstrong saw what Collins meant: a wrong movement on his part would easily launch the abort rocket, so he rolled his leg as far as he could from the handle. It wasn't far. Now he had to take into account one more of a thousand things that could go wrong.

Collins leaned back in his chair and pushed away his own fear of fears: a reschedule. Having to re-slog through the tedious process of recycling the fuel, of redoing everything, every detail, a second or even a third time…

Let's just—go!

* * *

Fritz Lang circled the bleachers in search of the VIP section. He spotted talk-show host Johnny Carson and former president Johnson with his handlers and decided to follow them. The temperature and humidity factor climbed but didn't bother the thousands of special guests from all over the world, along with nearly as many members of the press, who had come in their summer clothes to witness history. They brought canteens and sandwiches and lightweight cameras. Once Lang was up a few rows in the VIP section, he saw "Good luck Apollo 11" scrawled into the sand in huge letters on a nearby beach.

"We're approaching the two-hour mark in our countdown," blared the public affairs officer over the PA system. "I'm Jack King, and I'm informing you that the crew is aboard the spacecraft. The hatch is closed.

Now they're purging the cabin to provide it with a proper atmosphere for launch."

Lang heard a few people speaking German not far from him, but he didn't mingle. Dornberger, sobered up, recognized Lang.

Not so long ago his mad film united us all, Dornberger thought.

Professor von Kármán also understood the small talk around him but stuck to English. He chatted with colleagues from JPL and nodded to Oberth, who was perched next to Dornberger a few rows back.

"This is Apollo Saturn Launch Control," King continued in his slight Boston accent. "All elements are go at this time. Astronaut Neil Armstrong has just completed a series of checks on the big Service Propulsion System engine that sits below him in the Stack. We are nearly at the one-hour mark, and a series of radio frequency and telemetry checks will soon be in progress within the launch vehicle. Fifty-nine minutes forty-eight seconds and counting..."

* * *

Von Braun, behind a row of controllers at their video monitors, listened to the spacecraft test conductor ask if the astronaut crew was comfortable.

"We're comfortable," came Armstrong's intentionally bland reply over the radio.

Kraft and Gilruth heard the same words at the control center in Houston. They made their rounds among the four tiers of pale-green consoles. Kraft consulted with the engineer responsible for flight dynamics, "Fido," and with CapCom Bruce McCandless. Opposite them were two ten-by-twenty-foot plot boards and three large screens. Kraft and Gilruth had helped hone Mission Control into a state-of-the-art, real-time computer complex, but its carpet had been walked ragged and was stained from numerous coffee spills.

Gilruth shook hands with a few of the mission veterans seated in their gray plastic-and-chrome chairs. Gene Kranz idled in the back; his White Team wasn't on yet. The Green Team's technicians occupied their stations, supervised by Cliff Charlesworth, who had sandy hair and a slight paunch and a personality like an old sneaker.

The spacecraft would desperately rely on information generated by their large ground-based computers, as interpreted by experts and funneled through the teams.

Gilruth noticed Kranz's lips moving in a silent prayer.

He's not the only one.

We've done a helluva job, Kraft thought, joining him. *It just better be enough.*

He saw how the grueling process had aged his mentor. "Thank you," he said to Gilruth and detected the trace of a smile in response.

From their elevated position, they could see the whole amphitheater room. Kraft called controllers through his console to bug them about the countdown. He knew Armstrong and Aldrin were busy at myriad tasks and checks and wanted his team to do as much as they could to guarantee their safety.

After a few minutes of this, Charlesworth swiveled around and said, "Chris, if you don't settle down, I'm going to ask you to leave—you're making *me* nervous!"

* * *

Lyndon Johnson held court next to the grandstands, attended by about fifteen reporters. "If we can send a man to the Moon," he said, "we should be able to send a poor boy to school and provide decent medical care for the aged."

A reporter from TASS eagerly wrote down his words.

In the bleachers above him, journalist Oriana Fallaci, like thousands of tourists, sported sunglasses and a visor. She'd invited a former Dora inmate to the launch, one of the surviving slave laborers, Jean-Michel, and had bought him a plane ticket.

"I cannot see this without remembering our endless terror," he said. "The murders, the horror."

She squeezed his arm. She'd hoped the launch might somehow remedy his anger and depression. She still hoped it would.

The temperature mounted to a humid eighty-four degrees, with a six-knot southerly breeze and a few whitish-gray cumulus clouds.

"Four minutes, fifteen seconds," King informed the crowds over the PA system. "The test supervisor has told the launch vehicle test conductor that he is *go*. Repeat: we are *go* for Apollo 11."

In Launch Control, von Braun's seat wasn't far from Debus and Dieter. The last, true to form, went over the statistics in his mind: *The Stack, 5.6 million parts, 4 million in the command and service module. Those parts have proven 99.9 percent reliable, which still allows for 5,600 possible failures.*

Dieter scanned launch control, somewhat reassured by the 463 technicians and engineers huddled over their 450 monitors, backed by over 5,000 specialists scattered throughout the centers. Crew had oriented the rocket's platform so the booster would take the ideal path to the Moon 250,000 miles away. Its angle would be monitored until only a few seconds before launch so the turning of Earth, at 1,000 miles per hour, wouldn't take the Saturn V out of alignment. To put their two men on the Moon, they would have to accomplish around 10,000 separate tasks in a specific order, and—

It could easily become a gigantic fireball.

"On the launch team's behalf, we wish you good luck and Godspeed," the launch operations manager radioed the capsule.

"Thank you," Armstrong's reply crackled. "We know it'll be a good flight."

"Firing command coming in now. We are on automatic sequence," noted King on the PA system. "T minus three. We are *go* with every element of the mission. Repeat: we are on an automatic sequence. The master computer is supervising hundreds of..."

Von Braun's biggest disappointment was that he couldn't be in the capsule with them.

I am sure I could have done it.

He clasped his hands together.

"Our status board indicates third stage completely pressurized. T minus sixty seconds and counting. We have passed T minus sixty."

"It's been a real smooth countdown," Armstrong radioed.

"Power transfer is complete," King announced. "We're on internal power with the launch vehicle. All second-stage tanks are now pressurized. Thirty-five seconds and counting..."

"It feels good," Armstrong radioed.

Inside the capsule, he turned to his two fellow astronauts and said with uncharacteristic emotion: "This time we're not on no hand-me-down military rocket or popcorn firecracker—we're going to ride the Saturn V, a fire-spitting, thunder-clapping, *go-to-the-Moon machine!*"

Von Braun felt an alarming tension in the room and prayed silently.

Over two hundred million television viewers round the world held their breath.

"Twenty seconds and counting. T minus fifteen seconds, guidance is internal. Twelve, eleven, ten, nine, ignition sequence starts..."

Millions upon millions wished them well, including Maria on a bleacher bench in the VIP section. She also prayed. Not far from her, Ward Kimball leaned forward, spellbound.

"Six, five, four, three, two, one, zero, all engines running..."

The center F-1 engine fired first, followed at quarter-second intervals by the diagonally opposed pairs of titanic motors. The rocket strained upward but was held fast by four giant clamps like the strong hands of an invisible colossus stretching up from beneath the earth. They would be released only when the five engines amped up to their full thrust of 180,000,000 horsepower.

"LIFT OFF!"

"Roger. Clock," Armstrong said in the capsule.

The first few seconds' movement was imperceptible to the astronauts. They knew the rocket rose only because the cabin's instrumentation readings told them so.

Under the ascending rocket, millions of gallons of cold water was pumped into the launch area by the deluge system, sloshing over the walls and mixing with the engines' flames to produce giant billowing clouds of steam. Sheets of ice quickly formed higher up on the rocket's skin from the supercold fuel within and flaked off in mini avalanches.

Thundering shock waves reverberated outward and startled flocks of ducks and small birds in the blue sky.

The three astronauts, bumped and banged around in their helmets, couldn't hear anything through the earphones.

The Saturn V's elegant fins slowly rose past the tower, leaving a blackened and blistered edifice behind.

"Tower cleared," King said.

The spaceship belched out enough destruction to decimate several armies.

Those in the bleachers, on the beaches and the crammed highways, shielded their eyes from the light of the blast from the far-off spectacle, which made no sound at first. There were only cries of astonishment and fear, and the clicks of Instamatic cameras. Many wept with joy or craned their necks to see the rising behemoth. Fifteen seconds later the audio shock wave reached them, a crackling like the breaking of sticks—then a raging *boom, boom, boom!*

"Flight control is now passing from Launch Control at Cape Kennedy, Florida, to Mission Control in Houston, Texas," said King on the PA system. "Communication with the crew is being handled there by CapCom Bruce McCandless."

"We got a roll program," Armstrong radioed.

"Roger. Roll," acknowledged McCandless from Houston.

Houston's Mission Control PAO, Jack Riley, took over. Sitting only a few feet from flight director McCandless, he reported: "Down range one mile, altitude three, now four miles. Velocity 2,195 feet per second. We're through the region of maximum dynamic pressure."

McCandless told the crew at two minutes duration, "Apollo 11, you are *go* for staging."

"Inboard cut off," said Armstrong.

"We confirm inboard cut off."

The crew was hit by about four Gs when the first engine shut down. Shortly after, the other four engines stopped—and the second stage's five engines jumped on, jerking the astronauts forward against their straps.

At three minutes and seventeen seconds after liftoff, Armstrong ejected the abort rocket, whose handle's proximity to his pants would no longer be a threat. Because the abort rocket had partially sheathed their command capsule, *Columbia*, Collins now had an unblocked window.

At nine minutes, the second stage shut down and the three astronauts experienced a brief weightlessness before the third stage engine ignited smoothly.

"Armstrong has confirmed both the engine skirt separation and the launch escape tower separation," Riley said.

"Houston, be advised the visual is *go*," reported Armstrong.

"Apollo 11, Houston. You are *go* at eight minutes." Sixty seconds later, McCandless advised, "Stand by for Mode IV capability."

"Okay. Mode IV."

"Mark...Mode IV capability."

"Altitude is 100 miles, downrange is 883 miles. Outboard engine cut off."

"Staging and ignition," Armstrong said.

Aldrin and Collins were confident.

"Ignition confirmed. Thrust is *go*."

"We have a good third stage now!" Riley exclaimed for the public to hear.

At 11:42 mission time, Collins called out, "Cut off!" which triggered a scramble among the controllers in Houston, who had to recheck their displays for the orbital Go/No-Go decision.

A rapid-fire conversation with his teams, and Fido shouted, "*Go*, Flight. We are *go!*"

"Apollo 11, this is Houston," transmitted McCandless. "You are confirmed *go* for orbit."

"Roger."

The crew of Apollo 11 was in Earth orbit.

Kranz headed over to the Singing Wheel bar to have a beer with his White Team before going home. He'd be back when his guys were on. Charlesworth's Green Team had supported launch and would handle the moonwalk. Kranz's team would be called on for travel and descent to the lunar surface, while Glynn Lunney's Black Team would—*God willing*, he thought—shepherd the crew off the Moon. Maroon Team, led by Milt Windler, would take care of their return to Earth. Some shifts would be as long as twelve hours, some as short as two; each team would cover the nine-day mission events for which they had trained.

* * *

Several stories beneath the Pullach schoolhouse, Kammler lorded over his own command center built at great expense with American tax dollars and West German deutsche marks.

Behind him, on an elevated throne-like dais, men from the Group and other covert organizations watched technicians at their posts. Positioned in three concentric circles, small TVs followed the events of the Apollo 11 mission, each attended by two operators. Other screens, with telephones in between, had stenciled labels affixed below: Groom Lake, DUCC, Black SAC. One of them showed ground crews milling about airships that hovered in place.

A larger display wall pinpointed the location of the Luna probe; when a memo was handed to a woman in a matching gray skirt and top, she readjusted its marker.

Quincy Adams wore a headset and spoke in a low voice to one of the technicians. He then addressed Kammler, "All stations report ready for transmission of code word AH-1."

"Transmit," Kammler said.

The day and the hour are near.

Kammler's thoughts dwelled on von Braun's imminent public humiliation, so much better than physical punishment in his view, and their burgeoning breakaway government.

Chapter 116

"They're on the Way"

—The Pittsburgh Press

Command and Service Module, Space
Wednesday, July 16, 1969

The astronauts' heads pointed down, toward Earth, their feet up, at the stars, zipping along at 25,500 feet per second. Although up and down meant little, Collins patted his stomach and Aldrin swallowed to clear his inner ears, both relying on their anti-seasickness pills.

Air force jets circled below their rocket. They would serve as communications links to Houston leading up to the rocket's trans-lunar injection burn.

At Cape Kennedy, the launch job over, people celebrated quietly. So many things could still go wrong that their attention remained on the screen and the PA system. Von Braun shook a few hands and lingered. He decided to stay until TLI.

Controllers in Houston lit cigarettes and extinguished them, only to light another seconds later. Flop sweat proliferated, and several men had to fight what they called "auto shake" in their hands. They compulsively double- and triple-checked their monitors and went down lists. Minor errors were made and corrected. One technician on a break dialed his doctor at a public pay phone to complain of a developing ulcer.

"Apollo 11, this is Houston. You are *go* for TLI. Over."

"Apollo 11, thank you," Collins answered in a monotone.

The capsule's onboard computer took control and counted down Saturn V's third stage to trans-lunar injection. On Armstrong's control console the awaited light lit up on a gauge at the correct pre-programmed moment.

"Ignition!" he said. "Call it at fifteen."

"Ignition," Collins confirmed. "Okay."

"We confirm ignition for TLI. Thrust is go," McCandless radioed from Mission Control. "Guidance looking good. Velocity twenty-six thousand feet per second."

"Pressures look good."

"Flashes out of window five!" Collins shouted from his right-hand couch. "Strange lights. I'm not sure…could be lightning or something to do with the engine."

At Kennedy, von Braun's mind swung to Kammler.

Sabotage! Are they already dead?

He sucked in his breath and shut his eyes.

"Continual flashes…" Collins said, and when no word came back, he asked himself, *Am I the only one concerned here?*

He hoped it was merely evidence of the engine's operations more than a hundred feet behind them.

Nothing irregular showed on any of the gauges.

"I wouldn't worry too much about that," Armstrong said.

God, please… von Braun begged.

"About two degrees off in the pitch," Aldrin said.

"Apollo 11, this is Houston at one minute," McCandless radioed. "Trajectory and guidance look good, and the stage is good. Over."

I can't believe I'm still the only—"Don't look out window one." Collins tried to laugh it off. "If it looks like what I'm seeing out window five, you don't wanna see it."

Armstrong looked. "I don't see anything."

"You don't see those flashes out there?"

Let it only be exhaust from the motor… Wernher opened his eyes.

"Oh, I see a little flashing out there, yes," Armstrong admitted.

He's not going to let anything bother him, thought Collins.

“Yes, yes.” Aldrin saw it. “Damn, everything’s…Kind of sparks flying out there.”

“Yes, that’s—oopsedo.” Collins felt a lurch.

“Man, that’s really…” Armstrong felt it, too.

“That’s PU shift?”

“I don’t know, but it sure put a little blip in there. I think it increased in thrust.”

The ratio change in fuel to oxidizer flow to the engine, most likely, thought von Braun. *Is that it?*

He silently cursed Kammler.

McCandless came on the line. “Apollo 11, this is Houston. Thrust is good. Everything’s still looking good.”

“Roger.”

Collins leaned back to enjoy the rest of the burn. Nothing bad was actually happening.

After five minutes and forty-seven seconds, the engine shut down on schedule.

At two hours and forty-five minutes, they were speeding silently through the ether on their way to Earth’s solitary satellite.

“We have cut off,” Armstrong reported. “Hey, Houston, Apollo 11. That Saturn gave us a magnificent ride.”

Von Braun shook hands with Dieter and Debus. “I must go back to the hotel and find Maria,” he said. “I’ll see you in Houston.”

* * *

Tourists and VIPs vacated the bleachers, while those preparing sandwiches and hot dogs for lunch packed the beaches. Whether congregating with friends or going their separate ways, everyone asked each other and themselves one thing: Would the three astronauts land safely on the Moon and return home?

* * *

About 3,500 miles away, the command and service module, or CSM, stayed on course, at more than 35,000 feet per second. Blinding sunlight pierced a couple of its windows and ricocheted off their white astronaut suits, painful to their eyes. Collins noted that, true to form, Armstrong had prepared for such an eventuality and stuck into place a segment of precut cardboard over his window, a sun visor for space.

My turn.

That meant couch swapping. As he moved to the left seat, Michael's heartbeat increased; Neil floated to the center and Buzz to the right, slow and deliberate, keenly conscious of not wanting to puke.

"Apollo 11, this is Houston," McCandless radioed. "You're go for separation. Our systems recommendation is to arm both Pyro Buses. Over."

"Okay. Pyro B coming armed," Armstrong said. "My intent is to use bottle Primary 1, as per checklist; I just turned on A."

"Roger. We concur."

While hurtling away from Earth, Collins prepared to disengage the command and service module from their third stage.

Don't stray too far ahead, don't lose sight of that monster while I'm turning. The same thoughts scrolled through his mind as in the simulations. *Not too much gas.*

He pushed a button, and their CSM was gently expulsed. With his left hand, he nudged a small control handle forward to fire thrusters on the perimeter of the capsule.

Their CSM coasted in space.

"Flies like a spacecraft instead of a simulator," he said. "I hope that's good."

"Sure is beautiful," Armstrong assured him.

A hundred feet out. Going to use more fuel.

Collins rotated the CSM until it faced the lunar module nestled inside their third stage. Although racing away from Earth, the two ships hovered motionless relative to each other. One spaceship contained the three astronauts; the other held the smaller lunar module, in which two of them would descend to the surface of the Moon. The CSM had to dock with it before going on its merry way.

"That thing looks like a mechanical tarantula crouched in its hole," Collins described the LM. He thought its one black "eye" was peering at him malevolently.

"Just line it up," Armstrong advised.

Collins made delicate adjustments, firing short bursts, inching toward the gray and black contraption.

The computer numbers flipped erratically, nonsensical…

Probably overloaded.

…so he used his instincts.

"If you're looking for something to do, you might look over at my panels one and eight and make sure all the switches are to your liking."

"I'll do it," Armstrong said. "Looks good."

"Stand by… We're closing."

No word from Houston for a while, Neil thought. *Must not be a good angle for communication.*

Using the crosshairs as a guide, Collins gently inserted the CSM's probe into the drogue, or receptor, of the lunar module. Latches locked into position with a clunk, and they were docked securely, two distinct pieces forming one.

"Not the smoothest docking."

"Well, it felt good from here," Neil said. "Buzz, see if you can get Houston on the high-gain antenna."

Collins pulled the lunar module into space.

Armstrong talked to Houston: "You might be interested to know that out my left-hand window, I can observe the entire continent of North America, Alaska, over the Pole, down to the Yucatan Peninsula, Cuba, and the northern part of South America. Then I run out of window."

"Roger," Mission Control said over the high-gain antenna. "You're go for LM ejection."

"Houston, we are officially sepped. We have a Cryo Press light."

"Roger, 11. We recommend you turn the O_2 fans on manually and ensure that the O_2 heaters are in the Automatic position."

"Roger. O_2 heaters are on, and we're going to cycle the O_2 fans."

Having swung round to face the Moon again, they readied their big CSM engine, which would put some distance between them and the now derelict Saturn.

A three-second burst.

At more than 18,000 miles out and about 4.5 hours mission time, the three astronauts in their *Columbia* command and service module streaked to the Moon, the lunar module attached to its "nose" like a car pushing a trailer. They ascended toward the constellation Virgo at almost 15,000 feet per second, with the Earth rotating west to east behind them.

* * *

In Houston, Kraft and Gilruth caught the mood change. Controllers who had been glued to their chairs stood up and stretched or chatted with their neighbors. Kraft even heard one say, "No problem," and another, "Piece of cake!"

A few of Kranz's White Team prepared for the upcoming shift change. Kraft wanted to remind them it was far from over, but they knew it and it was okay to relax a little.

In Florida, von Braun couldn't unwind. He was listening to the PAO on his car radio when he turned into the hotel parking lot.

He embraced Maria in the lobby but was dogged by lingering, disquieting thoughts.

Back in their room, he carefully folded a blue dress shirt and latched a beige suitcase for their flight to Houston.

Damn, damn, damn Kammler! And damn whoever is behind him, pulling the strings...

Chapter 117

"World Watches as the Great Journey Begins"

—*The Sydney Morning Herald,* Australia

Langley Research Center, Virginia
Wednesday, July 16, 1969

"We've got to stop Kammler," Rachel told Angleton. "This isn't a crass assassination or coup—this is the future. All of us."

They were in Angleton's second-floor office, and she thought the career spy looked ill.

She leaned toward him between low stacks of documents. "You can't protect that murdering prick any longer. Tell me where he is, and I'll—"

"Let's be serious." Angleton fell back into his armchair and his old swagger. He lit a Virginia Slim. "Multiple wheels are already in motion. There's nothing anyone can do. Those above me…let's not forget they have confederates. There are other interested parties."

"I know more than you about all of that." She straightened. "The situation is not as dire as you think. It never is. Tell me what you know—and I'll fix it."

Angleton reflected. He'd been caught off guard. She had always affected him, had led him to betray his colleagues on several occasions.

What difference will it make? None.

He swore Rachel to secrecy.

Then he told her everything about Kammler and the Luna probe, about the explosive combination, about Pullach's underground control center and its link to larger ones. He wanted to divulge their reasoning.

About the war and its aftermath.

"Even if they knew the Soviets couldn't abort."

Command and Service Module, Space
Wednesday, July 16, 1969

"If we're late answering you, it's because we're munching sandwiches," Collins informed Mission Control.

"Roger." McCandless sounded rueful. "I wish I could do the same."

"Awww. You can't leave the console, pal."

"Don't worry, I won't."

"Flight doesn't like it."

In Houston, McCandless glanced back at Kranz. "Nope. He doesn't."

"Down there you might want to join us in wishing Dr. Mueller a happy birthday," Armstrong radioed.

"Roger. We copy. I'm looking in the viewing room right now, but I don't see him back there."

"He may not have arrived from the Cape yet."

"Roger."

Many NASA employees were in transit from Cape Canaveral to Houston on launch-day afternoon.

Von Braun, after several interviews and a press conference, had joined Maria, and they were being driven to the airport.

Over their car radio, the public affairs officer said, "We don't expect to hear a great deal more from the crew tonight."

"Can you please turn it up?" Wernher asked the driver.

At a louder volume, the PAO continued, "At about 11 hours, 20 minutes we said good night to the astronauts from Mission Control. They are beginning their sleep period early. Apollo 11 is 55,522 nautical miles from Earth, traveling at a velocity of 7,920 feet per second. Gene Kranz and his White Team here in the Control Center will be in charge for the next few hours."

* * *

Zipping through space in their crammed capsule, the three astronauts weren't sure if the notorious flicker-flashes might make them go blind. Several crews had experienced the flashes, and the weird, often bothersome lights had returned to harass the Apollo 11 mission.

Buzz settled down like the others in his light-mesh sleeping bag, having shed his pressure suit, and recalled that the phenomenon was mixed up with quantum mechanics. NASA scientists had thrown in the towel on the subject. The lights had become one more oddity the three men had to ignore because they didn't have a choice. Unless the flicker-flashes affected the mission adversely, the astronauts had been told not to discuss them over the radio.

Buzz and Neil stowed themselves under the couches, while Mike floated above them, tethered to a lap belt to keep from wandering off. He also had a miniature headset taped to his ear in case Mission Control should call. Before trying to sleep he'd put the CSM into "barbecue mode," its long axis perpendicular to the rays of the Sun, rotating at three revolutions per hour to prevent overheating or damage to its systems and surfaces.

If I don't want to see the lights, I won't, Buzz thought.

He saw a white one pass through Neil, exit the back of his head at high speed, and slip right through the wall of the capsule into space. They penetrated in and out of the spacecraft at will, speeding through their helmets and skulls—that was the rub. Buzz knew it worried Neil and Mike, too, but they weren't saying anything. Flashes of white or light blue with gray-white auras, they came in different forms, too: spots, stars, streaks…

At least they don't hurt.

To change his thoughts, Buzz listened to the whirr of electric fans and the *thump*, *thump*, *thump* of the attitude-control thrusters.

Mike, not able to sleep either, watched the Earth shrink in size but grow in brilliance; he judged it brighter than the Moon ever shone over Earth and wished others might one day see the beauty for themselves.

The majesty of their voyage did not escape any of them, but with the whole world listening, self-conscious, they downplayed it to the point of existential comedy. They reserved some observations for secure channels.

In his mind, Neil compared the Earth with other massive celestial objects: Saturn, Neptune, Jupiter. Earth, seen at a great distance, didn't look like it could put up much of a fight against whatever the universe might throw at it. A single globe so politically and culturally divided was absurd. From space, Earth was one. Buzz had reminded him that Jesus had taught his apostles that they were all one, whether they liked it or not.

Sure, we can fight forever. It doesn't mean a thing, except foolishness.

* * *

The Luna 15 entered lunar orbit at 10:00 UT on July 17.

Nixon and Borman had been informed by Moscow that the probe would remain in lunar orbit for two days while its controllers checked onboard systems and performed two maneuvers, before landing ahead of Apollo 11's astronauts.

No military or civilian officer in the Soviet Union or the United States detected anything abnormal in its flight or its telemetry.

Chapter 118

"Mighty Apollo Streaking for Moon; World Electrified by Dream Voyage"

—*Charleston Daily Mail*

Command and Service Module, Space
Thursday, July 17, 1969

On day two of the mission, ground control radioed a wake-up call to the astronauts but found they were already busy at their tasks.

"Apollo 11, Apollo 11, this is Houston. Over."

"Good morning, Houston," Collins replied. "Apollo 11."

Charlie Moss Duke, CapCom on the line, went over a number of straightforward jobs with the crew: checking dials, meters, lights, alarms, and indicators, looking for signs or fluctuations that spelled trouble. In a pretty near uninterrupted back-and-forth with Mission Control, they had to operate, control, and monitor the CSM's environment, fuel, propulsion, radiators, radars, sextants, antennas, timers, computers, purge valves, navigation instruments, pressure regulators, medical monitors, communication panels, and fan motors—interspersed with headlines Duke read them from a local newspaper in his North Carolina accent.

"Hey, Charlie, what's the latest on Luna 15?" Aldrin broke in.

"Say again, Buzz? Over."

"Roger. What's the latest on Luna 15?"

"Stand by," Duke said. "I'll get the straight story for you."

Collins verified food, sanitation, lights, fuel cells, guidance systems, telescopes, and wastewater systems, then floated from his couch to inspect the LM interior. He opened the hatch. It looked okay, but didn't smell good.

Like charred electric wiring.

Visible wiring checked out okay.

A past condition? Sure hope so.

Armstrong tracked down a camera that had become untethered, and Collins chose to mention the bad smell later.

Aldrin was growing impatient. He had to bite his tongue while Duke gathered the information.

We don't want to smash into the damned thing!

"Hello, Apollo 11. Houston. Over."

"Go ahead, Charlie," Collins answered first.

"Roger. Here's the skinny on Luna. TASS reported this morning that the spacecraft went into orbit, functions normal, at about sixty-two nautical miles above the lunar surface. We don't foresee any problems. Over."

"Roger. Thank you, Charlie. Over."

An orange light on the main control panel told the crew to switch over to a private channel.

"Apollo 11, Houston," came Duke's voice. "Over."

"Go ahead," Neil said. "Over."

"Intelligence reports the Soviets are having technical problems. Luna delayed and may land not far from you. We'll keep eyes and ears out—please do same. Over."

"Roger."

For Christ's—! Buzz thought. *Good thing I asked.*

* * *

In a motel room near the ocean Rachel pushed her mind into another dimension.

She'd reasoned that no amount of physical effort on her part could stop Kammler and the Group, so she was taking a different path.

At a higher frequency, her disembodied self encountered a snake-like entity, who studied her with sorrow, until she was catapulted back into her body, knocked off her chair.

Her nose bled.

The path was blocked; it wasn't working…

* * *

Aldrin saw it first, on the evening of the third day, shortly after 9:00 Houston time.

Strange. It's moving relative to the stars, but it's brighter.

"Mike, Neil, you see that?" he asked, pointing out of *Columbia*'s window three.

They saw it, but they didn't want to get Mission Control on the line. At least, not yet. They'd talk it over among themselves first, as planned.

Mike grabbed the monocular.

"It's about a hundred miles away."

Buzz used the sextant.

"It seems to be changing shape. Sometimes it's a cylinder…but when I adjust focus, it looks more like a lit-up letter 'L.'"

Neil silently assessed the object.

"There's a straight line," Buzz added, "a small bump in it and a little something off to the side."

Neil gave the okay and Buzz radioed Houston to ask how far away their discarded third stage had drifted.

"In the vicinity of six thousand miles."

Houston understood what they were asking and why. The crew didn't have to spell it out.

"Let's just say we saw one of the panels," Neil decided.

The three astronauts observed the unidentified object off and on for about an hour, in between "housekeeping" chores. Similar to the flicker-flashes, it had to be chocked up as another anomaly.

At about 177,000 nautical miles out, the Moon's gravitational force was pulling them in.

Chapter 119

"Apollo Flying Around Moon— Key Firings Are Crucial to Success"

—*The Bethlehem Globe-Times*

Houston, Texas
Saturday, July 19, 1969

When von Braun arrived in the crammed viewing room of the Manned Space Center, he detected an air of strained collegiality. Not far from birthday-boy Mueller, Gilruth, Kraft, assorted administrators, and other higher-ups conversed quietly. Astronauts John Glenn, Gene Cernan, Dave Scott, and Al Worden grabbed the last chairs in the front row.

Gilruth and his lieutenants were focused on every last detail of the ongoing mission. Kraft watched over Kranz and his White Team. On the control center floor, astronaut backup crew Bill Anders, Fred Haise, and Jim Lovell joined McCandless at the CapCom console, where Slayton had already stationed himself. They kept their eyes on the big picture and, if they thought of him at all, considered von Braun a passive observer, whose Huntspatch experts knew relatively little about the command module and LM. He'd be needed only if something unexpected occurred.

Yet von Braun lived the astronauts' voyage intensely, transforming their words and those of Mission Control into his own experience, enhanced by an intermittent TV feed. His enthusiasm, however, beat in contretemps to his terror. He still couldn't reach Rachel…

He recalled Kammler's specific threat, "*If they land…*"

I have to tell Gilruth.

He looked over but couldn't interrupt Gilruth's conversation with Mueller.

"We have loss of signal because Apollo 11 is behind the dark side of the Moon," PAO Riley announced. "We are showing a distance to the Moon of 309 nautical miles, velocity 7,664 feet per second. On this fourth day of the mission, we are 7 minutes, 45 seconds away from the LOI, burn number one, which they will execute behind the Moon, out of communications."

* * *

In the CSM, Armstrong asked Collins, "You have a patch ready in case you want it? You may have the sun in your eyes coming round the corner."

"Got it right here." Collins exhibited his cardboard slat. He looked out the window. "Yep, the Moon is there. In all its splendor."

"Man, it's…I don't know," Buzz said.

"Plaster of Paris gray to me."

"Man, look at it."

Seventy-six hours since blastoff, the crew went about prep for their first lunar orbit insertion burn, which would put their ship nearly close enough to launch the lunar module.

"What we need is a good performance from the ol' main engine," Collins said.

And I sure as hell hope we don't send ourselves into orbit around the Sun.

"EMS and G-n-N CALS together," Armstrong reported.

"Okay," Aldrin acknowledged.

"Pitch trim is up at 1.5 degrees," Collins said, "cycling about that, which is a little bit off the SIM value. Yaw trim is cycling, oh, about zero."

They checked, checked again, reconfirmed the computer's numbers, and rechecked. Another life-or-death moment.

The engine ignited on cue, and they kept an eye on the clock. Six minutes later, the motor turned off on schedule.

"That was a beautiful burn," Armstrong declared.

"Well, goddamn, I guess!" Collins said. "I don't know if we're at sixty miles or not, but at least we haven't hit it."

"Whoo!" Buzz whooped, looking down at the Moon. "Well, I have to vote with the ten crew: that thing there is brown."

"Looks tan to me," Neil said.

"It used to look gray," said Mike.

The great Moon loomed between them and the Sun, which cast a halo upon it. Collins sensed the celestial sphere greeted them with a whispered warning, a double-edged invitation to its scarred and pock-marked surface that seemed to burst through his minuscule window. Its physicality blew away his memories of a more anonymous, more remote nighttime friend. This huge Moon, scary and three-dimensional, disturbed his expectations.

"It changes colors easily," he said. "Now it looks blue."

"Depends on the light," Buzz said.

"It's a view worth the price of the trip," said Armstrong.

They'd achieved the proscribed sixty-mile-high elliptical orbit. From over two hundred thousand miles away, their miniscule capsule had hit a moving bull's-eye.

"Look back there, kind of behind us—sure is a gigantic crater," Collins said. "Look at the mountains up around it. They're monsters. Yes, there's a moose down there, the biggest one yet. God, it's huge, enormous. It's so big I can't even get it in the window."

"Yes, there's a big mother over here, too," Buzz said.

The two kept describing craters and mountains in codes or jokes, and though they'd been told to expect them, to see one of the crumbling superstructures stretched believability.

Armstrong said nothing until he heard Houston trying to make contact after they'd emerged from the dark side's shadow.

"Apollo 11, Apollo 11, this is Houston. Do you read?" asked CapCom McCandless. "Over."

“Yes, we sure do, Houston,” he replied. “The LOI-1 burn was just nominal as all get out. Everything’s looking good.”

The iterative multi-burn approach would give Mission Control enough leeway to confirm the effects of the Moon’s exact gravitational pull, which folks on the ground would recalculate based on the craft’s telemetry.

Static and radio problems prevailed for several minutes, however, until—“Roger. Reading you same, now. Could you repeat your burn status report?”

A stream of numbers, values, and angles.

“Roger. We copy. The spacecraft is looking good to us.”

“Roger. Everything looks good up here, too. We’re getting our first view of the landing approach. It looks like the pictures, but it feels like the difference between watching a real football game instead of one on TV. There’s no substitute for being here.”

“Roger. We concur, and we certainly wish we could also see it firsthand.”

* * *

Von Braun knew the CSM and its passengers would stay in their new orbit for a few trips around the Moon, which would take several hours. Mission Control would suffer a loss of signal each time and each time people would feign a wary nonchalance, but the anxiety wouldn’t go away.

He swallowed a few pills and went over to Gilruth.

“Bob, can we talk? I need five minutes.”

They took an empty office outside the control room. Gilruth stayed standing. Von Braun sat on a bare wooden desk and laid it out: “Something is in store for Apollo 11, something bad. I should not be telling you this, but there it is. I have this information from a reliable source.”

“Wernher, I don’t get it.” Gilruth rubbed his face. “What the hell are you talking about?”

“I’m sorry, Bob. I am not myself. How can I convey this? I have access to certain information. So do you. Have you heard nothing of a serious nature that threatens the mission?”

"A man-made danger?"

"Yes."

"From inside or outside?"

"Outside."

"Are you sure?"

"No."

"Oh, for—why are you telling me now?"

"Perhaps I'm wrong." Wernher clapped his hands. "I simply don't know. They have threatened me and my family."

Gilruth understood, and he didn't like it. "We've got to tell Webb. And the others. Right away."

"The problem is I don't know what to tell them. I have nothing real, nothing useful to say. I am confiding in you because I trust you, because I hoped that…I thought—"

"You were hoping I knew more than you. You were hoping I could fill you in. Well, I can't."

"Then I am sorry for both of us."

Wernher knew he'd opened a can of worms; he could see that Gilruth was pissed off at him for the worms and for having waited so long.

"They might not survive," von Braun said. "The astronauts could be killed. That is what my gut is telling me; that would be the worst outcome."

"C'mon. Let's make a few phone calls."

* * *

Although not in the flight plan, Armstrong and Aldrin prepared their equipment in advance for the following morning. Floating in their octagonal lunar module, the *Eagle*, which measured about nine feet high and twelve feet wide, they arranged their clothing, impatient for the next day. They went through a mental list of the many procedures they would follow.

Collins had his own chores.

When they knocked off for the "day," tired and excited, they forgot to look for the odd flashes of the previous two nights and slept fitfully.

* * *

Out of sight from their command and service module, but not far, the single red light of the Luna 15 flickered in the obscurity of the Moon's shadow. In its lonely unmanned orbit, the machine knew nothing of its hijacked purpose.

Chapter 120

"Moscow Says That Luna 15 Won't Be in Apollo's Way; Americans Check Module"

—*The New York Times*

Virginia Beach, Virginia
Sunday, July 20, 1969

Rachel hadn't been successful, had spent days trying, until the voice from the windmill had returned.

Still in her motel room, she shut her eyes, left her physical state, passed the sentry snake, and sent her astral body deep into space; she'd never sent it so far. She accelerated to something like half light speed and traveled without resistance except a buzzing in her ears.

Seconds later she saw a donut-shaped space station, perhaps two miles round, orbiting the Moon, though not in the same dimension. She saw it through her electric eyes. A small tube-shaped craft moved slowly toward the dark side.

She arrived at one of the space station's platforms, penetrated two large doors, and floated by gray large-headed automatons with long, bony fingers at intricate tasks. They paid no attention to her.

In a small white room, three short aliens with bulging black eyes dressed in white robes came at her quickly. They wanted to know who she was and how she'd found them. As quick as thought, they understood and let her pass.

Taller aliens occupied a laboratory of gold veneer walls and moved like praying mantises. Also in white robes they stared at her with curious insectile eyes. Behind them throbbed a delicate machine made of a transparent glassy substance. They knew about her, but they didn't know everything.

"We have a shared desire," Rachel pleaded telepathically. "This and your Moon base are in jeopardy."

* * *

Gene Kranz stopped by the bunkhouse, where controllers could shower and watch TV after completing their shift. He chatted with a few guys in T-shirts in the lounge and poked his head into a room full of men on bunk beds. A flight surgeon was handing out pills to those who couldn't sleep.

When Kranz entered Mission Control that morning, day five of the mission, he inhaled a familiar odor of cigarette stubs and pizza crust, bacon sandwiches and freshly burnt coffee. Von Braun caught sight of him making his rounds, blond crew cut, thin lips, square jaw. Kranz's eyes didn't smile when the rest of his face did. To keep his team communicating and motivated, he encouraged banter between them. He didn't want anyone to feel inhibited; he didn't want anyone to make a mistake more than once. Preferably not at all. Von Braun noted all this with approval, but most of his mind waited for Gilruth's return.

"This is Apollo Control at 101 hours, 54 minutes," PAO Riley announced. "We're now about twenty minutes, forty-five seconds from reacquiring the command module on its fourteenth revolution. Time until ignition for the power descent is 38 minutes, 55 seconds."

Kranz glanced at the viewing room and saw von Braun, on the phone, along with the biggest flock of space officials he'd ever seen. He shook hands with astronauts Lovell and Anders.

"You're up," said Anders.

He and Lovell left to hunt for a communications outlet to plug in their headsets. Everyone wanted to hear the transmissions.

Kranz weaved his way among the chairs and headset chords, shook a few more hands, stepped over a manual left on the floor, and took up his post in the middle of the third row. He sported a custom-sewn white vest, the color of his team, over a gray shirt and black tie; tan pants; and black shoes.

"The lunar landing site display is now up for the first time in Mission Control Center," Riley said. "A blow-up for Landing Sites 1 and 2."

Kraft walked up behind Kranz and patted him on the shoulder.

"Good luck, young man."

"Got enough milk in the fridge?" Kranz worried about Kraft's pre-ulcer.

"Sure."

Kraft joined George Low in the director's row. He looked for Gilruth, but his designated chair was vacant.

On the floor Kranz glanced at his board and saw each controller's light burning amber. As his White Team keyed in, were briefed, and flipped their display switches on, each light turned green. He put on his headset and plugged into a closed loop.

"Okay, flight controllers, listen up," he said. "Today is our day; we'll always remember it. The hopes and dreams of the entire world are with us and the crew up there." He leaned on his sweaty palms. "In the next hour we'll do something that has never been done before in the history of the world. Good luck and God bless us. Okay."

"This is Apollo Control," Riley droned. "Flight director Gene Kranz is going around the control center a second time, talking to his flight controllers, reviewing status in preparation for making the Go/No-Go decision for undocking."

In the viewing room, Rees leaned over to von Braun. "You wish you could be with them up there, eh, Professor?"

"Of course, you idiot. This is only the next best thing."

Kranz took a quick poll, and each controller shouted out, *"Go!"*

"Apollo 11, Houston," Duke radioed. "We're *go* for undocking. Over."

"Roger. Understand," Armstrong's voice came back.

He'd specifically requested Duke be CapCom for the landing because of his knowledge of lunar module systems.

"Starting a trim maneuver to AGS CAL attitude," Collins told Houston.

"Ground control, lock the control room doors," Kranz ordered security. "Take Mission Control to battle short. No controller can leave or enter the room. Main circuit breakers in the MCC are blocked and closed."

* * *

In the capsule, after sipping lukewarm coffee and eating a breakfast of bacon cubes, Armstrong and Aldrin took from a storage bin their lunar underwear: full-body johns plaited with hundreds of thin, flexible tubes sewn into a fishnet fabric. They put them on carefully while hovering.

The two then climbed into the dull-gray lunar module for undocking. Buzz glanced for a moment at the LM's innards—bundles of wires, rivets, and circuit breakers—all exposed to save weight. He switched on departure systems.

"How's the Czar over there?" Mike asked Buzz. He'd recently chosen that nickname for Armstrong. "He's so quiet."

"Just hanging on and punching," Czar Armstrong answered as he input data into the computer.

"Beware the revolution," Mike warned. "You cats take it easy on the surface. If I hear you huffing and puffing, I'm going to start bitching at you."

"Okay, Mike," Buzz said.

They sealed the hatch.

"We got just about a minute to go," Mike said. "You guys all set?"

"We're set when you are, Mike," Neil radioed.

"Fifteen seconds…okay, there you go. Beautiful."

The lunar module drifted away from the CSM.

"Looks like a good sep."

Although the three astronauts were unaware of it, the LM drifted out farther than anticipated. The tunnel between the CSM and the LM hadn't been completely vented, and excess pressure had given them an additional shove, invisible, even to Mission Control.

"Looks good to me," Collins said.

But it wasn't. The extra drift would throw off their calculations for landing.

"Okay," Armstrong said. "I've killed my rate, Mike. Starting my yaw."

He rotated the lunar module so Collins could inspect it in the black backdrop of space.

"You're looking good," he said.

Armstrong put the LM into a clockwise orbit so the sun wouldn't be in the eyes of its occupants.

"*Eagle*, Houston," Duke radioed. "We see you on the steerable. How does it look? Over."

"The *Eagle* has wings," Armstrong said.

Both *Eagle* and *Columbia* passed under cover of the dark side. When they came back around, Kranz would give the final Go/No Go for descent.

* * *

Near von Braun in the viewing room, Dieter reassured himself by noting numbers on a pad. When they next acquired the lunar module, it would be at an altitude of about eighteen nautical miles, or thirty-three kilometers, on its way down to a low point of about fifty thousand feet, where their powered descent to the lunar surface would begin.

News of the seemingly charred wires in the LM had worried von Braun, who considered the possibility of sabotage. His anxiety became acute when Mission Control couldn't pick up the LM on its scheduled reemergence from the dark side.

"Voice communications are broken," a controller said.

Von Braun looked down at Gilruth's still empty seat.

Where the hell did he go?

LM telemetry couldn't lock up. Kranz's team punched off the loop to call flight group, hoping for guidance from the back rooms, where the communication experts worked.

"*Columbia*, Houston. We've lost *Eagle*," Duke called Collins in the command module. "Have them try the high gain. Over."

"*Eagle*, this is *Columbia*." They heard Collins relay the message: "Houston's lost you. They're requesting high gain."

Does that mean he can still see the LM? von Braun asked himself.

Kraft's stomach burned. Armstrong and Aldrin had enough fuel for only two landing attempts—and in minutes they would lose that first window.

"Please, God, give us comm," Kranz prayed softly.

"Have them switch to the aft antenna," suggested the communications room over the loop.

"*Columbia*, Houston," Duke radioed. "Tell them to go aft Omni. Over."

Collins relayed the order, but his voice was garbled, too.

"Okay, we're reading you," Aldrin came through the static. "See if they have me now. I've got good signal strength in Slew."

"Okay," Collins radioed. "You should have him now, Houston. Over."

"*Eagle*, we've got you," Duke said. "Looking good."

Kranz exhaled.

Von Braun wiped the sweat from his brow.

Their words zipped 250,000 miles in an electromagnetic whisper without snapping the delicate filament.

"Keep the chatter down!" Kranz ordered and called up his team. "It's Go/No Go for lunar landing. Retro?"

"*Go*."

"Fido?"

"*Go*."

"Guidance?"

"*Go*."

"Control?"

"*Go*."

"G and C?"

"*Go*."

"EEcom?"

"*Go.*"

"Surgeon?"

"*Go.*"

Kranz looked at Duke. "CapCom, we are *go* for landing."

* * *

In the lunar module, Aldrin pivoted right to switch channels on the side panel.

"Proceed. One, zero," he counted down.

Contrary to procedure, he left the docking radar on, in case they had to catch up with the CSM because of an abort.

"Ignition," Armstrong ordered.

"Ignition. Ten percent thrust."

Static in Houston.

Too much static! von Braun thought.

"...just about on time..." Armstrong's voice barely came through. "...light is on..."

More static.

In the command and service module, Collins pressed his nose against the window like a kid for a good view of his colleagues making their powered descent. As his ship glided away from the LM, he glanced at the Sun. It would be at a fairly low angle for the landing, as planned, to provide good, sharp shadows for depth perception.

"How does *Eagle* look, *Columbia*?" Duke radioed, desperate for eyes.

"It's getting smaller."

Both astronauts stood in the LM. No seats had been installed for what, hopefully, would be two short flights: one down, one up. Nor did they have footholds. Buzz grasped a handhold, but their flight was expected to be smooth. At twenty-six seconds the engine went to full throttle and they detected motion.

Aldrin read out loud a long computer sequence and thought, *I must sound like a chattering magpie.*

"Okay, we went by the three-minute point early," Armstrong realized. "We're going to land long."

The undocking error was making itself evident, though neither astronaut had more than a second to think about how bad "long" might mean.

"Rate of descent is looking real good," Aldrin reported. "Altitude's right about on."

"Houston, our position checks downrange show us to be a little long," Armstrong repeated.

"Roger... Let..." Heavy static. "Copy."

In the viewing room, von Braun inhaled deeply on his cigarette.

Where the hell will they land?

Kranz's team did the math quickly, their displays switched from Earth-centered to Moon-centered.

"Three data sources confirm they're not going to hit the planned landing point."

Their runway is rough, crowded with craters and boulders.

But no abort order was given.

The two astronauts, in order to spot landmarks as they passed them in the LM, faced away from potential landing sites, flying backward toward something they couldn't see.

"Program alarm. It's a 1202." Armstrong's voice for the first time had fear in it.

"1202!" Aldrin confirmed.

Kranz and Kraft looked at each other.

"What the hell is a 1202?" Kraft shouted.

Because Mission Control was already processing a potential landing site disaster, it took a moment before they collectively grasped that a second, potentially mission-ending problem was occurring.

At the CapCom console, Duke's heart sank.

"Stand by, Flight," said Steve Bales, guidance officer of the mission.

Bales had been relaxing only a moment before in the belief that his job was done. Now this young man wearing black-rimmed glasses had to interpret the alarm message with his team. It could be one of thousands.

"Please advise," they heard Armstrong ask from afar, his voice weak. "Houston, please give us a reading on the 1202."

"Repeat, it's a 1202 alarm in question," Duke emphasized on the loop as calmly as he could.

C'mon guys!

We sure as hell didn't come this far to abort, Armstrong thought in the LM.

In the simulations, three seconds to respond had been considered far too long—and they were way past that.

Kraft and the others knew it, too.

Bales frantically ran down page after page of lists to see in what group the program alarm belonged—when Jack Garman, a backroom expert at another console, piped up, "We're go! *Go!*"

Even as he heard it, Bales realized 1202 was one of the new rules they'd recently trained for—and radioed, "We're *go* on that alarm!"

"*Eagle*," Duke relayed upward, "we're *go* on that alarm!"

"Roger," came Neil's reply.

"The computer is having troubles with data overflow," Garman quickly explained to Bales. "Something is making it process unnecessary radar data, so the thing's telling us it's dropping lower-priority tasks."

"Same alarm!" Aldrin shouted on the radio to Houston.

"We are *go!"* Bales shouted back nearly simultaneous with the alarm. "Tell him we'll monitor his altitude data."

Duke gave the all clear, but Bales, on a private loop, warned Kranz: "There is a danger. If they get a series of these alarms, the computer will go into idle mode—and abort the landing."

"Roger." Kranz switched loops. "All flight controllers, hang tight. We should be throttling down soon. Seven and a half minutes."

For the final Go/No-Go landing decision, he and his controllers verified once more they'd met the needed criteria.

"CapCom," he said, "we are *go* for landing."

"Roger. Copy," Duke said. "*Eagle*, Houston. You are *go* for landing. Over."

"Okay," Armstrong answered. "Three thousand at seventy."

"Roger," they heard Aldrin. "Understand. Go for landing. Three thousand feet."

"Copy," Duke said.

In the viewing room, von Braun squashed out another cigarette.

"Program alarm 1201!" Aldrin's voice crackled, and Bales cried out, "Go! We are *go!*"

No more alarms, please no more.

Each alarm in the LM distracted Armstrong, who had to clear them manually while flying the machine. Each alarm forced his eyes away from his primary duty: spotting strange landmarks on a strange lunar surface.

"Two thousand feet," Aldrin read out.

Armstrong confirmed landmark tracking, then rotated the craft around its thrust axis to acquire a partial view of what lay before them—a large, jagged crater, into which the automatic approach system was guiding them.

He switched to manual control.

"Give me an LPD."

Buzz gave him the angle: "AGS, forty-seven degrees."

Neil peered through a window inscribed with vertical and horizontal scales marked in degrees. While he scanned the gray lunar horizon, Buzz read out computer numbers indicating where on the scales the machine thought they should land, but Neil no longer cared about the computer's opinion.

Tempted to land short, he quickly changed his mind when they passed over a pale crimson light deep within a dark crater.

"Seven hundred feet. Twenty-one feet per second down, thirty-three degrees."

"Pretty rocky area," Armstrong said.

"I think we better be quiet from here on, Flight," Duke recommended in Houston.

"Roger," Kranz agreed. "The only callouts will be fuel."

"Eight percent."

Not much, but enough, Neil thought, two hundred feet from the surface.

"Low level!" exclaimed another controller. "Propellant is almost below point we can measure."

Driving on empty, Kranz thought. *They don't have more than 120 seconds to land.*

Von Braun willed the controllers to help the astronauts anyway they could, but he knew it was up to Armstrong.

Where the hell is Gilruth?

Armstrong spotted an area of flat, inviting ground.

"Okay. Looks like a good place here."

At twenty feet per second, he reduced the pitch to six degrees.

Final descent.

"I got a shadow out there," Buzz said.

They're hovering…

Kranz used body English in his chair to help them.

More than eleven minutes since they'd started descent—longer than they'd ever trained for.

"One-hundred sixty feet," Buzz said. "Six point five down."

"Sixty seconds of fuel," Duke radioed.

Everyone in the control room and the viewing room and the support rooms stood up. Von Braun saw Gilruth run in and fix his eyes on the board.

What did he find out?

"You're looking good," Buzz said. "Picking up some debris."

Outside the LM, a transparent sheet of moving dust that obscured visibility grew thicker and larger as they neared the surface. Both men strained their eyes to see through the gray-blue blur.

Are we clear of the rocks? Armstrong asked himself.

The peaks of three gigantic boulders showed through the dust storm to their right.

Jesus!

"Thirty seconds," Duke warned.

The controllers kept their eyes riveted on their consoles. A red warning light came on.

"Only five percent fuel..."

"Drifting forward a little bit..." Buzz said.

At thirty feet, Neil felt the craft slide backward and adjusted.

If it quits on us, we'll fall to the surface...

If we come down too hard, Buzz thought, *we'll damage the engine—and be marooned.*

He saw the LM's searchlights slicing through the dust.

Neil corrected their angle and speed...

"Only seconds left," Duke radioed.

"Contact light!" Buzz cried out.

One of the footpad probes had alighted on the Moon.

"Shutdown!" Neil shouted.

Like a helicopter landing. Smooth.

"Engine stop."

"We copy you down, *Eagle*."

The two astronauts gave in to their excitement only long enough to pat each other on the shoulders. Then Buzz initiated procedures for an immediate abort liftoff, in case one were needed, reciting checkpoints—but Neil interrupted him to radio back home: "Houston, Tranquility Base here. The *Eagle* has landed."

"Roger, uh, Tranquility," Duke replied. "We copy you on the ground. You got a bunch of guys about to turn blue. We're breathing again. Thanks a lot."

At first confused, Buzz realized that by naming their landing site and switching call signs, Armstrong had signaled an official status change: from insectoid flying machine to tiny, isolated outpost of the United States.

Not much, but a beginning.

"Tranquility Base," Duke said, "be advised there's lots of smiling faces in this room and all over the world. Over."

"Well, there's two of them up here, too," Armstrong replied.

"And don't forget one in the command module," Mike radioed.

"Roger," Duke acknowledged.

"Okay, we're going to be busy for a minute," Neil said and turned to Buzz. "Let's get on with it."

It took a few moments for the rest of those in Mission Control to grasp that the two-man lunar crew was going through their engine shutdown checklist.

They'd landed on the Moon.

As soon as it sunk in, spectators in the viewing room drummed their feet on the floor and cheered. In the network staff support room, people looked up from their communication panels, dazed, then broke into broad grins and whooped.

Kranz slammed his forearm on the console, snapping his pencil and bruising his elbow. *"Damn!"* he shouted.

Kraft heard more shouting, saw small American flags waved, felt backslaps. He saw Gilruth brush a tear from his cheek discreetly. With lumps in their throats, they shook hands.

Gilruth nodded to von Braun, who questioned him with his eyes. Gilruth replied with a sign to wait.

"Okay, keep the chatter down!" Kranz ordered, and his controllers went over their checklists again to verify system numbers.

"*Eagle*, you are stay for T1," Duke informed the two astronauts.

"Roger," Armstrong replied. "Understand, stay for T1."

Time for a walk.

Back in an empty office, Gilruth told von Braun: "Nothing. Webb and I went through channels, went to the top. Nixon confirmed his confidence in the Soviet information. The official response is there are no dangerous saboteurs around and the matter is closed."

"The CIA says nothing?" Von Braun lit a cigarette.

"Nothing."

"What about the others?"

"Are you kidding? They're not talking. I don't even know if I got through to them."

As von Braun feared, they were helpless.

* * *

In a low orbit, the Luna raced into the Moon's shadow. Its red light blinked twice, and a small yellow light above it flashed on.

Chapter 121

"The Moon Is Just One Step Away—All Systems Go for the Greatest Adventure of All Time"

—*Sunday Sun,* England

Tranquility Base, the Moon
Sunday, July 20, 1969

No one in Mission Control, or anywhere else in the world, knew precisely where Armstrong and Aldrin had landed, including Armstrong and Aldrin. Collins, high above, tried to help when in orbital vicinity, but he couldn't spot them either.

"No sweat," Duke told them.

For the moment, it didn't matter.

"It could explode," said programmer Tom Kelly. "They'd be stranded, dead."

His colleagues agreed—engineers in the Spacecraft Analysis back room huddled round a monitor. Pressure and temperature readings were rising at an alarming rate in one of the LM's descent-stage fuel lines, even though the motor was off.

"If it blows and damages the ascent engine…"

"What can we do?"

"We could burp it," suggested Kelly.

"We better—"

The pressure indicator dropped, then shot back up. Kelly's right eye twitched.

The indicator dropped back again to normal. When the temperature thermostat followed suit, they breathed easier.

No one told the astronauts about it.

CapCom did tell Collins about a potentially dangerous temperature malfunction in the CSM and directed him to his technical manual.

Again? Mike thought. *That long-winded thing?*

Instead he threw a switch from automatic to manual and back to automatic.

Betchya it fixes itself.

It did.

104 hours and 49 minutes, mission time.

"This is the LM pilot," Aldrin called Houston. "I'd like to take this opportunity to ask every person listening in, whoever and wherever they may be, to pause for a moment and contemplate the events of the past few hours. To give thanks in his or her own way. Over."

"Roger, Tranquility Base. Over," said CapCom Owen Garriott. Garriott twirled his mustache and pushed a button. "The world hears you."

In the lunar module, Buzz reached into his personal kit and Neil did the same. The former unwrapped three small packages: a small chalice of wine, a wafer, and his Freemason flag from Texas.

Neil held in his hand a small golden locket in the form of a heart, which had belonged to his daughter, Karen. Muffie.

Buzz took Holy Communion and read aloud from the book of John. "*I am the vine, you are the branches...*"

Neil asked Muffie to forgive him, and to pray for him and his colleagues from her celestial abode.

"*...he who abides in me, and I in him, will bear much fruit, for, apart from me, you can do nothing.*"

In his capacity as Special Deputy of the Grand Master, following the world broadcast, Buzz enacted another ancient rite, with the embroidered flag standing in for an old symbol. His lips moving but silent, he claimed the Moon as the latest territory for the Ancient Free and Accepted Masons.

Buzz couldn't tell if Neil approved of his actions but figured it made little difference to him as long as they stayed on schedule.

About an hour later Buzz couldn't help asking, "Neil, do you know what you're going to say?"

Neil shook a negative and turned back to his small window. The surface seemed to be made up of a chalky gray-white desert sand. Far beyond a wall of two-foot-high angular blocks, a bluish mountain surged up at least a mile.

Through the left-hand pane, Aldrin studied a level plain that had been devastated in eons past by a large number of meteorites and asteroids, ranging from five to fifty feet wide; a few of the darker craters sank to invisible depths. In the distance he saw long brown ridges twenty to thirty feet high.

It was providence that led Neil to a good landing spot.

"Neil, this is Houston." McCandless was back on CapCom duty. "What's your status on hatch opening? Over."

"Everything is go here," Armstrong radioed back. "We're waiting for cabin pressure to bleed, to blow enough pressure to open the hatch. Over."

Depending on the relative positions of the Earth and Moon, the two astronauts stayed in communication with Mission Control via three big antennas, at Honeysuckle Creek, in eastern Australia; another near Madrid, Spain; and a third at Goldstone Lake, in the Mojave Desert.

"I don't need to tell you both that your TV and radio audience is growing by the hundreds of thousands. Millions."

"The hatch is coming open," Armstrong said.

He'd found his words and gave the hatch a tug to break its seal.

Moist cabin air immediately formed into ice crystals and was sucked into the lunar vacuum. He and Buzz breathed safely in their pressure suits.

Neil got down on his knees and, with difficulty in the cramped quarters, maneuvered his feet backward toward the open hatch.

"You're clear," Buzz directed him. "Little bit toward me...straight down. To your left a little bit. Plenty of room... Okay, you're lined up nicely. Did you get the MESA out?"

Neil pulled on a lanyard just above the ladder, which released a latch at the top of the Modular Equipment Stowage Assembly, which dropped a TV camera into position.

Its orthicon pickup tube clicked on, and its low-velocity electron beam began sending a continuous photoactive mosaic to Earth, over two-hundred thousand miles away. Except in Soviet Russia, where the government instead broadcast a film about a deceased Polish singer, the Americas, Africa, the Middle East, and parts of Asia, five hundred million people, tuned in to watch.

"We're getting a picture on the TV," McCandless radioed.

In Houston's viewing room, von Braun also watched.

In the director's row, Gilruth worried about the walk and the camera, which he hoped wouldn't break down.

"Neil," McCandless said, "we can see you coming down the ladder now."

"I'm at the foot of the ladder." Armstrong's voice sounded confident to them, but suffered from static. "I can see the LM footpads are only...depressed in the surface about one or two inches. The surface itself appears to be fine grained. It's almost like a powder."

Buzz kneeled at the top of the ladder.

Go with God.

"Okay," Neil said. "I'm going to step off the LM now."

With his right hand on the ladder, leaving his right foot on the footpad, he placed his left foot on the Moon.

"That's one small step for a man," Armstrong said, "one...giant leap for mankind."

Von Braun bowed his head.

"*Nur wer die Sehnsucht kennt...*" he quoted Goethe. He thought in English, *A dream is fulfilled.*

Mission Control erupted in applause. Gilruth gripped Kraft by the arm, but their headsets kept them from embracing. A measured euphoria.

Neil put his right foot on the Moon and took a step.

"I can kick the surface powder up loosely with my toe. It does adhere in fine layers to the sole and sides of my boots. I'm only sinking in a fraction of an inch, maybe an eighth, but I can see the footprints of my boot treads in the fine, sandy particles."

A man is walking on the Moon, Kranz thought. *An American. One of us. We did it.*

9:56 p.m., Houston time.

109 hours, 24 minutes, mission time.

On an internal loop, Green Team leader Charlesworth asked, "Surgeon from Flight?"

"Go, Flight."

"How you look?"

"Looking fine, Flight." The flight surgeon read the gauges. "Data's good and crew's doing well."

Buzz had one leg out, about to join Neil on the surface. "I want to back up..." He withdrew his leg. "Making sure not to lock myself out."

Neil chuckled. "A good thought."

Standing on the barren surface minutes later, they took a brief moment to appreciate its foreboding beauty and history. About a half mile away, a structure didn't seem natural.

"Isn't that something!" Neil exclaimed. "A magnificent sight out here."

"Magnificent desolation."

Buzz stepped out of the LM's shadow, and the hard heat of the Sun pierced his suit.

Like punching through to another dimension. So different from Earth.

His backpack pumped water through the tubes of his lunar full-body underwear to cool him. He looked up and saw half of his home planet, divided by the day-night terminator, a faint blue orb against the black of space. He could make out the brown landmass of North Africa.

The soil I'm standing on may be older than those continents.

His flesh tingled with goose pimples. The Moon's sky appeared inky, and Neil…Neil looked brilliantly white, like no white Buzz had ever seen.

Colors are being reinvented.

Back to work.

A "laundry list" sewn into his left-hand glove read, "Lean/Reach/Walk; Best Pace/Start/Stop; Fast Pace/Traction/Dust; Close-up Photos/Cassette; Collect Environment…"

Armstrong snapped a photo of Aldrin with his Hasselblad Data Camera.

Whatever they did, they did carefully. Even a small tear in their spacesuit would result in their blood quickly boiling.

Although not on either's laundry list, they busied themselves with planting an American flag. Assembly kit, staff, and extendable crossbar. The telescoping part didn't cooperate at first.

"They've got the flag up now," McCandless described to the world what they saw. "You can see the Stars and Stripes on the lunar surface."

Only Collins in the CSM couldn't see it live on TV.

In the viewing room, von Braun's anxiety lingered. Something could still go wrong. Gilruth's face told him he had the same worries.

"Go ahead, Mr. President. This is Houston. Out."

Nixon had been patched into the LM and the two astronauts at 11:49 p.m., eastern standard time. Standing on the Moon, they heard his voice. "Neil and Buzz, I am talking to you by telephone from the Oval Office at the White House, and this certainly has to be the most historic telephone call ever made," the president said. "I just can't tell you how proud we all are of what you have done. For every American this has to be the proudest day of our lives. And for people all over the world, I am sure that they, too, join with Americans in recognizing what an immense feat this is. Because of what you have done, the heavens have become a part of Man's world."

"Thank you, Mr. President," Armstrong replied. "It's a great honor and privilege for us to be here, representing the United States and all the peaceable nations."

Both astronauts saluted the flag, then Buzz unveiled a plaque, which read, "Here Men from the planet Earth first set foot upon the Moon, July 1969 A.D. We came in peace for all mankind."

Armstrong glanced uneasily at a far ridge and recommenced his chores.

Aldrin became aware of his painfully full bladder.

I may have been second on the Moon, but I'm going to be the first to piss in his own pants.

* * *

In a Houston suburb, not far from the Manned Space Center, a news team had managed to corner a six-year-old boy. Michael Collins's young son held a garbage bag in his small hand, but a reporter pushed a microphone into his face and asked, "What do you think about your father going down in history?"

"It's fine, I guess," the little boy replied. "But what is history anyway?"

Out on Cape Cod another six-year-old squinted at the moonwalk on her parents' TV. Her dad had woken her up for the historic event. Even though the trees loomed darkly beyond their windows, she made up her mind.

"I can't see the picture," she declared. "It's all fuzzy."

The six-year-old's parents watched her open the screen door and go outside.

She stood in the driveway awhile looking up at the Moon, then stomped back in.

"I still can't see 'em. Where's the flashlight?"

* * *

At the Arlington National Cemetery outside Washington, DC, a caretaker in stiff overalls and muddy boots noticed a fresh bouquet of red and yellow roses. It lay on the grass next to the flat granite plaque of John F. Kennedy's grave.

When the old man bent down to move the roses from the wet grass to the dry tombstone, he noticed a card.

"Mr. President, the *Eagle* has landed."

Chapter 122

"Astronauts Plant Old Glory on Moon; Millions Watch 2 Scout Lunar Face, Make 'One Giant Leap for Mankind'"

—The Topeka Daily Capital

Tranquility Base, the Moon
Monday, July 21, 1969

The two astronauts installed a scientific equipment package on the surface, which would monitor lunar conditions. They took rock samples toward the end of their moonwalk and stacked them in a pyramid pile near the LM.

Neil ventured out farther than either of them had gone to visit a crater about eighty feet in diameter and twenty feet deep. Jagged rocks lined its bottom. He pivoted to see Buzz pointing at something—one of the larger craters about seventy yards to Neil's left. It glowed. A dim yellow light in the dark.

Damn, I bet that thing is hollow.

"Are you seeing what I'm seeing?" Buzz asked on a private channel.

"I sure am."

An imperious thought occurred to both astronauts at once: *return to your vehicle.*

They climbed back inside and shut the hatch.

They pressurized the interior and, with mechanical movements, began stowing their moon rocks.

"You're cutting out, Neil," McCandless radioed from Houston. "You're not readable."

In the viewing room, Debus rubbed the dueling scar on his cheek and leaned over to von Braun. "This could be bad."

Kraft fidgeted in his chair. The geologists had warned them that if the astronauts exposed moon rocks with iron filings to an oxygen atmosphere, they might burst into flames.

A minute passed.

* * *

High above Tranquility Base, having completed over fifty orbits at various inclinations and altitudes, the Luna 15 drone fired its main retrorocket engine. It would be a quick descent to the lunar surface.

* * *

In the Pullach control center, the woman in gray moved the marker representing Luna closer to a greatly enlarged, detailed photo of the Moon's surface. Another marker, not far from Luna's, was a little American flag.

The TV broadcast of the Apollo 11 mission was interrupted.

Kammler looked at the clock.

Behind him a phone rang and the stiletto-bearded Group member answered it.

At a monitor, one of the technicians held his palm over a red button in a metallic panel. His blinking communications system was connected to an exterior satellite dish.

"Transmit code word AH-2," Kammler ordered. "Prepare for *action* code word, all stations."

* * *

"Tranquility Base, this is Houston." McCandless sounded far too anxious to those around him. "We're reading neither one of you. Standing by…"

Another long minute.

A few of the controllers jerked up, agitated.

Kranz and Kraft felt paralyzed. They weren't sure if Neil and Buzz hadn't burned up on the Moon…

"Neil, this is Houston. Neil, this is Houston. Radio check. Over…"

No response.

"Buzz. Buzz…this is Houston. Radio check, radio check. Over."

No response.

More than three minutes.

Luna! von Braun thought. He'd put the robotic craft completely out of his mind, compartmentalized to a fault, but it came surging back. He wondered if it had crashed near the LM or worse.

Could they have tampered with it? Impossible.

"This is Houston…" McCandless perspired noticeably. "Radio check, radio check. Over…"

"Does anyone know something definite about the Luna probe?" von Braun asked out loud.

* * *

In the CSM Collins was as blind and helpless as Houston.

On the Moon, Buzz and Neil stowed more moon rocks, trancelike.

"This is Houston…radio check, radio check. Over…"

They continued their task, oblivious—when a bright flash outside the LM lit them up. They went to their starboard window, where another white flash made them look up into space.

They saw a glowing spot increasing in size.

"Whatever it is"—Buzz was awake now—"it's coming down fast and close."

"Luna," Neil said.

"Tranquility Base, this is Hous—"

Both astronauts fell back when something ultrabright shot by their field of view. They scrambled forward again and saw the object, the Luna, transformed into a pulsating spot.

It radiated outward, twinkling into tiny fragments, then melted into the black.

"Vanished!" Buzz said. "Vaporized."

Neil was silent.

"I think it came from that glowing crater."

Neil went to the radio and tried to raise Houston but got only static.

He tried again and—"This is Houston. I copy a transmission, but it was broken up," McCandless radioed. "If you read, we suggest you unstop one PLSS antenna. Over."

"Houston, this is Tranquility…" Neil came through to Mission Control. "How do you read?"

"Tranquility Base, this is Houston." McCandless was almost gushing. "Loud and clear. How us?"

"Loud and clear. We've been removing our pressure suits."

In the viewing room, Rees's expression went from controlled panic to comical. He figured he'd come close to a coronary, put his hand on his heart, and saw von Braun leave the room in a hurry.

In the LM, Neil and Buzz took off their helmets. Moon dust floated in the cramped space. It coated their hands and faces and lips, and penetrated their nostrils. The ancient powder had a pungent smell.

Wet ashes in a fireplace, Neil thought.

"Now we really have something for the debriefing," Buzz said.

"We may have been lucky."

* * *

At Pullach, Kammler was handed a phone.

"*Nein*," he said and paused. "*Nein*."

Group members and their associates waited behind him. Two of them exited through a door with a red light above it.

The woman in gray withdrew the Luna marker from the display board. Technicians murmured to each other, and Quincy Adams slouched in his chair.

Monitors showed the astronauts alive and well on the Moon.

"*Nein.*"

A few more men in dark suits filed out.

The bearded man appeared at Kammler's side. "I underestimated her."

Kammler sucked in his lips.

"Pissnelke!" he swore and slammed the phone into its cradle.

Chapter 123

"Was die Astronauten auf dem Mond Erlebten (What the Astronauts Experienced on the Moon)"

—*Der Abend,* Berlin

Tranquility Base, the Moon
Monday, July 21, 1969

Their schedule called for sleep, but inside the squeezed quarters of the lunar module, the two astronauts could not get comfortable. Neil jerry-rigged a kind of hammock out of a waist tether, which he could lean into when seated on the ascent-engine cover; Buzz curled up on the floor. Reflected Earth light glared through a window, despite shades, directly into Neil's eyes.

Cold and exhausted, they slept badly. A high-pitched whine from a glycol pump was unwelcome. Blinking orange, yellow, and bright white display lights made slumber unlikely.

What the hell happened out there? Buzz asked himself. *I wonder if they'll tell us, if we make it back.*

Neil put the whole thing out of his mind and thought about what they'd do upon waking. He peeked out the window and could see from his angle the ridge that bothered him, not far from the crater.

Would be nice to see Mike's face instead. Ascent engine never tried up here. Actually, never been fired. Couldn't be. Fuel and oxidizer too corrosive or…something. Hope to God it works. Never been tried. Should work. Has to work…

Orbiting above in the command and service module, Mike thought, *If I give in to my terror, it'll win out.*

He knew nothing about Luna and its end, yet he had to keep at bay persistent fears for his friends below—a recurring, horrifying image of an only-Mike return.

Two cadavers left behind.

An engine malfunction or who knows what, and they're stranded. They couldn't be more vulnerable.

"I'd like the grid square of this crater 130 prime. Over," he told Houston.

"*Columbia*, Houston," CapCom Ron Evans replied. "Say again about 130 prime."

"I'd like its grid square, please."

"Roger. Stand by."

Mike needed another task to keep himself busy.

In the back room reserved for analysis, Kelly and half a dozen controllers gathered again round a monitor.

"I still can't get a good read on that helium tank," Kelly reported. "It may have discreetly ruptured—"

"Or it may rupture on launch," Kranz interjected. "Or explode. *Shit.*"

"The readings fluctuate."

* * *

"Tranquility Base, how is the rest period going up there?" Evans radioed, about seven hours later. "Did you get a chance to curl up on the engine can? You're looking good to us."

Neil and Buzz had already been active for over forty minutes when Buzz discovered a problem during prelaunch checks: a broken-off switch on a crucial circuit breaker.

"The one that supplies electrical power to the ascent engine," he told Armstrong.

I must have snapped it off! Buzz scolded himself. *While suiting up?*

"Either we fix it or we're dead."

"Well, I snapped it, so I'll mend it."

He retracted the point of his Fisher space pen and jammed it into the mechanism.

The light turned green.

"Roger," Evans radioed. "Our guidance recommendation is PGNS. You're cleared for takeoff."

Von Braun stepped back into the viewing room, pushing back a desolate vision similar to Mike's: two dusty brown skeletons crumpled on the lunar surface adjacent to a tiny junkyard of mechanical debris.

At least the controllers had determined that the helium tank scare was due to faulty instrumentation.

In the LM, Neil thought of Muffie and put his faith in the people who had built the ascent engine.

"Roger. Understand," he radioed. "We're number one on the runway."

He pressurized the fuel tanks.

Small charges triggered the valves connecting helium and propellant.

"Both ED batteries are *go*."

"Roger."

"Nine, eight, seven, six, five," Aldrin counted. "Abort stage, engine arm, ascent."

Explosive bolts separated the ascent module from the descent stage. Additional explosive charges drove guillotine blades through electrical cables and mechanical plumbing.

Neil opened the engine valves. When he saw the computer display "Verb 99," he pressed the "Proceed" button and the ascent engine ignited. The fixed-thrust hypergolic rocket engine fired up.

Thank you…

Their data and voice signal lights switched off and switched on a moment later. They felt their ascent machine rise smoothly, increasing its thrust in modulated bursts, power to power.

"We're off," Buzz reported. "Beautiful."

"*Yeeaaaahhh!*" Collins shouted high above them, with his intercom off. "C'mon, guys! Seven minutes to my place."

Buzz looked down through the window and saw the American flag on the lunar surface blown over by their departure.

"This is a pretty spectacular ride!" Neil shouted.

Due to the Moon's relatively weak gravitational field, they rose like a balloon shot from a cannon, from 30 miles an hour to nearly 1,800.

Go, engine, go! Buzz cried out to himself…

"We're burning, Mike," Neil said.

"That-a-boy!" Collins exclaimed for all to hear in Houston.

He could already make out a faint blinking light in the darkness. A speck, growing bigger. Within moments the amorphous spot transformed into its old buggy self.

"*Eagle*, *Columbia*. I got a solid mark on you."

"Okay," Buzz replied. "Auto maneuver."

The *Eagle* was docking with the *Columbia*—when unexpected jolts shook the three astronauts sideways, then rattled them up and down.

Collins realized that each ship's automatic attitude system was fighting the other and swung *Columbia* round with his hand controller to keep pace—but the LM yawed to the right.

Have to outwait the automatic retraction cycle. Eight seconds…

Neil and Buzz tried to look at their controls with everything vibrating.

Bang! Bang! went something.

Docking latches slammed shut.

"Hey!" Mike said over the intercom. "All hell broke loose!"

"Oh, yeah." Neil sounded relieved. "It seemed to happen right when I put the plus-X thrust to it."

Day six, 128 hours mission time.

With a grin on his face, Buzz was first to step back into the familiar command module. Mike grabbed him and was about to give him a kiss on the forehead when his emotional programming kicked in. Neil followed, and Mike did the next best thing he could think of and took each of their hands.

"Welcome back!"

They looked at each other and jumped up and down like kids.

* * *

"Hello, *Columbia*. Houston," Duke called when the capsule emerged once more from the dark side. "Do you read? Over."

"Houston, this is *Columbia*. Reading you loud and clear," Collins called back. "The hatch is installed. We're running a pressure check, leak check. Everything's going good." He added to Neil and Buzz, "It's the hour for the get-us-home burn, the save-our-ass burn. The we-don't-want-to-be-a-permanent-Moon-satellite burn."

"Are we facing the right direction?" Neil asked. "I'd hate to use our last bit of fuel to head toward the Sun."

Their big engine fired for two and a half minutes, a flawless Trans-Earth Injection, which quickly put them more than four thousand miles away from the Moon.

Deke Slayton took the mike. "Fellows, congratulations on an outstanding job. You guys put on a great show up there. But a word of friendly advice—don't fraternize with any of those space bugs."

"Hello there, boss," Collins acknowledged. "Roger that."

Buzz looked in the vicinity of the alien rocks. *If it's not one thing, it's another.*

Kraft, Gilruth, von Braun, Debus, Dieter, and Rees adjourned to the best restaurant in town. They'd heard from their Soviet counterparts that the Luna probe had crashed somewhere on the surface of the Moon. At last, von Braun and Gilruth experienced a relatively calm hour, though the *Columbia* wasn't back home yet.

Chapter 124

**"Apollo's Crew Begins the Journey Home;
Luna Mystery Ends in Sea of Crises"**

—*The Guardian,* London

Houston, Texas
Wednesday, July 23, 1969

Von Braun stopped at a pay phone on his way to the Spacecraft Center. He put several coins in the slot and dialed. Waiting, he looked up and down the empty suburban street. A few seconds later he heard a voice on the other end.

"Rachel, you must tell me what happened."

"I can't, but one thing is clear. They want space to be a battleground."

"That is a terrible idea. Terrible. It would be a disaster of historic proportions."

"They'll be at it again. Always."

She paused.

"Are they safe now?" von Braun asked. "The astronauts, I mean."

"They should be."

Rachel hung up and pushed open the accordion door of the telephone booth. It was late morning in Manhattan's East Village, and she sensed danger up ahead. They weren't going to wait for nightfall. She passed by an alley midway along Avenue C and looked into the dark, moist corridor that stank of garbage.

Two men poised, sharp knives out.

Something held them back.

"Tell the Group I disappeared, that you couldn't find me," she said. "They'll believe you."

She continued down the block and turned right.

The two men normally followed orders, but understood that if they had tried, they wouldn't have survived.

Command and Service Module, Space
Wednesday, July 23, 1969

The CSM had become a foul-smelling hovel. In pursuit of a stray camera, Mike skirted the right side of the lower equipment bay, their reeking "forbidden zone," a repository of urine bags and fecal content in blue pouches.

Their drinking water was laced with unavoidable hydrogen bubbles, which led to endless farting.

After a loud one, Buzz laughed. "We could shut down the thrusters and do the job ourselves."

Their mood didn't sour during their multiday flight back home, yet their brief, spontaneous joy was replaced by a tired professional distance they'd established before leaving home. Close quarters in a capsule couldn't change that.

Maybe circumstances demand it. Mike packed up the camera. *Bowel movements with no privacy… Still, too bad we're not friends instead of business partners.*

He wanted to feel a strong connection with Buzz and Neil. The latter was feeding info into the ship's computer.

Look at him. A typical Czarino Leo, proud and distant ruler of a lunar jungle.

"If we carry this thing off," Mike said aloud, "we're going to really need each other."

He paused for a reaction, but none came.

"It's going to be a shitload of cameras and press," he insisted, "and we're only going to be able to rely on each other. No kidding."

"That's the truth," Buzz agreed. "You guys can count on me."

Peer pressure made Neil say, "Me, too."

"You gotta know what we're in for," Mike added. "It's going to be big. And I doubt it's going to be much fun. We'll only be able to relate to each other. For the rest of the world, we'll be freaks."

"I know it…" Buzz trailed off.

"We'll be able to handle it," Neil said.

At 3:56 p.m. Houston time, nearly 160 hours mission time, the trio passed the halfway point.

* * *

"*Columbia*, Houston," Evans radioed. "You're going over the hill shortly, but you're looking mighty fine to us."

"It was a great ride. See you later," Neil signed off before communications blackout.

Mike quietly rejoiced to see the service module disengaged and their space toilet float away…

At about 1,500 nautical miles above, the command module struck Earth's atmosphere at 6.5 degrees below the horizon, slipped through, and became a super-heated man-made meteor chased by a sonic boom.

Parachutes deployed and fifteen minutes later the capsule splashed down in the ocean.

Inside Mission Control, 11:15 a.m. Houston time, Dieter touched von Braun's arm and said, "Professor, do you realize that the original flight estimate projected touchdown at 195 hours, 18 minutes, 59 seconds. Impossible to predict, you might say, and yet our command module actually splashed down at 195 hours, 18 minutes, 35 seconds. A differential of a mere 24 seconds—in our favor! You must admit that is quite incredible."

"Yes, Arthur, I admit it. How long have you been waiting to tell me that."

"A long time."

Von Braun allowed himself to relax completely, at last.

The big television screen displayed the *Columbia* bobbing up and down in the Pacific with large words onscreen: "*Task accomplished—July 1969.*"

A jubilant crowd gathered at the flight director's console in a cloud of victory cigars and cigarettes. The viewing room emptied onto the floor; Wernher and his colleagues shook hands and slapped backs with Gilruth, Kraft, Kranz, and all the others.

Awestruck sailors transported Armstrong, Collins, and Aldrin via helicopter to the awaiting *Hornet* aircraft carrier and its mobile quarantine facility, a small trailer. There, cooks broiled real steaks and served genuine cocktails to the three astronauts, while the ship steamed toward Hawaii's Pearl Harbor.

Days later, with the trio housed inside, the quarantine facility was transferred via flatbed truck to a jet cargo plane, which flew them to Houston, where Aldrin, Armstrong, and Collins were put into the lunar receiving laboratory.

* * *

Guenter stopped by to deliver his homemade crescent-shaped key to Armstrong.

Von Braun and Dieter flew in to be among those first to visit during the astronauts' stay of eighteen days. On the threshold to the trailer, the two men crossed paths with a doctor, a well-known hypnotism specialist whom von Braun had first met at a medicine and space conference.

Inside, von Braun took something out of his pocket. "It's a telegram I received," he said to the astronauts. "I think you'll enjoy it. I know you have received thousands, but this one is special. It's from the children of the man who invented Buck Rogers."

"No kidding," Neil said. "I read that when I was a kid."

"We all did," Mike said.

Von Braun read aloud as they sipped cognac from plastic cups. "'We heard about the adventures of Buck Rogers on his flight to the Moon, firsthand, from our father… Although walking on the Moon was commonplace to us, it was a thrill to watch your flight: Buck Rogers finally coming to life. Our best wishes,' signed the children of Philip Nowlan.'"

He handed the telegram to Mike, who said, "From the imagined to the real. Maybe they're the same in the long run."

Buzz poured von Braun and Dieter a drink. "Not everything imagined becomes real, ol' buddy."

Neil examined his Styrofoam key and said, "Maybe when enough people want it to, it does."

Chapter 125

"From Coast to Coast: A Joyous Welcome for Astronauts—Chicago Cheers Apollo 11 Crew and Families; Armstrong, Aldrin, and Collins Warm to New York's Throngs; State Dinner in Los Angeles"

—*The New York Times*

Pullach, Federal Republic of Germany
Sunday, August 24, 1969

On a sultry afternoon, a man wearing gray Bermuda shorts, a clean V-neck white tee, and a yellow straw hat was watering his lawn. He held the warm green rubber hose in one hand and a lit cigarette in the other. To protect against the sun's glare, he had on Ray-Bans, because he liked how they looked on Roy Orbison.

For the last two decades, most of his German and American agency neighbors knew him as Hans Eckhard, a low-level engineer. He'd lived among them peacefully in their quiet compound. The nosier sort had often wondered why he never married.

He drenched the roots of a red rosebush as two black Chevrolet Impalas pulled up, followed by a shapely woman on a Triumph motorcycle, who parked across the street.

Four men stepped out of the two Impalas. They wore gray three-piece suits despite the heat. They also wore Ray-Ban sunglasses. The woman in a tight dark-blue jumpsuit approached, black helmet under her right arm, brown curly hair. The men stayed on the scorched sidewalk behind her while she stepped onto the manicured lawn and scanned the compound, west to east.

"Herr Kammler."

"I've been expecting you, Rachel." Kammler peered over his sunglasses. "Of course I have been abandoned, because of my poor performance. The Group, Angleton, the CIA, they have had enough of me. For I am no longer useful." He flicked his cigarette away and hosed the next rosebush. The water splashed off a yellow flower, scattering its petals. "It is too bad for me."

"Look at you," Rachel said. "Like Eichmann, you're the picture of banality."

"Insults? I thought about killing myself, but I am too old." He studied her. "You, however…you do not seem to age. You look the same as… Do you mind if I turn off the hose?"

"Go ahead. You should not be watering them in this heat anyway."

He considered her words. "Like I said, I am getting old." He walked over to a spigot near the garage door. "My clothes are already packed."

He went into his house and another car arrived. Angleton got out, more cadaver-ish than ever. Neighbors gathered, CIA wives and husbands, technocrats and accountants, to witness the arrest.

"The last thing anyone wants is a sensational trial," Angleton said to Rachel and lit a cigarette.

"That's the last thing *you* want. But Israel will honor the deal, as long as he's confined to one of their prisons."

Kammler reemerged with a brown suitcase in one hand and a bloody hole appeared in his forehead. A split second later a loud shot rang out, and several of the gawkers cowered. The four men on the sidewalk turned their heads toward a sniper on a nearby rooftop, who waved at them.

Kammler's lifeless body flopped to the lawn.

"Perhaps it's for the better," Rachel said.

"You called it," Angleton agreed. He motioned the four men to the corpse. "C'mon."

One man took the dead man's arms, another grabbed his feet, and they carried him to the lead car. A third opened the trunk, and they heaved the body in. The fourth started the engine.

"This could've been a lot of paperwork," Angleton said to those watching. "It's a good thing you saw nothing, because that man, well… he was never here."

Chapter 126

"Second Moon Landing Will Be More Challenging Than First"

—Logan Herald Journal

London, England
Tuesday, October 14, 1969

"If it's Tuesday, it must be London," Mike said to Neil and Buzz.

They'd disembarked from the presidential jet at Heathrow twenty minutes before and lounged in the back seat of a white Jaguar Mark 2. Their wives were in a second car behind them, being driven to the American Embassy, the next stop on a monthlong world tour. The three astronauts, in tailored suits, suffered from mild laryngitis.

"Paris, Amsterdam, Oslo, Brussels, Germany," Buzz counted on his fingers. "You're right, Mike."

"Brussels was before Oslo," Neil croaked.

They never discussed the stranger aspects of their mission with the endless train of dignitaries, politicians, and celebrities. Even in private, the trio didn't speak of the anomalies. Each of them wasn't completely sure of what he'd seen. Their memories didn't seem reliable.

At the embassy a huge crowd cheered their motorcade. A large contingent of journalists and photographers scribbled and snapped photos. NASA's senior security specialist surveyed the scene for potential problems; Mike and Buzz climbed out first.

"How do you feel?" one reporter asked.

"What did you see up there?"

It was the question that annoyed Buzz most. He sensed a wall between his memories and himself and was never quite sure how to answer.

When the throng spotted Neil, they rushed forward, screaming as they would for a pop star.

A small girl was pressed against the metal barrier and cried out. The astronaut quickly pulled her up.

"What's your name?" Neil asked.

The little girl looked afraid to say. She had blonde hair and wore a winter coat with leopard spots.

An English bobby waved the crowd back.

"It's okay, you can tell the man," he encouraged her.

"Wendy Jane Smith, sir," she said in a small voice.

"How old are you?"

"I'm almost three." No longer shy, she added, "My mum says that you're a spaceman, but I know who you really are."

Mike and Buzz saw Neil kiss the girl on her cheek. At the same moment, the astronauts' wives stepped out of the second car, accompanied by their public affairs officer. Mike caught Pat's eye, and she nudged Janet Armstrong, who saw the grin on her husband's face.

"Oh, my God!" she gasped.

The resemblance to their daughter, Muffie, was uncanny.

A photographer close to Janet followed her gaze and snapped a shot of Neil and Wendy together. The girl's father emerged from the crowd to reclaim his daughter, and hundreds of well-wishers waved photos at the first man on the Moon.

He took one and while he signed it, he thought, *I am forgiven.*

Chapter 127

"U.S. Space Program: Can It Pay Its Own Way?"

—San Antonio Express

National Mall, Washington, DC
Wednesday, May 10, 1972

It rained large drops, but not hard enough to discourage Wernher and Maria from taking their afternoon walk. They followed their usual cement path along the lake's south side, not far from the Washington Monument. He'd turned sixty a few months before and held a large black umbrella over their heads. Maria was worried about him. His father had died recently; his once golden hair had thinned into gray wisps.

Persistent antipathy toward her husband had also lingered longer than she'd ever predicted. Subtly, in Huntsville, and more blatantly in cosmopolitan DC, where Maria had assumed things would be different.

At first, things *had* been different. Exciting and stimulating. Her husband had been appointed number four at NASA, associate deputy administrator, before he was frozen out by politics and indifference. Maria had watched with sorrow his gradual fall from grace.

"My dear, *Liebchen*," Wernher said, "the fellow in the office next to me said something. He told me that others think I have the smell of death on me."

He handed the umbrella to his wife so he could fasten the top button on his black raincoat.

"It can't be that bad," she said.

"It is. At this juncture, it is."

He took the umbrella back, and they continued their leisurely promenade beneath a dark gray sky. He had no appointments to keep.

"It is all economics and penny pinching. Now that we have beaten the communists, they have no use for me."

"What about the space shuttle?"

"I told them what I thought and they thanked me. I don't know… they will use crazy Jack Parson's formula to power it. That has been the one bright spot, my dear."

She admitted to herself that Wernher's devotion to pushing space projects forward had become less passionate of late. Denied his old team of colleagues and stalwarts, he was a man without a country. For the last few weeks, nearly every day, they'd circled the Mall for hours after lunch while he confided, painfully, in his wife.

They skirted a shallow puddle on Jefferson Drive.

It upset Maria to see him so depressed. In the past, he'd waited all day and into the evening to talk to her when he got home. Now he couldn't wait so long.

"If only Gilruth would retire," he said. "I might have enough resources to get things going again. I could organize the Mars program."

"I suppose it's possible, dear. He is old."

But she saw that he felt old, too.

"My dear," he said, "even during the war my spirits were never so low."

They stopped, their umbrella dripping, and waited for a light to turn green. The rain had increased, and only a few adventurous tourists rambled about.

"I am afraid I may be losing the will to do these important things."

"It's just a phase. Maybe George Low can help."

"I don't think so."

He announced his retirement a month afterward with no fanfare and to Maria's great relief.

Alexandria Hospital, Virginia
Tuesday, November 30, 1976

Von Braun was dying.

"The doctors say it's kidney cancer," he explained to Arthur C. Clarke and Connie Ryan, who were visiting. "All those cigarettes maybe…I hear they're bad for you."

"This is a pretty elaborate way to avoid finishing your article," Ryan joked, but his smile didn't last long.

The two men had already been told von Braun had little chance of recovery. They would've known it by looking at his withered face. He'd lost so much weight. Maria sat knitting at the head of her husband's hospital bed, to his right; they approached on his left.

"Don't feel too badly," Clarke said. "Who else has seen in their own lifetime so huge a vindication of their dreams? I count it as one of the greatest privileges of my life to have known you."

"And I have always been an admirer of your Star Child." Wernher smiled. "Your Star Child would have…destroyed the satellite weapons. I only wish I could write as well as you. You know, my Mars book…" His eyes misted over. "I wish only—"

"Dear…" Maria warned him. "You must not."

Her husband had been prone to tears since his sickness began.

* * *

Ten days later, she allowed a small delegation of her husband's former colleagues to pay their respects. She abhorred any kind of public attention and kept visits to a minimum. No journalists allowed.

Arthur Dieter, Ernst Rees, and Kurt Debus saw the luster faded from von Braun's eyes. Careful of the tubes, they filed around their friend's ailing body, which lay hidden beneath a blue wool blanket Maria had brought from home.

They told old stories and laughed.

"Did you know, Professor," Arthur said, "that the astronauts' travel pay for going to the Moon totaled a mere forty-nine dollars and ten cents? They got so little because the government provided their food and lodging."

"No, I did not know," Wernher replied, and they laughed again.

"We have brought a surprise for you," Rees announced.

He opened the door and Hanna Reitsch charged in. "Wernher, it is so good to see you!" she exclaimed in German.

"We thought if you cannot go home," Debus said, also in German, "we will bring some of it here."

Maria had not been told and was not amused by the old woman's arrival, but only Arthur noticed her discomfort.

"My dear Professor von Braun," said Reitsch. "I heard that before your illness you went to London and had breakfast with the Englishman Duncan Sandys. Is it true?"

In a thick fur coat and a pearl necklace, she didn't want to talk about his cancer.

"Yes," Wernher replied. "It was quite something, I can tell you. There we were, having high tea and blueberry scones, two former enemies chatting about the war. You know, we had the English where we wanted them, but we didn't know it."

"Better to forget about that," Rees said.

Debus looked at his shoes. He, too, had grown old. "I will never forget."

"We should remember, yes," Reitsch agreed. She had become vain in her old age, and her face grimaced under a heap of makeup. "What have we now in Germany? A land of bankers and automobile makers. Even our once great army has gone soft. Soldiers have beards and question orders. I am not ashamed to say I believed in National Socialism. I still wear to parties the Iron Cross with diamonds that Hitler gave me. Today, you cannot find a single person who admits they voted for Adolf Hitler—but I will say so."

She paused. Wernher knew what she was going to say. They all did.

"You old men feel guilty, but no one wants to explain the real guilt we share—that we lost! We lost the war. This is our real shame. *Ein Volk, ein Reich, ein Führer!*"

Maria searched for an excuse to push them out of the room.

"I am not so sure," von Braun said in a soft voice. "Kurt, Arthur, Ernst, do you think it right that we developed the rockets?"

"Of course!" she gasped before they could reply.

"We did it for spaceflight, we did it for—" Dieter began.

"Do not lie to yourself. Not now," Debus said. "Do not change history. Each of us wanted to win."

"We must be cognizant, yes." Wernher lifted his head from the pillow. "We wanted to win, and we did not query. None of us investigated what we heard or what we saw."

"It was none of our business. What else should we have done? And do not forget, America is still fighting the Bolsheviks."

"Well, I am happy to think that our missiles have turned out to be guardians of peace, not more weapons."

"That remains to be seen."

"Oh, I almost forgot." Rees reached into his coat pocket and pulled out a book. "For you."

Wernher took the copy of Albert Speer's *Spandau Diaries*. On its first page was a handwritten dedication.

"Thank you."

"Speer is a traitor," Hanna spat out. "His book is full of half lies."

"Also, uh, Professor von Braun, we have come to share with you some bad news," Rees said, his eyes tearing up. "Poor Arthur is being investigated by the Justice Department."

"Investigated?" Maria was horrified.

"Yes," Arthur said. "For war crimes. I will be deported, it seems."

"We must fight it..." Wernher mumbled.

But he realized that Arthur had lost his will to fight and sunk back into his bed.

* * *

Neil Armstrong paid a visit after New Year's Day.

"Doctor von Braun, good to see you," the ex-astronaut said.

He kissed Maria on the cheek.

"Neil, how nice of you to come," she said.

The two had bonded over their mutual aversion to publicity.

"Doctor, I—"

"Please, I am Wernher now." He tried to prop himself up. Maria helped her husband, who weakened each day. "But you, I hear you are now *Professor?*"

"That's right. I'm teaching aeronautical engineering at Cincinnati University."

"Well, I am not doing much of anything." He gestured toward some papers on the bed. "Perhaps my last book."

"Wernher, I came to ask you about something important." Neil glanced at Maria, who was checking one of the IV lines.

"Maria, could you leave us for a moment, please?" her husband asked.

"Of course." She picked up her knitting and, after smiling at Neil, closed the door behind her.

Neither man said anything. Armstrong heard a bird's cry and through the window saw two large ravens perched on a tall pine tree.

"You know, Professor Armstrong, today I am as patriotic as you. I've got more than four hundred pints of American blood running through my veins."

Neil grinned. "In fact my question is about health. How can I put this?" He took Maria's chair. "I saw Buzz recently. It turns out he has the same problem as I do—trouble remembering exactly what we did on the Moon, or how we felt."

"Of course you cannot remember. You astronauts were hypnotized and drugged before each mission, and during your quarantine. They don't want you or anybody to spill the beans accidentally about what is up there."

"We weren't alone?"

"Of course you weren't alone. But you cannot remember it. No one can. It's true you did not see any great detail either. The transmissions were garbled, but it would seem you were helped to survive. That's my understanding."

"I knew something was missing, because no one is talking. It's been harder on Buzz, for some reason. I usually say the experience was similar to the simulations. But something is missing. Inside."

"Of course it is. They're playing a dirty game, and it will escalate. Listen, I don't want to be on the wrong side again."

Armstrong didn't like the idea of America being on the wrong side of anything.

"I know some of the things the military does is terrible," Wernher went on. "The extraterrestrials are not hostile. They helped you, but the generals and the intelligence agencies are concerned about what some other country might do. They believe they are fighting against the clock and see threats everywhere. They look for reasons, so that's what they find."

He coughed and drank some water from a glass.

"I tell you this because I trust you. And because you have tremendous influence. If you talk to the public, they cannot touch you. But… but, you see, I am afraid we are going down a road that leads to the militarization of space. Of that I am sure."

The idea wasn't a new one to Armstrong. He'd heard the concept debated, though not openly, and not by von Braun.

"The communists have been the enemy, but Neil, let me tell you, terrorists will be the next one. If this does not work, they will go on about asteroids. They will find any excuse to weaponize space, that's for sure. The most long-lasting threat will be alien invasion. That will be the final scare. We are going to militarize space against them, and all of it is a lie. A foolish lie. The real use for weapons up there is to control the population down here. I have met with an alien once or twice, and they are no threat."

Armstrong looked at von Braun, trying to gauge his mental health.

"Doctor von Braun, I hesitate to remind you, but you were an early advocate of nuclear weapons in space."

"I…what did you say?" his eyes searched the other's face.

"You wanted to weaponize space."

"Well, I…I have learned… Changed. Yes, I have changed. That was before I knew so much."

Wernher could see that the first man on the Moon wasn't convinced.

Maria knocked on the door. "May I come in?"

"Yes, my dear."

Neil got up to leave. Maria took back her chair and saw him hesitate. She looked at her husband, who didn't want to let his friend go in such a state.

"Statistically my prospects are poor, it is true," he said. "But you know how false statistics can be. According to them, you should be dead in space and I should be in jail on Earth."

Armstrong smiled and said, "They don't know anything, do they?"

He shook von Braun's hand and kissed Maria goodbye, then headed down an overheated corridor to the elevators.

* * *

In the spring, Sigismund's duties as West Germany's ambassador to France kept him away, but Magnus came to visit with his children. Upon seeing his older brother, he had to fight an urge to turn away. The person he'd venerated his whole life, who had always exuded such strength and poise, had sickened into a living skeleton, a poxy veneer of shiny flesh stretched taut over muscles and veins.

More family arrived with fresh flowers and crammed into the hospital room. Wernher's three adult children, Iris, Margrit, and Peter, as well as an assortment of cousins, gathered on a frigid afternoon. As usual Maria knitted on her yellow cushioned chair.

"Uncle Magnus, why aren't you as famous as Uncle Wernher?" asked one of his nephews.

Wernher didn't seem to hear the question, but Magnus replied to the seven-year-old, "Well, I'll tell you. One day, when we were only kids, Uncle Wernher and I strapped rockets to our little red wagon and—*zoom!* We crashed through our village and made a big mess." The boy's eyes opened wide. "When we were caught, we were severely punished. We were told never to do such a thing again, and I never did. But the following week Uncle Wernher did it once more. He went speeding through our village a second time. That is why he is so much more famous. Do you understand?"

The little boy did not understand but nodded that he did.

Magnus took his brother's frail hand in his. His own hair had whitened, and he needed rose-tinted glasses. "Do you remember that day?" he asked.

"*Ich erinnere mich, ich erinnere mich.*" Wernher replied that he hadn't forgotten. The pain in his words hurt Magnus. "Dear brother, do you think it right to do what I did for those many years? I spent my life developing…spaceflight. I persuaded thousands, maybe millions, to do the same. I spent huge sums of money with so much misery in the world. Was I selfish? Did I do the right thing? I am asking you… You were there."

"Yes, I think you did the right thing."

Wernher smiled with yellow teeth and thin, bloodless lips. "Did you see this?" He motioned with his right hand to Maria, who took a leather case from the night table and handed it to his brother.

"You must open it," Wernher instructed. "You see? You see? It is the Presidential Medal of Science." Two tears ran down his face. "Ernst brought it over before Christmas. Is it not wonderful? This is…certainly…a…wonderful country. Here I came, a foreigner, an enemy, and in the end they give me this great honor. Isn't it wonderful? Simply wonderful…"

"It is wonderful, you are right." Magnus handed the case back to Maria.

"Maria and the children are also…wonderful…" He cracked a ghastly smile.

At a sign from Maria, the cousins and nephews shuffled toward the door.

"…they take perfect care of me, Magnus. I cannot tell you how much I relish these visits."

He cried softly, with his brother still holding his hand.

"Only now do I realize what a terrible price I paid during those many years my work kept me away from my family."

He turned to Maria, who wiped his forehead with a dry towel.

His three children gathered nearer, Peter sitting on the foot of the bed.

"God saw fit to let me make rockets, but not to explore the planets. He saw fit to gather round me so many talented, intelligent people, and we worked so hard. So hard and so long…"

Visions of rockets blasting off flooded his mind, one after the other, each larger and more thunderous than the last. He looked at his children, one by one, and said, "A human being is so much more than a physical body…that withers and vanishes after it has been around for a few years. It is…inconceivable to me that there should not be something else for us, after we have finished our earthly voyage on this beautiful world." He let go of Magnus's hand to grab hold of his wife's. "Now I am going to know finally what comes after the end."

* * *

The next day, he was alone with Maria.

"I…" He covered his eyes with bony fingers. "I…see the mangled bodies of those blown to bits by my missiles. I see the prisoners dangling by their necks, thousands of them. Their purple tongues hanging out. These terrible corpses mock me…"

He lowered his hands to reveal a face that had come to resemble one of those tortured slaves. His body heaved, but tears no longer came. Maria held her husband to her breast and cried for them both.

As he died, the two black birds outside took flight. They flapped their wings heavily, rising up with each powerful stroke into the hazy sky, and disappeared.

Epilogue

Los Angeles, California
Wednesday, September 21, 1977

In his office at Twentieth Century Fox, where he had a film project in development, Buzz Aldrin sorted his mail. It consisted mostly of offers to join company boards, junk, and autograph requests. A letter from the Grand Master, however, made it official: to honor the Apollo 11 space mission, the Grand Lodge of Texas had established Tranquility Lodge No. 2000. The lodge would operate on Earth "until such time as it may hold its meetings on the Moon."

He put the letter down and reflected. He'd come to peace with most aspects of his adventure. NASA hadn't conquered or stolen anything. He and Neil had only absconded with a few rocks. The Apollo 11 mission had originated in the silliest kind of gamesmanship and politics but, by all standards, had been accomplished with great poise.

We've passed through this life while doing good.

The door to his office opened and George Lucas entered.

Buzz put the letter in a drawer and closed it. He'd been impressed with Lucas's film *Star Wars*; he'd returned to the cinema more than once, bringing friends to see the sci-fi space fantasy. Buzz intended to go to Grauman's theater again that night, because the story—particularly the Death Star, an enormous floating battle station the size of a small moon—stirred something dormant within him.

Before the shy, slight filmmaker, with black horn-rimmed glasses, could explain the reason for his visit, the former astronaut said, "You're one of them."

Lucas looked confused.

"I wish I was one of them," Buzz said. "I'm not."

Lucas thought it better to back out of the room.

Buzz followed him with his eyes. "But *you* are…"

The filmmaker shut the door behind him.

* * *

That same evening, Corso and Rachel watched from a control tower as three F-15s took off from Wright-Patterson AFB.

They saw the jets separate on radar and climb to over 38,000 feet.

At fixed intervals each of them launched a guided projectile that sped through space.

At precise locations, the projectiles fired accelerated particle beams at their designated satellites, alien and man-made, two of which orbited above the poles.

Their makers, a hostile extraterrestrial tribe and the Group, hadn't foreseen this precise scenario.

Their satellites were blown to bits.

* * *

Later in a motel room, bedside light switched on, Rachel sent out her mind to communicate once again with the voice from the windmill…

I have another mission for you, it said.

In disclosed reveries of past, present, and future, she glimpsed a specter sitting crookedly on his throne in a city beneath the desert.

She shivered.

Her vision expanded to encompass the Sun and the planets in their systemic gyrations. In our solar system's fixed journey, the whole neared the center, its cosmic hidden twin. The breath of expansive change blew through it all.

Adjusting her mind to the realm where things happen first, she beheld past ages of suffering, bondage, children beaten and raped. Minds beyond counting ripped to pieces.

She saw one age drawing to a close, while another waited in the wings, half felt.

The idea of rockets and space travel had taken only a little while to appear. Children not tortured by murderous parents would take longer.

But in that far-off future kingdom reserved for the daughters and sons of Earth, she saw them building homesteads and monuments on Mars, while from deep within the planet's core, starships sailed out silently on their way to Alpha Centauri…

End Quote

"I believe that these extra-terrestrial vehicles and their crews are visiting this planet from other planets, which obviously are a little more technically advanced than we are here on Earth…

"I would also like to point out that most astronauts are very reluctant to even discuss UFOs due to the great numbers of people who have indiscriminately sold fake stories and forged documents abusing their names and reputations without hesitation. Those few astronauts who have continued to have a participation in the UFO field have had to do so very cautiously. There are several of us who do believe in UFOs and who have had occasion to see a UFO on the ground, or from an airplane."

—L. GORDON COOPER, Col. USAF (Ret.), Astronaut (Mercury Seven), excerpted from his letter to Ambassador Griffith, Mission of Grenada to the United Nations, dated November 9, 1978

Acknowledgments

My heartfelt thanks to early readers,
enthusiasts and critics alike:

Genevieve Rinzler
Alan Rinzler
Ben Rinzler
Sarah Rinzler
Sohaib Awan
James Luceno
Tobias Meinel
Iain Morris
Reinhold Schubert
Richard Dean Starr
Rick Sternbach
Hans Wolf
Jesse Clark